DEAD WEIGHT

DEAD WEIGHT

John Francome

LONDON NEW YORK SYDNEY TORONTO

This edition published 2001
By BCA
By arrangement with Headline Book Publishing
A division of Hodder Headline

CN 1263

Typeset by Avon Dataset Ltd, Bidford-on-Avon, Warks

Printed and bound in Germany by
GGP Media, Pössneck

With thanks to Mary Bromiley, Nick Oldham, Michael Scott,
Marc Serfaty, Miranda Wolpert and Gary Nutting
(aka www.harrythehorse.net) for their advice

Keith woke up when the front door banged. For a moment he was relieved – his mother had come home. Then, as he listened to the heavy tread of a man's boots on the floorboards of the hall, he realised it was Dad. The clump, clump sound was softened by the new lino in the kitchen – black-and-white check, Mum kept it spotless – but Keith was scared all the same. He didn't know his father well – he'd been away for a long time. Mum had never said where he'd been but Keith knew, he'd heard things. And seven-year-old boys know what's meant by 'prison'.

He lay still, listening to his father move around in the kitchen. The cottage was small and the walls were thin. Granny used to say that if you rolled a marble across the floor you'd scare the crows off the roof. That was before she had a row with Mum and stopped coming round. The row was about his father, Keith knew that. Granny and Dad didn't get on.

There was a rattling noise from downstairs and a clink of glass on glass. His father was having a nip. Sometimes he called it a wee dram and other funny names – a docking doris, that was one. It was because he was Scotch. When Dad was in a merry mood he'd try and teach Keith Scotch words and Scotch songs. That was fun. When he'd first come home they'd done that a lot and Keith had learned all sorts of things. He could sing 'The Bonny Banks of Loch Lomond' and say the first verse of a poem called 'To a Moose', which was very hard. Maybe that was why Granny didn't come to see them any more. She said she hated the Scotch and why didn't Keith's dad clear off back north? There were enough old soaks in Somerset already without importing drunks from Dumfries.

'Susan!'

Even upstairs, under the covers, Keith flinched. He wasn't scared of adults just because they were bigger. He'd sworn at old Pinky Cook when he'd told him off for nicking strawberries, hadn't he? But his father wasn't just big and strong. When he was out of sorts he could be mean – nasty mean like he sometimes was with Mum. Then you wouldn't want to face him on your own. You'd want someone meaner and nastier on your side. Like the Beast.

'Where are you, woman? Come down here, you bloody whore!'

Keith began to shake. He didn't know what a 'hoor' was, but he knew it wasn't nice. He hated it when his father got like this. There were two Dads. One was kind and funny and gave him lots of things. The other was . . . like this.

'Susan – do I have to drag your arse out of bed?'

He was coming upstairs. Thump, thump, thump. He was looking for Mum but she wasn't here. She'd always been here before when he'd come home like this.

The door across the corridor crashed back on its hinges.

His father cursed, a string of bad words. It wasn't the words that upset Keith, he knew them anyway. It was the way Dad said them. As if he hated Keith's mum more than anyone in the world and he wanted to kill her.

But she wasn't there.

Smash!

Keith scurried deep beneath the blankets as light flooded his small room. But there was no place for him to hide.

A hand like a shovel picked him out of bed and dragged him into the open.

His father's face was red and ugly. The wave of hair above his forehead that he flicked back with a comb was all flattened and skew-whiff. It looked funny. But Keith didn't dare laugh.

'Where is she?'

He stared up at his dad, frozen with fear. He was like a little boy in a picture book, held captive by a giant.

'Where is your two-faced, whoring, cheating mother?'

Keith shook his head. He didn't know.

'Come with me.'

The Beast wasn't frightened of Dad. If his father yelled at the Beast like this and tried to push him around he'd be sorry.

The big man dragged Keith by the arm into the next room, the one his parents shared. The bed was made and the bedside lamp lit. The room was as neat and tidy as usual.

The man took hold of the counterpane and ripped the blankets from the bed. The sheets glowed in the pale lamplight.

'Where is your mother?'

'She's not here,' he blurted.

'I can see that for myself, you wee fool. You're lying for her, aren't you?'

'No!'

He threw Keith upon the bed and ground his face into the sheet.

'Smell that, son. Smell it!'

The faint whisper of his mother's scent filled his nostrils as his father pushed his head down into the mattress. Keith squirmed, his cheeks smarting.

'You know what it is, don't you? It's the stink of a whore.'

Keith coughed and spluttered.

'She's whoring in another's man's bed and you're lying for her.'

Suddenly his father let him go. 'Get up.'

He dragged Keith back into his bedroom.

When his father spoke this time his voice was soft.

'I'm going to give you one more chance to tell me the truth.'

Keith didn't like it when Dad's voice got small. Somehow things always got worse.

'Put the mice on the table, son.'

Keith's mum had objected to pet mice but Keith had begged and begged. And when Dad had come home he'd supported Keith, said there was nothing wrong with a few wee mice. That was when he'd taught Keith the Scotch poem, about the Moose. He'd even bought the mice for Keith, so it was out of Keith's mum's hands really.

There were three, two white and one black. Keith had called them Gemmell, McNeill and Johnstone, after Scotch footballers, to please his dad.

Keith put the cage on the table and watched as his father opened the door and took out Gemmell, the white one.

'Now, think carefully. I want to know the truth. Where is your mother at the moment?'

Keith stared at Gemmell, his white fur gleaming and his little pink

3

nose twitching as he crawled up and over and through the hoops his father made out of his big sausage-shaped fingers.

'Yes, son?'

Keith thought hard. He didn't know where she was. Sometimes she went out for a couple of hours after he'd gone to bed, but she said if he was worried he was to run next door to Mrs Shippam.

'I dunno, Dad. Honest, I don't.'

His father stared at him, his eyes dark and gleaming.

'Wrong answer,' he said softly. 'She's lying on her back in another man's bed and I want to know whose it is. Now just you watch.'

But Keith didn't want to watch. His father's fingers were flexing round the mouse and gripping. Then his hands were moving apart, a piece of Gemmell in each of them. Its white body writhed and wriggled, its squeaks filling the small room.

'There,' the Scots voice purred. 'Poor wee thing. That's what happens when you don't tell the truth.'

His father tossed the bits on to the floor.

'So – who's she with, son?'

Keith was silent. He couldn't speak, even if he knew what to say. His eyes were fixed on the little corpse, the white now stained with red.

'Let's try again, shall we?' said Dad softly, and he pulled another mouse from the cage.

As the man destroyed his son's pets, tears rolled down the boy's face. But in his eyes burned the anger of the Beast.

Chapter One

For as long as Phil Nicholas could remember, accidents only happened to other people. Like any jump jockey he'd had his share of falls and scrapes. He'd been dumped into ditches at thirty miles an hour, dragged face down through birch fences and kicked like a football as he rolled beneath the hooves of two dozen galloping steeplechasers. He'd paid the price in lost teeth, cracked ribs and broken collarbones and, on several occasions, spent the night in hospital at some doctor's insistence.

But overall he considered he was one of the lucky ones. He'd had friends who had been killed and a few who now did their racing from wheelchairs. Paralysis was the fear of every jump jockey. The moment you stopped rolling through the grass, regardless of what pain you were in, the first thing you did was to check you could move your legs. He'd been as shocked as anyone whenever tragedy struck but, deep down, it had no real effect. Like a soldier in a trench, no matter how many comrades fell around you, you had to believe that it would never happen to you.

Three years ago his brother had died in a show-jumping accident but, though Tim's death had turned his life upside down, Phil had never questioned the sense in riding horses for a living. As far as he was concerned, he was a guy who always got up and walked away. Then last September he'd ridden May Queen at Worcester.

A seven-year-old mare with a white blaze on her muzzle, May Queen was a favourite at Deanscroft, the large and successful West Country yard run by trainer Russell Dean. May Queen was embarking on a career over fences but she wasn't a natural. She found difficulty in judging where to take off and often ended up just guessing. At home she was always fresh and as a consequence could get herself out of trouble, but at Worcester on a beautifully sunny afternoon she took one guess too many.

Until the first open ditch in the straight, she'd jumped like a champion and the race was there for the taking. All Phil had to do was get safely over the last four fences. He'd even had time to glance over at the River Severn as they'd turned for home, noticing a pleasure boat full of people enjoying a free view of the race. He began to calculate the distance to the fence. May Queen was in an even rhythm which made it easy for him. With five strides to go he crouched lower into the saddle, preparing for her to spring forward, then for no reason she suddenly launched herself into the air.

They were at least two full strides away and there was nothing that Phil could do, except sit tight and pray May Queen could at least reach halfway up the fence. If she could have managed that they might have been all right, but they had no such luck. Her front feet just made it over the guard rail and she turned a huge cartwheel over the birch fence, firing Phil head first into the firm ground. The horse untangled her limbs with a snort of indignation and trotted off unscathed, leaving Phil with ruptured nerves in his back, a left arm fractured in three places and the knowledge that accidents no longer happened to some other poor sod.

Now, the following January at Wincanton racecourse, Phil was about to race with May Queen once again. But this time, thank Christ, he wasn't on her back. That dubious pleasure belonged to Russell Dean's second jockey, Mark Shaw.

Mark was tucked away in a corner of the weighing-room, pen in hand, reading the *Racing Beacon*. He looked up as Phil sat next to him and grunted hello – the kind of greeting that clearly indicated he was busy.

Phil could see the paper was open to a list of entries for the days ahead, many of them ringed and scribbled over.

'Not reading my column, then?'

Phil compiled a weekly diary for the *Beacon* – one of the perks of being last season's champion jockey.

'That load of old bollocks.' Mark's mouth twitched upwards at the corners, taking the edge off words spoken in a soft Irish brogue. 'Why should I bother to read it when I can get it direct from your big gob?'

Phil laughed. 'You cheeky monkey.'

Phil was the number-one rider at Deanscroft, and though there was only five years' difference between the two, that added up to a wealth of racing experience. He'd been imparting that experience ever since Mark had arrived as a green apprentice two seasons ago. Green or not, there had been no denying his ambition or dedication, and the first time Phil saw him on a horse he'd had a shock. The boy had clearly modelled his riding style on Phil's own. Phil had never referred to this – though plenty of others had – but he'd felt a special sympathy for the Irish lad and gone out of his way to help him along. Not that, these days, Mark needed much help.

'Watch out for May Queen at those ditches,' he said. In a two-and-a-half-mile race at Wincanton there are four open ditches to be cleared – more than any other course in the country.

'No problem.'

'She did me at a ditch at Worcester. Put her front feet straight in.'

'And so she did. I've got it on video. It's in my top ten.'

'Oh?' Phil had watched it once. It had not been an enjoyable experience. 'Well, be careful she doesn't go for a repeat performance.'

Mark grinned. 'Just you worry about your own horse and stop trying to put me off. I reckon I'm on the winner.'

Phil stood abruptly. He realised he'd got it wrong. Mark was actually looking forward to piloting a dangerous jumper over seventeen fences in the January mud. What was more he recognised the feeling only too well. Until Worcester it had been one he shared.

He clapped Mark on the back. 'Good luck,' he said. The words 'you'll need it' also sprang to mind.

In the parade ring Phil turned his thoughts to his own problems – all of which would be solved if only he could start riding winners again. Despite having the pick of the Deanscroft entries, he'd not been first past the post on any of them since his comeback at the beginning of December. No matter what spin he put on the facts – the after-effects of his injuries, a continuing problem with his left arm, the loss of racing opportunities to bad weather – he knew he was no longer the rider he had been before the accident. Though everyone at the yard had been vocal in their support, it wouldn't be long before someone else noticed that he had lost his touch. And that someone was liable to be the man now standing next to him, his expensive mackintosh flapping in the keen winter wind, his granite-grey eyes assessing Phil as earnestly as any of his runners: Russell Dean, master of Deanscroft, the most successful National Hunt trainer of the past five years.

Phil had begun riding for Dean just as he'd emerged as the top trainer in the land. Some called Dean lucky, others were suspicious of his methods, the envious simply complained he'd made it with his father's money. Phil knew how wrong they all were. Russell was a man who combined attention to detail with an obsessive need to improve. He took nothing for granted and was always willing to try something new. As a consequence Deanscroft was ever changing and constantly expanding – it had a heated indoor swimming-pool for the horses, mechanical walkers where up to eight animals could be exercised at the same time, and a covered exercise ring to beat any bad weather. This, together with on-site veterinary staff constantly monitoring weight and testing blood, made Deanscroft the best training facility in the country.

Russell Dean did not come from typical racing stock. The nearest he'd been to a horse as a boy was watching from the rail at a racecourse with a bookie's slip in his pocket. His father had been a Devon farmer who'd turned a couple of coastal fields into a caravan site and never looked back. When Roger Dean died he left his son a flourishing holiday-letting business with properties all over the West Country, including thirty acres of farmland and dilapidated buildings five miles north of Taunton in Somerset. Within two years Russell had sold the holiday business, christened the farm Deanscroft and set about converting himself from an afternoon punter into a full-time horse-trainer. And he'd done it. As he'd often said to Phil, what odds would he have got on that?

'How's the arm?' he asked as he gave Phil a leg-up into the saddle of his mount, Ashburton, an eight-year-old bay of impressive proportions who'd already won over fences.

'Getting stronger by the day, boss.' This was true enough.

The trainer ran an affectionate hand over the horse's flank. 'You'll be safe as houses on this boy.'

Phil was thrown by that – surely Russell wasn't implying he wanted to play it safe? But the trainer was looking up at him with a reassuring smile. 'I've got a hunch the pair of you are going to bolt up,' he said.

Phil hoped so. Champion jockey without a winner for four weeks. It was really getting to him.

*

Rain was beginning to fall from a leaden sky as they cantered down to the start. The ground was soft and getting softer, but that suited Phil just fine. With his huge feet and high rounded action, the big rangy Ashburton was made for heavy going, unlike many of his rivals in the upcoming novice chase.

They came alongside Adrian Moore on Chronicle and the young jockey pulled a face. 'Mine don't fancy this much,' he called over.

Phil could see for himself that the dainty Chronicle was looking far from comfortable.

'Tell you what,' Adrian continued. 'You can have this race and I'll take the last.' Adrian was due to ride January King, a renowned mudlark, in the final race.

'You're on,' Phil replied. He'd settle for one winner out of two starts any day, let alone right now.

But the outcome of the battle ahead was unlikely to have much to do with Adrian or Chronicle. There were tougher contenders in the fifteen other runners now massing behind the starter's tape. In particular, Phil liked the look of Major Tom, a sturdy chestnut horse who had won at three miles in the wet at Hereford before Christmas.

May Queen, on the other hand, now pulling out of the line and delaying the start, was surely not a contender. He watched Mark wrestling with the unruly mare, trotting her round in a tight circle and bringing her back to face the tapes.

Phil turned his attention to the task ahead – two miles and five furlongs of sticky, clogging ground punctuated with solid birch fences four feet high. Beneath him he could feel the bulk of Ashburton humming with energy, eager for the off, and the sensation began to flood into his own veins. Phil laughed out loud, attracting a curious glance from Adrian on his inside. Phil didn't care. This was more like it. This was how he used to feel.

I'm back, he thought with sudden clarity. *Now let's get on and win this sodding race.*

Julia almost lost track of time as she worked on Little Harry. When she massaged a horse she often lost herself in the task – it was as much mental as physical. She imagined the positive energy flowing from her hands, soothing jumping nerves, easing strained muscle and sinew, acting like oil on stiff and creaky joints. Little Harry loved the way she pacified his tired flesh, and so did all the other horses she ministered to at Deanscroft and here at Ridge Farm.

Now she gave the trapezius muscle at the base of the animal's neck a final stroke and reached for her sweater. Little Harry butted her gently with his big golden head. The message in his eye was plain – don't stop.

'Sorry, Harry,' she murmured as she pulled the shapeless woollen garment over her tousled blonde head. 'You wouldn't want me to miss Phil's race, would you?'

He would, of course, she reflected as she rushed from the old stable block to her muddy Fiesta. All horses were the same. No matter how cranky or nervy or just plain out of sorts they might be feeling, once she'd laid her hands on them they never wanted her attentions to cease. Which put them in line with pretty much all the men in her life.

A male pest was the reason she was running late now. She'd been over at Deanscroft working on a couple of recent runners who needed sorting out. Her plan had been to quit in good time to drive the ten miles back, attend to Little Harry and reach home for the build-up to the race on television. But one of the new vets had detained her. He'd watched her work, giving her the benefit of his unwanted advice, and, when she'd finished, asked if she'd mind taking a look at his swollen knee.

'I don't do humans,' she'd replied, which wasn't strictly true.

The vet had refused to take the hint and shifted the conversation to Portland Blue, the horse in the next stall, who had gone lame. As it happened she knew Portland Blue well, and it was hard to get away without being rude. And being rude wasn't in Julia's nature.

It irritated her, however, the way men continued to pursue her when she was clearly unavailable. Wasn't her wedding ring obvious enough? Perhaps she should hang a sign round her neck saying 'Just Married – Off Limits'. She guessed that some men couldn't help themselves.

A plain girlfriend she no longer spoke to had put it another way. 'You're so fucking gorgeous, Jules, guys just want to hang around you even if they're not going to get anywhere.' She'd said it in an envious tone which had upset Julia. How could she tell her she didn't want the attention of every heterosexual male in her vicinity? In Julia's experience, beauty – and she supposed she had it – was as much a curse as a blessing.

She drove faster than was sensible down the narrow track, drenching the hedges on either side with plumes of water from the standing brown puddles. Not that it mattered – there was no other traffic on the way to Barley Cottage, half a mile away on the southern edge of the farm. She could have avoided this rush by going up to the farmhouse, where the television in the parlour was tuned to the racing throughout the afternoon. But that would have meant watching with Phil's mum, Margaret, and she didn't feel up to that. She liked her mother-in-law well enough, but this race was too important, she wanted to be able to concentrate in private.

Barley Cottage was big and draughty. It looked particularly bare this afternoon in the absence of the Christmas decorations which had brightened the place only a week ago. Now they had gone there was no disguising the fact that the hall needed replastering and the kitchen required a complete refit – and that was just downstairs. Phil's parents had done a remarkable job getting the place in good enough shape for them to move in after their honeymoon in August. The engagement and the wedding had all been rather a rush, they'd said, but they weren't complaining. Margaret's bright eyes assessed her with fond anticipation every day and, if the in-laws had their way, there would be decorators upstairs now turning the back bedroom into a nursery. To Julia's way of thinking, talk of having a family was premature, but it was a topic Margaret could not resist. Maybe that was the real reason she had driven back here to watch the race.

She hurried into the front room and turned on the television. The runners were already off. Instantly all thoughts of children, decorators and in-laws were wiped from her mind.

The old feeling stayed with Phil around the first circuit. Ashburton was foot perfect and Phil could feel his confidence grow as they soared over the fences. Though new to jumping, he was a complete natural.

The main pack of runners were bunched on the inside, taking the shortest route home. Phil was keeping Ashburton wide to stay out of trouble and to avoid the worst of the ground, now badly churned up from the afternoon's racing.

Ahead of him, some five lengths clear of the pack, was May Queen.

Phil could see Mark working hard to get the mare round. She had schooled half a dozen times at home since her fall at Worcester but her jumping had not improved much. She was small and the soft ground made the fences that much bigger. She was hitting the top of most of them, bouncing off the packed birch, being knocked out of her stride. Yet there was no denying her spirit as she gamely kept picking herself up and working back into the race.

By the last on the far side the field had unravelled, and Ashburton was going well. Major Tom, the chief danger, was keeping pace just to his rear, with May Queen ahead by a couple of lengths. They were approaching the last open ditch, and Phil kept one eye on the fence and the other on May Queen. As he expected, the mare gave it a real thump and knocked out a cloud of birch. Ashburton swept past, sailing over the jump, and landed running. Phil caught a glimpse of Mark struggling to keep May Queen on her feet, but her nose was touching the grass and she looked about to keel over. He hoped to God Mark was all right.

They were galloping downhill now towards the fourth from last. Suddenly Phil was aware of Major Tom making a move on his inside. Ashburton was eager to go too but Phil kept the big horse in check. He knew this course well and was aware of the sharp bend to the right into the home straight that followed the next fence.

Major Tom shot past, coming down the slope like a car without brakes, and took the jump three lengths ahead. But he was too tight to the rail on the sharp right hand bend and, as a consequence, was forced wide into the straight. Phil kept Ashburton on the optimum racing line and swept into the lead. Now he had the benefit of the rail to run against.

Phil knew the race was his. Ashburton was tiring now but his jumping remained rock steady as he carried them over the next two fences. Phil kept squeezing with his legs, keeping the horse up to his work. All he had to do to win was get over the last. Approaching the fence, he became aware of the crowd in the stands to his left. For a wet and wintery afternoon they were demonstrating remarkable enthusiasm.

Suddenly he understood why. At his shoulder, unbelievably, was Mark on May Queen. Somehow the horse was still on her feet and Mark was urging her on, hunched forward in the stirrups, his hands working as he screamed in the horse's ear.

Phil assessed the situation in a split second. *Get stuck in NOW!* It wasn't a conscious thought, more a reflex – the kind of instant racing reaction that had rescued him many times before.

But he was slow to respond, his body frozen, somehow unable to communicate the urgency to his horse. In a flash the fence was upon them and Ashburton seemed to take for ever in the air. Beside them, Mark threw May Queen forward as if the fence didn't exist. For once the mare nailed it, and landed half a length clear.

And that was it. There's next to no run-in at Wincanton after the final fence. Even if Ashburton had had enough in the tank to catch May Queen he'd run out of room.

Phil crossed the line second, as downhearted as he'd ever been at the end of a race.

He caught up with Mark as he slowed his mount beyond the winning post.

'Well done,' he said. 'I thought you'd gone at the last ditch.'

Mark pulled his mud-spattered goggles down around his neck. His eyes sparkled. 'Told you I was gonna win, didn't I?'

Phil remembered. He'd thought it was just bravado.

Mark was regarding him shrewdly. 'I'd've won on your horse too, you know.'

Phil took most things with a smile on his face, but he wasn't amused as Mark rode off to the winner's enclosure.

The hounds were making a fair old racket out the back but Keith Jeffries didn't hear them as he stared at the television on the sideboard to the left of the empty fireplace. Even though he'd had nothing on this race, the drama of it gripped him, shutting out everything else. The unlit room was dark in the late afternoon gloom, and the reflection from the screen danced across the pages of the old exercise book open on the table in front of him, illuminating the neat rows of figures inscribed in blue and red ballpoint. A rank of reference books – *Chaseform, Chasers and Hurdlers, A Guide to Racecourses* – stood by his elbow; a calculator, pad and pencil lay directly in front of him; and, within easy reach to his right, newspapers were stacked, open to the racing pages. He was a man who took his betting seriously. As with everything in this life, it required forethought, organisation and luck – a commodity forever in short supply in Keith's experience.

But at least, he thought as the television camera cut to an interview with the winning trainer, he'd never considered putting money on May Queen. If he'd had the urge and then rejected it – which, on her form, he would have been bound to do – then he'd be cursing his luck right now to see her pull off such an unexpected victory. You often got one complete turn-up for the books in an afternoon's sport and Keith was rarely the beneficiary – unlike some he could think of. His system didn't allow for flukes. The best he could hope for was to avoid them and, thank Christ, he just had. The next race was the one that counted. With serious money at stake he was relieved to have the afternoon's freak result out of the way.

He was aware now of the hounds' commotion. Mind you, they always kicked up a racket – a pack of hunting hounds was never quiet. Most of the time he tuned the noise out. It was just background clamour, like the wind in the trees, though he'd taken comfort in it since Denise had left. He wasn't some sad sod living on his own in the middle of nowhere, not with a hundred hungry, rapacious creatures dependent on him. Denise had hated them, surprise, surprise. Now there was a lucky cow when it came to a flutter. She'd have piled on May Queen and picked up her windfall as if she deserved it.

The whore Denise. Walking out on him for an accountant, that was a laugh. She'd soon unbalance his books for him. Now it would be his turn to shell out for designer dresses and other expensive women's crap, like all that stuff gathering dust upstairs. If Denise wanted any of it back she'd have to come and get it herself – and somehow, after last time, Keith didn't think she'd have the guts.

The doorbell rang, diverting him from thoughts of his estranged wife. So that was why the hounds were kicking up a fuss – he had a visitor. He wondered why he hadn't heard a car engine. Keith heaved himself from his armchair. Whoever it was they could bloody well shove off sharpish. He had a lot – a heck of a lot – riding on the next race.

Keith didn't recognise the bespectacled old gent standing on his doorstep. The newcomer was togged up for a winter's walk: Barbour, wellies, walking stick and a cap with earflaps that looked like a family heirloom. He had a thin grey moustache and spoke like a toff.

'Mr Jeffries?'

Keith grunted, on his guard.

'Awfully sorry to drop in unannounced.'

'You got a car?'

'I'm parked out in the lane. Thought I'd stretch the old legs.'

So that explained it.

The toff hesitated for a moment before he spoke.

'Look, Adam Jellicoe gave me your name. Said you might be able to help me out.'

Captain Jellicoe, master of the Latchbourne Hunt – Keith's boss.

'Help you in what way, sir?' Keith dropped effortlessly into deferential mode. It worked a treat with Jellicoe's crowd.

'Adam tells me you've got a humane killer.'

Keith nodded. Part of his job was destroying old or injured farm stock to feed to the hounds.

'The thing is, my old hunter is too long in the tooth to ride out and I don't think he can cope with much more of this dreary winter. I can't put it off any longer and I wonder if you would take care of him for me.'

So that was it. He wanted Keith to kill his horse. He probably didn't dare ask the local vet who, at the very least, would question the necessity of ending the life of an old and faithful servant. For a second Keith's stomach turned over. Was this what he'd come to? Slaughterman? He deserved better than this.

'Of course, sir,' he replied. 'You'll have to bring the horse up yourself, though.'

The old boy looked relieved. 'Righto. No problem. And what will it, er . . .?'

'A hundred pounds.'

'Oh.' The man's face fell. Keith could see him calculating whether it was worth him risking the vet's wrath after all.

'Eighty for cash,' he added.

The other agreed quickly, offering his hand on the bargain.

'Bring him up tomorrow,' Keith said. The visitor nodded and would, Keith could see, have engaged him in further conversation – doubtless justifying his decision to get rid of his horse. But Keith was already turning back into the house. The runners in the last would soon be going down.

Phil sat in silence in the noisy weighing-room. He should have been more positive, committed Ashburton from the turn for home, but he hadn't, and he knew why.

For Phil, race-riding had always been simple. He never analysed his technique or agonised over tactics or spent his every waking moment studying form like some other riders. As far as Phil was concerned he got a leg-up from the trainer, listened to a few words of advice and then instinct took over. He knew he was lucky. He could climb on an unknown horse in the ring, take it down to the start and, in those few minutes, learn what kind of animal he had beneath him and how to get the best out of him. Owners had often been amazed at the performances he coaxed out of the most unpromising beasts. It was as if he were a musician able to pick up any battered old guitar and, after a few seconds of strumming, produce sweeter sounds than it had ever made before. He had no idea how he did it.

But now, though his instinct was still as attuned as ever, he wasn't able to act on it the way he had since his fall at Worcester. It was some kind of breakdown in communication between his brain and his body. When the going got tough these days, he just froze. He'd been brooding about it all through Christmas and every time came to the same conclusion: since the accident he'd lost his nerve.

He'd seen other riders lose their bottle. It didn't always follow a bad fall; sometimes it was an accumulation of minor injuries and the knowledge that it was only a matter of time before you copped for something serious. But when it happened to you there was no hiding from it. As much as you wanted to be brave, to go for gaps and throw caution to the wind when it was necessary, you couldn't make yourself do it. You only ever saw the short, safe stride into a fence. And when the race was over, everything seemed fine – until the next time.

Some jockeys managed to ride through the bad patch and regain their confidence. A rare few packed up straight away. Most just plugged on, going through the motions but never giving horses a proper ride. Eventually trainers' loyalty from past service wore thin and rides dried up. In that position, a jockey had no option but to find another job. Phil didn't want to end up like that. That was why he'd made the appointment at the clinic last week.

'Wakey-wakey, mate.'

Phil looked up. Mark was standing by his side in clean silks. Phil suddenly realised he'd been slumped on the weighing-room bench for nearly twenty minutes. He leapt to his feet – it was almost time to weigh out for the last.

'I must have nodded off,' he said.

'Too much shagging,' came a voice from the other side of the room. Adrian was putting out some dog biscuits for Beatle, his scruffy terrier who spent race afternoons asleep on a sweater under his peg.

'And who can blame him,' came another voice. Almost all present had been at Phil's wedding and admiration for his bride was universal.

'No wonder he's knackered,' said Adrian. 'All day riding horses and all night riding the lovely Julia.'

Phil joined in the laughter. Much better that they had no idea what was really on his mind. He'd never live it down if they knew he was seeing a shrink.

On the off-chance of finding an old packet of cigarettes, Julia rummaged through the downstairs drawers and poked in all the hidey-holes where household junk fetched up. She hadn't had a smoke since the wedding and, after the first few weeks, she'd not missed it. But now a sudden craving for nicotine gripped her. She longed to dull her disappointment in silky clouds of tobacco smoke. But she was out of luck. She banged the kitchen drawer shut with a petulant slam and returned to the sitting room.

She'd been involved with jockeys before, so she was familiar with the rollercoaster of emotion that went with watching them race. She was aware she had to take the rough with the smooth, to treat triumph and disaster just the same – and all the other well-worn clichés. But at the moment that was difficult. She knew how much it mattered to Phil to have a winner right now. And Ashburton had been his best hope for the day.

She returned to the sitting room to watch the last race. The television camera cut to a huddle of men in the parade ring, Phil among them. Julia tried to read her husband's face as he was caught mid-conversation with an owner she did not recognise. Phil had not mentioned his losing streak that morning but she knew he had been banking on Ashburton. He had to be bitterly disappointed. If so, he showed no sign. Just before the camera cut away, he put his head back and laughed in the uninhibited, full-throated way that was now so familiar to her. The sight cheered her up and she realised the nicotine pangs had disappeared. What right had she to wallow in gloom when Phil, ever optimistic, was obviously just getting on with it?

She knew he didn't fancy his mount in the upcoming race. He'd ridden Snowflake at Lingfield shortly after returning to the saddle in December and the horse had struggled to come last, ten lengths behind the field. 'Don't expect me back early,' he'd said as he'd left that morning. 'I'll still be getting round on Snowflake.'

Julia had laughed but she'd felt bad about it afterwards out of loyalty to the horse. She tried not to have favourites among the animals she worked with but it was hard to ignore her likes and dislikes. To her, horses were much like people, each with their own distinctive personalities. And, as with people, there were some with whom she just clicked – like Snowflake. When she'd first started her physiotherapy she'd been told he was lazy, that he was avoiding work after a lay-off from a stress fracture sustained on the hard courses of late summer. Julia had quickly come to the conclusion that the little horse was still in pain though, game fellow that he was, he was trying his best not to show it. To her mind it was no surprise that he was performing badly in races – he shouldn't have been running.

She'd said as much to Russell, who had promptly placed the horse in her charge. Since the New Year she'd been massaging the little grey and riding him out. In the last week he'd been working well and her impression was that Snowflake was finally getting his confidence back. She had the feeling he might be capable of springing a surprise. She'd kept that to herself, though – it was between her and the horse.

She watched the parade of runners circle the ring. Snowflake was looking alert and frisky. Maybe there was still hope.

Julia was on Phil's mind as he rode down to the start. He'd have guessed she'd been working with Snowflake even if he hadn't known. In his experience, all animals at Deanscroft benefited from her attentions, and the little horse beneath him was no different. The grey was taking a good hold on the way down to the start of the two-mile novice hurdle.

Phil noted that the animal was comfortable with the going, which was now heavy. On reflection this was not entirely a surprise – for a horse recovering from a stress fracture, soft ground was preferable to firm. And, though Phil was pleased the horse was happier in himself, it was not likely to make much difference. He doubted that Snowflake was going to run fast enough to stay in touch with January King or any of the other fancied runners in the race. The bookies had him at 33–1, and he had no reason to question their judgement.

Keith kept his betting book in two colours of ink: blue for the punts he fancied making and red for the bets he actually placed. Blue was the predominant colour in these pages, a fact that gave him a considerable degree of satisfaction. It demonstrated to him that restraint, self-control and discipline were now present in his life – which had not always been the case.

He had employed this two-tone method for the past three years and, whenever its frustrations became oppressive, he reminded himself that it was better than his previous system. In those days all bets were red – which is why he no longer owned his own home and worked as a rural skivvy in the back end of nowhere without even his slut of a wife to keep him company.

At least now he was no longer a slave to the bookmakers. The blue bets – his theoretical wagers – required the same degree of research and racing knowhow as before but they had the advantage of being risk free. Betting blue, as he frequently reminded himself, he couldn't lose. If his chosen runner nosedived then the only blow was to his pride. Without the pain in the pocket he could consider the loss as the mere statistic it was, a simple addition to the sum of racing knowledge required by a dedicated gambler like himself. And if a blue bet came off he had the satisfaction of knowing his judgement had been sound. Admittedly this was the difficult part – he'd be a bloody fool if he didn't admit he'd rather have the cash.

What was more, he could see from a tally of his blue bets where he used to go wrong. In the past he'd been too impatient; now he waited until all the factors in the betting equation looked good before he put his money on the table. It was hard work, constantly studying form, weights, breeding and the rest, but it narrowed the odds in his favour. And the blue bets put a brake on his gambling instincts. This afternoon, however, was going to be a red-ink race day, no question.

His eye was on the runners circling the ring. He picked out the black and yellow diamonds of January King. The horse looked in fine condition – lively, powerful and well turned-out – which was as well considering that there was £800 of Keith's money on him. Not that Keith had wagered £800 in the first place – this was the last leg of a treble. His initial stake had been £100.

Keith was sure January King would bring home the bacon. He noted with interest that the price had gone out to 7–2, making January King second favourite behind Skipjack at 7–4. Keith felt a stab of alarm but then reminded himself why he hadn't fancied Skipjack for this race. Though he'd beaten January King on this course as recently as November, he was now carrying five pounds more in weight, and the ground that day had been good. Today it would be a different ball-game. The ground was a bog – just how January King liked it. Keith congratulated himself on consulting the long-range weather forecast before he'd laid out his cash. At least if the bet went down he'd know he'd covered all the angles.

As Phil lined Snowflake alongside the other runners at the start the rain lashed into his face and body. There wasn't much protection from the elements in a jockey's lightweight racing silks. Once they were off, however, all thoughts of personal discomfort vanished and he thought only of the race.

There were a dozen runners and they bunched together in the early part of the race, passing the stands for the first time before heading out into the country. Phil eased Snowflake along at the rear of the pack, pleasantly surprised by the little horse's rhythm and neatness over the hurdles. As they turned into the back straight on the far side of the course, they met the worst of the weather, but even that didn't slow him down. On the contrary, Snowflake began to pick up the pace, and Phil was only too happy to let him forge on. The little horse was skipping across the heavy turf with relish, making his way through the field.

As they approached the sixth, Phil was amazed to find them drawing alongside the race favourite, Skipjack. The big bay was struggling and barely got airborne, ripping the hurdle from the ground. Through mud-spattered goggles, Phil could see his rider working hard to keep Skipjack upright. Then, turning for home, they passed the unhappy pair and the course was clear ahead but for the distinctive yellow and black of Adrian some way in the distance on January King. If he kept going like this, Phil realised, he could finish second.

Keith was not a man to count his chickens – he'd lived long enough to know that was how you got egg on your face. Still, surely the money was in the bag now with January King ten lengths clear and Skipjack run out of it. He allowed himself to relish the thought of picking up a cool £3,600. Enough to get Denise off his back for a while, pay a few bills and still have something left over to give him breathing space. Time maybe to plan a few more coups like this. He wouldn't mind making a living as a full-time gambler.

The sound echoed round the little room, drowning out the TV commentary.

'Go on, Snowflake! Go on, Snowflake! Go on, Snowflake!'

Julia was on her knees in front of the set, scarcely aware she was shouting. She didn't think that Snowflake could win from so far back but the horse that she believed in was coming good. And even if Phil only finished second, this heroic ride on an unfancied mount would surely prove to everyone that he was returning to form.

'Go on, Snowflake!'

He was catching January King, but going into the last there were six lengths between them. Surely that was too much to make up?

Phil never thought of using his whip. There was no need – Snowflake was as keen to catch the horse ahead as he was. He rode high over the little grey's shoulders, urging him on with his hands, amazed by the transformation in the animal beneath him. How he wished there were a couple more furlongs to go. As they jumped the last hurdle – farther out, thankfully, than the last fence on the chase course – they were fast running out of room.

Keith couldn't believe it. He'd been about to land the sweetest gamble of his life. January King had been four lengths clear and in sight of the post when the jockey had stopped riding! It was as if the horse was over the finishing line and the race was already won. But it wasn't. The rider – that twat Adrian Moore – had simply dropped his hands, sat still in the saddle and let some pathetic outsider catch him on the line.

It was incredible. Keith had never seen anything like it. It had to be a fix.

Standing in the winner's enclosure for the first time in a month, Phil felt relief rather than euphoria. Though his smile was broad as he accepted the handshakes and back-slaps, he told all who would listen that the horse deserved the real credit. In truth he hadn't had to do a great deal.

He found Adrian sitting in the weighing-room next to Beatle, the dog's head resting in his lap. He looked up as Phil approached, his face pale.

'I've just been booed off.'

Phil had heard the commotion at the end of the race. Not everyone had been happy with Snowflake's last-ditch victory.

'Don't worry about it. It's happened to everybody.'

'Not me.' Adrian looked close to tears. 'Some bloke called me a cheating bastard.'

Phil put his hand on the lad's arm. 'It goes with the territory. It's not your fault some clot's done his beer money.'

Adrian managed a grin. 'But it was my fault.'

'I wouldn't beat yourself up. You're not the first to do it and you won't be the last.'

'He was tiring at the end. Since we'd obviously won I couldn't see the point of racing him to the post so I dropped my hands. Didn't see you coming at all.'

Phil knew just how Adrian was feeling – something similar had happened when he'd lost on Ashburton. Sometimes racing was a pure lottery and this time his number had come up.

The television was off and Keith sat in the dark. He ought to see to the hounds but, for the moment, he couldn't move. Since the race had finished he'd sat frozen in shock.

He'd been robbed. That was the only way to look at it. It happened in all sport so it wasn't a surprise. The blatant penalty not given, the plum lbw denied – the horse stopped on the line. Everyone knew it went on. The reason was money, obviously. In this case, the winner was a rank outsider at 33–1. Some jokers would be celebrating tonight, and you could bet that included the smartarse riding January King.

Keith had never counted himself a fortunate man and he'd learned to live with the fact. These days he relied on graft and preparation and cunning – not luck. Like this red-ink treble that had just blown up in his face. That bet had not been based on good fortune but on the exercise of betting intelligence. And it had been about to pay off – until some little bastard on the take had robbed him.

He knew the little bastard's name and the training yard where he worked. It shouldn't be difficult to find out where he lived.

Keith slammed his fist on the table in front of him. He'd been playing by the rules, but where had it got him? Sod the rules.

The shock was fading now, to be replaced by other feelings. Deep, dangerous feelings of hurt and anger that he knew well and which lived inside him like a separate creature. The Beast, that was how he thought of it. He'd lived with the Beast all his life, and he'd learned the hard way how to control it. But sometimes the Beast wouldn't be penned in. Its need was too strong and too terrible. The way he felt now, after this humiliation, he didn't know whether he could keep it in check.

Chapter Two

'What do you think, Phil?'

Julia turned towards her husband, who was sprawling on the bed, watching her get dressed. A small, dark furrow of anxiety creased her brow. Selecting the right clothes for the evening ahead was a serious business. It was important to look her best.

'Phil?' She couldn't read his expression, which was hidden in shadow.

'Let's see the other one again,' he said.

Her mouth tugged downward in frustration, but she obediently slipped the straps of her oyster-pink dress from her slim shoulders and wriggled the tight garment over her hips. Beneath it she wore just a tiny satin thong – a Christmas present from Phil – and she was conscious of her near-nakedness as she stood directly beneath the overhead light. Across the foot of the bed lay her other possible choice – a black sheath which had been on and off a couple of times already in her search for the right outfit. As she reached for it again, she heard Phil chuckle.

She jerked upright, her bare breasts quivering. 'You pig,' she cried, the penny suddenly dropping. 'You just want to gawp at me!'

She could see his eyes now, glinting wickedly, as the chuckle grew into full-blown laughter. She threw the dress at him.

'Come here,' he said.

She went – she couldn't resist him.

He slipped an arm round her waist and pulled her down on top of him.

'We'll be late,' she protested.

His hands were on her. Strong, callused hands now tenderly stroking and teasing. Tracing the tiny tattoo of a daisy high on her left buttock – and other places. He did not speak but his lips were busy.

Julia could feel her heart pounding and a knot of desire gather in her belly. The anticipation before they made love was sometimes painful. It frightened her, the way he could turn her on so quickly, just as if he had flicked a switch.

'You said this evening was important,' she murmured.

'So it is,' he breathed into her open mouth, 'but it's not as important as you.'

The knot inside her drew tighter as she returned his kiss with heart and soul.

As they sped into town, Julia peered out of the window of Phil's luxury Saab – a prize for becoming last season's top jockey. Snug in leather-upholstered comfort, she made out vague shapes of houses and hedgerows along a road grown familiar to her over the last twelve months. It still seemed strange to her that her life had changed so fast. A year ago she'd been suffering a miserable existence at the other end of the country – working as a drudge in a café just to stay near a man who didn't love her. And now look at her: a valued member of the best training operation in National Hunt racing and happily – ecstatically – married to the champion jockey.

They were running late but she no longer cared about that. Given the choice she'd have stayed in bed, in Phil's arms, and finished what they'd barely begun. The depths of her physical passion for her husband surprised her – it seemed she wanted him all the time. She considered him surreptitiously as he concentrated on the wet road ahead. Did he look just a mite more relaxed now he'd won the first race of his comeback? Or was he, like her, still savouring the delicious way they had just made each other happy? She couldn't tell. Whatever he did, Phil looked at ease. She'd rarely seen him disconcerted. Even lying broken in a hospital bed, he'd raised a smile and told her it was all part of the job.

She'd always had a thing about jockeys. She supposed it followed from loving horses so much. Though she'd never actually owned a horse, she'd grown up with them, courtesy mostly of her mother's men friends. 'Mum's the original hippy,' she'd told Phil in their first serious conversation. 'Me and my sisters wandered around a lot.' They'd wandered from communes in the Home Counties to crofts in the Western Isles to a farm in Northumberland, where her mother still lived with Big Alan, the last and best of Julia's many surrogate dads. The one thing that could be said about the dads was that they all encouraged her passion for horses.

Most little girls like horses – Julia's sisters and friends were as keen as any but, when it came down to it, any cute furry creature with big eyes would do. Not for Julia, however. She couldn't understand how anyone could prefer a soppy bunny rabbit or fluffy kitten to a horse. Horses were noble, strong, magical creatures. Who talked to her.

The first horse to speak to her was a Shetland pony on the Isle of Mull when she was six. He was kept in a field near the caravan where they were living, temporarily, in the course of a domestic upheaval. Julia had gone to feed him with her sisters and had stood back as they thrust their hands through the fence, holding out pieces of apple and yelling to the pony. He shambled over, snaffled the fruit and then nipped the girls' fingers. They jumped back shrieking and screamed at Julia not to go near the pony. She ignored them and held out her offering calmly. She knew the animal wouldn't bite her and he didn't. As he gently extracted the apple from her little fingers, he looked her in the eye and his words took shape in her mind. 'I like you. Those others are too noisy.'

Julia was overcome with delight. She hugged the moment to herself but later, when their mother was telling the girls never to go near that bad-tempered animal again, she made the mistake of standing up for him. 'He only bit them because they were shouting,' she said. 'He told me so.'

She never heard the last of it. From then on, whenever her siblings wanted to be mean, she was the mad sister. 'Dotty', 'potty', 'crazy', 'flaky' – all these words and many more were hung around her neck. Sometimes, in the lonelier years of a misspent adolescence, they seemed to give her an identity that she herself could not provide. But she always found a purpose in horses – and then boys.

When boys had started to pay her attention – she'd been barely into her teens – the ones who caught her eye were those who liked horses. All her fledgling romances were played out against a horsy background. Hanging around stables, riding out, watching point-to-points with her admirer of the moment, she'd talked and breathed horses. But the boys who kept her on the floor longest at the hunt knees-ups were the jockeys. Lads with keen eyes, quick wits and wandering hands. She'd been in love with a rider, it seemed, since she was twelve.

The last of them – the one before Phil – had almost killed her, first with his kindness and then with his treachery. She'd been unhappy working at Jimmy Craig's stables in the Scottish borders, where the conditions were bad for the horses and worse for the stable staff. Though she'd got her own flat and was working closely with Eileen, the local horse physio, she couldn't ignore the way the grooms were treated. Then Jimmy's young brother Rob took an interest in her – he was the stable jockey, naturally. He listened to her when she complained that a horse was not being given time between races for a swollen hip to mend, and that another had been taken off the diet the vet had recommended – and he even promised to talk to Jimmy about the rats in the girls' hostel. He'd bedded her beautifully, too, and she'd fallen for him hard. His soulful brown eyes, his hot touch between the sheets, his sweet voice serenading her at midnight as he picked at his guitar – for a few weeks Rob was the love of her life. Then Jimmy told her Rob was engaged to his most important owner's only daughter and sacked her in the same breath. The job at the café lasted just ten days, time enough for her to hear – finally – from Rob himself that she'd just been a minor diversion from his chosen path in life.

A few weeks later, after she'd got some work at Deanscroft on Eileen's recommendation, she'd seen a photo of Rob's wedding in a newspaper cutting a friend had sent and cried as she mucked out Russell Dean's horses. She'd cursed the friend as she did so, thinking her cruel, but it turned out she had done her a favour. Phil had found Julia in tears and whisked her out on to the gallops on a broad-framed novice jumper who required all her attention.

After that, Julia had become aware of Phil keeping an eye on her, asking her opinion on horses, getting her to help him out, being a presence she couldn't ignore. She didn't fancy him at first, though she guessed he was keen on her – why else would the yard's top jockey bother with her? But after their first proper conversation, over mugs of tea in the tack-room when he listened patiently to her life story, she knew she'd end up in bed with him.

That event lay some four weeks in the future, by which time she'd formed the opinion that Phil was worth half a dozen feckless men like Rob. For one thing, he was the best rider she'd ever seen. He got the best out of horses without appearing to do much, as if they responded to him in a different way to other jockeys. And when there was a panic on at the yard, after a horse was found cast in his box and a lad lost it in a screaming match with the assistant trainer, Phil's sudden appearance calmed everyone down. She was impressed that he mucked in to sort matters out with the minimum of fuss.

The other girls were mad about him and jealous of the attention Julia was receiving. Through them she discovered his reputation with women. The press, it seemed, were always eager to feature him in the gossip columns with a new model on his arm. All of this changed him in her eyes from just a friendly shoulder to cry on into someone dangerous, mysterious – seductive. By the time he made his move on her, her feelings had come full circle and she was convinced he'd never fancied her at all. She fell into his lap like a ripe plum.

'You didn't rate me at first,' he told her once they'd become lovers, 'then you couldn't wait. You were gagging for it.'

'And I suppose you weren't,' she'd said, affronted.

'Of course I was.' He'd looked at her strangely, as if he were embarrassed. 'I've been in love with you from the start. Is that OK?'

It was indeed, and it had turned out better than OK. Much better.

They were half an hour late arriving at the restaurant but no one seemed to care. The group assembled to celebrate Snowflake's unexpected triumph were too busy downing champagne.

Jack Mitton, Snowflake's owner, pounced on them as they entered the private bar on the first floor, Russell Dean at his elbow.

'The guest of honour,' Jack exclaimed, seizing Phil's hand. 'Without you there'd be no party.'

Phil tried to deflect the compliment, as Julia knew he would.

'Very kind of you, Mr Mitton, but your horse did all the work.'

The owner's expansive grin vanished. 'Really? He's never done any before.'

He looked as if he might continue to argue the point but Russell cut in. 'This is Julia.'

Jack took her hand in a fleshy grip and studied her closely. 'I've heard about you,' he said, 'but Russell never told me you were a beauty.'

Julia blushed and took a glass of champagne from a waitress. What on earth had Russell been saying?

Around them milled familiar faces from the yard. Others, older and more smartly dressed, she assumed to be Jack's friends. The owner grabbed one of them by the arm, a man in his early fifties with thin grey hair and rimless spectacles.

'Here's Arnold, my personal orthopaedic surgeon. Fixed up my hip last year. I always drag him along when I'm going to get drunk in case I break any more bones.'

Julia laughed on cue and smiled her way through the pleasantries. This was one aspect of being a famous jockey's wife that she didn't welcome. She had little confidence in her social skills though, luckily, Phil could be counted on to keep their end up. Secretly she was longing to break away and have a giggle with Gary, Snowflake's lad. She knew he'd be thrilled about the afternoon's victory, and they hadn't had a chance to discuss it.

An elegant, dark-haired woman had joined them and Jack introduced her as Simone Brown, Arnold's wife.

Out of the corner of her eye Julia saw Phil's grin broaden as he took a step towards the woman.

'Nice to meet you,' Simone said, deflecting his greeting and turning to Julia. Her smile was mere politeness but her eyes probed, bristling with curiosity.

Then she'd whisked her husband off and Julia was aware that Phil was staring at her retreating figure in shock. For once, he looked genuinely put out.

Julia's mind raced. All her intuition told her that something significant had just taken place between Phil and that woman. Obviously he knew her, but she'd barely acknowledged him. Why?

There could only be one answer to that. Julia's sole reservation about throwing in her lot with Phil had been his reputation as a womaniser. However, he'd been transparently honest about his past affairs. He'd given her chapter and verse on the women who'd mattered to him and answered every question she'd put to him. He'd been out with dozens of females, from barmaids to Sloanes, attached and fancy free, young and not so young – but none she'd heard of had been called Simone.

Julia finished her drink in one gulp, aware the wine was going straight to her head. It did nothing to ease the nervous fluttering in her stomach. She knew the feeling well. After being put through the wringer with Rob, she was no stranger to the pangs of jealousy.

To Julia's dismay she was separated from Phil when they sat down to eat at two large round tables. As host, Jack decreed the seating plan, and she found herself next to him with Russell on her other side. Phil had been placed on the other table between Peggy, Russell's wife, and – predictably – Simone. Julia tried not to stare but the woman was directly in her eyeline. She'd removed her jacket to reveal smooth olive-skinned shoulders on to which tumbled a torrent of lustrous black hair. Her face was lean, with deep-set mysterious eyes and a long thin nose – a strong face, Julia decided. What was more, she filled her low-cut cocktail dress in a way that no man, let alone Phil, could ignore. All in all, the woman was thoroughly intimidating.

So far Phil and Simone hadn't spoken to each other. They were working hard – suspiciously hard? – at being neighbourly in opposite directions. Julia knew they couldn't keep that up. When they finally turned to each other she'd be watching.

'Russell tells me you're the young woman I have to thank for Snowflake's transformation.'

Jack Mitton's voice commanded Julia's attention as she toyed with the smoked salmon on her plate, her mind on events at the next table.

'I wouldn't say that, Mr Mitton. He just needed time to recover from his injury.'

'Rubbish,' said the owner, tearing a bread roll with purpose. 'You know what gets me about the horse business, my dear, you're all so bloody modest. That horse had been swinging the lead for years until you came along. It was off for pet food if it hadn't performed today, I promise you.'

'Did you say that to Snowflake? It probably made all the difference.'

Jack squinted at her in surprise and Julia added, 'I think horses understand more than we give them credit for. Snowflake's a very bright animal.'

Jack glanced at Russell on her other side, who was listening to the exchange. The owner's expression clearly said, 'This girl's a fruitcake.'

'Julia's winding you up, Jack. She put in a lot of work on the horse and it paid off.'

Jack chewed his roll for a moment. It seemed he was coming to a decision.

'Russell says you sometimes take on special projects. Outside of Deanscroft.'

'I sometimes stable horses with my father-in-law just a mile away, if that's what you mean. I can keep a close eye on them that way.'

Julia realised it was no accident she was sitting between the two of them. She was being set up. Not that she minded; she was curious to hear what was on offer.

'My wife's the keen horse owner in our house, not me, but she's not too well these days. Couldn't make it tonight, unfortunately. Anyhow, Yvonne's got a jumper who had a bad accident a couple of years ago. She nursed him back to health and she's always said that he could race again. I'm wondering whether to give it a try. Maybe you could take him for a bit, see if he's up to it.'

'How old is he?'

'Ten, but I reckon he's got a few years left in him yet.'

'And what kind of accident did he have?'

'He was six lengths clear in the Murphy's at Cheltenham two years ago and tried to fly the last. Tore all the ligaments in his hip.'

'Oh.' Julia reached for her glass, her mind racing. 'Surely you don't mean—?'

'Callisto,' Jack said quickly. 'The best horse we've ever had. A once-in-a-lifetime horse,' he added wistfully.

Russell chipped in. 'He was second in the King George at Kempton and he won the Murphy's the year before. He was the favourite the year he fell.'

'He'd have been put down at the course if Yvonne hadn't begged the vets to wait a little longer,' said Jack. 'She saved him and she'd love to see him race again. I don't care if it's at the meanest little gaff track in the country.'

'Gosh,' said Julia, overwhelmed by the thought.

'So what do you say?' Jack stared at her intently. 'Will you take a look at him?'

Julia downed the rest of her wine in a gulp. 'I'd love to.'

'Enjoying your evening, Mr Nicholas?'

Phil shot Simone a sideways glance. 'So you're talking to me now, are you?'

She smiled and inclined her head in the way that he was coming to know well. 'I didn't mean to appear rude earlier but I thought you wanted to keep our relationship between ourselves.'

'You know I do.'

'Then you mustn't greet me with open arms. We're not supposed to have met.'

He sighed. 'Sorry. It's just that you're the last person I expected to see here.'

'It's not a problem, is it?'

'No. Of course not.'

She chuckled, a low musical sound. 'Your wife is even lovelier than I'd imagined. She can't stop staring at you.'

'I'm a lucky guy, aren't I?'

Simone turned to him, her expression now devoid of humour. 'Why don't you tell her about us, Phil?'

He held her gaze but didn't reply.

She shrugged her shoulders. 'Let's talk about this another time.'

Then she turned abruptly to join the conversation on her other side.

Julia was too far off to hear what Phil and Simone had been saying but it was obvious from their faces that they had not just been swapping the niceties of first acquaintance. They appeared to know each other well enough to be in serious disagreement. The woman had something on Phil, Julia could tell that. She'd rarely seen him look so put out.

Her imagination went to work along predictable lines. Phil was obviously having an affair with her – or had been involved with her in the past. That would make more sense. He'd been such an ardent lover she couldn't see how he could have been carrying on with Simone recently. And now the pair of them had been thrown together again unexpectedly and she'd covered it up better than him. But it was plain the woman still had power over him and Julia could see why. Simone was intelligent, articulate, sophisticated – all the things Julia feared she was not. And the cow was showing too much chest.

Julia tried to focus on other matters. On Russell's conversation about all-weather tracks. On Jack Mitton's hunting yarns. On Yvonne Mitton and Callisto. But she wasn't having much luck. Her eyes were drawn magnetically to Simone's superior smile and gleaming cleavage. Her fingers itched to seize a cigarette from Russell's pack lying just inches from her left hand.

Instead she filled her glass and drank.

*

33

The letter took shape in Keith's mind as he loaded the soiled shavings of the hounds' dirty bedding into the incinerator. There were four pens and a dozen couples – twenty-four hounds – in each pen. He cleaned out one pen a day, and bloody tedious it was too. It was good to have something to think about while he performed his drudgery.

He returned to the cottage and drafted the letter in longhand to be sure he got it right. Then he turned on the computer.

He wasn't what you'd call a computer buff. He resented the way people went on about them – 'the new technology', 'e-mail', 'the information super highway' and all that bollocks. He'd only bought the darn thing to keep Denise quiet when she was going on about getting herself trained up on computers so she could go out and get a job. He'd got it off a bloke who owed him a few favours. The fellow had bought his son a smart new one so he'd been happy to pass the old machine on to Keith. Predictably, Denise had sneered at it, said it wasn't up to date, but he'd known that was just an excuse. The lazy cow had no intention of making herself 'computer literate', as she called it. As for getting a job, that was a joke. She thought marriage was a meal ticket. It was the best thing he'd ever done, kicking her out of the house.

So Keith had kept the computer for himself and gradually come to terms with it. He wasn't too clever on the keyboard but he could knock out a letter if he had to. Sometimes his self-taught skills came in handy – like now.

He sat down before the screen and, slowly, began to type.

The meal was drawing to a close and some people had already left for the bar, preferring more alcohol to coffee. Julia made her excuses and got up to join them.

She took the stool next to Mark Shaw, who was sitting on his own.

'So you've deserted the top table,' he said, his face lighting up at the sight of her.

'I've quit while I'm ahead.' She took a gulp from the wineglass the barman placed in front of her. 'Mr Mitton's just asked me to look after one of his horses.'

'Really?' Mark leaned closer. 'Does he know you have conversations with animals? Shall I tell him the truth about you, Mrs Dolittle?'

Julia punched him softly on the arm. 'Just you dare.'

He laughed, his sea-green eyes flashing, and she laughed too. Once, in her early days at Deanscroft, Mark had caught her in earnest conversation with a horse and she'd assumed he'd make fun of her like everyone else. Instead he'd quizzed her about her methods and she'd told him more than she'd ever told anyone.

'Sometimes,' she'd said, 'the horses tell me where they hurt, so I know how to treat them.'

He'd not said anything to that but, after riding an animal in her care who'd made an unexpected return to form, he'd sought her out.

'I could do with a gift like yours,' he'd said. 'The horses could tell me how they'd like to be ridden.'

Julia felt relaxed in Mark's company – she didn't have to watch what she said. Even Phil wasn't so understanding about her rapport with horses.

She pushed the thought of Phil from her mind. He was still sitting at the table, next to that Simone creature.

She studied his pale face. 'You're looking a bit glum for a man who rode a winner today. You were brilliant on May Queen.'

He turned his eyes on her full bore. 'We're here to toast Snowflake, remember? Anyhow, that's all history. I need more winners and I don't get enough rides.'

'But Russell's got plenty of horses.'

'And all the good ones go to Phil, don't they?'

Julia was taken aback. 'Surely there are enough to go around.'

'No, there aren't. When Phil was injured I got the pick of the bunch. Now I'm back in the queue. Making do with dodgy buggers like May Queen.'

'Oh.' Julia didn't know what to say.

Mark looked embarrassed, as if it had suddenly dawned on him who he was talking to.

'I'm sorry, Julia. I'm not having a go at Phil – he's the number-one man, I know that. It's just that you can't hang around in this business. If you're not getting on you're going nowhere.'

Julia had never considered how Phil's recovery might affect anyone else. She admired Mark's honesty in admitting to her how he felt. He looked so miserable her heart went out to him.

They were standing by the stairwell which led to the main dining-room on the ground floor. A handful of couples were moving around a small circular dance-floor and music floated upwards.

'Come on,' she said, grabbing his hand. 'Let's dance.'

'I can't,' he protested.

She ignored him and set off downstairs. He followed, muttering, 'I'm hopeless.'

He wasn't, of course. No man with his natural rhythm and balance was without hope on the dance-floor and when the fast stuff came on he threw her around with some flair.

'You fibber,' she protested as Ricky Martin faded out. 'You can dance all right.'

He grinned and put his arms around her for the next – slow – number.

'Won't Phil mind?' he murmured in her ear.

'Of course not,' she said. And to herself she thought, who cares if he does?

But Mark was still anxious. 'You won't tell anyone what I said about not getting rides, will you?'

'No, Mark. Your secret's safe with me.'

She felt his body relax against hers as they moved in time to the music.

The Editor
The *Racing Beacon*

Dear Sir

May I draw your attention to the 4.15 at Wincanton this afternoon, supposedly won by a rank outsider called Snowflake. I say supposedly because, to any honest observer, the race was plainly chucked by Adrian Moore on January King. Moore was four lengths clear going into the last hurdle, then he stopped riding so Snowflake could catch him on the line. In a lifetime of watching racing I don't think I've seen anything so blattant. I don't suppose the fact that January King was 7–2 and Snowflake 33–1 had anything to do with it?

To add insult to injury, when Moore was up before the stewards he was suspended for ten days and fined £500. Ten days! He should be banned for six months at least. And £500 is a joke – he probably got ten times that for pulling the horse.

No punter complains when he's beaten fair and square but this is as bent as a five-bob note and *it happens all the bloody time*. Six months ago at Sandown Park a jockey stopped his horse at the wrong winning post. At Fakenham the favourite lost because he was pulled up a circuit too early. And I've lost count of the times my horse has been second and the winning jockey has been banned for misuse of the whip – how is that fair? Why should I lose out to a jockey who has broken the rules?

I tell you why – it's because the whole thing is crooked. Racing is run for insiders and their cronies, a small cleek of crooked bastards who are milking the honest punter dry. But why should you lot care? You journalists go on about the 'sport' of kings and the 'rules' of the turf but you sit up in London stuffing your faces on expense accounts, tenners hanging out of your back pockets, because *you're in on it too*.

The *Beacon* claims to shed a spotlight on the sport of racing, doesn't it? And to be the friend of the average punter. It's about time you proved it. How about an exposay of cheats and charllatons? Naming and shaming bent jockeys and trainers like the *News of the World* did with peedophiles? I challenge you to live up to your name for once and give us a campagne for justice in racing.

If you don't do it then I bloody well will.

YOU HAVE BEEN WARNED.

It was strange for Julia to feel another man's hands on her body in the intimate clinch of the slow dance. Strange but not unpleasant. She closed her eyes, the alcohol in her system fogging her thoughts. Phil had become so much part of her in such a short time. One flesh, that was how people described the sensation, wasn't it? When they were close her husband's body was simply an extension of her own. Only this wasn't her husband's body she was holding now. It was another man's hands on her hips, his hot breath on her face, his leg pressing against her thigh.

She broke away abruptly in the middle of the dance.

'I'm sorry,' she cried. 'I can't—'

She ran from the dance-floor and blundered up the steps, aware of other people staring at her. It wasn't Mark's fault but she had to get away from him. It was wrong for her to be dancing with another man.

She tripped on the top step of the stairs and strong arms caught her. It was Phil.

'Jules, are you all right?'

'Take me home,' she blurted. 'Please, Phil. Now.'

Keith felt better now he'd written the letter – just a bit. It was as if he'd thrown the Beast inside him a scrap, a morsel to chew on that would keep his hunger at bay. But he knew the Beast all too well – it couldn't be appeased with scraps.

When he was a young man, the Beast had been a devil to control. A chance remark in a pub, a sly innuendo, sometimes an ill-timed glance across the bar, and Keith would be on his feet, swinging his big fists. He'd lost a few friends that way and a few teeth, and he'd seen the inside of a police cell more than once. But he wasn't a stupid man and he'd realised that the terrible anger that burned inside would end up destroying him unless he could put it on a leash. There had been some casualties on the way. His mother, God rest her soul, had borne the brunt of his callow rage. And Belinda, his first wife, had seen him at his worst before she too had left him – not that he blamed her. It was as well she'd run away or something really bad might have happened.

Of course, the one person he really wanted to harm, the one who had placed the Beast in his soul and turned him into its unhappy keeper, had cheated him. His father had died before Keith had had a chance to expend his adult fury on him. So now he never would and the Beast would never be tamed. Only kept at bay.

Julia woke in the dark. The hollow in the bed next to her was empty but warm.

'Phil?' she croaked, her mouth parched, her temples throbbing. She remembered this feeling. What had she been thinking of? It had been months since she'd had a hangover.

The bedroom door opened and a quadrant of light speared into the room.

'I've brought you some tea.' He placed a mug on the bedside table and sank on to the covers next to her. 'How're you feeling?'

'Oh, Phil.'

He chuckled. 'You're a dark horse. I've never seen you plastered before.'

'I'm sorry.' She struggled into a sitting position and noticed he was wearing jodhpurs and a sweater. 'Aren't you coming back to bed?'

'I can't. I'm running late as it is.'

Julia squinted at the bedside clock. The LCD read 7:44. At Deanscroft the team would have been hard at it for nearly an hour. Fortunately she wasn't due in today.

She put her hand on Phil's thigh. 'Please.'

'I promised Russell I'd ride work on Hollow Crown.' Hollow Crown was one of the yard's star performers, on a strict training regime that would, if all went well, put him in the winner's enclosure at the Cheltenham Festival.

Right now Julia didn't care about that. She was remembering painful things about the night before and she needed some reassurance. She took Phil's hand and held it against her chest.

'You minx,' he said, and kissed her throat, then her lips, softly at first but soon more urgently. His fingers took the bait, as she knew they would, and cupped the softness of her breast. She felt her nipple harden at his touch. Then he took his hand away.

'Sorry, sweetheart.' He kissed her forehead and stood up.

'I hate you,' she muttered.

He laughed as he bustled about, putting on his watch and grabbing loose change from the dresser.

Julia warmed her hands round her mug of tea and watched him. The events of the previous evening became clearer in her mind.

'I mustn't drink, Phil. I just can't hold it.'

'One drink and you're anybody's, eh? I saw you dancing with Mark.'

'Two drinks and I'm not capable.'

'That's true enough.'

He was standing over her now, smiling, concerned, his eyes full of love. She remembered him in much the same position last night, tenderly undressing her, putting her to bed.

'Tell me about Simone Brown.'

His expression froze. The affection in his eyes vanished to be replaced by – what? Caution? Fear? Guilt?

'Who?'

'The woman you sat next to last night.'

'Oh, her. She's OK.'

'What did you talk about?'

'Not much, darling, and I've really got to go.'

He bent to kiss her goodbye and she clung on to him like a child, reluctant to let him out of her sight.

Phil crouched low in the saddle and squeezed gently with his thighs, just a touch, like a feather-light pulse on the accelerator of a high-performance car. The effect was much the same. Hollow Crown powered up the schooling ground and took off like a bird, flying the fence. The north wind bit into Phil's face and he filled his lungs with cold air. He felt great. The sky was blue above, the animal beneath him was pure class – and yesterday he'd had a winner.

He slowed the horse at the end of the run, where Russell, muffled against the elements, was waiting for him.

'He's tiptop,' he called to the trainer. 'Jumping like a dream.'

'Once more,' Russell said, and Phil trotted the horse round, eager to take the three-flight practice run again. This wasn't work – it was fun. It was strange to think some people preferred lying in bed on a crisp winter morning. Of course, most people didn't have the privilege of riding a Gold Cup chaser.

He wondered why he was going off to see that shrink, Simone Brown. At this particular moment he couldn't imagine. Then he reminded himself he'd never had a fall when schooling a horse. His problem only seemed to surface during steeplechases. It didn't happen at every fence but sometimes, just a couple of strides from taking off, he would be gripped by lurid fears – of smashing into the hard-packed birch or being kicked like a football by the pounding hooves of the pack or lying buried and broken under half a ton of racehorse. At these moments he would just freeze and leave everything to the horse. On experienced animals that was fine but, on novices who needed assistance, he was an accident waiting to happen.

Phil put the matter to the back of his mind and tried to give himself some confidence. These practice fences were as big and challenging as any on the circuit, and he was steering Hollow Crown over them as fearlessly as he had ever jumped in his life. And, classy though he was, the animal needed treating with caution. He'd run out once over hurdles at Warwick and, given half a chance, Phil knew he'd do it again. If a horse thought he'd got away with something once, he'd be bound to repeat it, even if years had gone by.

It was as if Hollow Crown had read his mind. Coming in to the open ditch, the last of the practice obstacles, the horse suddenly cocked his jaw and swerved to his right. For a split second the pair were heading for the solid wooden upright that formed the end of the fence wing. Phil had seen more than one jockey smash his knee to pieces in that kind of collision. He already had his whip in his right hand and, without thinking, he cracked Hollow Crown down the right shoulder. The horse did not alter course; he seemed drawn towards the post as if to a magnet. Visions of losing his leg raced through Phil's mind and he jerked both his knees up to minimise an impact that seemed inevitable. In desperation he gave an almighty yank on the left rein, at the same time giving the horse another crack of the whip with the sort of force that only comes from fear. Hollow Crown took one more stride and then ducked back inside, skipping neatly over the ditch as if it had always been his intention.

Phil let out a long breath as he regained his composure, and then looked back towards Russell. From where the trainer was standing the incident had obviously looked insignificant. He gave Phil the thumbs-up and pointed down the hill, in the direction of the yard. Phil sat back in the saddle with relief and clapped the big horse on the shoulder, his heart still pounding.

So what was he going to do about Simone? Fancy her turning up last night – he could have done without that. He'd been caught on the hop and he knew Julia had picked up on it. Typical of her. It just went to prove that it had been a mistake to go and see Simone in the first place. His riding was OK now. He'd won on Snowflake. He'd laid down the law to Hollow Crown. He didn't need any psychiatrist to sort him out.

By the time Phil had walked the horse back down the path to the yard, he had resolved to cancel his future appointments.

Julia dragged herself down to the kitchen, the mug of cold tea in her hand. She must have drifted off after Phil had left. She didn't feel much better – in fact she felt worse.

She made coffee in a fog and then did the one thing she'd sworn to herself she'd never do again. She lit the cigarette she'd found at the bottom of a little-used handbag when she'd dressed last night. She'd laughed when she'd discovered it, being on a high from Phil and Snowflake's success and with the prospect of a happy evening ahead of

41

her. She'd thought herself fortunate in not remembering it earlier in the afternoon when she'd had the urge. Well, thank God she'd not smoked it then or she'd not have it now.

The stale tobacco scorched her throat, scrambling her thoughts for a few seconds. She held the smoke in, savouring the taste, the smell – the buzz – of the wicked weed. The first two drags hit her like a hammer blow. Maybe this was the way to smoke – one cigarette every six months.

The ringing of her mobile interrupted her reverie. Drat – bad timing. She wanted to concentrate on her vice without distraction. But it might be Phil.

'Is that Julia?' A woman's voice, cultured and gentle.

'Yes?'

'I'm Yvonne Mitton. I believe you are going to take a look at my horse.'

Oh my God, Callisto! Last night's conversation came flooding back.

'I'm so excited,' the voice continued. 'Jack tells me you're a miracle-worker. I know you'll have him running again.'

'I can't make any promises, Mrs Mitton.'

'Of course not. But you don't know Callisto like I do. He was going to win the Murphy's for the second year running before his accident. Jack thinks I'm a bit barmy but I can't help feeling it's not too late. Especially now you're on my side . . .'

By the time she rang off, some fifteen minutes later, Julia's precious cigarette was an ugly mound of grey ash. Saved from herself by an unknown horse – maybe it was an omen.

Keith considered Monty, the horse that Henry Carrington, the old buffer from the hunt, had just unloaded from his trailer. He was a big-boned animal who must have cut a dash in his youth. Even now he stood straight and carried his noble head high. He was still a handsome beast, even if he was a bit grizzled around the edges.

Not that that was of much concern to Keith, who had four £20 notes in his pocket for the trouble of turning the horse into dog meat. Carrington had stuffed the notes shiftily into Keith's hand before he'd driven off, and Keith had no doubt he felt guilty about the whole business.

'You'll make sure he doesn't suffer, won't you?' he'd said after spending a minute or so stroking the horse and chatting to him in an undertone Keith couldn't catch.

'Stay and watch if you like,' Keith had replied, which had drained the blood from Carrington's face and sent him scurrying back to his vehicle.

Men like Carrington were stupid, in Keith's opinion. He certainly wouldn't waste good money on getting someone else to do his dirty work. But then, being a gamekeeper's son, Keith had been accustomed to dead animals all his life.

He took the horse's rein and led him into the shed he used for slaughtering, the one with the blood channels and a drain in the centre of the floor. A few yards from the double doors the animal caught a whiff of dead flesh and planted his feet. Carrington had said he was twenty-four if he was a day and past it, but Keith wasn't so sure about that. The old horse looked like he had a few more gallops left in him. He had certainly looked a lot more lively since he had sensed what was about to happen to him.

Which was neither here nor there to Keith. He'd been paid to do a job so he might as well get on with it.

Unless. A sudden thought struck. Someone he knew might be persuaded to pay him a bit more to keep the horse alive.

He went into the house to make the call and returned five minutes later with a bucket of water.

'It's your lucky day, Monty,' he said as the horse drank greedily. 'Eleventh-hour reprieve.'

Keith was pleased. It was his lucky day too. Soon Monty would have a new lease of life on the hunting fields of Derbyshire and Keith would be a few quid better off. He'd asked his pal for £1,200 so, with luck, they'd settle on a grand. Provided Carrington never got wind of it, everyone was a winner.

Phil had a good feeling about the 2.30 at Folkestone – a three-mile, two-furlong handicap chase. He was riding an old friend, Wolf Patrol, who he'd successfully piloted round the course the previous January, in the days before Julia, before the wedding and before his accident. It seemed more like five years ago than one. But he well remembered kicking the tireless Wolf Patrol home in the teeth of a gale to win by three lengths. The victory had put him in the lead for the jockey's championship and he'd not been headed after that. Though he'd not ridden Wolf Patrol since – the horse had been sidelined for the rest of the season with a leg injury – he'd been looking forward to getting back on him. At nine years old, the powerful chestnut gelding was considered a seasoned campaigner. During Phil's absence, he'd carried Mark to victory at Uttoxeter and Catterick, and Phil was keen to get reacquainted. All in all, the omens looked good. It was even blowing another gale.

During a race, Phil always took the shortest route, around the inside of the course. There was no point in taking any other unless the ground was a bog and it was easier for the horse to gallop elsewhere. There were some days when he'd go miles wide just to find a firmer surface. The difference could be as marked as running on a beach, where it was firm at the water's edge or soft in the deep dry sand beyond the tide line. However, racing on the inside was much more dangerous.

Eighteen runners lined up, at least four of whom wanted to make the running. Phil was delighted that Wolf Patrol needed to be held up. He felt the now-familiar churning in his stomach and took a deep breath to fight the bile rising in his gorge. The thought of being jammed against the rail by a pack of horses filled his thoughts. The downside of taking the inner was that you could find yourself galloping flat out towards a fence and not able to see it because of the wall of horses in front of you.

There was also the wing of the fence to think about. If a horse decided to run out or got pushed out by another horse the result was guaranteed to be painful; even though most of the wings were now made of plastic. Phil had been through one at Hereford and the wing had shattered and carved through his boot and calf muscle. He remembered hooking the last piece of plastic out with a needle while staying in a hotel before riding in the Swedish National. That had been almost a year later.

As they galloped flat out towards the first fence, Wolf Patrol was swiftly into his stride but Phil was a complete passenger. He felt as if they were going a million miles an hour, but in reality they were only holding their position at the back of the pack, where they had started. He held his breath as the fence rushed towards them and prayed Wolf Patrol would get over safely. The big horse launched himself and Phil threw his weight back in the saddle ready for the fall, but Wolf Patrol landed cleanly on the other side, unaware of his rider's terror.

It took an entire circuit before Phil finally believed that his mount was not going to fall. Only then did he begin to relax and give the horse a ride.

At last Phil and Wolf Patrol were in harmony, eating up the ground and devouring the fences. The field had strung out and it was as if he were hacking the horse round on his own. Now the fear had passed, Phil could feel his breathing return to a more even pattern. He began to think about winning instead of his own safety.

He was on the right-hand curve leading into the home straight for the second time when he saw the leader begin to falter. With the gale now blowing directly into his face, it looked as though he were running through treacle. The lead he had enjoyed for so long was shrinking fast. The horse struck the top of the first fence in the home straight and veered right on landing, close to the rail on the inside of the circuit. The wall of wind had hit him and Wolf Patrol too, but Phil's horse was still full of running. With his head down he took the fence cleanly and quickly put some distance between himself and the rest of the field. He popped over the last and came home hard held.

As they walked back, Phil felt ashamed. Wolf Patrol had won despite him. He didn't know why his nerve had suddenly failed. This morning he'd almost believed he was over it – now he seemed worse than ever. He acknowledged the small crowd who came over to applaud his return but couldn't look any of them in the eye.

'Hey, maestro!' The shout came from the other side of the unsaddling enclosure, where Phil had just led Wolf Patrol to the berth reserved for the winner.

He forced a smile on to his face as a large bespectacled fellow picked his way across the boggy ground. It wasn't that he disliked Hugh Pimlott but the journalist's appearance was a reminder that he hadn't given a thought to his column for the *Racing Beacon* and his deadline was that afternoon. Still, that was where Hugh came in. Despite looking like a sixth-former on a skive, Hugh was adept at conjuring copy out of nothing. Phil preferred to write his column himself but sometimes the scruffy journalist was a saviour.

'Sorry, Pim. I haven't done it yet.'

Hugh was unperturbed. He pulled a notebook from the depths of his baggy overcoat. 'No sweat. Gimme an idea or two and I'll see what I can cobble together.'

'Well . . .' Phil's mind was suddenly blank.

'How about your return to winning ways? Great horses, great rides, great to be first past the post after a long lay-off.'

'It's a bit boring, isn't it? It's what you'd expect me to say.'

Hugh chewed on his pencil. 'What about commenting on the last at Wincanton yesterday? Adrian Moore dropping his hands and getting the bird. Enraged punters crying for his head.'

'I felt sorry for him. He was trying to save the horse and didn't see me coming. It could have happened to any of us.'

Hugh was scribbling. 'So it's "lay off the honest jock, he was only thinking of his horse and there but for the grace of God go the rest of us, I myself did something similar in the previous race" – that's right, isn't it?'

Phil nodded.

Hugh continued writing. 'I'll work in the stuff about Snowflake and Wolf Patrol, got to say something about them. You're feeling top of the world and back in the swing of things now the season's really hotting up and lots more winners to come. How's that?' His eyes looked huge, magnified in his smudgy spectacles.

'Don't make me sound too big headed, Pim.'

'Why not?' The journalist put away his notebook and laid a porky hand on Phil's arm. 'You're back on the victory trail, mate. Let's crow about it.'

The horse ambled slowly round the boggy paddock, familiarising himself with his new surroundings. He was big – some 17.1 hands tall – and he moved stiffly, as if testing the ground before he put his full weight on it. He favoured his left side, dragging his off-hind leg. He took no notice of the two people by the gate closely watching his every move. Even when his perambulation took him close up to the watchers he gave no sign that he saw them at all.

'What do you think, Ted?' said Julia. When she'd asked permission to stable another horse at her father-in-law's farm she'd not told him anything about her latest patient.

Phil's dad considered the matter as he dragged on his cigarette. Julia had deliberately placed herself upwind of him, terrified that her recent cravings would lead her to another lapse. Funnily enough, watching the big horse shuffle disdainfully around the paddock made her feel better about everything. She waited on Ted's words.

'Hmm,' he said at last, 'he's a bit grand, isn't he? Underneath all that muck.'

The horse's flanks were caked with mud, and there were brambles and dead bracken tangled in his black tail hair.

'He was clean enough when he arrived. When I let him out here he went for a bit of a roll.'

Ted laughed. 'I can see that.'

'Can you see anything else?'

Julia valued the farmer's judgement. He'd worked with horses all his life, some of them pretty good. He'd once run a medium-sized training operation, but the death of Phil's brother had changed everything. Julia knew the history. She also knew that sometimes you had to dig to get at what Ted had to say.

He turned to look at her. 'You're being deliberately mysterious, aren't you, young lady?'

She grinned. She liked Ted such a lot. He was better than all the dads she'd ever had.

'Something tells me I've seen this horse before.' Ted stamped out his cigarette. 'I reckon he used to be a top performer. It's the size of him.'

He took the animal by the head-collar and scrutinised his face.

'I've seen you in the ring at Cheltenham, haven't I? Named after one of the planets – Saturn? Pluto?'

'Callisto,' said Julia. 'One of the moons of Jupiter.'

Ted looked at her. 'Not a bad guess, eh? And I suppose you've got to get him fit enough to get back to Cheltenham?'

'Anywhere will do, they say.'

Ted scratched the horse behind his ear. 'What does Phil reckon?'

'He doesn't know about Callisto yet. It all happened rather suddenly.'

Ted looked at Julia gravely. 'I saw that fall on TV.'

They all had, it had been shown dozens of times – the horse losing his footing as he tried to fly the fence and landing with a sickening crunch to lie in a lifeless heap.

'You've got your work cut out,' the farmer said. 'Two years out of training is a long time.'

'But it can happen – horses do come back.'

'Give or take the odd miracle, they don't. It's the same in any sport. Gazza after his knee injury wasn't the player he was before. The same goes for any athlete. Horses are no different.'

Julia's spirits plummeted. She could tell this was a special horse and Yvonne Mitton's enthusiasm had been infectious.

'Cheer up,' said Ted. 'You don't want to look down in the mouth when the conquering hero returns.'

Her bewilderment must have been obvious.

'Phil's had a couple of winners this afternoon. Didn't you know?'

'Has he?' In her excitement at receiving Callisto she'd forgotten about Phil's rides at Folkestone. 'On Wolf Patrol?'

'That's right. And a two-mile hurdle on Stanley Spencer. So there's no call to look gloomy.'

Julia felt like pointing out that Phil was coming back from injury too, and he was doing all right, but she decided to hold her tongue.

Callisto was studying her, probably wondering whether she had anything tasty tucked away in her pocket. No chance of that, she thought. He was already carrying too much weight for an athlete on the comeback trail.

It was a tedious drive back to the West Country from Folkestone. As a rule Phil found some radio show to listen to, just to occupy his thoughts. Today he drove in silence – his thoughts were already occupied.

Notwithstanding the wind and the heavy going he'd had an easy ride on Stanley Spencer. The favourite had led on the first circuit and then, unaccountably, fallen. Since the other runners weren't in Stanley's class that had handed him the race on a plate. Phil had hunted round to the rear of a group of four then put his foot down with a hurdle left to jump, leaving the other horses gasping in his wake.

The result should have been thoroughly satisfying. In his last four races he'd had three wins and a close second – good going in anybody's book. Hugh Pimlott had certainly thought so.

'Fantastic, mate. I'll tweak the old copy so the punters know you're really firing now. And don't worry, I'll keep it humble.'

Phil watched Hugh shamble off. Little did he know that, whatever the outward appearance of things, the champion jockey was far from back to his best.

An old jockey had once said to Phil that the moment your

imagination joins you out on the course you've had it. At the time he hadn't understood what the other fellow meant. Now he did.

As he drove silently cross-country Phil was glad he had not cancelled his appointment with Simone after all.

Chapter Three

Hugh Pimlott dumped his bulging briefcase on the floor next to his desk and, in a well-practised movement, flicked on his computer. Click, click, click – printer, terminal and screen. He kicked back his chair with one foot, stood his double-strength cappuccino on the mouse mat, shrugged his coat from his shoulders and slung it on top of the filing cabinet. With his left hand he seized the almond croissant protruding from his mouth, biting off a soggy chunk as he did so, and walked his right hand across the keyboard, inputting his log-in codes and password. Within sixty seconds of shouldering his way through the door, he was poised to begin work. At school he may not have been much of a sportsman but on the office playing-field Hugh was a world-beater.

It was 8.30 in the offices of the *Racing Beacon* and Hugh had the place to himself. His co-workers would not be seen for at least an hour, which suited Hugh down to the ground – he had a load of stuff to get through. Since his colleague Bernard's sudden retirement – a thinly disguised culling by the new management – certain tasks had been dumped on him which only a quiet hour of slog could resolve. Like trawling through the readers' letters.

Bernard used to have the letters page down to a fine art. He could sniff through a pile of illiterate Basildon Bond, simultaneously scanning the latest batch of e-mails, and come up with a balanced and entertaining page of precisely the right length in the half-hour between elevenses and opening time. This responsibility had now been handed to Hugh, and it took him a darn sight longer than that.

A backlog of epistles from Joe Public were piled haphazardly in a red wire basket – at least Hugh didn't have to open the envelopes. He began to flick through them. This morning he needed only a couple of 'unknowns' as a trainer had buttonholed him at Newton Abbot the day before. After bending Hugh's ear about his pet scheme for revising the handicap system, the trainer had pulled an envelope from his jacket pocket and pressed it into Hugh's hand.

'It took me bloody hours to work out so make sure you print it,' he said.

Hugh intended to. Dropping a horse's handicap mark by seven pounds if the animal finished unplaced in three consecutive races made sense to him.

He'd also received an e-mail from a former groom who recalled a trainer showing a horse to his owner during an evening tour of stables. The owner had been thrilled by how much the horse had improved since it had left his farm and had said so at length. The trainer was basking in the owner's praise until a sixteen-year-old lad piped up. Not only were they looking at the wrong horse, but it wasn't even the right sex. It was a bit of an old chestnut but usable just the same.

What he needed now, he decided, was a relatively literate offering from a reader with a topical point to make. Soon he thought he'd found it, buried halfway down.

But as Hugh read the neatly printed page he realised that the writer was not someone whose opinions could be given licence in the pages of the country's top-selling racing paper – or any paper, for that matter. A smile spread across his face as he reached the end. 'YOU HAVE BEEN WARNED.' Oh yeah? One of his father's sayings sprang to mind – 'They're not all locked up, son.'

He chucked the page into the wastepaper basket, then changed his mind. He opened his desk drawer and pulled out a scuffed old folder packed with stray bits of paper. This had been one of Bernard's prized possessions – a collection of bizarre and silly letters from the public amassed over the years. Hugh had been quite touched when the old journalist had handed it over with mock ceremony and told him he was now the keeper of the flame.

Hugh retrieved the letter from the bin and added it to the office Loony Letters file. Really, it was too good to chuck out.

Phil took his seat in Simone's reception room, torn by doubt. He couldn't believe he was doing this. He felt so foolish, sneaking off to see some shrink, asking for help like a little boy. *Please, miss, I'm a professional jump jockey but I'm worried I might fall off my horse and hurt myself.*

If any of the other jockeys got to hear about him seeing a psychiatrist they would rip the mickey out of him for months. He thought about getting up and leaving, but suddenly the door opened.

He was summoned into Simone's office: beige carpet and curtains, framed seascapes on the walls – decor designed to soothe. Simone looked completely different from the last time he'd seen her. She wore a dark-patterned suit, small tortoiseshell spectacles and no discernible make-up. The glamorous dinner companion was well disguised.

'Hello, Phil.' She smiled and indicated the seat facing her desk.

'I've decided not to go on with this.' The words came out in a rush.

'Really?' Her expression did not change.

'The riding's going OK now so . . .' He paused, anticipating some kind of objection, but she said nothing. 'So there's not much point in me coming here, is there?' he added.

'Not if the symptoms you were complaining of last week have disappeared.'

'I've had a few winners since then.'

'So you're no longer suffering from flashbacks to your accident? You're not waking in the night with chest palpitations and tingling in your arms and legs?' She dropped her eyes to the folder open on her desk. 'And at crucial moments during a race you no longer turn rigid with fear?'

Phil felt a flash of resentment at hearing his words quoted back at him. It was as if the bloody woman had caught him in a lie.

'It's been going better,' he said. 'Honest.'

'Phil.' Her voice softened. 'Sit down. Please.'

He did as he was told.

Keith gunned the quad bike up the hill along the edge of a ploughed field, drenching the hedgerow to his right with muddy puddle-water. The four-wheeled motorbike ate up the terrain in pursuit of the hounds, who were on the scent of a fox over the brow of the hill. Keith cut off the corner of the field, careering across the ruts, exhilarated by the power of the hungry vehicle. He'd ignored Fred, his helper's, request to cadge a ride, pretending he hadn't heard as he'd zoomed away from the knot of hunters edging their Land Rovers along the lane. He'd buy the old fellow a pint later. Today he didn't want any kind of company.

At the top of the hill he spotted the pack behind a group of farm buildings where they must have cornered the fox. The hunt itself was spread out across the fields and paddocks below him, most of the riders way out of touch with the action. Not for the first time Keith wondered exactly what they got out of it. His own horse-riding days were behind him.

He'd been a keen rider once, when he was fifteen and chafing at the bit to get out of school for good. His mum had an old flame with contacts at a yard in Gloucestershire, and he'd got taken on as a lad. He'd fancied being a jockey, of course, even when it was obvious he'd end up the size of his father. So that hadn't worked out. And after he'd knocked the number-two jockey's teeth down his throat at chucking-out time it had been *adios*, Gloucestershire.

To his mind these days there was nothing to beat mechanical horsepower.

He shot full throttle down the rutted gravel track to the farm. He guessed the hounds would have killed the fox by now, and it was his job to retrieve the corpse. At moments like this he felt truly alive. Even his misfortunes were fuel to his fire. He abandoned the quad bike by the farm gate and grabbed his sack. As he strode across the muddy yard, the excited yapping of the hounds was loud in his ears. Three fields off, on the downslope of the hill, he could see the leading horses of the hunt. They'd be too late for the action.

Those bastards at the *Racing Beacon* hadn't printed his letter. It didn't surprise him – he'd expected as much. They probably thought it was the work of some nutter, someone who got their rocks off on a bit of paper, some toothless twit you could safely ignore. Well, they weren't going to ignore him.

He found the pack milling around the remains of a stone barn. The fox was long dead, and Keith grabbed the bedraggled corpse from a pair of boisterous hounds.

He'd get cracking tomorrow. The day after a hunt was a good day to do a little hunting of his own. He hefted the sack, now weighed down with the disembowelled fox, on his back. Its end would have been quick and he doubted it had suffered. Not like someone else was going to suffer tomorrow.

*

Phil had been doing all the talking so far. At their first session Simone had asked him to describe his problem and he'd done so at length, focusing on his accident the previous September. She'd also probed him for details about his family, his career, his recent marriage. She was trying to build up a case history, she'd said.

Today she was making him retrace some of the ground, digging more deeply, which took Phil by surprise. He'd been rather hoping she would come up with some kind of treatment. Pills? Hypnosis? Some marvellous new way of defining his race terror so he could deal with it?

'Tell me about your brother,' she said.

He didn't want to do that. He'd outlined the story briefly but he really didn't want to revisit the circumstances of his younger brother's death in an equestrian competition three years earlier. But what option did he have? It was hardly insignificant.

Phil had not been at Blenheim when Tim died, buried under Forester, his much-loved horse, after a catastrophic fall during the cross-country phase of a three-day event. The news had come through while Phil was racing at Doncaster. There'd been a phone call for him when he was still out on the course, and by the time he reached the weighing-room details of the accident were already being broadcast.

His valet, a former jockey, had intercepted Phil the moment he'd weighed in and broken the news with the compassion of a man who has seen it all. He'd offered to make Phil's arrangements, to find a driver and whisk him home immediately. Phil had said no thanks, changed his colours and ridden in the next race. On the long drive back to the West Country he'd stopped his car once and cried softly in a lay-by. That had been the extent of his outward show of emotion.

'It wasn't that it didn't affect me but I had to stay in one piece for Mum and Dad. Tim's death turned everything upside down. It was like they were suddenly the kids and I was the parent. Dad had a terrible time and had to be treated for depression. I took charge of the farm, sorted out Tim's affairs, kept an eye on Mum. I couldn't afford to let go.'

'What about the way your brother died? Did you dwell on that at all?'

'I looked at the video, trying to understand how the accident came about. If I was being absolutely brutal, I'd say it was Tim's fault. So I never thought it could happen to me, if that's what you mean.'

'And do you think about his accident now?'

Phil said nothing for a moment. He focused on the folds of the copper-coloured scarf she wore at her throat and the amber brooch in a silver setting that held it in place.

'Yes.'

She waited for him to elaborate but he didn't. 'Do you think about Tim's accident differently now you've been badly hurt yourself?'

He nodded. He'd rerun it constantly in his mind. Forester coming fast downhill out of the trees, Tim pushing him, trying to claw back time penalties. The big horse getting into the bottom of the solid fence and not having the room or time to manoeuvre himself over it. Why in God's name had Tim kept on pushing? The entire event had been worth only a few hundred pounds. Tim had been thrown to the ground and, a split second later, had been buried beneath the bulk of his mount. Phil retained a cartoon image of the accident in his head, in which he was Tim and the horse was a giant's foot, about to descend and flatten him. But in the cartoon he used to always get away. Used to. When he'd replayed it the other night the giant had stamped him into oblivion.

He didn't want to tell this to Simone. It trivialised Tim's death. It was shaming. But if he wasn't going to be honest, why on earth was he here? More to the point, if he didn't tell the truth, how could she help him?

Adrian Moore gave Beatle his lunch, cleaned out the boot of his car and thought about packing. Then he hung around the house. It was the first day of the ban he'd earned for dropping his hands on January King and he didn't know what to do with himself. He'd booked a last-minute skiing trip for the following week but that still left him with a couple of days to twiddle his thumbs.

He made himself a cheese-and-pickle sandwich and thought about heading into town, but he knew he'd only end up in the bookie's watching the racing. The two other jockeys he shared with were busy at Ascot. He could have gone along to watch but he wasn't much of a spectator. To be honest he didn't like the idea of racing going ahead without his being involved. If he had his way, the entire country would be buried under blizzards for the next ten days with all race meetings abandoned. At least next week he'd be out of the country.

He picked the cheese out of the leftover half of his sandwich and chucked the bread in the bin. Beatle trotted over and snaffled the cheese from his fingers. Then he plonked his furry brown head in Adrian's lap and made his most winsome doggy face.

'What do you want?' Adrian scratched the animal under the chin. Beatle ran excitedly towards the door. He stopped and looked back.

'A walk, is it?' Adrian grinned. The dog did everything but talk.

The lane was empty and the dog lolloped on ahead, turning by habit off the made-up road along the footpath into the wood.

Adrian mooched slowly along some fifty paces behind, deep in thought. It wasn't so much the unfairness of the ban – to be honest, there were times when he should have been punished but had got away with it – as the timing. He'd had some cracking rides lined up over the next week, and if he could have just kept his nose clean he might have grabbed some headlines. Now the headlines would be grabbed by someone else – specifically by his housemates this afternoon at Ascot. Frankly the flight out couldn't come quick enough.

'Beatle?'

There was no sign of the dog on the path ahead. He'd probably spotted something interesting in the undergrowth and gone exploring. Adrian wasn't that bothered. You couldn't blame a dog for enjoying himself – besides, he'd be back soon.

But he wasn't. Adrian called a couple of times in his stop-mucking-about voice, which usually brought results. Whatever excitements Beatle might have unearthed he knew when his master meant business.

Not this time, however. Adrian shouted the dog's name, serious now, preparing to lay down the law to his shaggy brown friend when he chose to show up. There was still no response.

Adrian picked up his pace and strode purposefully down the path. Beatle must have got farther ahead than he'd expected.

The trees on either side thinned and gave way to brown, wintery fields. Above the crunch of his boots he heard something – a high-pitched yelp. The sound of a dog in pain.

Adrian stood still and cast around for the direction of the noise. It was clearer now, a piteous mewling and squealing. Beatle was in trouble. Perhaps he'd got tangled in some barbed wire or caught in a trap. Poachers snared rabbits in all sorts of cruel ways.

He broke into a run. Through the fringe of woodland, over by the stream, something caught his eye. A brown wriggling object suspended from the branch of an apple tree, standing in the garden of an abandoned cottage. The wriggling object, dangling in the breeze, was horribly familiar. He was sprinting now, fired by a rush of anger. What the fuck had someone done to Beatle?

Adrian plunged off the path and scrambled over the old stone wall, relief and fear churning in his guts. As he got closer, running with difficulty over the boggy meadow, he could see Beatle hanging by his hind legs about four foot off the ground.

Adrian reached him at last, hugging the squirming dog to his chest, making soothing noises even as the uncomfortable questions formed in his mind. This was no accident. A blue nylon cord had been used to bind the dog's hind legs together. It had been looped over a solid branch six feet up and tied off round the trunk.

Adrian picked at the knot tying the dog's legs, while keeping an eye out for whoever had committed the crime. The cord had bitten tight and Beatle squirmed and whimpered.

'Calm down, old boy,' he muttered as he worked. 'It's all right now. I'll soon have you down.'

At last he was able to ease the pressure on Beatle's legs. The cord was tied in a slipknot and now, by taking the dog's weight off the noose, Adrian was able to wriggle a finger beneath the cord and work it loose. Any second now the dog would be free and he'd be able to look for the bastards who'd done this. Some mean-spirited local kids, he had no doubt. He'd slaughter the little sods if he got his hands on them.

The blow to his thigh took him by surprise. He didn't feel pain, just the sensation of his entire leg being jerked from beneath him.

Suddenly he was sitting on the ground. Beatle had scrambled free and was hopping around in a frenzy, as bewildered as Adrian was.

Then he was hit again, in the other leg as it stretched out in front of him, and this time it did hurt. A lance of fire licked through his body, sucking the breath from his lungs as he stared down at himself in bewilderment.

His jeans were changing colour, from pale blue to dark wet purple. Adrian stared in disbelief at his left thigh. There was something sticking through it, at the centre of the wetness. A metal tube projected from the wound with feathers on the end – like the flights on a dart, only bigger and meaner looking. In some compartment of his brain Adrian realised that he had been struck by some kind of arrow. An arrow powerful enough to knock him off his feet. He closed the door on that thought – it made no sense.

But he couldn't move and the fire in his body had taken hold now as the blood began to pool around him on the leaf mould and wormcasts of the old garden.

'Help!' he shouted. His voice echoed back to him, small and feeble.

The afternoon light was beginning to fade, there were no dwellings within a mile, and the only person in the vicinity had crippled him with some foul medieval weapon.

Adrian had never been more petrified in his life.

That night Keith watched all the news bulletins. It gave him a considerable degree of satisfaction.

Adrian Moore's assault was the lead item on every channel, with the focus on the heroic behaviour of his dog, Beatle, who had led rescuers to the stricken jockey. A police spokesman revealed that Adrian had been wounded in the legs but, while refuting that he had been shot, had refused to say what precisely had made the wounds. Keith was amused by this coyness, though not displeased. Two of his crossbow points had been embedded in Moore's legs, and he didn't believe the police would have any problem identifying the kind of weapon they came from. But it was well known that the police habitually withheld details of crimes – it was all part of the game.

Much of the television coverage was taken up with talking heads from the racing world, all expressing shock and disgust. Adrian Moore, it turned out, was universally loved throughout the jumping fraternity, and a finer sportsman was yet to take to the saddle – except when he was chucking races and screwing the punter. The punter's views, naturally, were not recorded.

Amidst the schmaltz and honest-citizen outrage, windswept outside-broadcast reporters wondered aloud who would want to harm this honest lad setting out in the morning of his career. Their conclusion was that simple bad luck had placed him in the path of a sadistic lunatic. But for his racing ban Adrian would have been exercising his precocious skills at Ascot; now it seemed he would be out of the saddle for the rest of the season – at the very least.

All in all, Keith reflected, it amounted to a good start. As yet the media had no idea that there was a reason behind the jockey's misfortune, but he'd soon put them straight on that score. For now, he had grabbed the country's attention in the most sensational manner possible.

When he went to bed that night, the Beast inside was content.

Phil woke, terrified, in the black of night. He'd been on a horse he couldn't control at a course he didn't recognise, racing under instructions he could not follow. He'd been told to hold the animal up but the horse wouldn't obey. The harder he tugged on the reins the faster his mount had gone, past the other runners, scarcely jumping the fences but crashing through the birch fills, past the stands and the winning post and – in the way of dreams – galloping along a railway track and into a tunnel as dark as pitch. Phil began to scream.

Thankfully he hadn't shouted out in his sleep. He'd done that before and woken Julia, but not this time. It took him a while to realise where he was. The T-shirt he wore was clammy with sweat and his heart was pounding. He felt for his pulse – it was getting to be a habit with him – and registered the life throbbing fast, much too fast, in his veins.

He felt ashamed. Here, in the night, there was no escape from the truth – he was a coward.

He listened for Julia's breathing and heard it, slow and rhythmic. She was still asleep, unaware of his turmoil. She mustn't know about his night frights. She mustn't know about any of it.

He needed to get up – go downstairs, watch the television, maybe just stand barefoot on the cold kitchen floor and look at the stars through the window – but her warm bottom was pressed against his hip, the smooth skin glued to his. He shuffled to his side of the bed and she seemed to follow him, her weight shifting as he pulled away. She rolled on to her back and there was a change in her breathing.

'Phil?'

He said nothing.

'You're awake, aren't you? Can't you sleep?'

'I'm all right, Jules.'

She turned towards him under the covers. 'Poor old you. Are you thinking about Adrian?'

'No.' He reflected for a moment. 'Well, maybe.' Of course he was. The news about Adrian was enough to give anybody nightmares. 'I've got to get up. Make some tea or something.'

'OK.' She slipped an arm round his chest. 'Bring it back to bed. We can have a cuddle.'

He pushed her away. 'When are you going to realise, Julia, that you can't solve everything with a quick fuck?'

He regretted it instantly. They were the first words in his marriage he'd wished he'd never uttered.

Hugh read the letter with disbelief, horror and mounting professional excitement.

The Editor
The *Racing Beacon*

Re: Adrian Moore
You are in receipt of my recent letter which you chose to ignore. You did not even have the curtesy to print it let alone start telling the truth about the cheating and corruption that goes on in racing.

Like I warned you, I have been forced to take matters into my own hands. The stewards gave Adrian Moore a slap on the wrist for chucking that race at Wincanton. A 10 day ban is just a holiday for a bent jockey like Moore. But he's not sipping champaine in 5 star hotel now is he?

You should have heard him scream when I knocked him down with my broadpoints. He sat in the mud and wepped for his mummy. He won't be riding again for a while will he? He should have got six months in the first place and now he has.

That's what I call justice.

Are you going to start blowing the whistle on the racing cheats or will you leave them to me?

I'm just starting.
YOU HAVE BEEN WARNED.
AGAIN!!!

'Bloody hell,' said Hugh aloud to the empty office as he pulled the Loony Letters folder from his drawer.

Julia wept softly as she bandaged the mare's front leg. The tears had not been far off all morning, and she let them fall when she was sure they could not be observed. As always the yard was busy, but there were moments like this, in the shadows of a horse's stall, when it was safe for her to let go.

When Phil had pushed her away last night she had frozen in shock. Now she was trying to come to terms with it. They'd had rows, naturally, but this wasn't a row, just an expression of anger and contempt that she didn't recognise as coming from the man she loved. He'd sounded like someone she didn't know. Is this what was meant when people said marriage wasn't easy? That you woke in the middle of the night next to a cold and distant stranger? Welcome to the real world, she muttered to herself.

Though she'd been keeping herself busy all morning she wasn't sure she'd been much use. She knew the horses were alert to her distress and that didn't help. How could she relax and heal them when she herself was in turmoil?

A voice disturbed her. 'Fancy a cup of tea?'

Julia raised her head. Mark was standing outside the stall, holding two mugs. For a moment she didn't register the offer, she was so immersed in her own thoughts. Suddenly she felt stiff and weary.

'Thanks.' She patted the little mare's rear quarters. There wasn't much more she could do for her.

They sat on the bench by the tack-room.

'I enjoyed our dance the other night.'

'I'm sorry, Mark. I had too much to drink.'

'You sure it wasn't me throwing you about?'

'Did you? I don't remember.' She remembered all right. It wasn't the fast dancing that had unnerved her, it was the slow.

'How are you getting on with that horse of Jack Mitton's? I heard he used to be a bit tasty.'

'He still is. He's a bit of an old rogue but a real star.'

'Like Jack Nicholson, you mean?'

'Actually, he's more like Sean Connery. Stylish, with good manners, but full of danger. And with a dodgy hip.' She found herself grinning. She couldn't talk to anyone else like this – not even Phil.

Mark was obviously intrigued. 'So you're going to get him fit to race?'

'I'll try. He never really recovered after his accident. He's been treated like a family pet. I think he needs firm handling and some dressage work, to get him into a disciplined frame of mind. Make him use himself. He moves like a complete slob at the moment.'

'I used to ride dressage a few years back. I was on the show-jumping circuit back in Ireland before I got into racing.'

'Really?' Julia liked the sound of that – it could be useful. On the other hand, she ought to see whether her husband would help her out first.

'Actually, I've got to talk to Phil about it. He knows a bit about dressage techniques.'

'Of course.' Mark nodded and drained his mug. 'Let me know if there's anything I can do. I'd be happy to give you a hand with him.'

'Would you?'

Mark turned to her, his green eyes lit by excitement. 'Callisto's a legend, isn't he? It'd be a thrill to sit on his back.'

'Ruth.' Hugh stood three feet inside the office door, farther than he usually ventured.

Ruth Walters, the editor's elegantly dressed, well-spoken guard dog, peered at him over the top of her spectacles, her fingers still flickering over her keyboard. 'He's busy.'

Hugh took another pace into the room. 'I've got to see him.'

'I wouldn't advise it.' She swivelled her eyes towards the editor's office and Hugh followed her glance. Through the open slats of a Venetian blind two men could be seen: Duncan Frame, the editor, broad shouldered and bulky, and pink-faced Pat, a greyhound-racing specialist and drinking-buddy of the absent Bernard. Frame perched on the corner of the desk, looming over Pat, jabbing his finger in the air. Hugh drew the obvious conclusion. The ritual early-morning bollocking had been a prelude to Bernard's departure – it looked like Pat might be following in his old friend's footsteps.

'I'm going in,' he said.

Ruth stopped typing. 'I thought you wanted to carry on working here.'

'That's why I'm going in.'

Whatever unpleasantness Frame was uttering was cut short by Hugh's entry. The editor stared at him, his finger suspended mid-jab, as the journalist burst through the door.

'Sorry, Duncan,' he said, 'but this won't wait,' and he pushed the letter he'd received that morning into the editor's hand.

Frame read it slowly. After a minute, without taking his eyes from the page, he said, 'You still here, Pat?' and the pink-faced man slipped out of the door, glancing gratefully at Hugh as he did so.

Frame looked up. 'It says there's another letter.'

Hugh handed it to him and the editor read it carefully, grinning as he did so. Hugh knew he would be calculating all the angles, of which 'How can I best exploit this to the paper's advantage?' would undoubtedly be the most important. He placed the two pieces of paper side by side on his desktop and considered them. Finally he said, 'Do you open the envelopes to the readers' letters?'

'Jemma does. She doesn't read what's inside them, though.'

'How do you know?'

'I asked her when I went to look for the envelope for today's letter. It was in her wastepaper basket. Postmarked Taunton.'

Frame nodded. Hugh could picture the cogs in his big square head revolving.

'I presume you decided not to use the first one.'

'I didn't think it was suitable.'

'But you kept it?'

'Bernard told me to save the dotty letters.'

Frame pulled a face at the mention of Bernard. 'That old soak.'

'He gave me his Loony Letters file. I put the first letter in there and dug it out just now. I'm afraid I never saw the envelope to that one, though.'

'Have you talked to anyone else about this?'

'No.'

Frame nodded. 'Right,' he said. He picked up the two pieces of paper by their corners, holding them between thumb and forefinger.

'Put these and the envelope in separate plastic folders. Then photocopy them. Don't show them to anyone else and don't, under any circumstances, breathe a word to a living soul about any of this.' As he picked up the phone, he added, 'And don't leave the office. You and I are going to talk to the police.'

Detective Chief Inspector Charlie Lynch of the Avon and Somerset Constabulary had promised himself a Saturday morning at home for once. More to the point, he had promised his daughter, a Bristol student, that he'd drive over with some items for her new flat.

'Of course, Dad,' Claire had said, 'if you'd bought me a car for Christmas then you wouldn't have to bother.'

He'd laughed and so had she, but the remark had struck home. Some of these new friends of hers at university appeared to zip around in brand-new Golfs and Clios, and it touched a nerve to think he couldn't provide for his offspring in the same way. And now she'd moved into a Georgian terrace in Clifton with a group of them. He hoped she'd be able to hold her own.

So the phone call from DS Petrie at Maybrick Street nick was hardly welcome.

'There's been a development in the jockey case, guv. I've just had some super from Scotland Yard on the phone.'

The jockey case had already caused a disproportionate amount of fuss in Charlie's opinion. If the unfortunate victim hadn't been a jockey in the public eye no one would have paid much attention. Which is not to say that it wasn't high on the list of the DCI's priorities, particularly after a visit to the boy's hospital bedside.

The upshot was a flurry of phone calls and a change to Charlie's plans. To his surprise, Claire did not kick up much of a fuss.

'Why don't I pop over tomorrow instead, sweetheart?'

'OK. Jennifer's parents are coming too so we could have lunch together. Her dad's a QC so you'll have lots in common.'

If Charlie had known that, he'd have put off Scotland Yard till next week.

It was strange for Hugh to be stuck in the office on a Saturday afternoon. As a rule he'd be at a racecourse somewhere, preferably not more than a two-hour train ride from London, giving him time for a decent night out before heading home to Clapham. Today, for example, he should have been at Kempton Park, checking out a variety of contenders, all jostling for position in the midwinter run-up to Cheltenham. As it was, he had to make do with watching the action on the television in the smokers' room while he waited for the coppers to turn up.

Fortunately they didn't do so till after a top-notch two-mile handicap hurdle, which saw an ex-flat racer, Devious, home by a length from his nearest rival despite carrying a full stone more. Afterwards his trainer, Gerry Fowler, told the TV audience that the horse's next outing would be the Tote Gold Trophy at Newbury. Hugh was pleased for Gerry, whose yard, Greenhills, was one of a number of West Country establishments. In the background Hugh spotted Gerry's remarkably pretty daughter, Louise, making a fuss of their winner. For a moment he regretted not being on the course in person.

Then Ruth's face appeared in the doorway, wrinkling her nose at the smell of stale smoke.

'He wants you,' was all she said.

The three policemen were already in Frame's office and Hugh was introduced swiftly, so swiftly he failed to catch all the details. The young one in the smart suit was from Scotland Yard. Hugh soon came to the conclusion that he was there for form's sake, representing some police brass of Frame's acquaintance.

The other two had travelled up from the West Country. Adrian Moore had been assaulted on their patch and so this was their investigation. The younger detective, John Petrie, wore a scuffed suit and a tie like a nasty Christmas present. His boss, Charlie Lynch, made no concessions to formality at all; his denim shirt and navy fleece were the Saturday wear of the weekday office slave. Being an everyday scruff himself, Hugh had no objection.

It seemed Frame had already laid out the basic situation and Hugh had been summoned to corroborate and to answer questions about his discovery of the letters. All of which was accomplished in no time. Then they discussed arrangements to fingerprint all staffers who might have laid a hand on them, presumably to inform the forensic examination to which the letters would be subjected.

Charlie and John sat side by side on the visitors' sofa, pouring over the two documents lying on the low table in front of them.

'Not much of a speller, is he?' said John. 'Of course, it could be deliberate,' he added. He seemed keen, Hugh thought.

Charlie said nothing but gave his colleague a warning glance, doubtless to shut him up. The officer was obviously well aware he was sitting in a newspaper office.

'What else have you got in this Loony Letters file?' Charlie asked.

'Nothing like this,' Hugh said. 'I went through it. It's full of suggestions like adding novelty jumps to steeplechases and staggering the start in handicaps. Crackpot stuff.'

Charlie grinned. 'You don't mind if we double-check?'

'The *Racing Beacon* will cooperate in every way, Inspector,' announced Frame. 'Our only concern is to catch whoever is responsible.'

'That's much appreciated,' said Charlie matter-of-factly. Hugh had no doubt that similar remarks had been exchanged before he'd arrived.

'Do you really think this bloke might have done it?' he asked. 'I thought the ones who blew off steam were generally harmless.'

Charlie turned towards him. 'You're probably right but we're duty bound to follow everything up.'

'You think there's something in this, though, don't you?' Hugh persisted. 'Is it the stuff about broadheads? Whatever they are.'

There was a small silence. Charlie appeared not to have heard. Then the London policeman broke in. 'There are some details of the investigation that I'm sure DCI Lynch would prefer not to divulge at present.'

Charlie switched his gaze to Frame. 'We have an agreement, don't we? None of this information appears until we say so?'

The editor nodded gravely. 'My newspaper is at your disposal.'

Lying toad, thought Hugh. Even in circumstances like this it was hard to give Frame the benefit of the doubt.

The policeman appeared to take the editor at face value, however. He nodded and said, 'The fact is, Mr Pimlott, Adrian Moore was hit in the legs by two aluminum arrows, about seven inches long, apparently fired from a crossbow. The tips are made of three razor-sharp blades which expand on impact to make a hole in the flesh about an inch and a half in diameter.'

Hugh winced. Poor lad.

'These arrows are known as broadheads,' Charlie added. 'Does that answer your question?'

It did indeed.

Chapter Four

Louise Fowler surveyed her father's office through a mist of fatigue and last night's overindulgence. The gunmetal-grey filing cabinets, painted breeze-block walls and a wastepaper basket brimming with yesterday's wadded-up tissues and brown apple cores made a depressing sight. The desk was a mess of scattered papers and open files – evidence of an early-morning visit by her father. Whatever he'd been searching for, she doubted he'd found it. He was useless in the office – which was why she'd been ordered off the gallops and told to fill the vacuum caused by Helen, the office secretary's latest failure to appear.

Louise filled the kettle and spooned instant coffee into a mug. Crisis or not, she needed to get her head together before she could tackle the chaos. Last night, having a giggle with Rebecca and those two new lads who'd chatted them up in the Cat and Fiddle, she'd shrugged aside the thought of the following morning. And back at Rebecca's later, holding a post-mortem on the evening, though she'd known it was daft for Becky to open another bottle of wine, she'd drunk it all the same.

What she hadn't bargained for was standing in for Helen. Surely flu didn't strike that quickly? Anyhow, here she was, on Dad's orders, sitting at a desk instead of riding out on her gorgeous grey filly, Skellig. Louise could cope with a hangover on horseback in the open air, but suffering in this poky room under the glare of a humming striplight was a different matter. No wonder Helen was ill so often.

She began to tidy the papers on the desk, pettishly chucking them into a filing tray. Honestly, if she'd wanted to be a secretary she could have got a job in an office in town and be earning some proper money.

As she waited for the computer to boot up, the phone rang. It was just after nine, about the time that jockeys' agents began to call.

'Morning, Greenhills Yard. Louise speaking.' Her voice sang out cheerfully. Perhaps she should be an actress? 'Oh, hello, Mrs Davenport – how can I help you?'

As the owner of one of their hurdlers prattled on, Louise continued to tidy the desk. Where was that list of things to do that Dad had been going on about?

Charlie Lynch sat glumly opposite John Petrie in the trendy coffee bar round the corner from the Maybrick Street nick. They'd spent the first hour of the day reviewing progress on the Adrian Moore case and John had suggested a change of scenery from the canteen. Personally Charlie would have preferred a pint but the Maybrick Arms wasn't open yet.

They had returned from their trip to the *Racing Beacon* full of optimism. The letters – with that reference to crossbow arrows – had looked like leading them to Adrian's attacker. But that had been almost two weeks ago and since then they'd not got much farther. Forensic analysis of the paper and print of the letters had yielded nothing useful. The only fingerprints had been identified as belonging to *Racing Beacon* staff. The notepaper was bog-standard A4, available at every stationer's in the country, so too the envelope. The letter had been generated on a computer and printed on a standard ink-jet printer like hundreds of thousands of others.

They'd also drawn a blank – so far – with the materials used to assault Adrian and his dog. The blue cord with which the attacker had tied Beatle was common. The same could not be said for the crossbow and its lethal broadheads, in the sense that they were not everyday items like paper or printers. On the other hand, as John had pointed out, specialist sporting goods were easily acquired these days courtesy of the internet. They were trying to find the source of the vicious little arrows that had made such a mess of Adrian's legs, but they weren't having a lot of luck. They could have been purchased from the website of some store situated halfway round the world.

Charlie watched John happily stuffing his face with a long brown jobby, first dipping it into his frothy drink, then sucking it down with relish. A *biscotti*, he'd called it, some kind of fancy Italian biscuit that went well with a double-strength *café latte*. Charlie wasn't impressed. All he knew was that a cup of tea and a digestive in the canteen cost a fraction of the price.

'What next, guv?' said John, wiping crumbs from his chin.

Charlie shrugged. 'Officially, we keep plugging away. The investigation is on-going.'

'But between you and me?'

'I think we're at the point where we trust it's a one-off. That our nutter has satisfied his personal grudge and that's the last we hear of him.'

'That's what you think?'

'It's what I sincerely hope.'

'So it's not what you think.'

Charlie didn't say anything. He had a bad feeling about this. He didn't believe the author of those letters was just a piss-and-wind merchant. And the nutter had made it clear that this was just the beginning.

Just before ten the phone went for what seemed like the hundredth time and Louise sailed into her customary greeting. Keeping upbeat was becoming a bit of a strain.

The voice on the other end was youthful but weary – her drinking-companion from the night before.

'Bit early for you, isn't it, Becky? I thought you students never got out of bed before midday.'

Rebecca groaned. 'Who says I'm out of bed? I'm only awake because someone rang me.'

'So?'

'So don't you want to know who that someone was?' She didn't wait for Louise to reply. 'Leo.'

Leo was one of the boys from the night before. The one Rebecca had fancied. She was now in full flow. It seemed she and Leo had talked for some while and, weary or not, she was prepared to divulge every detail. Louise cut in.

'Can this wait a bit, Becky? I'm supposed to be working here.'

'So you don't want to know about next Wednesday?'

'What about it?'

'Valentine's Day. Me, you, Leo and Kit.' Kit was the other boy, the moody one with the sky-blue eyes. He hadn't taken them off Louise all evening. 'They want us to go to a club in Bath.'

Suddenly the day had become less dreary. 'Wow – fantastic!'

'I said we might be busy.'

'Becky, I'm not doing *anything*!'

'They don't know that. Let them sweat. Honestly, Louise, you're clueless about men.'

'Louise—' Her father was standing in the doorway pulling off his gloves; his cap and Barbour were glistening with beads of rain.

'Gotta go, Becky,' said Louise hastily. 'Catch you later.' And she smartly replaced the receiver.

'Don't you spend enough of your life in that girl's company without tying up my phone line?'

'Sorry, Dad. She just rang me.'

'Did you do the things on that list?'

'I couldn't find it in all this mess. And the phone hasn't stopped.'

'So you haven't rung Weatherby's?'

'I didn't know I had to.'

There was a silence. Louise could see that her father's usually cheerful face had taken on a look of panic. Cold fury, she knew, would soon follow.

He yanked the phone from its rest and began to punch in numbers he knew by heart.

As he waited for the connection he looked her full in the eye. 'If we're too late to declare Devious at Newbury tomorrow, there will be trouble.'

Louise glanced anxiously at the clock on the wall. As every trainer's daughter knew, declarations had to be in by ten o'clock the day before the race. The authorities were not known to be flexible.

The time was now six minutes past ten.

Her heart sank.

'Have you told your wife yet?'

It was almost the end of the session and Phil was tired. He felt as if he'd spent the morning in the gym lifting weights rather than an hour in a softly padded armchair in the beige haven of Simone's office. Mental exercise, he was discovering, could be more exacting than physical exertion.

Her question took him by surprise. It was the first time she had raised the subject since the dinner for Snowflake.

'I don't want anybody to know I'm seeing you,' he said. 'I'd be finished as a jockey if it got out I'd lost my bottle.'

'Julia is not just anybody.'

'All the same, I don't want her to know.'

'Why not?'

Her words hung there. He'd asked himself that question more than once and shied away from answering it. He struggled to put what he felt into words.

'Before I met Jules, she'd had a bit of a rough time. Men had really buggered her around. I swore I'd never do that.'

'How would sharing your problem "bugger her around"?'

'I can't tell her I've got mental problems. She relies on me. I'm supposed to be the man of the house.'

Simone considered this. 'So you're the big tough guy sheltering her from the winds of adversity?'

'That's a bit of a poncy way of putting it.'

She smiled but stared at him keenly, still expecting an answer.

'Well,' he conceded, 'I suppose that is how I see it.'

'Has it not occurred to you, Phil, that the pair of you might be more effective as a partnership if you faced the wind together?'

His first impulse was to say that he didn't know what the hell she was talking about, but he held his tongue.

She got to her feet, signalling the end of the session.

'Just think about it, Phil.'

He nodded. Like hell he would.

Mark had never thought of himself as the jealous type but, sitting in Phil's fancy car on the way to Newbury, he felt a sudden surge of envy for what his friend had in life. The car was the least of it.

Julia had seen them off from Deanscroft in dirt-spattered jeans and a shapeless sweater that failed to conceal her shape. She was the kind of girl who'd look good in a coal sack. Phil had kissed her goodbye carelessly, casually palming the rounded curve of her hip as she lifted her heart-shaped face to his. Mark had looked away hastily, a stab of desire lancing through his gut. She was the loveliest woman he'd ever met, all the more so because she seemed totally unaware of her appeal.

She'd kissed him goodbye too, a chaste touch of her plush pink lips on his cheek as she'd said, 'Good luck this afternoon.' To think that Phil went home to her every night. Lucky bastard.

He promised himself that one day he'd be champion jockey with a top-of-the-range car, a woman to make your knees go weak – and the best horses. That was the catch. You needed the best horses to become champion, and the way things were now Mark wasn't sitting on enough of them. He was back in the queue at Deanscroft behind Phil, trying his heart out on the second string. Mark had every confidence in his riding ability, but the fact was you could be the most gifted rider on God's earth but no one would ever notice if you were riding a donkey.

Julia gave herself half an hour to clear up the cottage. She'd always been a bit of a messy person – she'd grown up in households where no one gave two hoots about keeping the place tidy. And Phil, being a man who'd always lived with his mother, was even worse. It was really only the thought of Phil's mum popping in unexpectedly – as she often did – and seeing the place in complete disarray that drove Julia to these bursts of industry.

Things had almost returned to normal after their quarrel in the middle of the night. Well, it hadn't exactly been a quarrel, but his outburst had shaken her to the core. The way he'd sounded – as if she were a pest, asking for sex all the time, and stupid as well, too dumb to realise there were other ways of responding to distress apart from offering her body.

But when she'd thought about it more rationally she'd realised he had a point. Often, in a relationship, sex had been her stock-in-trade. Her response to a man's anger or sorrow or pain had invariably been to offer him the comfort of her embrace because . . . well, because that rarely failed. She wasn't the most confident woman in the world, but she knew that her body was what men liked. Ever since she'd developed curves, boys had made it clear her shape had pleased them.

So the outburst from Phil, shocking though it was at the time, had maybe done her some good. He had a point. In a proper, long-term relationship, she couldn't solve every crisis by opening her legs.

'I won't be offering you a bonk when I'm ninety, will I?' she'd said to him the next evening when they'd talked it through. 'You'll be in trouble if you don't,' he'd replied. 'I'll ask for a divorce.'

Then he'd made love to her on the sofa with a tenderness that made up for his early-morning bad temper. Afterwards she'd lain in his arms, looking at the vase of sumptuous roses he'd bought her as a peace offering, and breathed a sigh of relief that their first real breach had been mended.

Since then things had almost been back to how they used to be. Except now when she heard him wake in the middle of the night she lay still, pretending to sleep even as he slipped from the bed and out of the room. She mustn't make the mistake she'd made before.

There'd been one other change. When it came to sex, she'd stopped making the first move. Before, she'd often given Phil the come-on. An impulsive kiss, a hand on his thigh, a certain kind of look – these were second nature to her. Now she consciously cut these gestures out in case she should be rejected again. As a result they made love less often than before. It's inevitable, she told herself. We've been married six months – sex appeal wears off. She herself didn't feel any different about Phil, but maybe he was going off her?

Today, as she cleaned up, her thoughts turned once more to their love life. Phil hadn't laid a finger on her for four days – five maybe. That had to be a record in their relationship – except when he was laid up by his accident, of course. But even then they'd found ways of expressing their desire. She'd even pleasured him in hospital once or twice.

She was surprised to find his personal organiser under the bed as, along with his mobile phone, it was a toy he carried everywhere. The organiser had been her Christmas present to him, and it had been a big hit. He used it all the time – though not so he could organise his life. He'd fallen in love with a game feature which looked to Julia like a lump of frog-spawn; the idea being to eliminate sequences of shaded blobs till you achieved a blank screen. He'd explained it helped while away the time between races.

Julia opened up the organiser and the game screen came on automatically. She chuckled indulgently – he'd be missing this at Newbury.

She touched the 'Phone' icon at the bottom of the small screen and brought up a page arranged in columns for names and numbers – only there weren't any. She touched 'Contacts' and a different format appeared, laid out for names and addresses. It was also empty. She tutted to herself. She'd been nagging Phil to copy these details from the old loose-leaved diary he carried around but he'd obviously preferred to play frog-spawn. Perhaps she'd take pity on him and offer to input the information herself.

She moved on to 'Agenda', arranged in days like a diary page. At least there were entries here – times, places and names, indicative of a busy life. Today was full of details of his Newbury rides, but it was the morning entry that caught Julia's eye.

'10.00 Simone.'

That was all it said. But it was enough.

The talk of the press room at Newbury racecourse was the list of declared runners for the following day's big race, the Tote Gold Trophy. The absence of Devious was a shock to all, and Gerry Fowler had been quizzed closely about the disappearance from the card of the antepost favourite.

Hugh was among the group of journalists who waylaid the trainer on the way to the stables to check on his runner in the third race. Gerry was as affable as usual, explaining that a last-minute injury had ruled the horse out.

'What exactly's wrong with him?' asked one writer.

'He's got a bruised foot.'

'How's Mr Rose taking it?' asked Hugh. The horse's owner was a theatrical impresario well known to the press and public – and to the bookmakers.

It seemed to Hugh that Gerry's affability faded a degree or two. 'He's disappointed, naturally, but he only wants what's best for the horse.'

More questions rained down on the trainer as he moved off.

'Any idea what caused the injury, Gerry?'

'What did Mr Rose say when you told him?'

But Gerry refused to answer. 'Enough now, lads,' he said as he moved off, adding apologetically, 'That's racing.'

Arnie Johnson, a tabloid reporter next to Hugh, muttered, 'I bet that's not what Rose said.'

'No?'

'He had Devious antepost at ten to one. Apparently he's just kissed goodbye to twenty grand.'

Hugh was still musing on Gerry's comments when, in search of a drink, he spotted a familiar tangle of red hair on the other side of the ground-floor bar. Louise Fowler was nursing a cup of muddy brown coffee and exuding gloom.

He pushed through the crowd towards her. This was too good an opportunity to miss.

Despite his shambolic appearance – or maybe because of it – Hugh got on well with women. He was not overawed by attractive girls and he never tried to impress them. Most women found that a relief.

Louise managed a wan smile as he came over.

'What's it to be – more coffee? Large gin? Or a bacon sandwich?'

'Ugh. A couple of aspirins maybe.'

Hugh liberated a cardboard packet from inside his coat. 'Paracetamol – best I can do.'

He watched as she took two pills from the packet and washed them down.

'What are you doing out here? Shouldn't you be mucking out or currycombing or something?'

'I'm keeping out of Dad's way, if you really want to know.'

'Any special reason?'

She looked up at him soulfully and Hugh noticed that her milky-blue eyes were red rimmed and moist. 'I've done something awful.'

The words took him by surprise. He didn't know her that well – though he always kept an eye out for her at meetings. He'd have been intrigued even if he wasn't a journalist.

'Really?' he said and, to his amazement, she told him she had been responsible for not declaring Devious in time for the Tote Gold Trophy.

'So the horse isn't injured?'

'No. Where did you hear that?'

'Your dad just told half the press corps. Said he had a bruised foot.'

'Oh, shit.'

Her face crumpled and she began to cry. For a second Hugh stared nonplussed, then he moved instinctively into action. He took the half-empty carton of coffee from her hands and dropped it into a nearby bin. Then, with his arm around her heaving shoulders, he manoeuvred her into a corner, shielding her with his bulk, and offered her a pack of paper handkerchieves. The newsman in him was elated by this discovery, but he was touched by her distress.

She blew her nose hard. 'What I've just told you is absolutely off the record, understand?'

'OK, but aren't you and your dad talking any more?'

'He's really angry with me. He had a terrible row with Mr Rose about it.'

Hugh wanted to tell her he was the last person she should confide in, but he wasn't that much of a saint. If a Titian-haired angel wanted to cry on his shoulder and serve up a good story, it would be unprofessional not to listen. He'd worry later about exactly how he would use the information.

Mark's discontent had been building all afternoon. He was still in a stew of envy over Phil, and its intensity puzzled him. When he'd first joined the yard as a conditional rider he'd been overawed by Phil, then thrilled to be accepted by one of the country's top jockeys as a fellow professional. When Phil had become champion jockey he'd been delighted for his friend, and he'd toasted his health at last summer's wedding as whole-heartedly as anyone else. But now, suddenly, those warm feelings had been replaced by distinctly colder emotions.

When Phil had had his accident Mark had been shattered. He remembered sitting in the weighing-room at Worcester in a trance, his limbs like lead, muttering a prayer for deliverance that he wasn't aware he still knew. All his thoughts were focused on the ambulance bearing Phil to hospital and on how soon they would hear news. Then he'd been summoned to see Russell out in the paddock. 'You're on the rest of Phil's rides,' he'd been told. Instantly all tiredness had evaporated, and concern for his injured friend with it. He'd ridden a first and two seconds and at the end of the afternoon, when he'd heard Phil was going to be OK, his first shameful thought had been *I hope he doesn't come back too quick*.

Things had not been the same since then. Mark had got used to the best Deanscroft had to offer in the months of Phil's absence. He wasn't proud of it but now, when Phil had the pick of the rides, a voice inside Mark's head muttered, 'I should be on that horse.'

Take this afternoon. Phil was lined up for five rides, all for Russell, which left Mark on just two Deanscroft horses, both novices having their first runs and as green as the grass they were about to race on. His agent had secured him a couple of other rides for different trainers but the mounts were plodders. The afternoon would be like going to work in a factory. Turn up, do your job, get the wages and go home. There would be no bonuses in the form of winning percentages. In comparison, Phil was riding four favourites. Mark resented it – he couldn't help himself. The time when he had been in awe of Phil had long since passed. To his mind, Phil had lost his edge since his accident, and Mark was certain that he was now the better jockey.

Hugh found a quiet corner and rang Crispin Rose's office. He'd talked to his PA once or twice before, Rose being happy as a rule to pontificate to the racing press. Hugh gathered he wasn't quite so generous with show-business correspondents.

'He said he wasn't talking to the papers,' said the PA, 'but since it's about a horse, you might be in luck.'

Nevertheless the great man sounded thoroughly fed up when he came on the line.

'Look, I don't know what I can tell you. The trainer tells me the horse is sick and it can't run.'

'So there's no truth in the rumour that Devious is in tiptop shape but just wasn't declared in time?'

'Who told you that?'

'Only, if that's the case, I wonder if you'd like to comment, especially bearing in mind the antepost bets that have gone west. I understand you yourself have lost a fair bit of money?'

'Has Fowler been talking to you?'

'I can't reveal my sources, Mr Rose, but I am anxious to represent all shades of opinion about a matter of importance to our readers.'

There was a prolonged silence on the other end of the line.

'Mr Rose?'

'Look, sonny, I'm in the business of mounting complicated and spectacular entertainments for a demanding public. Last-minute cockups are my speciality. In my world, whatever fiascos occur before the curtain goes up, the show goes on. But *horseracing* . . .' He spat the word out contemptuously. 'If some idiot is five minutes late in making a phone call the day before the race, then I'm stuffed. What kind of business is that?'

'So you'd like to see a change in the rules—?'

Rose cut him off. 'I'm not interested in monkeying around with petty regulations. I'm sick of them. I'm thinking of quitting racing altogether.'

*

The afternoon had gone much as Mark had predicted and his mood had not improved, even though the trainer of his third mount had been thrilled with the way he had ridden.

'That's the best he's ever run,' he'd said as Mark pulled his muddy saddle from the heaving animal. 'But not good enough,' he added.

Mark was tempted to tell the trainer that the horse was hopeless. Instead he smiled and said that he'd love to ride him again if he could. As he made his way back to the changing-room he heard that Phil's mount had won in a common canter, which only added to his frustration.

As they lined up for the sixth race of the afternoon, a two-mile handicap chase, Mark was on Alone Again, a one-paced stayer with stamina but little else. He usually raced over longer distances but Russell felt he was swinging the lead a bit and a run over two miles might sharpen him up. The idea being that when he reverted to his regular trip he might find the slower pace more comfortable and his enthusiasm would be rekindled. At any rate, that was theory. Mark was sceptical but he wasn't the boss.

Phil was on Russell's other runner, Funland, a crabby customer inclined to give anyone a nip or a kick if he got the chance. He was a big, powerful horse with plenty of ability, but also – in jockey parlance – pig ignorant. Mark had won on him at Uttoxeter in his last race but he hadn't enjoyed the experience. Even he, who would ride almost anything with four legs and a tail, had been pleased just to get the race over with.

Funland had come to Deanscroft from Ireland. The horse had been moved to England because his owner believed he'd benefit from better opportunities. The groom who dropped him off reported that he was a really nasty individual and the whole yard were pleased to see the back of him.

Uttoxeter had been his first run for Russell. Funland had pulled his lad all over the paddock beforehand and then shoved him hard against the railings as he'd tried to lead the horse with Mark on board out on to the course. As the lad let them go, Funland had plunged forward with his head low to the ground. Mark had used both hands on one rein and given him a good yank in the mouth. He'd hated doing it but he'd had no choice. Another split second and the horse would have been into his stride and Mark would never have got him back under control. As the steel bit jarred against Funland's mouth Mark felt him give slightly and he pulled again, twisting the horse's head sharply around to the left so that his nose was almost against Mark's foot.

It was a battle between the pair of them. By the time Mark had wrestled Funland to the start, his arms were hurting with the effort of trying to restrain him. The horse had been just as intractable in the race itself. Mark had kept him jammed in behind a wall of other runners but, by the time the race was over, he was exhausted.

Funland wasn't even a good jumper. He was a bit of a guesser who would launch himself from anywhere unless his rider made it clear where he was supposed to take off. It seemed to Mark that the animal thought he was invincible so he didn't need to bother himself. What he needed was a bone-shaking fall to knock some sense into him. The question was, which poor sod would be on his back when he took it?

Hungry as he was, this was one ride that Mark wouldn't miss. As the starter called them in, Mark looked across to see how Phil was coping. Funland was dripping with sweat and tugging his rider's arms out. Phil looked as white as a sheet.

Mark shouted over to him. 'He's the biggest yak I've ever sat on.'

'Thanks a bunch,' was all Phil could manage before the tapes went up.

At least when Mark had ridden Funland there had been plenty of other runners and he'd been able to hide him behind a few. Today there were just seven, and Mark knew that Phil's chance of getting Funland to settle were zero. The horse might be favourite but, if he ran away, Mark knew that he would win nothing. And that was just what he did.

Mark watched as, ahead, Phil sawed at Funland's mouth, desperately trying to hold on to him. When they got to within a dozen strides of the first fence the horse lifted his nose in the air and took off like a rocket. From the safety of Alone Again's back, Phil turned to the jockey on the horse galloping alongside him. 'Rather him than me,' he said.

The words were barely out of his mouth when Funland made as if to stand off the fence but lost his nerve and crashed straight through it instead, sending birch flying in all directions. Phil was thrown forward on to Funland's neck and 'called a cab' with his right hand, as the horse's momentum jolted him back again. Then Funland was into his stride and running away towards the next.

Mark expected to see Phil lean back in the saddle and fight to get Funland under control, but he did nothing. It was as if he were paralysed.

Mark knew that if Phil didn't at least try to hold on to Funland's head there would be an accident. When a horse bolts, the most important thing is to keep contact with his mouth. That way, when he gets into trouble, at least you can help him stay balanced.

Funland galloped straight through the water jump and then powered on around the bend into the back straight. Mark knew that Phil was now in trouble, and he silently implored him to try something, anything, to regain control of his mount. To his amazement, Phil didn't do a thing.

Funland was burning up the grass, thundering towards the next fence, going too fast to jump with any accuracy, that was for sure. Then, suddenly, Phil stood up in the irons and gave an almighty tug on the right rein, pulling Funland away from the fence and on to the hurdle course.

At first Mark thought Phil had felt the horse go lame and taken him out of the race. But when he looked across at Funland, now racing upsides them thirty yards to the right, the horse looked fine. There was nothing the matter with him.

Suddenly the truth dawned on Mark and, for a moment, he couldn't take it in. Phil had deliberately yanked his horse from the race because he was scared. The tough guy of jump racing had bottled it. Mark could hardly believe it.

Phil slipped from Funland's back in a daze. He tried to concentrate as Russell and the owner, Lavinia Morris, opened the inquest on the race.

'What the hell happened?' said the trainer. 'I thought he must have broken down.'

Russell was staring at Phil, giving him his famous glare, reserved for staff who had ballsed up.

'I thought I felt something give.' Phil avoided Russell's eye. 'I'm sorry, folks.'

Lavinia Morris, a plump, good-hearted sort who had been making a fuss of the horse, said loudly, 'For God's sake, there's no need for apologies. It's not the end of the world, is it, Russell?'

'No, Lavinia,' he replied, but his eye was still cold and Phil knew he would have to account for himself later.

But how could he explain it? The last thing he was prepared to say to Russell was that his nerve had failed him. He thought of some of his finer moments, but past triumphs were no consolation to him now – they were simply a measure of how his talent was slipping away, a yardstick of present failure.

'Cheer up, man,' cried Lavinia, slapping him heartily on the back. 'You can't win 'em all, you know.'

How true that was.

Julia was exercising Callisto in the indoor school. The roof leaked a bit and there was still some broken-down farm machinery in one corner but it wasn't too fanciful to call it an indoor school. Ted had said he'd used it exclusively for horses in the old days, before Tim's accident. He'd cleared a lot of junk out of it so Julia could make use of the space.

The surface was ordinary builder's sand with some shredded rubber added to give it some bounce. The school was almost as useful in the summer, when the ground was baked hard outside, as it was when it was snowing a blizzard in winter. There was no doubt in Julia's mind that horses learned twice as quickly when you had them indoors, away from any outside distractions. She used the area for jumping, schooling and breaking in youngsters – for just about everything, in fact.

It was ideal for Callisto, whose fitness regime was proceeding steadily, if hardly spectacularly. The old injury to his sacroiliac joint had healed following cortisone injections, but the horse had been left with a legacy of weakness in his quarters down one side. This meant that, when he pushed himself forward, he tended to veer off a straight line. If the horse were ever to race again he would have to regain the strength in his right side, and Julia had designed a training programme to this end. At the moment he was wearing a special binding on his off-hind leg, just above the fetlock, incorporating three pounds' worth of weights. By lunging him for an hour each day with the weights and taking him for long uphill trots, Julia was gradually building up his muscles.

As she walked she talked to him. Not all horses were good listeners, she'd found. Some of them, the younger ones, would rather fidget and play. Callisto, on the other hand, was a mature animal, one who'd suffered and survived. As she told him that the person she loved most in the world had betrayed her, he nodded wisely, as if taking in every word.

*

Hugh asked Gerry Fowler for a moment in private then, without mentioning Louise, told him what Rose had said. Gerry did not attempt to deny it.

'Look, I was only trying to save a bit of embarrassment. It was a slip-up in the office and it's a damn shame for everyone.'

'I've got to report it.'

The trainer looked up at him. He was too proud to beg but Hugh could read the appeal in his eyes. 'Have you really?'

Hugh didn't like this. It occurred to him that even if Louise didn't hate him after today, her father certainly would. 'It's my job, Gerry. Besides, some other hack will get hold of the story and run it if I don't.'

The trainer sighed. 'God forbid someone else should beat you to it.'

'I'm sorry, Gerry.'

The trainer nodded. He appeared resigned.

'I knew I shouldn't have tried to wriggle out of it. Sometimes you've just got to put your hand up, haven't you?'

'Is that what you'd like me to say?'

'Yes. I want you to make it clear that this whole business is entirely my fault.'

Julia had returned Callisto to his box and was rubbing him down.

'What shall I do about Phil?' she asked.

Of course, what she *should* do was confront him. Fling it in his face the moment he walked in the door. What's going on with you and Simone? Are you sleeping with her? Do you love her?

But suppose he said yes, he was in love and that was the reason he didn't hunger for Julia any more. That he'd had enough of neurotic blonde girls and wanted a sophisticated grown-up woman like Simone.

Then the whole mess would be out in the open and their marriage would be smashed in bits on the floor, beyond repair. What would she do after that?

She could leave him. Pack her things and never look back. Find a good lawyer and take the bastard for all she could get. Her friend Eileen would approve of that – and lots of other women too.

'I can't do that,' she said to Callisto. He cocked his head to one side. He understood.

*

The house was empty when Phil arrived home. There was no sign of Julia. He had tried her mobile a couple of times on the journey back but it had been switched off. Julia always turned it off when she was with a horse. Phil had an idea where she would be. He got back into the car and drove down the track to his dad's farm.

He found her sitting in the corner of Callisto's stall, one light bulb spreading a dim glow on the scene.

'What are you doing down here?' he said.

She remained where she was, her face a white smudge in the gloom. 'Hello, Phil.'

'Are you all right, Jules?'

She didn't reply.

'Come on, sweetheart, time to knock off. Not much you can do for old loppy legs at this time of night.'

She got to her feet. 'Don't you dare call him that.'

The vehemence of her response took him by surprise.

'It was just a joke. You've got to admit he is a bit lopsided these days. It'll be a miracle if he ever runs in a straight line again.'

She leaned out of the stall, her face an unrecognisable mask of fury as she hissed, 'Don't you ever talk like that in front of him again.'

'What are you on about? He doesn't care – do you, boy?' And he reached past her to pat Callisto's neck.

Julia smacked his hand away. 'Just go, Phil. Go back to the house and leave us alone.'

Phil stared at her. The full, kissable mouth was now set in a thin hard line, the small pointed chin thrust out in defiance. Her eyes bulged in anger. She looked nothing like the soft, pretty companion who graced his life.

'I'm sorry,' he said, aware now that she wasn't joking and that something was terribly wrong. He put his hand gently on her upper arm. He could feel the tension in her body. 'What's the matter, Jules?'

'Just go up to the house. I'll be back later.'

She turned away abruptly, back into the shadows of the box, leaving Phil standing empty handed.

He opened his mouth to say something but shut it again, fearful of making things worse. What the hell had got into her?

The horse stared at him implacably, standing like a sentry at the entrance to the stall. Phil raised his hand automatically to scratch the animal's ear, then thought better of it.

He turned and walked back to the car.

Keith's hands shook as he read the headline on page five of the *Racing Beacon*. 'Devious fails Newbury deadline – "All my fault," says trainer.'

He'd heard on the news the day before that the horse was out of the race, but this put a different slant on events. Keith had kept his eye on Devious all season and blue-inked him consistently. His antepost wager of £50 was the first time he'd ventured into red ink and handed over real money. When the news broke of the horse's injury it had pained him, but it was sod's law and he'd simply cursed his luck. But now he saw that it had been nothing to do with luck after all.

It still amazed him how naïve he was. He'd actually believed that stuff about a bruised foot, but now the truth had come out – the trainer had simply forgotten to declare the runner in time. At least, that was what it said in the paper. So Keith's bet had gone down, his and many others. The paper reckoned some £50,000 of punters' money had been lost in stakes never to be returned – one of the hazards of betting before the day of the race.

The trainer, this Gerry Fowler, had apologised in the paper to all the punters who had lost money on his error – but that was just hot air. He hadn't offered to pay them back, had he? Fowler had said he'd made an honest mistake, but Keith wasn't so sure.

Suppose a big bookmaker says to a trainer, there's something in it for you if your horse doesn't run? So the trainer makes a song and dance about how his horse is certain to walk off with a particular race – which pulls in a load of antepost bets. Then the trainer scratches his horse the day before the race and takes a backhander from the bookie for doing so.

It was plain that fifty grand had been unfairly extracted from punters, and Keith had no doubt than Mr Gerry 'I'm so sorry' Fowler had been given a share of it.

The trainer had made a mistake, though – he'd not let his owner in on the scam, and it turned out he was one of the losing betters. He was so furious he was thinking of quitting racing – he certainly wasn't bothered about keeping a lid on things. So the truth about the horse's non-existent injury had come out and Gerry Fowler's bent behaviour had been exposed.

The man was a con artist, a swindler.

It shouldn't fucking well be allowed.

The paper cited similar instances in the past of fancied horses who'd not been declared 'due to oversight'. 'It's happened before,' the article concluded, 'and it will happen again.'

Why? Keith wondered. *Why will it happen again?*

It was that kind of complacency which guaranteed that the rip-offs in racing would continue. No one, it seemed, had the will to do anything about them.

'Except me,' he said to himself.

Chapter Five

Gerry was first into the yard at 5.30, as he was every morning. Even on a Sunday there was still work to be done.

Most mornings at this time of year he was reluctant to steal out while the household was still in bed. He'd take his wife, Anne, a cup of tea before venturing into the dark, grumbling under his breath. But today was different. The memory of last night's quarrel still poisoned the atmosphere, and he quit the house without a backward glance.

Bloody women.

He knew he'd been out of order last night, shouting at the pair of them. It wasn't like him – but a man was entitled to lose it once in a while. Especially when he'd been made to look a fool in public for something that wasn't his fault. The evening phone-call from Crispin Rose hadn't helped. No wonder he'd lost his rag with Louise – the entire fiasco was down to her. He was quite entitled to refuse her the loan of the Peugeot for the foreseeable future.

Anne had thought he was being spiteful. After all, the girl shouldn't have been in the office in the first place – she was only helping him out. Well, if she's so bloody mature, he'd replied, why was she out on the piss the night before with that little madam Rebecca?

And so it had gone on, with Louise running off to bed in tears – 'Very mature,' he'd shouted after her – and he and Anne saying things to each other that, he knew from past experience, would fester in the memory. Nobody, it turned out, had behaved in a mature fashion last night.

He took the gravel path around the big square lawn at the back of the house. It would have been quicker to cut across the grass but it was boggy from the rain. He passed through the gate in the hedge that served as a boundary between the house and the yard and walked towards the stables. It was as black as night with no lightening of a sky banked with cloud. Flecks of rain whipped into his face.

How he wished he'd kept his mouth shut. Guilt lodged in the pit of his stomach like an indigestible meal. Louise was a good kid – loyal, hard working, conscientious. She'd slipped up, but it had been his responsibility and he shouldn't have taken it out on her. Why hadn't he been able to be as noble in private as he had in public?

Now, in the gloom of the morning, he blamed Rose. That phone-call had done the damage. The impresario had decided not to abandon racing after all but he was abandoning Gerry. He was moving his horses out next week, bringing a ten-year relationship to an end. That hurt.

The trainer reached the American barn, a building which housed both horses and office space. As he put his hand in his pocket for the keys, coarse material suddenly descended over his face, like a shutter cutting him off from the world.

He was too shocked to shout or struggle and, by the time he did, the material – it felt like sacking – had been pulled down to his waist, as the weight of a man slammed him against the door. The cry in his throat was cut off as the breath was expelled from his body. His feet were kicked from under him and he sprawled on the wet flagstones of the yard. He felt something tighten around his chest, pinning his arms to his side.

The first blow landed in his ribs. It felt like a kick, a thunderbolt from a boot of steel that propelled his body across the stones. There were more kicks as Gerry tried vainly to get to his feet and run. He felt a lance of fire in his chest as something gave way inside him.

'Help me!' he yelled, but the cry was feeble, lost in the foul, filthy sacking.

The kicking continued, the boot crashing into his head. Gerry tried to curl up and protect himself but his arms were caught up in the material and the blows were too precise. That was the one thing that stuck in his mind as he lay on the wet stones and took the punishment. This was not a wild, frenzied, heat-of-the-moment attack. This was a calculated assault. Intended to maim and cause maximum pain. Maybe to murder. He was terrified.

'Please!' he moaned. A pathetic appeal.

The blows stopped.

Thank God, he thought. *I'm still alive.*

Then the hammer fell again, exploding against his skull, and blackness claimed him.

Julia put together a tray of breakfast things – orange juice, toast, a single boiled egg, a cup of black coffee – to take upstairs to Phil. She'd left him in bed playing that infuriating game on his personal organiser. Since she'd discovered the entry about Simone she'd conceived a hatred for the little machine. She wished now she'd never given it to him.

They usually had a lie-in together on Sunday mornings. They'd make love, eat breakfast, then maybe fool around again, pawing each other with buttery fingers, toast-crumbed sheets tickling their naked bodies. But that had been before things started to go wrong. There'd be no fooling around today. Julia had already dressed and the tray was laid for one. She intended to be out of the house within ten minutes – she had a rendezvous with Callisto.

She entered the bedroom holding the breakfast tray. She expected Phil to be surprised to see her dressed, but he appeared not to notice. He was listening intently to the radio, his face drawn.

'Gerry Fowler's in hospital,' he said. 'He got beaten up.'

The news shocked her. She knew Gerry – everyone did.

The newsreader's voice echoed around the bedroom.

'Mr Fowler's condition is described as serious but not life threatening. He has yet to regain consciousness and his wife and daughter are waiting by his bedside.'

Julia sank on to the bed, the tray on her lap, and listened to the remainder of the bulletin.

'The trainer has recently been involved in controversy following his failure to enter a fancied runner for yesterday's Tote Gold Trophy at Newbury. This is the second time that a member of the horseracing fraternity has been attacked and hospitalised. Just over a fortnight ago, jockey Adrian Moore was assaulted while taking his dog for a walk. A police spokesman said it was too early to tell whether these events are connected.'

'Poor old Gerry,' said Phil, shutting off the radio as the next item came on.

A single thought petrified Julia. 'You will be careful, won't you?'

'What do you mean?'

'If there's someone going round attacking racing people . . .'

Phil laughed. 'Don't you believe it. Who'd want to do that?'

'But it's a bit of a coincidence, isn't it? First Adrian, then Gerry Fowler.'

Phil shook his head and removed the tray from Julia's lap. 'Aren't you having some?'

'I'm not hungry.'

'What have you got dressed for?'

'I'm working Callisto.'

'No you're bloody not.' He hooked an arm round her waist. 'I'm not having you going off on your own with these mysterious assaults on racing personnel taking place.'

'That's not funny, Phil,' she protested, but she couldn't deny she welcomed the feel of his arm around her.

'I don't mean any disrespect by it. Gerry's a bloody good bloke. Gave me a few rides as a conditional. I wouldn't mind meeting up with the character who's done this.'

'Phil!'

'Don't worry.' He pulled her down next to him on the bed, so she lay almost on top of him, his lips brushing her cheek. 'I'll keep a good lookout on dark mornings.'

It was heaven lying there with him. The horrible news and his closeness had put her misgivings about their relationship to the back of her mind. She couldn't think about their differences with his mouth on hers and his fingertips tracing the stem of her neck.

They came up for air.

'Callisto can wait,' he said, and began to tug her shirt from the waistband of her jeans.

It was a blissful twenty minutes. Just like it had always been. Better, in fact. But when it was over and she lay naked in his arms, she caught sight of that damned personal organiser on the bedside table and all her doubts and fears came flooding back.

Did Phil lie in bed with Simone like this? By not confronting him, was she condoning his other woman? Shouldn't she have it out with him right now?

No – she didn't dare.

She lay there more confused than ever.

*

Louise sat in the small room next to the hospital bed and the swathed and bundled body that was her father. She clasped his hand in hers, a bony horseman's hand, callused and rough. She'd know this hand anywhere. It struck her that it was about the only part of her dad's body that wasn't battered out of recognition. He'd sustained a broken pelvis, a fractured cheekbone and a punctured lung, courtesy of three ribs snapped like chicken bones.

It was one o'clock in the early hours of Monday morning, and she still wore the grubby work clothes she'd thrown on at 6 a.m. the previous day. She felt travel worn, as if she'd been on a long journey. Since finding her father, bloody and barely conscious, she had been living on nervous energy. She'd talked her mother into going home for the night and arranged to change places with her later in the day. Despite her fatigue, she knew she wouldn't be able to sleep; though her body was tired, her mind was still working overtime.

Louise was convinced the whole nightmare was down to her, beginning with her slip-up over the declaration and escalating through her unguarded confession to Hugh Pimlott. She was horrified by news reports speculating that the attack on her father was connected to Devious not running at Newbury. At least Dad wasn't going to die, so they said. If he did, it would all be her fault.

She hadn't even had time to make up with him. Saturday night's row seemed a year ago and yet it still cast a shadow. She'd never seen Dad so angry. After Crispin Rose had called to say he was taking his horses away, Dad had been speechless. Then he'd taken it out on her and, on reflection, she couldn't blame him. She'd brooded on it all that night and, when she'd heard him leave the house, she'd decided she had better try and mend fences. That was why she'd got up so early – to say sorry – and she'd found her father lying in a pool of blood in the courtyard. At least she'd been able to summon help at once. Of course, if she'd got up even earlier maybe she could have prevented the attack taking place at all.

There was a sudden change in the rasping note of her father's breathing. She leaned over him anxiously and saw, beneath the skullcap of bandages, that his eyes were open. His head looked the size of a melon, the skin stretched tight over his swollen flesh. It was the face of a stranger; only those eyes were familiar. They focused on her and his puffy lips stretched wide.

'Loo?' His pet name for her. He never used it when he was angry – he'd not called her that on Saturday night.

'Oh, Daddy.' She squeezed his fingers. 'I'm so sorry.' Sorry for everything, she meant, and started to cry.

'Ssh,' he mumbled, stroking her hand.

This was the first time he'd been conscious when she was with him. He'd spoken to Mum that afternoon, while Louise was in the canteen, sipping a cup of tea. He'd also managed a word or two at the same time with a female detective called Patsy, who'd been keeping discreet attendance. When Louise returned she'd been miffed that she'd missed her father's few minutes of lucidity. He'd been lying sedated ever since.

When he next spoke his voice sounded stronger and his grip on her fingers was firm.

'Do me a favour, Loo. Look after the yard.'

She was surprised. Surely he wasn't lying there worrying about the business?

'What about Chris?' she said. Chris Blackmore was Gerry's assistant trainer.

'Keep him sweet. Listen to what he has to say but you're in charge. OK?'

She nodded. 'If you say so, Dad.'

He didn't speak any more, just squeezed her hand and, in a few moments, dropped back to sleep.

Louise sat in the half-light, mulling over his words. She knew what to do. She'd let Chris get on with training the horses and organising the stable staff, and she'd deal with the owners herself. First thing tomorrow, she'd phone all of them and reassure them it was business as usual – almost.

She felt better than at any time during the past two days. She swore she wouldn't let Dad down again.

Julia heard Phil get up in the night – it was getting to be a habit with him. As usual she lay still, not daring to reveal that she too was awake. She stared unhappily into the pre-dawn gloom, alert to every sound he made downstairs. She heard his footsteps on the tiled kitchen floor, the gurgle of the kettle as he made himself a drink, then the creak of the kitchen door. Would he come back to her? He didn't, as a rule, return to bed but, in what little glow remained of that morning's intimacy, she hoped that he might. Then she heard the scrape of a chair in the living room and her hopes were dashed.

What did he do by himself in the middle of the night? Ponder how his life had gone wrong since he'd married her? Pine for his lover? Or plot how he could get free of silly, fragile Julia, who was nothing to him now but a burden?

She longed to go down and talk to him honestly. Maybe there was still something she could do to mend things between them. Maybe she'd got it all wrong and there was some other reason why he had removed himself from her emotionally. Maybe.

With Julia safely asleep upstairs, Phil laboriously worked at the task Simone had set him, writing on a lined A4 pad on the living-room table.

Phil had been dismayed when Simone asked him to write an account of his accident on May Queen.

Why? he'd asked her, and she'd explained at some length, though he wasn't sure he'd followed all her reasoning. But did that matter? He wasn't the kind of man who quizzed the doctor about what was in the medicine he'd been prescribed. All he cared about was, would it work?

'It's going to take some time,' Simone had said, 'but I'm sure there are things we can do to help you.'

One of those things, it transpired, was to record in as much detail as possible the events of that day at Worcester last September. He was now on his third version, condemned to keep returning to it until Simone was satisfied he had captured every last memory on paper.

Flashes of it kept returning to him as he wrote. He remembered the taste of earth in his mouth as he lay on his back after the fall and the view of horses' underbellies as they galloped over him, showering him with grass and dirt. As the sound of them receded – the drumming of hooves, the shouted curses, the slapping of whips – he'd felt surprisingly peaceful. There'd been a floating sensation in his body as his head tried to work out what had happened.

'A bit of me was thinking, Oh, sod it,' he wrote, ''cause I thought I was in with a chance in the race. But I also thought, I haven't blacked out, so I won't be disqualified for the next. Then through my goggles, which were all steamed up, I saw paramedics rushing over. Alongside them was a steward I knew, a stout fellow, and he was running too. I thought suddenly, Christ, I must be bad if he's running over. At that point I realised I had no feeling in my legs. I tried to lift my head to look down and see if they were still there but I couldn't move a muscle. The first thing I said to the medics was, "Have I still got my legs?" I had a picture in my mind that I'd left them behind, stuck in the fence.'

Phil put his pen down and reached for his mug of tea. His hand was trembling.

So this was supposed to help him feel better? He couldn't see how.

Louise returned home the next day with a clear sense of purpose. She'd managed to doze in the chair by her father's bed for a few hours so, after a shower and change of clothes, she got straight to work. First she sought out Chris. He seemed relieved when she explained the division of labour – he'd have more than enough to do managing the yard without being polite to owners. She omitted to mention her dad's wish that she take charge but said that she would be visiting hospital every day to keep Gerry in the picture. Then she hit the phones.

Naturally enough, everyone she spoke to was sympathetic and the calls followed the same pattern. First she ran through the events of yesterday – the attack on her father, the hospital vigil, the extent of his injuries – then assured them that Greenhills was functioning as normal and (briefed by Chris) moved on to discuss their particular animals.

She left Crispin Rose to the end. She wasn't sure exactly what she was going to say – she felt as if he were the enemy now. However, while Devious and his three other horses remained in the yard he was still a Greenhills owner. She found herself repeating what she'd told everyone else. She finished off by asking when he would like to remove his horses. His response took her by surprise.

'I don't want to remove them at all,' he said. 'This terrible business has put a few things in perspective. Would you tell Gerry I can't imagine working with any other trainer and ask him if he'll keep the horses after all?'

'I don't need to ask him, Mr Rose. He'd be delighted.'

She realised she'd just made her first executive decision as temporary boss of the yard. It felt pretty good.

Finally she called Rebecca. Apart from her need to unburden herself of all that had happened, she had a proposal to make.

'How much would I have to pay you,' she said, 'to get you to shift your bum out of bed at six in the morning?'

'Why would you want me to do that?'

'To ride a few horses.'

'You're offering me a job?'

'Just to help out for a few days. Can't you miss a few lectures?'

'You bet. But won't your father mind? I know I'm not flavour of the month.'

'Don't worry about Dad. He's put me in charge while he's away.'

Hiring Rebecca was her second executive decision. She could get used to making them, she thought.

The Editor
The *Racing Beacon*

Re: Gerry Fowler
As you may have noticed, I've been busy.

Mr Gerry Fowler is guilty of cheating and lying to the betting public. He pulled Devious out of the Tote Gold on a trumped-up story and got caught out, robbing honest punters of their antepost bets. He probably thought he was being clever when he banked his backhander from the bookmakers, but I bet he's not laughing now I've taught him a lesson.

The cheaters in horseracing are soon going to sit up and take notice – the ordinary punter is fighting back.

So when are you lot going to take your finger out and do something? I've just about had it with the *Racing Beacon*. You claim to be the punter's friend but your not.

Like I said before I want a proper campagne for justice in racing. You'd better start taking the lid off racing scams quick or there will be more like Gerry Fowler with a sack over their heads.

I'm giving you till Thursday morning.

PS If you're not interested there's others who will be. This is your last chance.

'Hmm,' murmured Charlie as he stared at this latest letter. He was aware that the three others in the room were expecting a dynamic response but this was all he could come up with. He needed thinking time.

They had convened once more in Duncan Frame's office – Frame, John Petrie and that shambolic-looking reporter, Pimlott. By tacit agreement of both parties, Scotland Yard was not represented – though Charlie had no doubt Frame would be on the phone to his contacts if he failed to get what he wanted. Charlie was well aware that the editor had his own agenda. So far, however, he had been remarkably restrained in presenting it.

'A question,' said Frame, obviously keen to move things along.

Charlie looked up from the letter and waited.

'Is the person who wrote this letter responsible for the attack on Fowler?'

Charlie decided to be frank. 'Almost certainly.' He needed Frame's cooperation and he couldn't see any point in prevaricating. Besides, if he started playing games with some tricky newspaper editor he'd probably end up on the losing side. Honesty – in selected doses – was usually the best policy.

He indicated the paper in front of him. 'We haven't released precise details about the assault on Mr Fowler. His attacker put a sack over his head before he beat him. So, either the letter-writer has inside knowledge of what happened from the emergency services or the family – or else he's the one who assaulted him.'

'So it's been dropped in to convince us he's genuine, like mentioning broadpoints in the last letter?' said Hugh Pimlott.

'It looks like it.'

'But the letter is addressed to the paper,' said Frame.

'He knows you'll have gone to the police. He's quite smart enough to assume we'll be talking to each other.'

Frame cleared his throat. Here it comes, thought Charlie, he's going to make his pitch.

'I think you'll agree, Inspector Lynch, that the *Racing Beacon* has been fully supportive of the authorities in this matter.'

Charlie nodded. 'I appreciate that you've agreed not to print any of this.'

'Quite. However, I'm not sure that it is in the public interest for the paper to remain silent much longer.'

Frame's small black eyes stared at Charlie out of his square red face. He was putting a polite gloss on it but he was saying he intended to break the story.

At last Charlie said, 'I agree with you.'

Petrie shot him a startled look. In all their discussions so far, they'd agreed to try to keep the letters out of the public domain.

'My reading of this bloke,' said Charlie, leaning forward in his seat, 'is that he wants publicity. He's dying to be the centre of attention for once in his life – I don't know why exactly. Anyhow, he's giving you an ultimatum. Start writing about punters being cheated or he'll beat up more racing people.'

'And he'll deal with some other newspaper,' said Frame.

'That too.' Charlie knew this was probably the most significant point for the editor. Whatever Frame might feel about the public interest, Charlie had no doubt that commercial imperatives would colour his thinking. The idea of losing the inside track on a hot story to a rival newspaper would be unthinkable.

'Would it be possible,' Charlie continued, 'for you to run a few articles on this fellow's pet subject?'

Frame screwed up his face. 'We can't go around accusing people of cheating – I'd end up in the courts faster than the man you're looking for. And I don't suppose the Avon and Somerset Constabulary would care to indemnify the newspaper against libel damages.'

'Box a bit clever. Give him a little of what he wants and buy us some time.'

Frame turned to Hugh, who had been scribbling on a notepad. 'What do you think?'

'Should be possible,' the reporter said, looking up from his notes. 'There's all sorts of stuff we could do safely.'

Charlie grinned at him gratefully. So the fellow wasn't a useless lump after all.

'Why don't we actually use his words?' Hugh continued. 'Flash "Justice in Racing" as a banner on the page.'

'Great,' said Charlie quickly, as if it were a done deal.

Frame nodded grudgingly. 'OK, but I'm running a separate news story linking Moore and Fowler. Our readers have a right to know there's a madman out there with a grudge against the racing community.'

Charlie couldn't disagree.

They caught a fair amount of traffic heading out of London on the M4. Not that Charlie much cared. John was looking after the driving chores, being the kind of fellow you couldn't prise away from the wheel. Personally, Charlie would be happy if he never sat in the driving-seat of a car again. He'd never cared for them. He remembered being given toy cars as a boy and leaving them untouched in his bedroom till his mum got fed up and gave them away. He'd bet John's mum never gave away her son's toy cars. He'd have pushed them till the wheels fell off.

The irritating trill of 'La Cucaracha' filled the vehicle. John's mobile phone was another toy Charlie would rather not play with. It had its uses, however. He fished it out of the sergeant's jacket and took the call from DC Patsy Preece.

'I've got a preliminary report from Forensics on the sack, guv.'

'And?'

'Apart from Gerry's, they've found blood. Animal blood, probably from a fox or a dog. There's fur and feathers, too.'

'No other human blood?'

'They don't think so. Just animals and maybe a bird or two, given the feathers. The sack itself is bog-standard. It looks like it might have originally contained wood because there's lots of splinters buried in the material. You know those sacks of kindling you buy at garages? That kind of thing.'

'What about the cord?' A length of blue nylon cord had been used to tie the sack around Gerry Fowler's body.

'It's like that used on the jockey's dog. But it's common stuff. You can buy it everywhere.'

They exchanged further information: Patsy on Gerry's condition (improving, but still no helpful recall of his attack) and Charlie on the latest letter (postmarked Bath, on the eastern edge of their area).

John shot Charlie a curious look as he finished the call and the DCI relayed the information on the sack.

'So it sounds like we're looking for some kind of countryman. Earns his living off the land and does a bit of hunting,' the DS said.

'Who follows the horses and has access to a computer,' Charlie added.

'And doesn't take kindly to losing money.'

The traffic slowed as warning signs flashed a reduced speed limit. The roadworks ahead were eight hundred yards off and they were already at a crawl.

'We'll be late for dinner,' said John.

Charlie shrugged. With Claire off in Bristol, the timing of his evening meal was an irrelevance. He pursued a train of thought.

'Just how many blokes like that do you reckon there are on our patch, John?'

'God knows – thousands. Tens of thousands. Half the male country-side population, I'd say.'

'So would I.'

Neither of them spoke for a few minutes.

'We're going to catch him, though, aren't we, guv?' said John finally.

'You bet we are. I just hope we do it before some other poor sod ends up with his head smashed in.'

Keith was running on pure adrenaline, getting through the many mechanical tasks of his day on nervous energy alone – exercising and feeding the hounds, cleaning out the pens, collecting dead stock from nearby farms. The attack on Fowler had taken the best part of Saturday night, what with an evening recce before nailing the bastard on Sunday morning. That had been four separate trips of forty miles each – and he'd had a hunt on the Saturday where there were plenty of nosey parkers who'd notice if his mind wasn't on the job.

He'd spent a lot of time on Sunday cleaning up. He'd worn his most clapped-out clothes for the trip to Fowler's yard and put them in the incinerator, just to be on the safe side. He'd even incinerated his old boots, which was a pity because they had a few months left in them. Cleaning the car took time too, but it had been necessary. He'd read about what the police forensic people could find, just from analysing some microscopic piece of dust. Frankly there probably wasn't any way he could make the car entirely safe, but what the hell – he could hardly put that in the incinerator, could he?

Then, after the clean-up, there was the letter to write and get in the post. That wasn't something he could rush, even though he'd been planning what he was going to say for days. And he had to make sure he didn't get careless and do something stupid, like leave a fingerprint on the letter or the envelope. No chance of that, though; he'd worn surgical gloves and only removed them after he'd driven all the way to Bath to put the letter in the post. That had been in the early hours of Monday and by rights he should have been dead on his feet. No chance. He was loving every minute of it.

And the best bit – even better than toe-ending that thieving sack of shit Gerry Fowler across his stable yard – was reading the newspapers. The coverage of the Fowler hit had been good – he liked the way the papers were beginning to make the connection with Adrian Moore. 'Who's next for racing's avenging angel?' was the headline above one article. 'A dark shadow of suspicion lies across the small world of National Hunt racing,' began another. Keith was pleased.

Wednesday's *Racing Beacon*, however, brought the breakthrough he wanted – a double-page spread headed: IS THERE JUSTICE IN RACING?

That was more like it.

Dinner in the restaurant was a sombre affair for Julia and Phil – which shouldn't have been the case considering it was a celebration for Valentine's Day.

The day had got off on the wrong foot when he'd given her a pair of red silk knickers and a silly card – which had seemed like a good idea when he'd bought them, in a rush, on his way back from his appointment with Simone the day before. Her present to him, on the other hand, was a discreetly wrapped box containing a pair of gold cuff links, obviously not a spur-of-the-moment buy.

Then the postman had arrived with a bundle of cards for him – all from fans. It happened every year – assorted pictures of canoodling teddies and winsome kittens, all adorned with messages of adolescent hero worship.

She had also received a card in the post, a painting of a horse's head with a white diamond on his forehead, like Callisto. It was unsigned – he'd looked.

'My fan club's bigger than yours,' he'd said, but he could tell she'd not been amused.

She toyed with her food and refused the champagne he offered her. Since the Snowdrop dinner she'd not drunk any alcohol at all. For once he was tempted to have a glass, but what was the point if she didn't join him?

He knew he wasn't exactly great company himself. It was that bloody Simone's fault. At their last appointment she'd brought him back to the matter of talking to Julia about his treatment.

'What do you think would happen if you told her?'

'It's hard to say.'

'I'd like you to try, though.'

'She'd think I was weak.'

Simone digested this and continued in the low, measured tone that he was now accustomed to. 'Why do you think she would find your behaviour weak?'

'You know.'

She'd looked at him with those gleaming black eyes, like she was judging him. 'No, I don't know, Phil. Tell me.'

'Because I'm meant to be brave. She married a top jockey, not some wimp who runs off crying to a shrink when he can't hack it.'

She smiled at the mention of the word 'shrink', and then continued to probe.

'After your accident, she didn't think you were weak because you accepted medical help, did she?'

'Of course not.'

'And if you had refused treatment for your injured body, would she have thought more or less of you?'

'She'd have thought I was a bloody fool.'

She sat back, savouring his reply. 'So where is the evidence, Phil, that she would think differently now? Might she not think all the more of you because you had the sense to seek help for your mind?'

In the end, he'd agreed. He should tell Julia.

But in the here and now, looking into his wife's unhappy face across the table, his resolve deserted him.

Maybe tomorrow.

Hugh had been feeling bad about Gerry. Whichever way he rehashed events in his head, he still ended up bearing some responsibility for the attack which had put the trainer in hospital. After all, it was down to him that the real story of Devious's withdrawal had been made public. And the consequence of that was that the mad letter-writer had gone after poor Gerry.

And there was another thing – it hadn't occurred to him that he was putting the trainer physically at risk by writing the story. But maybe it should have done. After what had happened to Adrian, Hugh of all people should have been aware of the danger he was placing racing people in by publicising their errors.

He'd been among the journalists who'd assembled at the hospital some ten miles from Greenhills Yard. Eventually they'd heard statements from the police and a family spokesman, a solicitor, who'd asked them to respect family privacy at this terrible time, etc. Hugh gave the solicitor a short note of sympathy for Gerry, offering personal support. He didn't see what else he could do. Then he'd returned to London, leaving some of his competitors to poke their noses round Greenhills. He didn't have the stomach for that and Frame would have to lump it.

By the Thursday after the assault, Gerry Fowler was off the news pages of the national papers. Hugh was aware that several Greenhills horses had been entered for the meeting at Taunton and, playing a hunch, he made the pilgrimage to Somerset. He could see that it had paid off as soon as he observed the horses in the parade ring for the first race.

He hadn't worked out what he was going to say to Louise. Sorry didn't exactly cover it. On the other hand, it wasn't his fault she'd told him about the Devious fiasco. He'd had to follow it up and, fortunately, he'd kept her name out of it. Otherwise – and this was the truly frightening thought – it could have been her lying in a hospital bed instead of her father.

Louise was standing in the centre of the ring talking to a middle-aged gent in a camel coat and dark brown brogues – an owner, obviously – and the jockey. She wore trousers and a yellow anorak and her hair hung loose to her shoulders in a deep auburn cloud. She helped the rider into the saddle and muttered a few words to him. She did not look like a girl racked with trauma; she looked like a woman with a job to do.

As the horses were lead out of the ring, the owner left Louise and strode off into the crowd. Hugh moved into position to intercept her but hung back as the stablegirl who had been leading the horse round came over to join her. Hugh had not seen the other girl before. She was about the same build as Louise but with dark hair. She put her hand on Louise's arm and squeezed encouragingly. Hugh had decided now was not the moment to interrupt when Louise looked up and saw him.

He couldn't read her expression as she approached. Her head was held high and her jaw was firm. In the course of his job Hugh had often been on the receiving end from irate trainers and jockeys – it came with the territory – but it had never bothered him. Right now, however, he knew he would not be able to shrug off a verbal assault from Gerry Fowler's daughter.

Her first words, however, disarmed him.

'I'm glad you're here. I've been looking out for you.'

'Oh.' She was smiling at him, which was about the last thing he expected. 'I'm terribly sorry about your father,' he began, but she cut him off.

'He's going to be OK. I read him your letter, you know.'

Hugh nodded, unsure how to react. He'd been prepared to grovel but she didn't seem interested.

'I'd like to take you up on your offer to help out. Are you able to put something about me in your paper?'

Hugh was quickly recovering his footing. 'What exactly did you have in mind?'

Chris had volunteered to return to the yard in the horse-box so Rebecca could travel with Louise.

'I still don't see why you spoke to Hugh Pimlott,' said Rebecca as Louise manoeuvred the Peugeot on to the M5 slip road.

'Because he can put the message out that we're still in business.'

'But there's other reporters. This one stitched you up.'

It was a discussion they'd been having since they'd climbed into the car.

'It was my fault really. Anyway, he owes me because of that.'

'Sure it's not because you fancy him?'

'Oh, please, Becky – you've got sex on the brain.'

'It's not me who mentioned sex – you obviously fancy him.'

Louise laughed. It was great to have a giggle with Rebecca, even in these circumstances. It wasn't healthy to be serious all the time, was it?

'So tell me about last night,' she said.

Rebecca had accepted the invitation from Leo and Kit to spend Valentine's eve in Bath. She had made an effort to get Louise to go with her but Louise had turned her down flat. She was due at the hospital.

That didn't mean to say that she wasn't curious about what had happened.

'It was OK,' said her friend without enthusiasm. 'It would have been better if you'd been there. Carol was a bit of a pain.'

Carol, Louise gathered, had been Kit's date – substituting for her. Kit of the sky-blue eyes.

'So,' she said, 'do you think I've blown it with Kit now?'

Rebecca hesitated.

Louise ploughed on. 'I mean, how was he with Carol?'

'Men can forgive a lot if you've got a cleavage.' Rebecca shrugged. 'Sorry, Louise.'

Louise drove on in silence.

'Chris wants you for first lot tomorrow morning.'

The other girl groaned. 'I really need a lie-in.'

'You agreed to stand in for me, Becky.'

'Yes, boss.'

Louise put her foot down on the accelerator.

What were so special about sky-blue eyes anyway?

Hugh was more than happy with the way Louise's interview turned out. He'd got a local photographer to capture her leading one of the Greenhills runners at Taunton and Frame had run it in colour on the front page. It was a photo that caught more than her youthful prettiness. The shadows beneath her luminous, wide-set eyes and the determined set of her chin spoke of maturity and inner strength. Here was a young woman who looked the world in the eye, unbowed by fear or ill fortune – which was the tone of the interview carried within.

Louise spoke simply of finding her wounded father and of his progress in hospital. Despite his horrible injuries, she stated that he would be back at the yard before long. In the meantime it was business as usual – the Greenhills staff were performing as well as ever under the expert eye of Chris Blackmore, and she was acting as go-between, keeping her dad up to speed on events in the yard. She thanked all the owners for their support, in particular Crispin Rose, who had reversed his decision to train his horses elsewhere.

As for the person who had assaulted her father, she knew nothing of his motivation and cared less. He was obviously sick in the head and she had every confidence the police would soon catch him. In the meantime, she and her family were deeply grateful to all the racing people who had sent messages of support. She believed that bad times brought out the good in people and racing folk were the best of all.

'Quite the plucky little heroine,' Frame muttered as he read Hugh's copy. 'Got your leg over yet?'

As a rule Hugh never responded to the editor's jibes but this time he was stung. 'For God's sake, Duncan, her father's been half killed.'

'So she'll need a game laddy like you to take her mind off her troubles.' He looked appreciatively at her photo. 'I'll say this for you, you know how to pick 'em.'

This time, Hugh kept his mouth shut.

Keith also dwelt closely on Louise's interview in the *Beacon*, though he was less impressed with her sentiments.

'Stupid cow,' he muttered as he read her remarks about her father's attacker being sick in the head. A bolt of white anger flamed within him. It was a pity the prissy little miss had not turned up earlier on Sunday morning – he'd have given her some of what her father got. A couple of black eyes and she'd not be on anyone's front page.

On the whole, though, Keith was satisfied with the way the *Beacon* had responded to his suggestions. This was the third day of the Justice in Racing articles. They weren't entirely what he wanted. He'd envisaged mugshots across the page of the leading lights of National Hunt, with captions underneath, spelling out their crimes. To be honest, these pages were a bit soft – light-threated yarns from days gone by, unsubstantiated rumours, done-and-dusted cases.

At least he'd got their attention. Part one of his plan had been accomplished.

Beating up jockeys had never been the limit of his ambition. Though there was a lot of satisfaction in dealing out rough justice, it wasn't enough. Where was the profit in it? And how did it get him out of this hole? He was too smart to spend his life cleaning up dog shit.

They were dancing to his tune now.

Time for them to pay the piper.

Chapter Six

After the fiasco at Newbury, Russell had accepted Phil's explanation that he thought Funland had gone lame in his off-hind from over-stretching at the water. Phil had been embarrassed. He'd never lied to Russell before and it wasn't an experience he wished to repeat. He felt dirty deceiving someone who was providing him with his living.

By way of making amends, he began riding out every morning. Normally he was only at Deanscroft on work days and when there was schooling to be done. Now he was in at 7.30 on the dot with his boots polished.

The daft thing was that Phil never had an anxious moment schooling, no matter how bad a jumper he was sitting on. Of course, they always jumped at home at a much slower pace and, if he did happen to fall, there wouldn't be any horses thundering up behind to trample him.

He brought his mount back to where Russell was standing, having watched Phil put him over nine large fences. The trainer looked more than satisfied.

'Get this fellow jumping like that tomorrow,' he said, 'and you might have half a chance of winning.'

Army Blue was just the type of horse Phil needed to give him confidence. You could boot him into the fences as hard as you liked, but you'd never get him do anything he wasn't capable of. In other words, he was safe. The kind of horse you'd put your daughter on for her first point-to-point. Phil made up his mind that tomorrow at Ascot he would give the horse a ride that Russell would be proud of. A ride to settle both their minds.

So Phil was in good heart as he drove home mid-morning. He hoped to catch Julia before setting off for Sandown that afternoon.

Now he felt he was getting to grips with his problem, Phil had finally got up the nerve to talk to her about it. He knew he'd been a moody bastard of late, and she deserved to know the reason why. Besides, it was about time he treated her with the respect she deserved as his wife. She wasn't just some pretty companion to be kept in a separate compartment of his life, where he could pick and choose which emotions to share. That was how he'd treated his past girlfriends, he realised. But he was married now and things had to change. For better or worse – that was it from now on, wasn't it? Well, this was definitely for worse, but he'd see what she made of it.

He knew she'd be down on his dad's farm with Callisto. It was amazing how much of herself she'd poured into that animal – if the old horse was a bloke, Phil thought, he'd be jealous. As it was, he felt a pang of guilt. He'd meant to give her a hand with him but so far had fobbed off all her requests, preferring to devote his time to the horses at Deanscroft. They, after all, were his bread and butter. With the best will in the world, he couldn't see Julia's old crock getting round a racecourse in one piece ever again.

As he parked the car in the lane he was surprised to see another motor beside Julia's little Fiesta. He knew who it belonged to – what was Mark doing here?

There was the sound of hooves from the nearby paddock, and Phil looked over the gate. The big field was used for schooling, and Julia had laid it out with practice jumps of all shapes and sizes. Mark was on the far side on a horse Phil did not at first recognise. The pair were moving at a brisk clip towards a wooden barrier, and the horse seemed to flow over it before slowing. Only when the rider halted his mount at the opposite hedge and turned him in Phil's direction did he see the white star on the animal's forehead.

Phil was amazed at Callisto's progress. He watched in a daze as Julia rushed over to make a fuss of the horse. He couldn't catch what she said but Mark's laughter rang out loud and clear.

The pair separated and horse and rider took off again, back towards the poles from the opposite direction. Phil had his hand on the gate. His impulse was to charge over and ask what was going on. But it was obvious. Julia had got fed up asking him to help out with Callisto and had turned elsewhere for help. If he were honest, he couldn't blame her. He couldn't say he liked it, though. Especially since Mark was doing such a good job. The old horse didn't look so old now. The way he was moving into the jumps, it looked like he still had the talent.

Abruptly Phil turned away.

As Julia let Mark into Barley Cottage she could see he was in pain. The session with Callisto, which had gone so well, had ended on an unfortunate note. Mark had taken him over a final jump and the horse had stumbled on landing, pitching the jockey to the ground. It was just one of those things.

Mark had sprung up, looking sheepish and holding his left arm. 'That woke me up,' he said, grinning. 'He's such a smooth ride, I must have gone to sleep.'

Julia had been concerned but he'd brushed away her attentions and had insisted on helping her stable Callisto. As she'd finished giving the horse a rub-down, she noticed Mark flexing his arm and feeling his collar bone. She'd offered to take a look at it back at the cottage.

She made him strip to the waist in the front room and raise his arm. His skin was milk white, like a young boy's but for the fine black hairs on his chest – and the muscles. Men who steered tons of horse-flesh over jumps for a living had rare power in their arms and shoulders.

'What's the verdict, Doc?'

'I'm no doctor, silly.'

'You're pretty good with horses, though. It's just flesh, blood and bone, isn't it?'

She laughed and put her hand flat on his skin. It was smooth and warm.

'Have you broken that collar bone?'

'Three times that side. It's not bust this time, though, is it?'

She pressed her fingers into him, looking deeply into his eyes. She saw discomfort there but not the involuntary contraction of the pupils that would indicate sharp pain.

'You're just a bit bruised, I think. I'll get you an ice pack.'

'Not the all-over body massage then?'

Lights danced in those sea-green eyes, and she realised with a stab of surprise that he was flirting with her.

'No,' she said, pushing the tip of her forefinger into the hard centre of his chest. 'Put your shirt back on.'

He held her gaze, smiling at her. Her finger was still pressing against his skin and she pulled it away, as if breaking an electrical contact.

When she went into the kitchen and opened the freezer cabinet she realised her cheeks were burning. *For Christ's sake*, she thought, *I'm a happily married woman*. She found what she was looking for and closed the freezer. *At any rate*, she corrected herself, *I'm a married woman*, and she pulled a bandage from the first-aid kit she kept in a cupboard.

Mark was buttoning his shirt as she returned.

'What's that?' he asked, indicating the white plastic object in her hand.

'A chiropractic cold pack. The gel inside retains the temperature and moulds itself to the shape of your body. I can't put it directly against your skin so I'm going to bandage it on over your shirt.'

'I always use a packet of peas myself,' he said with a grin. 'Not that I'm complaining.'

She was now acutely self-conscious as she set about fixing him up, wrapping the bandage round his chest to hold the compress in place. Their faces were agonisingly close, and the warm smell of him was in her nostrils – a lemony hint of aftershave mixed with a faint trace of sweat from the morning's toil.

'You've got a fair pile of Valentines,' he said, with a nod towards the table.

The cards from Wednesday lay in a heap – she hadn't got around to chucking them out yet.

'They're from Phil's private pony club,' she said with more acid in her voice than she intended.

'Not all of them, surely?'

'Phil gave me one.'

'That's all? Don't tell me you've not got your own admirers.'

He was grinning at her, but there was something in his voice – what was he getting at? Surely he couldn't know about that other one, the card with the horse? Unless . . .

She fixed the bandage with a safety pin – not an easy thing to do with shaking fingers.

'What about you?' she said. 'I bet you got loads.'

His smile faded. 'Not the one I really wanted.'

Oh, shit. She stepped smartly away from him. The sooner he was out of her house the better.

*

Phil did not join in the regular changing-room banter at Sandown. He'd genuinely convinced himself that morning that he was getting his nerve back, but now he knew differently. The afternoon had been another of complete torture – a succession of rides in which his phobias had surfaced to undermine his confidence and defeat his best intentions at every turn. He was sure that people who'd watched him ride over the years would soon notice his problem. It was tormenting him more than any physical injury he had ever suffered.

When the afternoon's work was over, he avoided his fellow jockeys and headed for the car park with indecent haste. He was turning into someone so obsessed with himself that he seemed to be on his own, even in the middle of a crowded room. He'd never behaved like this before.

But if cutting himself off from other people was what was going to get him through his bad patch then he had no choice. It seemed to him a natural consequence of his sessions with Simone. She'd made it plain that no quick fix was available to him.

He'd finished his written version of the accident on May Queen to Simone's satisfaction and, as instructed, had recorded it on an audio tape. Now he was supposed to listen to it over and over. The theory, as she had explained it, was that by exposing himself repeatedly to his worst fears, he would eventually become desensitised and no longer respond negatively.

'You mean,' he'd said to Simone, 'that I'll get so bored with hearing myself whinge on that I won't care if I have another accident.'

She'd liked that. 'Phil, if your reaction to this trigger event were to be one of boredom then I think your troubles would be behind you.'

He'd played the tape only once so far, putting it on as he drove to the racecourse. As he heard himself describe the scene at Worcester last September, he'd begun to panic. He'd pulled into a lay-by and forced himself to listen. He was conscious of his heart beating faster and his breath coming in short gasps. He was there, on May Queen, in a pack of horses, heading for the open ditch, about to make that foolhardy leap. Only this time he knew the disastrous consequences of throwing a fast-moving, small-brained, half-ton animal who couldn't jump at a four-foot fence.

He turned the tape off and jabbed the button to lower the window. He gulped in fresh air as the terror slowly receded, and found himself staring at a middle-aged man leaning on the bonnet of his car, clutching a mobile phone.

'You all right, mate?' said the man. 'You look bloody awful.'

Phil forced a smile on to his face. 'Not half as bad as I feel,' he said, and drove off slowly.

'Thanks a bunch, Simone,' he muttered to himself as he did so. But she'd told him not to play the tape in the car and, he realised, that was precisely why he had put it on. It had been a small act of rebellion against a woman who he saw partly as a friend but mostly as a petty-minded schoolmistress.

'What makes you think you're going to fall off your horse?' she'd asked him at an early session.

'Because jockeys come off all the time,' he said.

'But do you?' she asked. 'Do you keep a record of how often you fall?'

Phil didn't, though he knew plenty who did. He also knew someone who followed his career with the dedication of a schoolboy train-spotter. His dad would know how often he'd been unseated.

'Apparently,' he told Simone at his next appointment, 'my average is a fall every eighteen rides.'

She'd thought about this. 'How many of those would be bad accidents?'

'Not many. You get bashed around a bit, maybe break a small bone in your hand or get badly bruised, but until last year I'd never had a serious injury.'

She made a note on her pad. 'I thought, from what you'd been telling me, that it was more dangerous than that.'

He shrugged. 'I've been lucky.'

'In more ways than one, I imagine. Apart from these bad experiences in races, do you still enjoy working with horses?'

That took him by surprise. 'Of course. It's all I've ever wanted to do.'

'Do you earn a decent wage?'

'I'm not complaining.'

'And there must be other good things in your situation.'

He thought for a moment. 'I meet plenty of interesting people. And get invited to all sorts of events.'

'So—' She put her pen down. 'Do you see what I'm getting at?'

He shook his head.

'I'm pointing out the benefits of your situation – you're doing what you want to do, you're successful at it and you make a good living. You may feel that these positives outweigh the risk of a minor fall every eighteen rides.'

Phil considered this. It was all true.

But so was the conviction, every time he galloped towards a steeplechase fence, that he was about to break his neck.

Simone must have read it in his face. 'It's OK, Phil,' she said softly, all trace of the schoolmistress now gone, 'it might take time but you're going to be all right.'

He wished he shared her confidence.

Julia had not intended to go to Ascot on the Saturday afternoon. As a rule she preferred spending time with horses to watching them run, and she could catch the racing on television.

Phil had already left for the course when she received a phone-call from Mark.

'Hi,' he'd said in that now-familiar Irish purr. 'I've got a free afternoon.'

'Oh.' Her mind filled with the image of him standing stripped to the waist in the front room, laughing into her eyes, as she studied his firm, pale body.

'I was wondering if you wanted me.'

Jesus, was he being deliberately ambiguous?

'To help with Callisto,' he went on.

She panicked. She didn't dare spend the afternoon alone with him.

'That's kind of you,' she said. 'But I'm going to Ascot.'

'How about tomorrow morning, then?'

Oh, God, what should she say? 'Yes – OK.' She regretted it instantly, but knew she would have felt worse if she'd said no. 'Look, I've got to leave now,' she blurted, and put the phone down, barely managing a polite goodbye.

She called Ted at once. 'Do you and Margaret want to come to Ascot with me? I've decided to surprise Phil.'

Her father-in-law hadn't taken much persuading, though Margaret declined. What was more, Ted insisted on taking his car so Julia could drive back with her husband.

All in all, Julia thought as they set off, things had worked out for the best. She pushed Mark firmly to the back of her mind.

The 2.25 at Ascot, a two-and-a-half-mile chase, commanded a prize purse of around £40,000 and attracted some of the best steeplechasers in Europe. The Irish favourite, Never Too Late, had already been heavily backed for the Gold Cup at Cheltenham in March; so too the French challenger, Cresson. Most of the press speculation surrounded the outcome of a head-to-head between this pair. Army Blue, Phil's horse, had also received some positive attention and was tipped in some quarters to upset the apple-cart.

Phil's column that morning had increased the speculation. 'The competition may be tough but Army Blue's a talented individual who doesn't hide on the gallops at Deanscroft. After his impressive win at Wetherby at the end of last year, here's a chance for him to measure himself against the best.'

The Wetherby performance had indeed been impressive – the horse had jumped like a stag and burnt off the field, winning as he liked. Mark had been on his back that day, and Phil was well aware his stablemate had coaxed a career-best performance out of the horse. The least he must do was to equal it.

Russell underlined the point as he gave Phil a leg-up into the saddle. 'You know what to do with this character. Get hold of him right at the start and set him alight.'

'Right, boss,' Phil said – he already knew the plan.

Army Blue was a good horse to sit on, with nice wide shoulders and plenty of neck in front of the rider. You felt safe the moment you were astride him. As they walked around at the start Phil remembered what he'd promised himself the day before. This would be the ride that put his career back on course.

But as the tapes rose and the runners thrust forward towards the first, Phil could only go through the motions. His riding had no conviction and, while he might be fooling most of the people in the stands, he wasn't fooling himself – and he certainly wasn't fooling Army Blue. The horse took his time at every fence, and after they had gone a mile he was too far back to ever be competitive.

Get him stoked up, shouted a voice inside Phil's head, *show the lazy bastard who's boss!*

Phil waved his whip, smacking Army Blue on the quarters without conviction. There was no change in the horse's pace. Unless you took Army Blue by the scruff of the neck, as Mark had done last time out, he never showed his true colours.

Phil couldn't bring himself to knock the horse into the action. He knew that Russell would be watching and cursing, analysing his performance, wondering why the horse wasn't doing his job – and probably wishing he'd given Mark the ride.

Get a grip! Phil screamed to himself. For the first time ever in a race he was conscious of his own body – of the thumping in his chest and the sweat on the back of his neck. He was in a blind panic.

Hugh got a message in the press room that Louise was looking for him and immediately stopped filing his race report to step outside. He'd spotted her earlier and wanted to talk to her, but hadn't been sure of his likely reception.

She was standing on the balcony overlooking the entrance, her curls bundled under a black felt hat. The dark smudges under her eyes spoke of sleepless nights, but she grinned quickly as she spotted Hugh.

'I wanted to say thank you for the photo.'

Hugh had ordered a blow-up of the print used in the *Beacon* and sent it to her.

'Dad's put it by his bedside,' she said.

'How is he?'

'Mending slowly. He spends all day shouting at the nurses. And your name's still mud.'

Hugh could believe it.

'How long will he be in hospital?'

She shrugged. 'He'll be in for a few weeks yet, I imagine. To be honest, I'd rather he stayed where he was. He needs twenty-four-hour care.'

'Are you sure that's the real reason?'

She looked at him quizzically.

'I mean,' he went on, 'with Gerry away you're in charge, aren't you?'

'So?'

'I think you rather like it.' He enjoyed teasing her.

'I suppose I do, but I'll feel much better when Dad's back.' She looked at him suspiciously. 'You're not going to write this in your paper, are you?'

He shook his head. 'I promise.'

She put her arm through his. 'If you buy me a coffee I'll tell you all about the problems of being a trainer.'

As Army Blue plodded on in his own time, carefully watching where he put each foot, Phil's fear gradually eased. There were no horses close enough to him to do him any harm, even if he did happen to fall off. He was six lengths behind the horse in front and some twenty from the leaders.

Finally, as they came out of Swinley Bottom, he hit Army Blue a meaningful blow. The effect was immediate. The horse quickened his pace and his jumping. He cruised past the labouring animal ahead and lengthened his stride.

But it was too late now for Phil and Army Blue to make an impression on the race. Though they began to pick off the tiring backmarkers, the leaders were uncatchable. As they jumped the last, the cheers were for Cresson, who, with a magnificent final burst, was overtaking the Irish horse on the line. Army Blue finished fourth, but Phil knew they had never threatened and he was acutely conscious there was still plenty of petrol left in the horse's tank.

Russell greeted Army Blue with warmth but said nothing to Phil. And even the unexpected sight of Julia and his father did nothing to lighten the cloud of dejection that settled on him. He nodded to his wife and made smartly for the weighing-room.

As Hugh sipped his almost-cold coffee and listened to Louise, he struggled with his conscience – not a familiar experience in his professional life.

She was telling him about an owner who, despite public statements of support for Greenhills, was on the brink of removing two horses. News like that wouldn't help her dad's recovery. She stopped in mid-flow.

'I'm doing it again, aren't I? Telling you too much.'

'Look, Louise, there's something I should tell *you*.' He looked around the bar, passing over several familiar faces. 'But not in here.'

They walked outside, away from the crowd. She took his arm again.

He wondered whether she'd feel quite so friendly when he'd finished.

Then he told her about the letters. The shadows under her eyes grew darker as she listened.

'So there really is a connection between the attack on Adrian Moore and my dad?'

'Yes.'

'And you knew about this maniac before you wrote that stuff about him not declaring Devious?'

'Yes.'

She removed her arm from his. Those milky-blue eyes glared at him in reproach.

'It never occurred to me it would put Gerry in danger. I'm sorry, Louise.'

'Why haven't these letters been reported?'

'Because the police want to keep them secret and the *Beacon*'s cooperating. The other news media don't know they exist.'

Louise digested this information, biting her lower lip. She looked like a puzzled sixth-former. It occurred to Hugh that she'd probably only left school last summer. She was having to grow up fast.

'So,' she said at length, 'I could take this information to another paper.'

'You could. But the police wouldn't like it and neither would the *Beacon*.'

'Would you get the sack?'

'Only after the editor had worked me over with a rubber truncheon.'

She grinned. 'They might put you in hospital next to my dad. That'd be a laugh.' Her expression changed. 'You needn't worry, I shan't tell anyone. You may find this hard to believe but I *can* keep my mouth shut when I want to.'

Then her face seemed to crumple, the determination and defiance leaking out of her. She looked very young as she murmured, 'I just wish I'd entered Devious like I was supposed to. None of this would have happened.'

Hugh hesitated, then put an arm round her shoulder. 'It's not your fault. And it's not mine either. We're not the crazies putting people in hospital.'

They walked back together to the mass of people milling around the grandstand, his arm around her still.

*

Phil had barely spoken a word to Julia at the racecourse and the atmosphere in the car as they began the journey back was pure poison. Julia was shocked by the antagonism that seemed to flow from her once happy-go-lucky husband. Each time she tried to initiate a conversation he ignored her, or simply grunted, which was even worse. Her unexpected appearance had obviously thrown him. She wondered why. Maybe he'd had other plans. Perhaps he'd intended to slip off for an hour or two with someone before returning home.

She stared out of the car window at the dreary fag-end of the February afternoon. She wished fervently that she had not come. And to think she had done so out of loyalty to her husband, to avoid the temptation that Mark represented.

Two people could play Phil's game. If he could take his pleasure elsewhere then so could she. It would have been easy to have spent the afternoon with Mark. First, schooling Callisto together, feeding off an interest in the horse that Phil obviously didn't share. Afterwards she'd have invited Mark back to the cottage, offered to look at his bruised shoulder – and then? 'Then' was not something she should think about. In the past, whenever she'd contemplated making love to an admirer, it was tantamount to making the act come to pass. She couldn't allow herself to imagine being in bed with Mark – it was one step closer to the real thing.

She leaned forward and pushed a tape into the car cassette. She didn't care what it was – anything was better than sitting in this dangerous silence.

A familiar voice filled the small space. Phil's voice.

'It's like I'm trapped but there's nowhere to go. I know I've got to get away but I can't—'

'Turn it off!' Phil cried, and took his hand off the wheel to jab at the buttons. The car swerved violently and a van behind them hooted.

'Fuck off, you bastard!' screamed Phil in the mirror as his recorded voice continued: 'I'm just lying there, helpless, and I know it's the end—'

'Stop it! Stop it!' he shouted, his face white.

She'd never seen him like this. Frantic, out of control.

She shut off the tape and put her hand on his arm. He was shaking. There was a service station ahead.

'Pull off the road, Phil,' she said firmly, and he did so.

He drove past the petrol pumps, his chest heaving, his breath coming in gasps. He stopped the car in the shadow by the back wall. His face was silhouetted in the lights of a fast-food restaurant, and when he turned towards her he seemed unrecognisable.

'Julia,' he said. 'I've got something to tell you.'

A fist gripped her insides.

What had he said on the tape? *It's like I'm trapped – I know it's the end*.

She knew with awful certainty that their marriage was over.

DCI Charlie Lynch made himself a cup of tea he didn't want and sipped it, staring through the french windows into the garden. It was too late now to get out there and attempt a few chores, tidying dead shrubs or whatever you were supposed to do in late February. Jan used to take care of all that. She'd been first rate in the garden and, since she'd died, he'd tried to keep it up because that was what she would have wanted. In practice, this meant asking Amy Baylis from over the road to come in and rescue it every so often. He supposed he ought to employ her properly but he wasn't keen on handing bright-eyed Amy an excuse to gain entry on a regular basis.

He'd been watching the racing from Ascot, not his usual practice but justifiable in the present circumstances. He didn't follow racing, which was maybe an advantage, he told himself – he could look out for things of relevance without being distracted by the sport. But what things? Were any of the faces in the crowd the man he was looking for? It was possible the letter-writer attended race meetings, sizing up his victims. Charlie looked closely every time the camera lingered on the parade ring and the unsaddling enclosure. Was his man one of those leaning on the rail, eyeing up trainers and jockeys rather than the likely winner of the next race?

It was impossible to say. And, despite his lack of interest, he found himself caught up in the atmosphere of the race meeting. He'd opened the morning paper to the list of runners and listened to the TV pundits' assessments. He mentally saluted the French horse who snatched victory in the big race and listened to the French jockey mangle the mother tongue in a post-race interview. And the more he looked at the cheerful, well-behaved crowd revelling in their afternoon the harder it was to imagine that any of them could be his vengeful letter-writer.

The camera was attracted to a few familiar faces – a couple of ex-footballers turned owners and a pop star with an underdressed girlfriend. Charlie noticed Louise Fowler as well, acting the part her father would have played. She was laughing with a group of owners and helping her jockey into the saddle with a few whispered words. He'd met her in different circumstances, after she'd given a long and difficult statement about the discovery of her father. He knew she blamed herself for the business of the horse that hadn't run when it should have. She was a plucky girl.

He found he was holding an empty cup. He must have finished his tea without tasting it. From the hall came the sound of a clock ticking. The evening stretched ahead of him like a void. What was he going to do now? He considered ringing Claire but rejected the idea. He'd spoken to her that morning. She had better things to do on a Saturday evening than worry about her old dad.

His eye moved to a dun folder at one end of the long kitchen table. He'd been resisting its call. He'd promised Claire he'd try not to obsess about work while she was away in Bristol. He'd said he'd get out more, see a few old pals, maybe take up bridge again.

He pictured himself at a card table, partnering Amy Baylis instead of Jan. Oh, no. One kind of partnership could easily turn into another.

He opened the folder and arranged the papers around him, the three photocopies in the middle. He began to read the letters again. In order. Slowly. Over and over. What kind of man had written them? What motivated him? What did he really want?

And what was he going to do next?

The silence in the car seemed to stretch on for ever.

'I know about Simone,' Julia said at last.

Don't make it easy for him – let him do the dirty work. She cursed herself for being the first to crack.

'You do?' He seemed startled. And embarrassed.

She nodded. She didn't trust herself to speak.

'I didn't have a choice, Jules. I just lost my nerve.' He grabbed her hand. 'A shrink was the only answer.'

'A shrink?'

'You know, a psychiatrist.'

Julia was confused. *What's her job got to do with it?*

'She says she'll get me through it but it'll take time. Apparently it's like people who survive car crashes and things. It's called Post-Traumatic Stress Disorder.'

She lost the sense of his words as relief, like a warm blanket, wrapped itself around her. She snuggled into its comforting embrace. *I've got it all wrong!* she thought jubilantly. *He's not in love with her after all.*

He was still talking.

'Stop, Phil.' Her voice was sharp. He obeyed at once.

She took him by the shoulders and stared intently into his face. He looked bewildered, unhappy, like a lost little boy.

'I love you so much,' she said. 'Whatever's wrong, I love you.' And she slipped her arms around his chest to hug him as hard as she could in that awkward cramped space.

She felt some of the stiffness leave his body as he submitted to her. She squeezed him tight, clinging to him like a drowning woman to a raft. She could so easily have betrayed and lost him. She felt so foolish – and so happy. Whatever was wrong with him, it could not be as bad as the thing she had feared.

'Jules, sweetheart—' There was a familiar warmth in his voice – he sounded more like himself. 'Is this your imitation of a boa constrictor?'

She let him go, but very reluctantly.

Julia ordered a sandwich in the service-station restaurant, as much for form's sake as anything else. But, as she listened to Phil unburden himself, she ate it ravenously. It was the first time she'd felt hungry for days.

He told her about the moments of panic during races which had driven him to seek Simone's help. He described the other symptoms – the flashbacks of his accident, the fearful moments in the middle of the night when he'd wake in a sweat with a pounding heart. He apologised for his recent bad temper and the way he'd cut himself off from her.

Suddenly it all made sense. It was as if she'd been trying to read an enciphered message and misinterpreting its meaning. And now he'd handed her the code.

'I'm sorry,' he said finally. 'It's not what you bargained for when you married me, is it?'

'I never took anything for granted. Jockeys get hurt.'

123

'But not like this. Mental problems and shrinks. I didn't want you to find out.'

'But, Phil – you could have been killed at Worcester. You could be in a wheelchair for the rest of your life. This injury is not as bad as that. You're going to get over it.'

'So you're not disappointed in me?'

'Of course not. I'm a bit disappointed you didn't tell me about it, though.'

'Actually, Simone's been nagging me to tell you for weeks but . . .' His voice trailed off.

Julia understood. Of course Phil wouldn't want her to know about losing his nerve. No man would.

'No secrets from now on, Phil.'

'No.'

In which case . . .

'I was jealous when you sat next to Simone in the restaurant that night. It was obvious you knew each other but she pretended you didn't. Then I saw her name in your organiser and I thought . . . well, you know.'

'Do I?' He looked bemused.

'I thought she was an old flame of yours. And that you still fancied her.'

'You thought I was having an affair?'

'Yes.'

'With Simone?'

'Yes.'

His laugh was rich, full throated.

'She's very attractive,' Julia said defensively.

He got himself under control but his eyes were brimming with amusement as he stared at her across the Formica tabletop. 'Compared to you, she's not attractive. Who'd eat mutton over the road when there's fillet steak at home?'

She felt foolish as he continued to chuckle. But foolish was good – very good.

'Come on,' he said at last. 'I'm taking you back. I'll show you who I really fancy.'

Phil was in the thick of a race, on a horse he'd never ridden before. All he knew was that his mount was lazy. Russell's words rang round his head. 'You've got to get after him. Get stuck into him like you've never done before. Show me you've still got the balls.'

He knew this was his last chance. All he'd done for Russell in the past counted for nothing now. He hit the horse with his whip and hit him again; even though they were in the lead he couldn't let up.

The chasing pack was close behind. The drumming of hooves and jockeys' cries were in his ears. He could hear what they were shouting to one another – 'He's scared shitless, the little yellow bastard' – and he knew they meant him.

A fence loomed up, menacing and huge – bigger by far than any normal obstacle. He froze as his mount took off. The horse crashed through the top of it, stumbling on the other side, miraculously staying on his feet.

The chasers were right behind him now, and he glanced to one side. A big black beast was upsides, eating up the ground. As it surged past he saw the rider's face. A woman with long black hair that streamed in the wind of her passing. It was Simone. As she flashed by, she smiled and said, 'This is fun. I thought you told me it was dangerous?'

Then she was gone and the other riders were all around him, jostling and yelling as the next fence loomed up, mountainous and threatening – a wall of packed and sharp-pointed birch, higher by far than anything he'd ever attempted. His horse was labouring beneath him but Phil threw him at the mighty obstacle all the same, closing his eyes and preparing for the terrible impact. Then he'd parted company from the horse and was spinning through the air, bracing himself for a landing that never came.

He jerked awake in the dark. Instead of wet turf there was a soft mattress beneath him, and the drumming in his ears was not the pounding of hooves but the hammering of his heart. The green glow of the clock read 3:20. The pillow beneath his head was damp with perspiration.

Not again.

When would it end? Surely things would get better soon. He'd done all that Simone had asked of him. He'd even told Julia. He'd thought, naïvely, as he'd fallen asleep in the warm glow of their reunion, that somehow it would all be different. But it was just the same. No one, he realised, could share his night terrors.

He stared at the ceiling, as depressed as he had ever been in his life.

125

But, as the knowledge that he was truly on his own formed into words in his head, Julia's fingers twined round his and squeezed.

He returned the pressure and cancelled the thought.

Mark drove to Ted's yard in high spirits. The sun was shining and there was a touch of spring in the air. An hour or so on the old champion Callisto in the company of the fair Julia was worth getting out of bed for. Not that he wouldn't rather spend the time with the lady between the sheets, but that was just a wet-dream fantasy he'd better keep to himself. Especially with her husband around. He'd watched Phil's ride on Army Blue the day before with amazement and some glee. It was a pity he and Phil couldn't have a race-off for Julia. Her old man wouldn't stand a chance.

He found her in the big barn leading the horse round with his specially weighted pads. She was wearing jodhpurs and a sleeveless fleece to keep out the cold. Her mane of hair hung loose, its spun gold highlighted by her turquoise shirt. It shouldn't be allowed.

'I wasn't sure whether you were going to turn up,' she said. 'I should have rung you.'

'Oh yeah?' She seemed different to the last time he'd seen her. More confident and more nervous, both at the same time. He wondered what was up.

'I'm afraid you've had a wasted journey. I don't need you to ride him out.'

'He's all right, is he?' The horse looked tiptop to him. Just what he would have expected after Julia's treatment.

'Yes, he's coming on well. In fact, I've decided to send him racing again.'

'That's great. So surely you want me to keep working him over jumps. Like you said.'

She looked a bit embarrassed but her voice was firm. 'I'm sorry, Mark, but Phil's going to help me out. It's the first chance he's had.'

Oh really? Mark thought. *Since when did he give a stuff about Callisto?* Julia hadn't exactly come out and said so but he knew that, so far, she'd had to handle the horse on her own.

He looked around. So where was Phil? Not in evidence, that was for sure. Julia was looking at him uncertainly. She seemed to know what he was thinking.

126

'Phil's having a bit of a lie-in but he'll be along later. I'm really sorry to have dragged you down here.'

'That's OK.' He forced a smile to his lips. He hadn't been sure how things were going to develop this morning but he hadn't foreseen this. Disappointment nagged at him like a sudden toothache. This wasn't how Julia had been the other day. There'd been something on offer then. Phil must have got at her – or else she was running scared.

In either event he knew he should back off graciously. If she were really interested she'd come running in a day or so, and if she weren't . . . well, what the hell was the point in getting involved with another man's wife? *Walk away, you eejit. Quick.*

He was never much good at taking advice. Even his own.

He took a step towards Julia and said, 'Are you sure Phil's up to it?' Her mouth opened in a little O of alarm.

He carried on. 'You know he's lost it, don't you? That race yesterday was a disaster. He sat on the horse like a pudding till it was all over then started showboating. You don't want him on Callisto. He can't hack it any more.'

His words had stripped away her self-assurance like dead skin. She looked raw and uncertain. 'That's not true. He's taking his time getting back after the accident.'

'Pardon me, Julia, but that's bollocks. I've seen him charging round the gym – he's perfectly fit. But race-riding's a different matter. You ride races in your head and his isn't working these days.'

'Mark, please.' She put her hand on his arm. 'Don't say those things.'

He could feel her shaking as she gripped him. Her touch brought him to his senses.

'I'm sorry. I never meant to say any of that. I don't know why I did.'

'I do.' She looked up at him, her honey-brown eyes big in the pale circle of her face. 'It's because you're his friend and you care about him.'

Mark felt ashamed. She couldn't have been farther from the truth.

'He's going to be all right, Mark. Honestly. He's seeing someone about it.'

'What do you mean?'

'He's seeing a psychiatrist to get him over this bad patch. He'll be back to normal soon, I'm sure.'

Jesus, Mary and Joseph! Mark slipped an arm around her. A brotherly hug seemed permissible in the circumstances.

She hugged him back and he enjoyed the push of her breasts into his chest.

'Is there anything I can do?' he said at last as they stepped apart.

'Just be a friend to him.'

'OK.'

'And you won't tell anyone else, will you? It's a secret.'

He nodded. He didn't trust himself to speak.

When the doorbell rang at 10.30 Charlie was in the act of shaving. He was a wet-shave man by habit, and the interruption caught him with a face striped by foam.

Who the hell is that?

He peeped surreptitiously through the net curtains in the front bedroom – like some curtain-twitching old biddy, he thought.

He looked down on a head of bright blonde hair tied back in a plait. Amy Baylis wore a scarlet sweater and jeans, and in her hands she carried a gardener's trug from which protruded the handles of a fork and trowel.

Charlie stepped quickly back from the window. He wasn't going to show himself like this. The bell rang again. He stood stock still. She'd have a fair idea he was in – he never bothered to park in the garage these days – but that was too bad.

After a few moments he heard her footsteps recede down the garden path and he forced his body to relax. Then he returned to the bathroom.

Later, in the kitchen, he glimpsed movement outside. He saw the flashing blonde plait, the square, scarlet shoulders, the firm heft of a spade. Amy was digging in his garden.

She was two years younger than him and had also lost her other half to cancer. In the summer, when she worked in his garden, she sang in a low, beguiling contralto, and her fingers were quick and skilful as she nipped unwanted buds and tied back errant stems. There were lots of reasons why he should open the back door, thank her for her hard work and offer her some coffee.

Not yet. He wasn't ready to share this house or himself – the things that had once been Jan's – with anyone just yet. Maybe not till he was done with policing – and that wasn't far off.

Before then, however, he had a job to do. He rang John Petrie.

'I thought it might be you,' said the DS.

'I'm sorry, John, this racing vendetta's been going round my head all weekend.'

In the background he could laughter and squealing. John's children were nine and seven. He'd seen quite a bit of them recently.

Petrie was having a muffled conversation with someone else, then he spoke. 'Suzy says you can come for lunch provided you don't talk shop in the house. Frankly, boss, there's not much more to say about it. He's had his kicks and now he's packed it in – that's what I reckon.'

There's wishful thinking for you, said Charlie to himself. John was a great bloke and a solid by-the-book copper but he didn't have a lot of imagination.

'So, are you coming over or what?'

Looking back down the hall, through the kitchen and into the garden, Charlie saw the heavy blonde plait swinging in the sunshine. His problem was he had too much imagination.

'Tell Suzy I'd be delighted to accept her kind invitation. And so as not to upset her, John, I'll say this now and then shut up. I think you're dead wrong. I think there's no way our man has packed it in. He's enjoying himself too much.'

Chapter Seven

Hugh had a lot on his mind as he sat at his desk first thing on Monday morning. He didn't regard himself as thin skinned – he would never have survived his schooldays, let alone life as a journalist, if he had been sensitive to personal remarks – but occasionally a comment pierced his defences.

Last night at his brother's, his sister-in-law Emma – of whom he was fond – had tried to pair him off with one of her friends. Halfway through dinner this Mandy had abruptly announced she had to leave, pleading a headache. In Hugh's opinion, she'd been making rather a lot of noise for a person who supposedly wasn't well, and he'd volunteered to fetch her a taxi. Then he had returned to the flat to find Tom and Emma in the middle of a disagreement. He was about to step into the room when he realised they were disagreeing about him.

'No wonder your mother's given up,' Emma was saying in an intense low tone that carried clearly into the hall. 'No one over the age of ten goes round with ink on their fingers. And does he really only possess two shirts? I don't know what I'm going to say to Mandy tomorrow.'

'I told you she wasn't Hugh's type, darling.' Not the most spirited of defences by his brother but better than nothing.

'Who the hell would be? I don't know any women who fancy podgy slobs in National Health glasses with a wardrobe from the 1950s. He looks a fucking disgrace.'

Hugh had made his excuses shortly afterwards and had been brooding about the insults ever since. 'Podgy' was cruel but justifiable – and he'd avoided the almond croissant this morning in consequence – but did women really care that much about clothes? It was depressing.

He couldn't face phoning Emma to thank her for what had been a less than lovely evening. Then he had a sudden brain-wave. He dialled Interflora and ordered an expensive bunch of flowers to be sent to his sister-in-law's office. He might be overweight but he wasn't cheap. Let Emma spend all day with his roses and then call him a disgrace.

He was still grinning as he saw Gemma approach. She held a tray with the day's post and plonked it on his desk.

'There's another one,' she said softly.

As instructed, she had left the letter sealed. It was postmarked Exeter, Saturday morning.

Hugh opened it carefully, the smile now gone from his face.

Louise answered the phone just as she was on her way out of the house to join third lot. She didn't recognise the voice at first.

'Hi, Louise, it's Christian Curtis.'

Who? 'I'm sorry, do I know you?'

'I'm a friend of Leo's. Obviously I didn't make much of an impression when we met.'

Oh, God, it was Kit! She flustered an apology, her words rushing out. Fancy not knowing it was him.

'It's OK. Only guys I went to school with call me Kit. It sounds sort of babyish, don't you think?'

'I think it sounds great.' She groaned silently – had she really said that?

'You can call me what you like, Louise. I was just wondering if you liked French films.'

'Um, I don't know.' That didn't sound bright – she qualified it hastily. 'I like films. And French food.'

He chuckled, a low, gravelly sound that conjured up a picture in her mind of his grave face and the lock of blue-black hair that fell over those piercing blue eyes.

'There's a Truffaut festival on at the Arnolfini in Bristol. I wondered if you'd like to come. I'm sure I could find a French restaurant as well.'

He was asking her on a date. Fantastic! Then reality kicked in.

'Kit, I'd really love to . . .'

'But?' She could hear the disappointment in his voice.

'But with Dad away I don't think I can go.'

'It's just for the evening.'

'Yes, but I go to the hospital in the evening. Dad needs to know what's going on in the yard. And I need his help with the entries. You'd never believe how difficult it is to find the right race for the right horse.'

'Oh, I see.'

But it was plain from his tone that he didn't. And though he went on to ask how her father was doing it sounded to her like mere politeness.

After that, she didn't even enjoy her afternoon ride on Skellig that much. What had happened to Dad was bad enough, but they were all paying the price.

She wondered whether Kit would ever call her again.

The Editor
The *Racing Beacon*

Very nice. I like the way you use Justice in Racing on the top of the page. Maybe I should have gone into newspapers – I'd be pulling down a better screw than I am now.

The artacles are crap, though that's what I expected. You don't have the nerve to take the real villains on, do you? How about dishing the dirt on the top trainers. Dean and Greenhoff have got to be up to something. You should start digging.

Still, it's a beginning. Maybe I won't pay a visit to a certain starter who let the tapes go early at Ascot last year and left the favourite standing. I wasn't the only one who saw his hard-earned cash go down without even the pleasure of a race.

Then there's that jockey at Fontwell who rode round the last flight of hurdles when he was ten lengths clear. He said the sun was in his eyes, I say he had his hand out and some bastard stuffed it with reddies. A five-day ban was nothing. On second thoughts, I might still have a little talk with him. Fix him up so he won't see the sun again, let alone a flight of hurdles.

Now we're partners I think it's time you spread some of the perks of your trade my way.

No, I don't want a free lunch. I want a fee in recognition of my services.

Consider these facts.

1. the effort I have put into this campagne.
2. the contribution I have made to your paper.
3. the fact I am owed big-time for the stake money conned out

of me by cheating bookmakers all my life.

Considering the above, £100,000 (one hundred thousand pounds) is not excesive.

The money must be prepared as follows. Half in used £50 notes, £30,000 in 20s, the rest in 10s, wrapped in three seperate bundles in clear sellophane and put in a dark-coloured shoulder bag.

On Wednesday evening, Miss Louise Fowler will drive to Scratchwood Melmoth shopping centre taking the bag containing the money. She will wear the yellow anorak she sometimes wears on the TV. Her car must contain enough petrol for at least 150 miles driving. She will park in Tesco's supermarket by 7.00 pm and walk across the road to the pay phones by the bus stop. At precisely 7.30 the phone farthest away from the bus stop will ring and she must pick it up to receive her instructions. If someone is using the phone she must wait until they are finished.

She must be alone. NO POLICE. NO RADIOS. NO CARS. NO HELICOPTERS. I will know if she is being followed.

Once the money has been received I will call off all my operations and you will never hear from me again.

But if these instructions are not carried out to the letter, MY OPERATIONS WILL CONTINUE. I have a long list of racing cheats. This time I won't go easy on them like I did with Gerry Fowler.

Duncan Frame put off the phone call for a few minutes while he considered his position – or rather the *Beacon*'s position – in the light of this new development. Pimlott had brought him the letter just a few minutes ago, looking a bit green around the gills. Frame had put that down to the mention of Louise Fowler.

The editor had already made one phone-call, not to the police but to his proprietor. Persuading Sir Gavin Hoylake to put up the hundred grand had not been as difficult as he had feared. As yet the *Beacon* had not moved to exploit its inside track on the case, but it was only a matter of time. And when that time came there were other media outlets in the Hoylake News Group which would also cash in.

Of course, no mention was made of Hoylake's TV and tabloid holdings in the course of their short conversation, but Frame was only too aware of them. There was little brotherly love in the Hoylake family of businesses – bitter sibling rivalry more accurately characterised relations between the group members. It gave Frame considerable satisfaction to think that, for once, he sat in the hot seat on a potentially big news story. If it all went well he wouldn't mind a move within the group. In the world of journalism a horseracing paper was something of a ghetto.

His dilemma at the moment was when to break the story. Soon – or else it would surface elsewhere. But even if it did, the *Beacon* had the letters and that gave him the edge. For the moment he'd play the conscientious citizen and stay hand in glove with the police. So when all this did come out into the open the *Beacon* would look good. It would look even better when it was known they had volunteered a hundred grand to keep a madman from persecuting the racing community. As Hoylake had said, only a few minutes before, 'Money invested in reputation is never wasted.'

Charlie put down the phone and ran into the outside office to stand over the fax machine. Hurray for Mondays – a heretical thought for most of his colleagues, but for Charlie it had been a long and tedious weekend and now, at last, something was happening.

The fax began to chunter and the LCD read 'Receiving'. DC Holly Green looked up from her desk and started to get to her feet. Charlie shook his head at her. No one was reading this fax before him, even if he did already know what it said.

He pulled the two sheets from the machine and read them on the hoof, disappearing back into his office.

Frame had described the contents accurately, though he hadn't conveyed quite the extent of the writer's gleeful arrogance. Charlie felt a little gleeful in turn. Though it presented enormous challenges, he knew where he stood with a ransom demand. Greed was a motive anyone could understand.

So now the vicious little bastard had stuck his head above the parapet. He was demanding a cash drop. Big mistake. When it came to the handover they'd have him.

Most of the police briefing was spent in discussing the geography of Scratchwood Melmoth, once a small town serving the local agricultural community of north-west Somerset. In the last ten years, however, a five-acre site outside the town had been turned into a 'retail park', boasting most of the national supermarkets and fast-food outlets. At its centre was a three-storey shopping mall, surrounded by car parks. A network of roads brought in shoppers from all directions, with the M5 motorway less than ten minutes away. At any time during opening hours – from eight in the morning till ten at night – the place was teeming with people and their cars. Charlie had already put in his request for extra bodies.

'We're going to need a load of back-up vehicles,' muttered DS Ivan Stone. 'He could send our girl in about a dozen different directions.'

Charlie nodded – he was well aware of it.

'Plus an army on the ground,' Ivan continued.

DC Terry Jenkins, three months into his transfer out of uniform into CID, look puzzled. 'What's the point of that? It's obvious he's going to tell her to drive somewhere a long way off. That's why he's asked for a full tank of petrol.'

The others had laughed and Terry had looked puzzled. 'What's funny?'

'Just suppose he's lying,' said Ivan. 'Suppose that's what he wants us to think. Then he tells her to go inside the shopping centre and has the bag off her in the check-out at M&S.'

'Oh.' Terry looked miffed.

'Think about it, pinhead, there's God knows how many ways in and out of that building.'

'And we will cover them all,' Charlie said firmly. He didn't want them scoring points off each other like a bunch of kids. There were more important issues to discuss.

John Petrie raised one of them. 'We're not going to use Louise as the courier, are we, boss?'

Charlie shook his head.

'Got anyone in mind?'

'It's not easy. We need someone who can pretend to be Louise, if necessary. She's going to have to think on her feet, stay flexible and not panic if she ends up driving half the night.'

There was silence in the room. Then Ivan said, 'That lets you out, Terry.'

Charlie joined in the laughter and added, 'I might have a word with SO10.'

Scotland Yard's undercover squad.

After the meeting, Charlie sat in his office with one eye on the clock. He reckoned he'd give it ten minutes.

The knock came well within that limit. As expected, DC Patsy Preece stuck her head round the door.

'Have you rung SO10 yet, guv?' she asked.

He shook his head and pointed to the seat facing his desk.

'I'll be the courier,' she said. 'I can be Louise better than any outsider. I could put my hair up like she does sometimes, and I reckon I sound like her.'

Charlie grinned, then began to chuckle.

'Don't laugh,' she cried. 'It's not a joke, I'm dead serious. Sir.'

Charlie stopped laughing. 'OK,' he said. 'The job's yours.'

'Just like that?'

'Of course. You're the obvious person.'

She looked puzzled. 'Why didn't you tell me at the briefing, then?'

'Because you've got to volunteer, Patsy. This could be bloody dangerous. Suppose you end up in the middle of nowhere with this lunatic? He might not be content with taking the money – especially when he finds out you're not Louise Fowler. He half killed poor Gerry.'

'But I won't be on my own. There's going to be back-up.'

'Of course. But things can go wrong, that's all I'm saying. There's the slight chance you could be on your own with him. You've got to realise that.'

'Sure.' She beamed, showing off her even white teeth and the dimples in her cheeks. Patsy was a woman of twenty-four but, for a moment, she looked even younger than his daughter. 'Thanks a lot, guv. I won't let you down.'

He nodded. He had every confidence in her, but this kind of thing filled him with misgiving. He'd had a long career in policing, and an operation like this – lots of bodies, a sackful of someone else's money and a vicious, clever nutter calling the shots – was a minefield.

He brushed aside negative thoughts and looked the young detective in the eye.

'Right, then. You and I have work to do. Do you know where Louise is today?'

'She's at Fontwell this afternoon. Mucky Molly's the favourite in the big hurdle race.'

Charlie looked at her sharply. 'Are you serious?'

She nodded. 'I saw Louise at the hospital and she told me it was worth a bet. She's worried about the going – the horse doesn't like it too heavy.'

This was more than Charlie needed to know, though, obviously he'd picked the right woman for this assignment.

'How often does she go to the hospital?'

'Every night, I think.'

Rebecca felt a mixture of emotions as she replaced the phone after a most unexpected conversation. Her dominant feeling, she had to admit, was one of excitement – but it was mixed with a big dollop of guilt which, now she thought about it, was ridiculous. A boy had simply asked her to go to the movies with him and she had agreed. What was so terrible about that? Anyway, it wasn't just the latest blockbuster you could catch any old time. She'd missed *Jules et Jim* when the student film society had shown it last term and she'd really wanted to see it. Now she had the chance to do so. And, since she was working darned hard to help Louise out *and* trying to keep up with her college work, she really needed a night off.

But – the boy was Kit.

Rebecca knew how much Louise liked him. How thrilled she had been when Kit had phoned her that morning and how disappointed she'd been to turn down his invitation.

Louise had told her all about Kit's call before she'd gone off to Fontwell for the afternoon's racing. In turn, Rebecca had dashed back home and tried to pick up the threads of the essay that was due in on Friday. There wasn't a hope in hell she'd ever manage that, even before the phone rang with another distraction – Kit's offer to take her to Bristol on Wednesday night.

So, was she going to ring back and say she couldn't go after all because (a) she couldn't afford the time, (b) she was sort of seeing Kit's friend, Leo, and (c) it would be disloyal to her best friend, Louise?

The answer was (d), none of the above. Because, mixed in with the excitement and guilt, was just a teensy bit of triumph. Kit was just so damn gorgeous. Gorgeous enough not to have to put himself out, make conversation, try to make the girls laugh, rush to the bar and get in drinks. A boy like Kit could sit and smoke and look broody all night, then walk off with his pick. And, irritating though it was that she was second on his list, on Wednesday Rebecca was his pick. She wasn't going to turn that down out of any misguided sense of loyalty.

Anyhow, Louise would never find out.

That settled, she turned back to the textbooks scattered across the table in front of her and forced herself to concentrate.

Hugh wouldn't normally have bothered with a Monday meeting at Fontwell but he was gambling on Louise attending. Greenhills had a few runners and a strong contender in the National Spirit Hurdle. She was bound to be there, he reasoned.

He spotted Louise in the crowd from out of the press-box window. The copper curls stood out; so too did that yellow anorak. It was ironic that she should be wearing it today.

He rushed for the door, his swiftly moving bulk causing some confusion among his colleagues.

'Watch it, tub,' complained Arnie Johnson as Hugh hurtled past, dangerously close to the open laptop on the table. Hugh ignored him, though the insult, of the kind normally forgotten in an instant, was still pricking as he rushed across the paddock lawn to the small parade ring.

He tried to catch her eye from the rail but she was busy. Hugh recognised the owner she was talking to, Mrs Davenport, a pernickety type. Louise would have trouble shaking her off once the horses went down to the start, particularly as the Davenport horse, Mucky Molly, had a good chance of winning.

And so it proved. Mrs Davenport remained glued to Louise's side and the pair watched the race from the stands. Hugh took up his station behind them. He knew Louise was aware of his presence but, after one eye-rolling glance, she had ignored him. It was obvious he would have to wait his turn.

The race turned out to be a thriller. Mucky Molly made heavy weather of the sticky conditions and didn't look at all interested for the first half of the race. With a mile to run she was last out of eight, and Hugh was writing her off as a contender for the Champion Hurdle at

Cheltenham in a few weeks. He could read the frustration in the two women in front of him.

Then, suddenly, Molly woke up and began to stretch out, overtaking the horse ahead. Hugh noticed that the jockey was taking his mount round the outside in search of some firmer ground. The question was – had he left it too late?

Even taking the long way round, she was too good for her rivals, bar one – Lord of Light, a big-boned old stager with a liking for heavy ground, ridden by Phil Nicholas.

Molly was breathing down the front-runner's neck as they rounded the last bend into the home straight. By sticking to the inside rail, Lord of Light increased his advantage and popped neatly over the penultimate hurdle a length and a half ahead.

Mrs Davenport was clinging to Louise's arm now, and the pair were jumping up and down with excitement as Molly began to close the gap.

Phil urged Lord of Light through the wet with a couple of taps of his stick, and the old horse hung on to his slight lead as they approached the last flight of hurdles.

Molly's jockey was hard at work, balanced high on the horse's shoulders. He hit her hard on the right flank and the horse veered slightly to the left, back towards the rail, where the ground had been most heavily used.

Hugh knew that the issue was settled there. Lord of Light took the last hurdle in front and held on to win by a head. He saw Phil raise his face to the skies and his whole body seemed to slump, before he bent to smack his mount's neck and whisper a few words of praise. It occurred to Hugh that, before his accident, Phil used to punch the air in victory, a grin splitting his face in half. Now he simply looked relieved.

Hugh caught up with Louise and Mrs Davenport in the unsaddling enclosure and asked for a quote for the paper. The owner, to her credit, displayed only slight disappointment.

'To be honest, after the way she started, I think we're very fortunate to have come so close.'

Hugh encouraged her to prattle on, with one eye on Louise. His chance came as Arnie Johnson drifted over, notebook in hand. When Mrs Davenport began to repeat her remarks, Hugh was able to place a hand on Louise's arm.

'I've got to talk to you,' he muttered.

She nodded, obviously struck by his urgent tone.

'Let me just finish here,' she said, and turned back to the mud-spattered jockey waiting by her side.

Phil was feeling better with himself as he took his mount down to the start for the next race. He'd not expected to win on Lord of Light, and holding off a good horse like Mucky Molly, one of the Champion Hurdle favourites, would have been more satisfying only if Russell had been on hand to see it. Unfortunately, the trainer had opted out of the trip to Sussex in favour of an afternoon in the office. Cheltenham was just around the corner and there was plenty of planning to be done. Lord of Light was entered for the Champion Hurdle, but no one thought he had much of a chance. Phil imagined that today's result would see the horse's price shortening. He'd love to see him repeat the performance at the Festival. He had a soft spot for the canny old bugger – maybe because he was turning into a canny old bugger himself.

This whole business with Simone had forced him to take stock. She'd said curing his failure of nerve would be a long haul, and at first that had terrified him. He wanted his trouble sorted out instantly, before anyone found out, before his career went up in smoke. But now he knew that wasn't possible. He had to be patient.

She'd also forced him to see that all was not doom and gloom. He hadn't lost his skill in the saddle. He could still win races – like this victory on Lord of Light. Riding out and schooling were fine, so too was racing over hurdles. Some chases were OK – when he was on a horse he could rely on, and when he could keep out of a bunched-up pack hurtling *en masse* towards a fence. The funny thing was, that was just the kind of situation he used to relish.

The starter called them to attention as the last runner was forced into line. The tapes went up and the fifteen horses set off to race more than three miles up, down and around the distinctive Fontwell figure-of-eight course, over twenty-two fences. Phil's horse was called Soft Centre, which about summed him up – a gelding with a history of joint problems who tended to peck on landing.

All things considered, this was just the kind of race Phil didn't want to find himself in. Already, as they turned into the downhill stretch and began to gallop to the first of its three big fences, Phil could feel a bubble of panic forming in the pit of his stomach.

He'd hang in, though, even if it killed him. He prayed that it wouldn't.

Hugh and Louise had walked to the middle of the course, away from the crowds. He could feel the wind of the pack of racehorses as they thundered past. That was the advantage of a course like Fontwell – you could get right up to the action. It was a thrill to see the runners this close and suck up a bit of the speed and danger. He wondered why he and the other members of the press box didn't do it more often – probably because it was a bit of schlep from the bar.

'Come on, Phil,' he roared after the runners as they sailed over the last fence together, like a single multicoloured creature. 'He didn't look too cheerful,' he said to Louise, who stood by his side, her face flushed with the wind and excitement.

'Is he a friend of yours?' she asked.

'I do his column. Well, to be fair, he does it, but I'm there when he needs help.'

'Tell him he's a rotten sod for keeping Molly out. Clever riding, though,' she added ruefully.

The horses had turned and were now galloping back towards them, up the hill this time, to complete the first circuit. Phil and Soft Centre were in clear space, a couple of lengths behind the leading pack.

'So what's this all about?' said Louise as they watched the runners head towards the bend at the top of the course.

Hugh looked around. A handful of other hardy souls were dotted over the muddy inner field, watching the race, but none of them was within hearing distance.

'Have the police spoken to you today?'

'No. Why?'

'We got another letter this morning. He's asking for a pay-off – a hundred grand to go away and not harm anyone else.'

'Gosh. A hundred thousand pounds?'

'It's not a lot if you consider the risk he's running. He could ask for a heck of a lot more, I reckon. A million maybe.'

'Why didn't he, then?'

'I don't know.' Hugh thought for a moment. 'Maybe because someone will actually pay a hundred grand. The *Beacon* are going to front it. They'd never stump up a million.'

Their conversation was cut off by the horses returning on the downward run. The field had spread out now, and Phil was still about halfway down. His face was tense and drawn as Soft Centre jumped the fence directly in front of them. The horse's knees seemed to buckle as he hit the ground, and his head sank almost to the turf. Phil was leaning back in the saddle like a rodeo rider, hauling on the reins to keep Soft Centre upright, his jaw set in a firm straight line. It flashed through Hugh's mind that this was a heck of a way to make a living.

They watched the horses run away from them without comment.

'Thanks for telling me,' said Louise.

'There's something else you ought to know, Louise. He wants you to carry the money.'

Her eyes grew large in her face. He pressed on.

'The letter says you've got to drive to a shopping centre in Scratchwood Melmoth and wait for a call on a public phone for instructions.'

The horses swept by them again, heading uphill once more. They stared at them almost without seeing, waiting to resume their conversation.

'Why does he want me?' she said, when she could be heard. 'How does he even know about me?'

Hugh laughed. 'You've been all over the newspapers. And on TV when you're at a televised meeting. You've probably got websites dedicated to you.'

'Me? Don't be stupid.'

'The thing is,' said Hugh, 'you mustn't do it. If the police ask you, say no. You'd be risking your life.'

'But they might catch the man who attacked my dad.' She turned to him, her jaw set. 'If they ask me, Hugh, I'm saying yes.'

His objections were drowned in the sound of thundering hooves.

Phil was still hanging in. The race lasted seven minutes but it seemed like an eternity. It was the downhill run that was the problem, with its three stiff fences and the slope that caused Soft Centre to overbalance. Each jump terrified Phil, as there was no certainty the horse would land safely and he had to yank his nose off the deck with all his strength just to keep the pair of them upright.

But now the last downhill run was over and they were still in one piece, still in the race. As they cut across the bottom of the course, Phil could feel his old confidence returning. There were three more fences left to jump, including his old bugbear, an open ditch, but they all lay on the uphill slope. Few horses fell on this stretch of Fontwell, where the gradient kept them steady and made the landings just that fraction higher.

They were lying about tenth going into the open ditch and, just as in the old days, Phil threw his horse at the fence. They flew the obstacle and landed upsides of a labouring runner. Phil gave Soft Centre a whack on the shoulder and got after him going uphill. The horse responded, and the pair of them made a late charge through the field which won him no prizes – they finished fourth – but pleased the owner no end.

'I never thought old Softy had it in him,' he said, clapping Phil on the back.

His wife kissed Phil on a muddy cheek and said with sincerity, 'You were absolutely terrific.'

Later Phil sat in the dressing-room, her words floating round his head. He hadn't been terrific at all but today had been better. Was it coincidence that he'd now sorted things out with Julia? He didn't know. All he knew was that he wanted to get home to his wife.

Louise wasn't altogether surprised to see Patsy Preece waiting for her at the hospital as she left her father's room that night. Next to Patsy was an officer she'd met on the morning of her father's accident. He seemed to be in charge but Louise couldn't remember his name.

'Charlie Lynch,' he reminded her as he shook her hand. 'I'm sorry to waylay you like this but you're not easy to track down.'

Louise nodded. It had been a long day. She'd driven straight from Sussex to report to her father on the day's racing. She was tired and, she realised, in need of food. Though she was nervous about the forthcoming conversation, she knew she ought to eat something.

When she said as much, Charlie's face broke into a broad grin and within ten minutes they were sitting in the back booth of a pizza parlour. It turned out Charlie had sometimes brought his daughter here, and he prattled on about her while Louise demolished a thin-based Four Seasons. He'd be a nice father, she decided, and she appreciated his concern to set her at ease.

Within a couple of minutes, it seemed, she'd cleared her plate. The waitress brought all three of them coffee and Charlie looked her full in the eye. Here it comes, she thought.

'Louise' – they'd progressed beyond 'Miss Fowler', thankfully – 'there have been some developments in your father's case that are not public knowledge. I'd like to take you into our confidence because, frankly, we need your help.'

She was tempted to say she already knew about these mysterious developments, but kept her mouth shut. She would be interested to hear the police version of events.

It didn't differ much from what she'd already learned from Hugh. Charlie told her about the letters and his belief that the assaults on Adrian Moore and her father had been perpetrated by the writer. She'd been hoping he might show her copies of the letters themselves but he didn't.

She listened in silence. All the time she was wondering what he was going to say about the latest letter, the one Hugh had told her about. Would he ask her to act as a courier, as the letter demanded? And what would she say if he did? Would she have the courage to agree? She'd been bold enough when talking to Hugh, with the horses charging past and the wind in her hair. She didn't feel so bold now.

'We heard again from our friend this morning,' Charlie said. 'He's asking for money or else he says he'll continue to assault people who have earned his displeasure. The letter is quite detailed in its instructions. He's asking for you to deliver the cash.'

'Me?' She felt like a hypocrite as she injected surprise into her voice, but she had to say something.

'He names you in the letter and even specifies what you must wear. That anorak, as a matter of fact.' He glanced at the yellow garment lying on the seat beside her.

'I'll do it,' she heard herself say.

The police officers glanced at each other, seemingly shocked by her words. Charlie opened his mouth to speak but she beat him to it.

'I'll be the courier. That's what you want my help for, isn't it?'

'No, Louise, that's not what we had in mind.' He grinned. 'You're a brave girl, I'll say that.'

'So what do you want me to do, then?' A bit of her felt disappointed. As if she been promised the lead in the school play and then discovered she was only the understudy.

'Allow us to borrow your car and some of your clothes,' said Charlie. 'Patsy here is going to pretend to be you.'

Louise turned towards the other woman. She'd been wondering why she'd been sitting there, not saying much.

'You don't have any objection, do you?' said Patsy, breaking her silence.

The two police officers stared at her, and Louise's bravado vanished in an instant. It was stupid of her to think she could go up against the man who'd reduced her tough, indestructible father to a pathetic bundle lying in a hospital bed.

'No,' she said. 'No objection at all.'

'Any news?' Hugh asked Louise when he got her on the phone the following morning.

'I'm not sure I'm talking to the press today,' was the reply.

'This isn't an official press-type call.'

'What is it, then?'

'Just a friendly enquiry.'

'I thought that was the same thing.'

'Stop mucking me about, Louise. Are you doing it or not?'

'No. They've got a policewoman.'

'Thank God for that.'

She laughed. 'You're not much of a newsman, are you? If I'd done it, you could have got an exclusive interview about my ordeal.'

'Only if you'd survived.'

After this conversation, Hugh rang Emma. He'd been ducking her calls. Her assistant put him straight through, so she must have been looking out for him. Guilt, he presumed.

'Thanks so much for the wonderful flowers,' she said at once. 'I'm not sure I deserved them – it was only shepherd's pie.'

'It was a bit more than that. I'm sorry I scared your friend off.'

'Oh.' She was surprised by his frankness. 'It's true Mandy can be a bit—'

'Next time, Em, I'll supply my own partner.'

'Great.' The surprise was instantly replaced by curiosity. 'Is there something I should know, Hugh? Or somebody, should I say?'

'No,' he replied quickly, and finished the call, feigning a summons from the editor. Let her stew on that for a bit.

*

Just after five o'clock on Wednesday afternoon DC Patsy Preece left Greenhills driving the Fowler Peugeot. Though the days were lengthening as spring approached, it was a murky afternoon and almost dark. She intended to fill up with petrol closer to her destination and to be well ahead of schedule. She wore her thick dark hair pinned up. On the passenger seat lay Louise's anorak and her black felt hat. A brown shoulder bag with a hundred thousand pounds in notes was locked in the boot of the car. She'd never been responsible for that amount of cash before, but she had more pressing things to worry about. Like how she would react when she had to answer the phone and talk to the man who had put Adrian Moore and Gerry Fowler in hospital – and might do the same to her.

She'd spent a lot of time with DCI Lynch, trying to anticipate this man's demands. They had discussed whether it might not be better for her to come clean. She could say Louise was too frightened to act as courier and that she was a friend who had taken Louise's place. That sounded reasonable – but would that make any difference to their man? Reasonable was not likely to cut much ice with a nasty bastard like him.

In the end they had decided that, if unmasked, Patsy would fall back on the 'friend' excuse, but, initially, she would simply behave as if she were Louise. The chances were she would simply be given directions to a destination where she would leave the money.

Charlie had made her run through a variety of test calls, and he'd played the part of the extortioner.

'*Turn off your fucking microphone!*' he'd shouted the first time, taking her completely by surprise.

Next he'd peppered her with personal questions – Louise's full name, date of birth, her mother's maiden name.

'How's he going to know any of that, though, boss?' she'd complained.

He shrugged. 'He might not but you've got to sound like you do.'

Now, as she drove towards Scratchwood Melmoth, with these matters tumbling around her head, she consciously tried to shut the turmoil out. She slowed her breathing and focused on her driving. She knew her colleagues were watching her but made no attempt to look for them. A lot of money and man-hours were depending on her performance. And, if she played her cards right, there was a chance they'd soon have their hands on the bastard who'd caused so much misery.

She'd joined the police to experience life at the sharp end. To make a difference. That was why she'd volunteered to stand in for Louise. She was determined not to let anyone down.

Louise was confined to the house. Since she was supposed to be in Scratchwood Melmoth at 7.30, Charlie had deemed it prudent she stay at home with DC Holly Green to keep an eye on her. It would be the first night Louise had not visited her father, but she'd warned him not to expect her.

'Got a date, have you?' he'd said.

'No, Dad,' she'd protested.

'That's all right, sweetheart, you have some fun. You deserve it.'

She'd badly wanted to tell him the truth but had held her tongue. The whole business was secret – even her mother didn't know what was going on, though she must have wondered why a policewoman had taken up residence.

Ironically, she could have been on a date tonight. It was the evening Kit had offered to take her to Bristol.

She rang Rebecca to take her mind off things – Holly said it was OK – but her friend wasn't at home.

She turned on the television and watched a soap she was long out of touch with. She couldn't make much sense of the programme any more. Her thoughts were elsewhere.

Patsy reached Scratchwood Melmoth just before seven. She'd made the journey the day before to check out the location, and now she drove straight to the rear of the Tesco car park and placed the vehicle as she had planned, close to the exit.

She'd already disguised herself in the hat and anorak when she'd stopped for petrol, so now there was nothing for her to do but wait. She knew she was being watched by her colleagues – she assumed that some of the other cars around her would contain police surveillance teams. But it was possible she was also being watched by the letter-writer. It was a scary thought.

What was to stop him suddenly appearing at her car door and demanding the money now?

Well, he'd be out of luck because by the time she'd got it out of the boot her back-up would have arrived.

She flicked the lock on her car door.

Suppose he pointed a gun through the window? A shotgun or a .22? An arrow from the crossbow he'd used on Adrian Moore could shatter the glass and go straight through her head. Like a skewer through a melon.

She glanced fearfully from side to side.

If he appeared with a weapon, she'd have no choice but to let him in the car. She'd have to drive wherever he told her. They'd have police on their tail but she'd be a hostage – and hostages sometimes didn't survive.

She looked over the barrier ahead of her at the road and the steady stream of traffic sailing by. An old lady was waiting at the pedestrian crossing, her destination possibly the bus stop thirty yards along the road on the other side. Patsy could see a knot of people standing by the shelter. Five buses had already come by in just over ten minutes. The shopping centre was well provided for.

Suppose he made her get on a bus? They'd not discussed that. She didn't know the bus routes – would that matter? Buses were slow. But buses looked pretty much the same, apart from numbers and destinations. There was plenty of room for confusion. She hadn't realised when she'd volunteered that she'd be vulnerable to such negative thoughts.

She took a deep breath and forced herself to think positively. If he made her get on a bus she would simply report it. She was wired up to an incident room and also carried a mobile phone. She was prepared to jettison the phone if required. She would deny all knowledge of the concealed transmitter unless she had no choice – like being on her own with the bastard in some dark and lonely place.

Suppose – and this thought had taken root in her mind without ever showing itself till now – he wasn't just interested in the money. It wasn't that much, all considered, as everyone had agreed. Suppose he was mostly interested in furthering his crackpot cause, getting revenge for racing events that had gone wrong. That would explain why he wanted Louise to deliver the money. Charlie Lynch said it was because the guy was a game-player, a manipulative bastard who liked putting people through hoops to show how superior he was. But suppose the DCI was wrong. After her father was attacked Louise had been quoted saying the Devious affair was really her fault. Suppose this creep wanted to take it out on her too.

Suppose the real point of this was to spill Louise's blood.

Which means my blood, thought Patsy.

She glanced at her watch. Ten minutes to go.

Deep breath.

Think positive.

At 7.25 Patsy got out of the car, took the shoulder bag from the boot, ran a quick mental check – ransom money (yes), mobile (yes), loose change for the bus if needed (yes) – locked the car and left the car park. She crossed the road and walked to the public phones. There were two of them, side by side, with a Perspex partition between them and a roof to keep off the rain. Neither was occupied. Even the bus queue had gone. Patsy felt exposed and vulnerable.

She focused on the phone farthest from the bus stop and watched as the hand on her wristwatch crept past the half-hour. At any second the phone would ring.

It didn't.

Another minute crept by.

She heard the sound of footsteps. A teenage boy in baggy sportswear was strolling towards her, wheeling a bike. Could this be him? He was only sixteen or seventeen but big enough to be a threat. He could strip the bag from her shoulder in a flash and be off on his bike, down some back alley.

The lad ambled past without a glance, lost in his own world. Just a harmless kid. She felt mean for being so suspicious.

Seven thirty-five, and no sound from the phone. She lifted the receiver to check it was working and heard the gentle buzz of the dialling tone.

More time went by. It looked like the operation was off. The guy had probably got cold feet. She stamped hers. He wasn't the only one.

The ringing tone took her by surprise, and it was a few seconds before she snatched up the receiver. As she pressed it to her ear, the ringing continued.

'Hello?' she said, and at once felt stupid. She was talking to the dialling tone.

She put the receiver down and realised it was the other phone, the one closest to the bus stop, that was ringing. Had she got the instructions wrong?

She lifted the other receiver.

'You took your time,' said a man's voice. Soft, almost a whisper. Was that an accent?

'Sorry. I thought it was the other phone.'

'That's what you were meant to think. Who are you?'

'Louise Fowler. I'm sorry – I'm terribly nervous.' That was true enough.

'Is your brother with you?'

What? 'I haven't got a brother.' The bastard was trying to trick her.

'OK.'

There was a pause. Was that it? Had she passed the test?

'Who came fourth in the Gold Cup last year?'

Jesus! How the hell was she meant to know that?

'Oh, please,' she protested. 'Can't we just get on with it?'

'You answer my question.' The voice wasn't so soft now.

She thought. She remembered watching the race. A big, black Irish horse had romped home in the fastest time since the war.

'Holy Moses won it,' she said.

'That's not what I asked, Louise.' There was a sarcastic emphasis on her name. He knew.

'I've got the money here,' she said quickly. 'Made up in different notes just like you asked.'

Another silence. Then his voice bellowed out of the receiver at such a volume she yanked it from her ear.

'You can stick it up your arse, COPPER!'

Then there was just a buzzing on the empty line.

Keith drove back carefully, deliberately suppressing his urge to put his foot down. He knew he had to stay in control, keep the Beast in check till he got home.

He told himself he'd done the right thing. He'd made a plan and he'd stuck to it. He knew they'd try to trick him and he'd caught them out.

The cheating bastards.

But she'd had the money. He hadn't been greedy, he'd just asked for enough. Enough to right the wrongs he'd suffered. Enough to set him free.

And he'd been cheated again.

*

Half an hour later Patsy was sitting in the back of Charlie's car on the other side of the car park. She had a blanket over her shoulders and was sipping slowly at a carton of hot soup – her second – held in shaking fingers. She didn't feel like she'd ever be warm again, though it wasn't the February cold that chilled her.

'I'm sorry,' she said for the umpteenth time.

'It's all right,' said Charlie, as he'd said many times before. 'You're not hurt, we haven't lost the *Racing Beacon*'s money and we live to fight another day.'

'But why did he ask me that? How could I be expected to remember what came where at last year's Cheltenham?'

'*You* can't.' Charlie was keying a number into his phone as he spoke. 'That's the point. Hello, Holly, it's Charlie Lynch.'

Patsy could hear the tinny sound of a voice through the receiver. Even from the back seat she could detect her colleague's anxiety.

'It didn't work out, I'm afraid, he hung up. But Patsy's fine. She'd like a word with Louise.'

Charlie passed the phone between the seats. Patsy put her soup on the floor and took it.

'Louise, can I ask you a question? Which horse came fourth in last year's Gold Cup?'

'Paris White. Why?'

Patsy was amazed. 'How on earth do you know that?' she asked, but suddenly it was obvious. She had guessed the reason even as the answer came out of Louise's mouth.

''Cos Dad trains him.'

Of course.

There was more to impersonating someone than simply borrowing their coat.

Keith butchered the carcass with unnecessary ferocity, raising a mist of flesh fragments and splinters of bone with each downward smash of the cleaver. There was no point in treating the dead calf like this – finesse in the dissection of a carcass made for a better job – except that the thrusting and jabbing of the blade helped relieve some of the fury raging through his skull.

The Beast demanded it.

He flung the bloody chunks into the hounds' feeding trays, imagining it was the body of that policewoman who'd tried to fool him at the handover. Police – did they think he was stupid? Hadn't he made it clear enough that he was not to be pissed about?

Maybe he hadn't. Maybe they needed a further demonstration that he meant business.

The cleaver rose and fell. Separating flesh from bone. Severing muscle and tendon. Dicing dead meat for the hounds' dinner.

Maybe it was time for the Beast to show his real face.

They'd do everything he told them after that.

Chapter Eight

Rebecca woke with a smile on her face. Milky sunlight lit the curtains, filtering around the edges, sneaking across the carpet. The alarm clock on her bedside table told her it was 8.40 – two hours past the moment it had first summoned her from sleep. She'd shut it off then and fallen back into desperately needed slumber. Now she was late, but that wasn't her only sin. She'd been a bad girl. Her smile grew wider as she recalled the details. It had been worth it.

Kit had left her bed before dawn. His goodbye kiss still lingered – the scrape of stubble on her cheek and the sleepy taste of him on her lips. She spread her naked limbs across the bed, burrowing into the hollow where he'd been. She'd get up and face the day soon, but for the moment she couldn't bear to break the spell. After all, how often did you have a perfect first date?

They'd hit it off from the moment he'd picked her up. On his own, he was talkative and funny and, well, rather wicked. They'd had a few laughs at the expense of Leo. Rebecca had felt a bit disloyal, but it was true that Leo was a bit of a fusspot, and he did have a habit of mentioning his uncle, who was a half-famous actor, at every opportunity. And when they finished pulling Leo apart, Kit had moved the conversation on to Carol, the girl who'd been with him on Valentine's night. Rebecca had rubbished her gleefully, and Kit had laughed so hard at her impersonation of Carol's goofy giggle that he'd pulled the car over to the side of the road so they wouldn't have an accident.

All that had been before they'd even reached Bristol. *Jules et Jim* was a bit of a museum piece but sort of sexy, which set the mood for their candlelit dinner. Kit told her she had a mouth every bit as beautiful as Jeanne Moreau's, but he said it in a French accent so she wasn't sure whether he was joking. Later, outside her flat, he'd said he meant it and proved it with a long, serious kiss.

She shouldn't have invited him up, not on a first date, but it was an hour's drive back to his parents' house and it didn't seem fair just to send him packing after such a great evening. So she hadn't and had sneaked him inside, the pair of them giggling as they tiptoed past Mrs Mason's door, before tumbling on to her bed in a sudden fever, all joking set aside. And there he'd remained, in her arms, until dawn.

The phone began to ring. It had gone once before but she'd ignored it, pulling the pillow over her head and stuffing her fingers in her ears until it finally stopped.

This time she reached for the receiver. She knew who it would be.

Time to face the music.

'Sorry, Louise,' she began. 'I overslept.'

'Are you all right? I rang earlier.'

'I know. I was too tired to answer.'

'I shouldn't have asked you to do this job. I know you've got a ton of college stuff to do.'

Ouch. Now Louise was really making her feel bad.

'I'll be there in twenty minutes.'

'If you're sure. Pick up the *Western Echo* on your way.'

'Why?'

'You'll see.'

Rebecca thought no more about it as she pulled on jeans and a sweater. She splashed water on her face and wound her thick brown curls into a single strand which she pinned on top of her head. At least working at a stable meant she could look like a scruff. What would Kit make of her now? she wondered. She didn't look much like a French film star this morning.

Oh, Lord, Kit. How on earth was she going to tell Louise? But she must, and the sooner the better. She'd not mentioned Kit's invitation on the basis that it could well have been a one-off, so what would have been the point? But now it had turned out to be something special she ought to come clean. Unless, and the thought punctured her afterglow like a knife between the ribs, it was a one-off after all. He'd not said anything about a next time.

Sod it. Now was not the time to worry about that. She'd give him twenty-four hours. And if she'd not heard from him she'd turn up at his house and kill him. It was simple.

Mrs Mason gave her a sniffy look as they passed on the stairs and Rebecca offered her biggest grin. Every silver lining had a cloud, but she wasn't in the mood to worry about it.

The *Western Echo* led with the story under the banner POLICE FOILED IN HORSE-RACE STAKE-OUT.

Over 100 police officers surrounded Scratchwood Melmoth retail park yesterday in an attempt to capture a man holding horseracing to ransom.

At 7.30 p.m. a female detective posing as the daughter of trainer Gerry Fowler answered a prearranged phone call at a public phone close to the Tesco car park. The caller was demanding £100,000 to cease a campaign of violence against racing people. It is believed the conversation was cut short when he realised he was talking to a policewoman.

Last night the police issued a short statement confirming that an operation had been carried out at Scratchwood in connection with an on-going investigation. Unofficial sources claim that the attempt to hoodwink the extortionist was doomed to failure because the detective who took the call did not know enough about horseracing. 'It was a farce. He asked her a question about last year's Gold Cup and she didn't know the answer.'

Regular shopper Mrs Mavis Ford, 61, said, 'I wondered why Tesco's was so busy. You couldn't move for all these young men cluttering up the place. I suppose they were all on overtime.'

Questions about the cost of such a fruitless deployment of manpower are sure to be raised at today's press conference. So too are concerns about the direction of an investigation that appears to be no closer to apprehending the man responsible for the recent attacks on trainer Gerry Fowler and jockey Adrian Moore.

As the *Western Echo* had anticipated, the questions flew thick and fast at the press conference convened at Maybrick Street police station. Charlie Lynch, in a suit that could have benefited from an iron, kicked off proceedings while, on his right, Chief Superintendent Howard

Tomkins lent moral support. On Charlie's other side, to the initial surprise of the assembled company of journalists, sat Duncan Frame. A nervous-looking press officer hovered near the dais on which the principals sat.

Charlie's opening statement provided a frank précis of the events which had led up to the operation of the previous evening. Both he and Tomkins had agreed there was no point in holding back – not now some rat on the team had spilled the beans to the *Western Echo*. Predictably, the letters received by the *Racing Beacon* soon became the dominant issue for the members of the press.

'How do you know the letter-writer attacked Adrian Moore and Gerry Fowler?'

'How many letters have been received from him?'

'When will you be issuing the full texts?'

Charlie answered briefly and then referred them to Duncan Frame. He was keen to see what a journalist made of being on the other end of press curiosity.

Frame began in pompous mode. 'Since it became clear that this individual had singled out the *Racing Beacon* as a conduit of communication, my colleagues and I have put the interests of the racing community above all other considerations.'

'Why haven't you published the letters, Duncan?'

'Because of legitimate concerns about the sensitivity of some of the content.'

'You mean the police didn't want you to?'

'Our priority has always been to assist the police in their attempt to catch this highly dangerous individual.'

'But you just said you wanted to look after the racing community first. Shouldn't you have told them there was a psycho on the loose with a vendetta against racing?'

Frame was beginning to look a little flustered.

'All of us in the press have a duty not to panic our readership.'

Charlie kept a straight face. In his opinion, most papers dealt in panic – pandering to people's anxieties was a good way to sell more copies.

Frame's questioners returned to the main topic.

'When can we see these letters, Duncan?'

Frame grinned. 'I'm not making any promises, but if you buy the

Beacon tomorrow there's a strong possibility you might get a glimpse.'

That sparked off a row. The question-and-answer format became submerged in noisy protests from journalists who were not employed by the media group who owned the *Racing Beacon*. They demanded that the police hand over the letters, even if Frame wouldn't. Charlie pointed out that they weren't his to release and, even if they were, he was not sure he would publish them at this stage of the investigation.

A tabloid reporter asked when the constabulary had decided to get into bed with Sir Gavin Hoylake, and the press officer began to shuffle his feet and look at his watch. As the *Western Echo* reporter began to ask pointed questions about the cost of the Scratchwood operation, it occurred to Charlie that he wasn't going to get any favours from this bunch from now on. But then, when had he ever?

Thankfully the Chief Super stepped in to cover the finance angle. He managed to sound fully supportive of Charlie and also combative on the rigorous process of deploying precious police resources.

The issue of the ransom money was raised and Charlie confirmed the quoted figure of £100,000. At which point Frame butted in.

'Please don't give our friends in the police a hard time about raiding the public purse. The ransom money was supplied by the *Beacon* at the express wish of the proprietor.'

Some of the journalists groaned, and Frame beamed in triumph. Charlie imagined that this snippet of information was not destined to feature prominently in many reports.

Which left the matter of Patsy's role in the affair.

'Inspector Lynch, can you confirm that the extortionist specified that Louise Fowler should carry the money?'

'He did.'

'So why did you use a policewoman?'

'Because it would have been unfair to expect Miss Fowler to place herself in a potentially dangerous position. Especially considering that this man badly injured her father.'

'Did you even ask her?'

'No, I did not.'

'But the operation failed because he recognised the policewoman wasn't Louise – isn't that right?'

'I wouldn't call our initiative a failure. We have opened communication with this individual and that's a significant step forward.'

There was a contemptuous snigger from someone in the front row and a fusillade of queries followed.

'Is it true he asked her who won the Gold Cup?'

'Couldn't you find anyone who knew about horses?'

'Do you think he's going to carry on beating up jockeys?'

'Is the money still on the table if he gets in touch?'

Charlie had had enough. He brought matters abruptly to a close with an appeal to the public for information, though he knew it would be buried in a bog of sensational reporting. Yesterday he'd had a shot at catching his quarry; today he'd not only lost him but the whole business was out in the open, subject to the scrutiny of this lot. Just wait till he caught up with whoever had been telling tales out of school.

Of course, it wouldn't have mattered if the extortionist hadn't twigged Patsy last night. Not that he could blame Patsy. She was his choice and maybe he should have chosen differently.

There was no getting away from it, the buck stopped with him.

Rebecca had no opportunity to talk to Louise about Kit when she arrived at Greenhills. For one thing, the article in the *Western Echo* and the details Louise was able to supply in addition, drove the matter from her mind. They'd read it together in the office the moment Rebecca arrived. Then one of the lads burst in to warn them that a group of cars were held up on the lane behind the horses returning from third lot. From conversations with the drivers it was apparent they were newspaper people who wanted to talk to Louise.

'You've got to help me, Becky,' she said. So, while Louise tried to get hold of Charlie Lynch for advice, Rebecca marched out to forestall the gathering of hacks.

After a couple of minutes Louise appeared, walking into a wall of questions. Without thinking about it, Rebecca thrust herself in front of Louise and demanded silence. She told the reporters Louise would make a short statement and then answer one or two questions. To her surprise, they backed off and allowed Louise to speak.

After that things passed off without drama. Louise said she fully supported the police operation and the use of a stand-in. She paid tribute to the officer who had taken her place and said that she had been unlucky to be caught out.

'Becky, you were brilliant,' said Louise after they'd gone, and Rebecca was on the brink of seizing the moment and confessing about Kit when Chris suddenly appeared.

'She's not that brilliant at getting her fanny down here on time, though, is she? I've got horses that could do with some of her brilliant mucking out.'

Rebecca got the message. Her confession would have to wait.

Charlie was worried. Not so much by the irritations of the morning or the exposure of his investigation to the press – that was spilt milk. His real concern was how to catch this character who had successfully hospitalised two men without being seen and had backtracked smartly out of the trap Charlie had set. How would he react to the events of last night?

Unfortunately there was no record of the man's voice – he'd avoided the phone tap by calling on the adjacent line. However, Charlie had a record of Patsy's responses and her impression of his voice. She'd described it as 'ordinary – not posh, maybe a touch of Bristol in the accent'. She said he'd started off softly but had got louder and shouted at her by the end. She'd not been able to get an impression of his age – 'Not young and not old, guv. I wish I could say more.'

But that was OK. It fitted with the impression Charlie was building up. He pulled a notepad from his desk drawer and began to make some notes.

How old would the target be?

A man in his middle years – thirty-five to fifty-five, say. So far he'd planned every step of his campaign with care, so he was unlikely to be a hot-headed youth. Maybe he'd learned from experience how to take his time.

He was above average intelligence, certainly, though he didn't seem particularly well educated – the spelling mistakes in the letters were a giveaway. Unless, of course, they'd been put in deliberately, which was always possible. It seemed the kind of trick he would be capable of. He obviously liked playing games.

Charlie hoped his man wasn't as smart as he obviously thought he was.

His train of thought was interrupted by a knock on the office door. Damn.

'What is it?' he shouted irritably.

161

DC Jenkins stepped hesitantly into the room. Charlie regretted his irritation. The lad was diffident enough already.

'Yes, Terry?'

The young detective's mouth was open but he seemed to have difficulty getting any sound out. There were freckles across the bridge of his nose, and his cheeks were so smooth Charlie wondered how often he had to use a razor. Not every day, that was for sure. All those cracks about policemen getting younger certainly applied to this lad, yet he'd already done a stint in uniform before transferring to CID. Charlie noticed that he held an envelope in his hand.

Finally Terry spoke. 'It was me, boss. I'm sorry.' He placed the envelope on Charlie's desk. 'That's my resignation, if you want it.'

Charlie was perplexed. He looked suspiciously at the rectangle of white paper. It was addressed to DCI Charles Lynch and bore the sweaty imprint of a finger in one corner.

He pointed to the chair opposite him and said, 'Why would I want your resignation?'

More hesitation. 'Because I told the *Western Echo* about the Scratchwood op. All that stuff in the paper's because of me.'

For a moment, Charlie didn't know what to say. He'd rather assumed the leak had come from one of the outsiders they'd roped in. Someone who'd probably resented being pulled off another job for the fun of kicking his heels in Tesco's car park. Charlie had not seriously thought it would have come from one of his own team. To be frank, the name of Terry Jenkins would have been about the last on his list of suspects.

'Tell me,' was all he said.

It all came out in a rush. After the aborted Scratchwood episode, Terry had met a girl called Jo in a pub. She'd been impressed to hear he was a detective and, over a pint, he'd coughed the story of the stake-out. The next morning he'd read the *Western Echo* with a horrible sinking feeling. There'd been more to Jo than met the eye, and her full name, he gathered from the byline, was Josephine Benson.

So here he was, offering himself up for sacrifice.

Charlie couldn't find it in his heart to be that judgemental, though he did his best to read the Riot Act. Jo Benson's innocent blue eyes had sapped the strength of more experienced men than Terry Jenkins. And her sharp-edged questions from the front row at that morning's press conference had caused him as much discomfort as any.

Charlie tore the envelope in two and tossed it into the wastepaper basket.

'Get out of here,' he growled, cutting off Terry's stuttering expressions of gratitude.

Rebecca felt like a hypocrite. After she'd mucked out, she'd busied herself tidying the tack-room. Rugs, saddles, bridles – everything was put in its proper place. Then she'd looked for Louise to get the Kit matter off her chest. But Louise was deep in conference with Chris about plans for the weekend.

'I really need a word, Louise,' she'd said, but Louise had looked at Chris and he'd glared at her. Obviously she wasn't back in his good books yet.

'It can wait,' she'd said. Then Louise had suggested she take Skellig, her grey filly, out for some exercise, and they could talk later.

'It would be doing me a big favour, Becky. I don't know when I'm going to get out on her today, and she'd love it.'

So here she was, hacking comfortably over the gallops on Louise's little horse. The sun shone low in the sky, picking out the first glimpses of blossom in the lanes down in the valley. A thrush was singing fit to burst in a hedgerow. Despite the continuing chill of winter there were signs that the season might soon be changing. There was not a soul in sight.

'Don't know what they're missing, do they?' she said to the horse.

She imagined being up here with Kit, the pair of them racing side by side. Not that she could imagine Kit in a riding hat and breeches. It was funny how much she didn't know about him – she didn't even know whether he could ride. When they'd first met – the four of them in the pub that night – they'd talked horses a bit. But Leo had made most of the noise. All she could recall about Kit's contribution was that he studied form. So he liked a bet. Well, she could live with that. She couldn't imagine having a serious relationship with a man who didn't have some kind of interest in horses.

So now, after one lusty night, she was having a serious relationship?

'Get real, woman,' she said out loud. 'Not you,' she added as Skellig pricked up her ears.

She turned the horse upwind and urged the filly into a canter. Time to blow the cobwebs out of her brain.

*

Keith knew he was taking a risk being over here, near the Fowler yard. Revisiting the scene of his assault on the trainer hadn't been part of the plan. But if the plan had gone right, today he'd be a hundred grand better off.

He'd been cheated again and someone had to pay. He'd made his instructions clear and they'd disobeyed him. But he'd anticipated that. He knew they'd try to double-cross him somehow, and he'd caught that police bitch out.

But that wasn't enough. He had to show them he couldn't be mucked around. Action was called for – something swift and terrible.

He'd brought the crossbow again. From up on a small ridge behind a hedge he could get a clear sight into Greenhills Yard and the first row of horse-boxes. Suppose he shot a horse? That would have the so-called racing fraternity running scared.

He hesitated. Putting a couple of blokes in hospital was one thing – they'd deserved it.

But now an alternative target had presented itself.

Up there, in the field beyond the copse where he was now parked, was a horse he recognised. He'd seen that little grey with the dappled quarters and white knee patches before, when he was watching the Fowler yard the night before he did Gerry. And the girl riding it had been the daughter, Louise.

He watched the horse and rider through the screen of trees. He was certain that was the horse. And the female on its back – young, athletic, leggy – would be the Fowler girl.

He could get a good shot at them from here. He couldn't miss.

On the other hand . . . He still had some of the cord in the car.

Forget the crossbow. He had a better idea.

Skellig had had enough, Rebecca decided, and she couldn't put off her showdown with Louise any longer. She turned her mount towards the corner of the field, where a path led past the trees down to the road.

Maybe Louise wouldn't care that much about Kit. After all, she'd had her chance to go out with him and she'd said no. Also, Louise had not had a proper boyfriend for six months. It took a special guy to even raise her interest these days. All that occupied her attention was horses, the yard, her father—

Damn, Rebecca thought, I hate having to justify myself.

She knew how much Louise had wanted to go and knew the reasons why she hadn't. They were fine, praiseworthy reasons.

She reached the gate by the road and dismounted.

'Just take your time,' she said to Skellig, who was keen to get home and hindering her attempt to pull back the five-barred gate.

Suddenly the little horse raised her head, startled.

Something slammed into Rebecca's face, blocking out the light and stuffing up her mouth. At the same time, she was grabbed around the waist and lifted off the ground.

She shouted and fought but her cries were lost in the coarse, foul cloth over her mouth, and the unyielding bulk of her attacker was implacable.

Whoever it was who gripped her wasn't going to let her go.

Keith had caught and subdued many wild creatures in his life. He was used to the primal panic that gripped a flapping fish on the riverbank or a squealing rabbit in a snare. All the same, the frantic strength in the girl as she flailed and kicked in his arms took him by surprise.

He lifted her and slammed her down on the tarmac of the road, crashing on top of her to pin her down. But still she fought and squirmed. He yanked her head back hard, gripping her face through the cloth. Her riding helmet jerked back into his jaw and he tasted blood in his mouth.

At any moment a car could appear or a walker or a kid on a bike – anything – and then he'd be in deep shit.

He put his knee in the small of her back and pinned her down with all his strength.

'Lie still,' he muttered, 'or I'll break your fucking neck.'

Suddenly she went limp.

With his free hand he pulled the cord from his pocket.

'I'm going to take my hand from your mouth. If you make a sound, you're dead. Understand?'

She nodded; he could feel the movement through the cloth.

He took his hand from her face and the gag with it. She gasped for air even as he leaned his whole weight on her. He doubted she was capable of making much noise in this position, but he had to work fast.

The strap of her helmet had come loose in the struggle. He pulled the hat from her head and slipped the noose around her throat. She jerked and thrashed feebly as he tightened it, jerking on it cruelly to subdue her. Even so she tried to resist as he captured her wrists, binding them hard and tight. He shifted round to get at her legs, tying the ankles together, still with the same length of cord. When he was finished she was trussed up like a Christmas turkey. He used the cloth to blindfold her.

The car was a few yards off, the boot already open. He dumped her inside and pulled an old tarpaulin right over her. As he began to close the door of the boot, she stirred, frantically twisting beneath the dirty material.

He slid his hand into his toolbag and grabbed the jack.

He bent down close to the mound of her head.

'We're going for a drive. If you shout or try to get out, I shall come back here and beat your brains out with this.'

He dug the heavy jack hard into the tarpaulin over her thigh.

He could hear her making little mewing sounds and panting with fear.

This time, when he began to close the boot, she lay immobile.

He drove off, slowly at first, aware that his heart was hammering and his hands were shaking.

By God, this would show the bastards he meant business.

It wasn't till he was twenty minutes into the journey that he realised. It hadn't been obvious while she was wearing her riding hat but the girl in the boot had the wrong colour hair.

The discussion with Chris had dragged on. First class though he was at his job, he was obviously feeling the strain of shouldering the training burden at this crucial time of the year. Louise found herself, a girl almost half his age, in the bizarre position of trying to boost his spirits.

'Dad thinks you're the reason we're starting to achieve things at last,' she said.

It was true – Chris's arrival at the yard had coincided with signs of real encouragement. Paris White had not been the only eye-catching runner at last year's Cheltenham; Devious had won three out of six and Easy Does It had been in the lead two fences out in the Grand National before being brought down by a loose horse. Dad had told her having a dependable back-up man like Chris was the missing piece in the jigsaw.

They'd all been looking forward to this spring, expecting to turn the previous year's promise into solid achievement. The removal of Gerry from the equation had been a body blow to their ambition.

Louise, however, was determined not to let things slide without a fight. Her dad was still a physical wreck but his mind was unaffected and the horses were in good shape. If Chris could remain on top of the training programme, if she could be an effective go-between and stand-in for her dad, and if they could avoid any new disasters, then it could still be a triumphant season. If, if, if.

Chris looked dead on his feet. His face was pale and drawn, with dark hollows beneath his eyes. Unlike some jockeys who piled on the pounds after they quit the saddle, Chris was probably as light as in his riding days. Louise wondered whether he looked after himself. Since her dad had been gone, Chris appeared to work twenty-four hours a day. He lived in a flat over the lads' hostel but never seemed to go home. Louise cursed herself for not noticing this before. No wonder his morale was flagging.

But at least this was one thing she had an idea how to fix. A word to her mum and Chris would never be short of a square meal. Her mother was desperate to make a contribution. Louise would ask her to keep an eye on Chris when she returned from her afternoon stint at the hospital.

Other things were not so easy to deal with. They could really do with a top-notch stable jockey. So far they'd relied on a canny old hand, Patrick Daly, who was skilled at squeezing the best out of a horse. But Pat had fractured his wrist at Uttoxeter before Christmas and taken himself off to his father's farm in Ireland. From what Gerry said, Louise doubted he was coming back. Since then they'd hired in freelancers and put up their apprentice when they were really stuck. It was hardly satisfactory, but Chris thought they should wait for her father's return before finding a regular rider. Louise was happy enough to agree; she was more worried about losing owners in Gerry's absence.

Justin Delancy, who owned Easy Does It and the promising hurdler Nobody's Perfect, was still considering whether to remove his horses. Not that he'd come out and said so, but she knew he'd talked to another West Country trainer about the possibility of moving them to him. The trainer had told Delancy he would be unhappy about taking them in the current circumstances and had then rung Chris to warn him what was afoot. Louise knew not all their competitors were likely to be so scrupulous.

Perhaps she'd better talk to her dad about it after all. Maybe he could ring Delancy and convince the banker that the yard would be back to normal soon. If only that were true.

Louise made sure they finished their discussion on an upbeat note. 'This time next week, Chris, I bet we'll have had half a dozen winners and Dad will be back home yelling at us like usual.'

He raised a smile. 'You really think so?'

'Why not?' She pushed him out of the office door. 'Go home and put your feet up. Catch up on your beauty sleep.'

He grunted. 'I'll have a quick look round and think about it.'

Louise watched him go with a mixture of relief and concern. Now, where the hell was Becky?

By the time the kettle had boiled, Louise realised Becky must have got fed up with waiting and gone home. But as she looked out of the small office window, sipping her tea, she noticed Rebecca's bicycle leaning against the wall.

She stepped outside, mug in hand, and shivered. It was chilly now, and the afternoon light was thickening. Chris appeared out of the murk, his face drawn and irritated.

'Skellig's not in her box,' he said. 'Your friend Rebecca takes some liberties, I must say.'

Louise frowned. 'Do you think she's all right?'

'Yeah, she'll be fine. It's the horse I'm worried about.'

Chris was not Rebecca's greatest fan, but Louise held back the defence of her friend that sprang to mind. She was more concerned about finding her.

'You go home,' she said. 'I'll drive up the lane and see if I can spot them.'

He accompanied her to the car and climbed in on the passenger side.

'It's OK, Chris. I can manage on my own.'

'Suppose the silly cow has fallen off and broken her neck? How will you manage then?'

Louise shrugged and started the engine. Chris was definitely one of life's pessimists.

*

They followed the network of small country roads around Greenhills for ten minutes without a sign of horse or rider, Louise trying to keep a lid on her anxiety.

'We'd better get out and walk,' she said as she drove back down the lane to the yard. 'I'm sure she'd have gone up on the gallops.'

She parked by the gate that opened on to the bridle-path. They'd looked closely at the hillside as they'd driven by the first time and seen no sign of Rebecca, which was why they'd driven on. But there were dips and folds in the land and scattered stands of trees which could hide a horse and rider – especially in the gathering gloom.

'Just as well we're looking for a grey,' she said, trying to lighten her spirits as much as his. Chris said nothing but took the flashlight he'd found in the glove compartment.

The gate into the field was not fastened. It swung back on its hinges at Chris's touch.

'Becky!' Louise called. 'Where are you?'

The shout was swallowed up in the emptiness around them. Louise felt a little foolish.

Then they heard something. The reassuring footfall of a horse's hooves on soft turf. Ahead, through the fading light, appeared the familiar shape of Skellig. Thank the Lord for that.

But as Chris's torch beam played over the little horse they could see that she was riderless. There was no sign of Rebecca.

Charlie had been in the house only five minutes when the front doorbell rang. He'd just had time to kick his shoes off and contemplate another night of beans on toast and a hot bath.

Amy Baylis had her hair loose this evening. It fell fair and lustrous on to the shoulders of her black silk blouse. She carried a paper carrier bag in one hand and a half-empty bottle of wine in the other.

'So, have you finally finished fighting the lawless, Charlie?'

'For today, Amy,' he replied, and couldn't resist adding, 'We guardians of the public virtue rarely put down our arms.'

'So I've noticed. You're not at home much, are you?'

He didn't reply to that. He was regretting his previous remark. Somehow Amy always lured him into making a fool of himself.

'Anyhow, Charlie, I've brought you supper. I cooked too much and couldn't finish it. You can throw it away if you like but I couldn't bear to.'

He didn't know what to say. This was precisely the kind of gesture he was expecting from Amy – a full-frontal assault on his domestic solitude. On the other hand, it was thoughtful and generous and he was damned hungry.

At that moment the telephone on the hall table rang.

Amy thrust the bag and the bottle into his hands. 'Goodnight, Charlie,' she said as she retreated down the garden path.

Saved by the bell, so to speak.

It was Holly Green, on late at Maybrick Street.

'Sorry to disturb you, guv, but I've had Gerry Fowler's wife on the phone. She says one of Louise's friends has gone missing.'

'Who?'

'A Rebecca Thornton, aged nineteen. She was helping out at the yard and went off riding mid-afternoon. When she didn't come back, Louise and a guy from the stables set out to look for her and found the horse wandering on its own. They're still out there looking.'

Charlie's stomach knotted. All thought of food and relaxation had vanished in an instant. He had a bad feeling about this.

'Have they informed the local police?'

'They're sending someone up there but they've not showed up yet. Rebecca's only been gone a few hours. Mrs Fowler wanted you to know, though.'

'Ring her back. Tell her I'm on my way.'

As Charlie put his shoes back on, he scrabbled in his inside pocket for his address book and quickly dialled a number. It rang half a dozen times before it was picked up.

'Yes?' The voice sounded dull and dispirited. In the background Charlie could hear a squeal of voices and the crash of theme music.

'Patsy, it's Charlie Lynch.'

'Boss?' She sounded startled. 'What's up?'

He explained. Patsy knew at once who the missing girl was.

'She's Louise's best mate. They're thick as thieves.'

'Have you met her?'

'I just said hello to her up at the yard.'

'Are you up for a drive or do you want to get back to your movie?'

'It's crap. I'll be ready by the time you get here.'

*

They spent most of the drive to Greenhills in silence. Patsy was grateful for the chance to get out and do something. After the cock-up of the night before, Charlie had told her to go home and forget about it. That had not been possible.

Neither of them had mentioned the obvious but it hung heavily in the air. This had to be connected to their horseracing case. It was too great a coincidence, surely, for a stablegirl at Greenhills to suddenly go missing. Particularly within twenty-four hours of the aborted handover.

If that was true, Patsy thought, it only made her failure of yesterday more damaging.

'Have a snooze,' Charlie suggested. 'We'll be another half-hour at least.'

Patsy stared out of the window at the motorway traffic with sightless eyes, sleep an impossibility.

Greenhills was alive with a blaze of light as they parked in the yard. Charlie noted the presence of a squad car amidst a throng of young men and women carrying torches, heading up the lane. Obviously a search party composed of stable personnel. So they hadn't found the girl.

'There's Louise,' said Patsy, rushing towards the knot of people leaving the yard.

Louise was next to Chris Blackmore, who was trying to prevent her joining the search party. 'You've done enough,' he said. 'If Rebecca's out there, they'll find her.'

She seemed to be about to argue the point when she saw Charlie and Patsy.

'Becky's missing,' she blurted at once. 'They've found her riding helmet but she's gone.'

Patsy put an arm round her. Charlie looked at Chris. 'Where was the helmet?'

'On the road near where we found the horse. The police are up there now and all the lads are going to have another look for her. Me and Louise couldn't see her, though.'

Charlie didn't envy the police trying to secure the site. It would be chaos in the dark with all these people. He ought to get up there.

He turned to Louise. 'Why don't you go back to the house? Patsy will go with you.'

She nodded. She looked beat. But she stepped close to him and said quietly, 'He's taken her, hasn't he?'

'It's far too early to say.'

'He has. I know he has and I know why too.'

Charlie had a feeling he knew what was coming.

'Becky was on my horse. He took her because he thought it was me.'

By Louise's side, Patsy's eyes registered surprise. Obviously the thought hadn't occurred to her. But it had to him.

'Don't jump to any conclusions, Louise. She could be found at any moment.'

But, in his heart of hearts, he doubted it.

Chapter Nine

Charlie Lynch felt a distinct sense of déjà vu as he took his seat for another press conference. Here he was at the same time, on the same dais, facing the same set of journalists as the day before. Only this time he had just the press officer for company – and the disappearance of a young woman to explain.

Once again he tried to make it short – sweet was not an option – but inevitably there were questions.

'Do you think Bernie's got her?' was the first.

That morning's *Racing Beacon* had run four pages on the whole saga, reproducing almost all the text of the letters. The nature of the writer's disillusion with racing and his allegations of corruption were now public property, as were new details of his assaults. The crossbow attack on Adrian had captured people's imaginations and reporters were now referring to the letter-writer as 'Bernie', after Bernie the Bolt on an old TV game show called *The Golden Shot*. Charlie remembered that contestants had to tell Bernie how to aim an arrow to win a prize. He had no doubt the name would catch on.

In answer to the question he sounded the same cautious note as he had with Louise – that the girl's disappearance might be completely unconnected with the Fowlers' troubles and that all avenues of inquiry must be kept open. He painted a quick word picture of the missing girl – Rebecca Thornton, aged nineteen, a first-year law student and temporary stable-worker – released a photograph they'd unearthed from her flat and appealed for help from the public. That was the point of the press conference, of course – to stir up public interest and get some cooperation. Someone out there had to know something.

'One last question, Inspector.' It was Jo Benson, in the front row, swinging her long legs. 'If Bernie has taken her, from your reading of his personality – what do you think are her chances?'

Charlie didn't rush to reply. He certainly didn't intend to speculate in front of a room full of journalists.

'All I'll say is that, if this man is responsible for Rebecca's disappearance, I appeal to his better nature and ask him to release her immediately. This young woman bears no responsibility for any of his grievances.'

He knew this wasn't the kind of answer La Benson was looking for but, after her trick on Terry, she wasn't getting any favours from him. Nevertheless, as he took the stairs two at a time to the CID room, an idea occurred, based on his reply to her question. He'd have a word with Duncan Frame about it.

Ivan Stone and Terry were waiting for him. They'd been round at Rebecca's place, talking to her landlady.

The sergeant was obviously bursting with news. 'I don't think our man took her.'

Charlie took off his jacket and loosened his tie. At 10.30 in the morning the room was already baking.

'The girl had a new bloke on the go, boss. Spent all night with him, apparently.'

Charlie nodded. 'Do we know who he is?'

'We don't have a name but, according to Mrs Mason the landlady, he took Rebecca out on Wednesday evening in his car, some kind of red convertible with an S and a W in the licence number. They returned about one in the morning and went upstairs to her flat on the top floor. He didn't leave till five-thirty. And from the noise they were making they weren't just drinking coffee, if you get my drift.'

'So she's got a boyfriend.'

'Boyfriends plural, boss. There's a string of them in and out, according to Mrs Mason. She doesn't miss much.'

'She's more like a jailer than a landlady,' offered Terry. It was his first contribution to the conversation.

Charlie glared at him – the young detective wasn't yet back in his good books. 'Anything else?'

'We had a look around. It's just a couple of rooms. Bit of a mess, like she'd left in a hurry. Two dirty mugs in the bedroom and an ashtray with some dog-ends. Mrs Mason says Rebecca doesn't smoke. There's condom wrappers in the bedroom wastepaper basket and a message on the answerphone timed at one-thirty-five yesterday afternoon. It's a bit funny.'

'In what way, funny?'

Ivan looked at Terry, who reached for his notebook. 'It's in French, guv. I made a note of what it said – "*Chérie, c'est moi. Hier soir c'était le meilleur de ma vie. Je t'adore.*" '

Terry's French accent wasn't bad. Charlie was impressed. 'Meaning?' he asked the lad for Ivan's benefit.

' "Darling, it's me. Last night was the best night of my life. I adore you," ' obliged Terry. 'But he didn't sound as if he was a proper Frenchman. It started off like a bit of a piss-take.'

'And finished up?'

'The *je t'adore* bit sounded serious. As if he was embarrassed to come right out and say how much he liked her.'

Charlie nodded.

Rebecca was the same age as his daughter. Was this the kind of thing Claire got up to now she was living away from home?

Ivan brought him back to the matter in hand. 'See? I bet the girl's disappearance has got nothing to do with our fellow. This Rebecca obviously puts it about a bit. Maybe she's just run off with the new boyfriend. He pitches up at Greenhills in his fancy car and in she hops.'

Charlie shook his head. 'She wouldn't leave the horse in a field. She could take it back in five minutes and then be on her way.'

But Ivan was not deterred. 'OK. She's not as keen on the new bloke as he is on her. He finds her out riding, she tells him to get lost and then he gets shirty. Whichever way you dice it, I bet this is just a young lovers' argy-bargy and she'll reappear in a day or two.'

Charlie hoped he was right – though he doubted it. However, all avenues had to be explored.

'We'd better find this boyfriend, then. I presume Mrs Mason gave you some kind of description?'

He jotted down the details as Terry once more consulted his notebook.

Keith put his foot down as he drove the wagon back to the kennels. He had two dead ewes in the back from a farm ten miles off and he was in a hurry. He'd got the girl safely secured but he'd feel better once he was home.

On the drive back the previous evening after he'd snatched her, he'd planned how he would arrange things. There was a small shed that had once been used as a kennel, before the pack got bigger and the new pens had been built. He'd kept his Rottweilers in there when he'd first taken the job – until that arsehole Jellicoe had objected and made Keith give them away. The chain leads he'd used on Rocky and Rusty were still in place, so that was handy.

The first thing he'd done, before he'd even opened the boot and got her out, was go in the house and find his Balaclava. He'd decided to wear it all the time when he was with her so she couldn't identify him later. It was either that or keep her blindfolded, but he couldn't risk her dislodging it. It would be awkward enough keeping her gagged during the day when he was off, like now, picking up dead stock, and when there was the chance of other people showing up – like Fred and Jeff, who were due later on to help him exercise the hounds.

When he'd moved her into the shed last night, all the resistance had gone out of her. She'd moaned and complained about her legs hurting, and he'd had to drag her out the back, past the pens, with the hounds jumping up and down and going bananas at the late-night excitement. She'd said a lot of stuff, asking him why he was doing this to her and begging and generally bleating on. He'd ignored it while he chained her up, then he'd belted her on the leg good and hard, told her to shut the fuck up or he'd fix it so she'd never walk again.

After that he'd been able to sort things in peace, though he'd hardly slept. He'd lain awake half the night, listening out for her. He'd warned her there was no point in her shouting or screaming because no one would hear, apart from the dogs. They were fighting dogs, he'd said, and if she made a noise he'd set them on her.

He'd not been sure whether she'd taken it in – she looked pretty much out of it – and he'd not heard a sound from her through the night. This morning she'd been lying curled up. He'd had to shake her awake so she could drink the tea he'd made her and use the bucket he'd supplied as a toilet. She'd not even raised much of a protest when he'd taped up her mouth.

As he parked in the yard he looked round anxiously for Fred's bike – sometimes the old twerp turned up early – but it wasn't in its spot by the back door. The place was just as he had left it.

He picked the bundle of newspapers off the passenger seat and headed indoors. He'd had a quick shufti at the news. The girl's disappearance was already making waves. HAS BERNIE STRUCK AGAIN? was the headline in the *Echo*. He read it with interest. Bernie the Bolt, eh? So he had a nickname. He supposed he should be flattered.

There was also a picture of Louise Fowler, saying how this Rebecca was her best friend.

Rebecca. He'd got used to the idea of her now. When it came down to it, what did it matter which girl he had?

For all his planning, the kidnap had been a spur-of-the-moment thing, but now he could see it was exactly the right thing to do. Better than another blow for vengeance. They wouldn't be able to ignore him now, would they? Not now he had Rebecca.

Louise had tried to keep herself busy all morning, which wasn't hard. She rode out with the first two lots, despite protests from Chris, who looked as exhausted as she felt. When she got back to the office, Helen, the secretary, gave her a list of callers. Her heart sank when she saw the name at the top – Justin Delancy.

'He wouldn't tell me what it was about,' said Helen, but Louise could guess.

Delancy could wait for the moment. She dialled the second name on the list.

She was put straight through to Charlie Lynch. He came to the point at once.

'Did Rebecca say anything to you yesterday about what she'd been up to on Wednesday evening?'

'No.'

'Has she got a boyfriend?'

'There's Leo. She's been out with him a few times.'

'Can you tell me what he looks like?'

Louise was puzzled but complied. 'Short spiky blond hair, about five eight, round face, slim. A puff of wind would blow him over.'

She could tell at once that it wasn't the information Charlie was after.

'According to Rebecca's landlady, a young man took her out on Wednesday and stayed in her flat until five-thirty yesterday morning.

He's six foot tall, with thick dark hair that falls over his face and, in Mrs Mason's opinion, very handsome. She says he thinks he'd God's gift to women.'

Louise was dumbfounded. It could only be one person.

'He also drives a red convertible with an S and a W in the registration.'

That settled it.

'That's Kit, Leo's friend.' She thought for a moment. 'His full name's Christian Curtis.'

'Do you know him well?'

Evidently she didn't know him at all. Not like Becky did, it seemed.

'No. Becky and I met Leo and Kit in a pub one night. After that I spoke to him on the phone once. I didn't know that he and Becky were—' What exactly? *Lovers, of course, dummy.* '—all that friendly.'

She made an effort to keep the shock out of her voice as she answered more questions. She didn't have Kit's number, but the police had taken charge of Becky's bag and it might be in her address book. Leo's certainly would be – Leo Mackay, he lived near Wellington.

She put the phone down in a daze. It came back to her vividly how Becky had looked at her yesterday when she'd interrupted her meeting with Chris. She'd wanted to talk, hadn't she? She could guess now what Becky had wanted to talk about.

Louise stepped out of the office, away from Helen's curious gaze, and found herself looking into Skellig's box. The little grey nuzzled her happily.

Was she jealous?

Yes, a bit. In fact, more than a bit.

Did this make any difference to how she felt about Becky?

No.

In these circumstances, her feelings of jealousy were nothing. Just self-indulgence. And Mrs Mason was right – Kit did think he was God's gift to women.

Skellig licked her cheek. She patted the horse's smooth neck and stared into her translucent eyes. If only Skellig could talk.

Louise didn't care what Becky had done. She just wanted her back.

Rebecca lay on the straw, listening to the protests of her pain-racked body. The abrasions round her neck from the cord stung like fire, and a steady throb licked through the swollen tissue of her left knee. But it was the deep-seated ache at the base of her spine that really consumed her. Inside the ache was a saw-toothed agony that seemed to shriek through her bones whenever she tried to move her legs. He – the hulk who'd taken her – had done some serious injury to her when they'd fought, crushing her with all his weight and breaking something deep inside. The pain robbed her of breath.

But pain was good. She liked it. It blotted out the worse stuff – the fear that gripped her. She was in hell. And she knew what she'd done to deserve it.

She had dared to believe in happiness. Dared to glimpse a blissful future. Dared to expect.

It was hard to imagine that the day before she'd woken in the arms of a loving man, safe and warm. Now all her certainties had been stolen from her. She lay chained in an outbuilding, on a bed of straw, like the dogs she could hear in other buildings near by. There was a bucket in the corner for her to pee into and a chipped mug of water for her to drink. And somewhere not too far away was the man who'd snatched her away from her life.

Who knew what he intended to do with her? She had a vivid imagination – what woman didn't have in these circumstances?

So she concentrated on her pain. That was tangible. Understandable. And when it gripped her, sucking the air from her lungs and sending an electric jolt through her brain, it blocked out everything else. Like the thought of what might happen to her next.

Julia rang Phil when she heard about the missing girl. He'd taken a bang on the knee so he was at home, resting up ahead of the next day's meeting at Haydock.

His voice was flat, a depressed monotone so unlike the real Phil. She heard it a lot these days as, after his confession, he no longer tried to hide how he was feeling. In her less kind moments she thought he could have made more of an effort.

For the moment, though, Phil's troubles were not uppermost in her mind as they discussed the latest disaster to strike Greenhills.

'It makes me mad,' said Phil, suddenly animated. 'I'm also going crazy stuck in here with my knee up.'

'Do you want me to come home?'

'It's OK, sweetheart. Anyhow, you've got your work cut out with your other old warhorse, haven't you?'

That was true enough. Callisto was making a comeback at Kempton Park the next day.

'I'll be back as soon as I can. Perhaps Rebecca will have turned up by then.'

'There's a chance.'

But she knew from the tone of his voice that he wasn't holding his breath.

It seemed to Hugh Pimlott that he had been working non-stop for days on end. He'd left the office the past couple of nights just in time to grab a takeaway and fall into bed. The ramifications of the Bernie story and the demands of Duncan Frame – which amounted to the same thing – had monopolised his time. Since he'd been the only staffer in on the drama from the beginning, Frame had insisted that Hugh write the whole article, and he'd personally scrutinised it line by line. The editor wasn't the easiest man to please, especially when he was in a mood – and he'd been in a mood ever since the *Western Echo* had broken the Bernie story.

Hugh had tried to get hold of Louise but without luck. Her mother and the Greenhills secretary were screening her calls, and neither would believe him when he said his interest was purely personal. He guessed all press callers were being treated with suspicion. And since he'd been stuck in the office, churning out copy, he'd not had the opportunity to see her face to face.

He wondered how she was managing now Rebecca had disappeared. He hoped she was holding up. He would have liked to have offered her a shoulder to cry on and an ear to bend. That was what friends were supposed to do in a crisis, wasn't it? He'd keep trying.

Right now he was on the phone to Phil Nicholas. Frame had issued another edict. Instead of Phil's Saturday column being the usual mixture of stable gossip and the jockey's forthcoming fancies, something different was required.

'We can't ignore what's going on,' Hugh said to Phil, paraphrasing the editor. 'We think an open letter to this man from someone of your stature in the game might get his attention.'

Phil's response was typically forthright. 'I'd like to get his attention, all right. I'd like to horsewhip him round Aintree for what he's done.'

'I don't think you can say that. You've got to appeal to his better nature.'

'He's got one, has he?'

'The editor's keen on the idea.'

'That's just because he thinks it'll make the paper look good, not because it will have any effect.'

'You're a cynical bugger, aren't you, Phil?'

'I know how you lot operate.'

Hugh couldn't blame him for thinking that way. On the other hand, he had his orders. He tried another tack. 'To be fair to Duncan, he's been talking to the police about a direct pitch to the kidnapper. They're all in favour.'

That made a difference, he could tell. He pressed on. 'Why don't you talk to the guy in charge?'

So that was how they left it. Hugh promised to get Inspector Lynch to ring and, as a fall-back, set about writing Phil's column himself – just in case.

Phil was surprised how quickly the policeman got in touch. Twenty minutes after talking to Hugh, Charlie Lynch was on the phone.

'I'm very grateful you've agreed to help us, Mr Nicholas.'

Had he? Phil didn't recall committing himself. He wasn't keen to take part in some newspaper stunt. But, as the detective outlined his plans, Phil was impressed.

'One of my problems,' the policeman began, 'is that we've no line of communication with this fellow. He writes letters to the *Beacon* and makes demands. So far that's it. But if you were to address him directly, that might spark something off.'

'You mean if I offered to be a kind of go-between?'

'Yes. You've got to phrase it right, though.'

'I'll say whatever you want me to say.' So, he had committed himself after all.

'It's got to be in your own words, you understand.'

'I'll do my best, Inspector.'

'Good man. Have you got a pen? You'll need to make a few notes.'

Phil found a notepad and did as he was told. At least he now had something to do.

*

Either Christian Curtis – Kit – was a bloody good actor or he was one of the few people in the West Country unaware of the missing-person drama on the front pages. Terry's instant impression was that he lived in a world of his own fabulousness, unaware of other lives being lived around him. So when they caught up with him – working in a music shop in Wellington at a gap-year temp job – Terry believed the incredulity that stole across Kit's face. The news of Rebecca's disappearance seemed to come as a complete surprise.

'This is a wind-up, isn't it?' Kit said as they took their seats in a greasy spoon next to the shop. Ivan reached for an abandoned copy of the *Western Echo* lying on the next seat and laid it face up on the table.

The self-confidence seemed to drain out of Kit as he read the story.

'Oh, shit,' he said, repeating it several times as he fumbled in his pocket for his cigarettes.

Terry offered him a light, noting that he smoked the same brand as had been found in Rebecca's bedroom. Of course he did – Kit didn't deny his involvement.

He confirmed he'd been out with Rebecca on Wednesday. He told them he'd spent the night at her flat and had got up early the next morning to go to work. Later, he'd left the message in French on her phone.

'I wondered why she hadn't called back,' he said tonelessly. 'I thought maybe she'd, you know . . .'

His voice tailed off.

'Maybe she'd what?' Terry prompted.

Kit shrugged. He was now looking very sorry for himself. 'Regretted letting me stay the night, I suppose. Girls don't like things to go too fast, do they?'

Terry left Ivan to answer that. Female responses were his department. But Ivan didn't want to play.

'Mr Curtis, can you account for your movements between three and six o'clock yesterday afternoon?'

'I was in the shop – you can ask Ian. Why?' The penny took a moment to drop. 'Oh, Jesus, you don't think I've got anything to do with this, do you?'

As a matter of fact, they didn't. Terry could see from Ivan's expression that he'd gone off the idea now he'd met Kit in person. This was a spoilt little rich kid. As soft as shit.

'Like they say in the movies,' Terry said, 'we'd like to eliminate you from our enquiries.'

Kit didn't appear to have heard. His hand shook as he lit another cigarette from the butt of his previous one. 'Do you think she'll be OK?' he asked. Then, to Terry's astonishment, he began to cry.

Ivan rolled his eyes. 'I'll just have a word with this Ian,' he murmured as he got to his feet.

Terry watched enviously as his partner walked to the door, leaving him alone with the snivelling Kit.

Julia put her foot down as she drove back to the cottage.

She'd been delayed by a call from a farmer whose hunter was hopping lame. A neighbour had recommended her and the man had sounded so desperate she'd not been able to put him off. She'd been glad that she hadn't as she'd been able to cut into the sole of the animal's near forefoot and release pus from a corn. The result had been rare and satisfying, as the dull glaze of pain vanished instantly from the horse's eyes. It didn't often work out like that.

She applied a poultice and made a fuss of her patient, who nuzzled her gratefully.

'He's a bit overweight,' she'd said to the farmer.

'That's my kids,' he'd replied, feeding the horse a Polo mint, 'they spoil him rotten.'

She'd also spent more time than she'd planned with Callisto, talking to the old champion about Kempton the next day. She was confident about his physical condition – the muscle imbalance had responded well to her treatment and he was now back to a racing weight – but she had no idea how he would respond to the atmosphere and excitement of a racecourse.

Actually, looking at his great white-starred head, she did have a shrewd idea.

'I'm feeling good about Callisto's race,' she announced to Phil as she sat down next to him on the sofa, dislodging a notepad from his lap.

'Oh yeah?' he said, slipping an arm around her waist.

'I think he's going to love it.'

*

Later, sitting in the kitchen, Julia told herself off for barging in on Phil, prattling about her horse. She'd not thought she was interrupting something important. When she'd found him scribbling away, she'd assumed he was doing one of his exercise tasks for Simone. It turned out he was writing an open letter to the sicko who'd kidnapped Louise Fowler's friend.

He'd asked for her help and she didn't know what to say. How do you appeal to a lunatic? Phil's instinct, she knew, would be to confront him, to demand this girl's immediate return. But he couldn't do that. He had to get on the kidnapper's side. 'How do you do that?' he'd asked her, and she'd not been able to help.

She'd promised to leave him alone to think.

At moments like this she craved a cigarette.

She got to her feet and opened the door to the front room. He looked up at her expectantly.

'Have you thought,' she said, 'of calling Simone?'

Keith was anxious about the girl. Every time he looked in on her, she was lying comatose, not responding to his pokes and prods. At first he'd thought she was doing it just to spite him, but when he'd given her a bit of a slap she'd scarcely protested. It was a worry – he didn't want a seriously ill person on his hands.

At least her condition made it easy to conceal her presence. There were comings and goings all afternoon, with Fred and a couple of dog-walkers turning up. The feeling was that the next day's hunt would be called off because the ground had been frosty all week. When the confirmation came through it was a relief. Now he wouldn't have to worry about dealing with the girl on a hunting day.

He took her some tea in the evening and, to his relief, she drank it. She refused to answer when he asked how she felt, but he wasn't bothered by that. At least there was more colour in her cheeks.

He had a job for her but that could wait until tomorrow.

'I'm cold,' she said, and he fetched an extra blanket – not that she thanked him for it. Ungrateful little bitch.

Phil's column appeared next morning on the front page of the *Racing Beacon*, beside a story combining speculation about Rebecca's disappearance with a discussion of prospects in the day's big race ('CLOUD OVER GREENHILLS AS EASY DOES IT HEADS FOR HAYDOCK').

Phil's contribution – 'CHAMPION JOCKEY APPEALS TO STABLEGIRL'S KIDNAPPER' – was by far the most difficult piece he'd ever written. He'd listened closely to Charlie Lynch and had also taken Julia's advice by phoning Simone. Then Hugh had lent a hand, to the point where Phil couldn't be sure exactly who had suggested what. Even so, it was his name on the front page. And his neck on the line.

The article was set out like a letter and attempted to talk straight, as one man to another.

'You have to show him some respect,' Simone had said, 'even if only by implication.'

'Respect!' Phil had been appalled. 'He's a scumbag.'

'I suggest you don't refer to him as such. If, as you say, you want to open a line of communication.'

In the end, it read as follows:

Dear Sir

I don't know you but, as you are obviously a follower of racing, there's a good chance you know of me. You've probably backed some of my horses – and cursed me when your money's gone west. And sometimes you'll have been right to do so. We jockeys do make mistakes, as do trainers and starters and everyone else involved in the racing game. But believe me, no racing professional ever deliberately sets out to cheat the average racing fan.

Even if you find that hard to believe, I'm sure you'll agree that the last person who deserves to suffer because of the industry's faults is a part-time stablegirl like Rebecca Thornton. If you are responsible for Rebecca's disappearance, I beg you please to release her at once. You cannot possibly have any quarrel with an innocent young woman whose only crime has been to love horses and to offer a helping hand to her friend, Louise Fowler.

Right now you might be regretting your actions. Or maybe you need to talk to someone who will listen to your side of the story – someone from inside racing who can make sure your voice is heard. In that case, I offer myself as a go-between. I have no axe to grind. I just want what's best for a missing girl who is in all our thoughts.

Please call the number below and let's discuss how we can all get out of this mess – and return Rebecca safely to her family and friends.

Keith read the article in the car outside the shop. He'd gone down to collect his papers first thing, as he did every morning. He forced himself to stick to his routine – somehow it seemed important.

The front page of the *Racing Beacon* immediately grabbed his attention. Jesus Christ, the letter from Phil Nicholas was addressed to him!

He read it once through fast, hardly taking it in. Then he started again, slowly. Exactly what was going on?

He knew Phil Nicholas, of course, in the way that every punter knows the stars of their sport. He was one of the best, no doubt about that, though maybe not as good as he once was. He'd been the bastard on Snowflake who'd pipped January King at Wincanton. That was what had kicked it all off for Keith – and the Beast – but he'd not held it against Nicholas. The jockey was just a pro, doing an honest job.

Despite his contempt for the racing establishment, it was still something to get the attention of the champion jockey.

It was tempting to ring the number in the paper. To speak to the top man and reassure him the girl's life was not in danger. What would he say?

Don't worry, Mr Nicholas, you'll get Rebecca back.

When you've paid me my money.

After he'd cleaned the hounds out, he went to see her. He took with him a pencil, paper and tomato soup in a mug. And, as always, he wore the Balaclava.

She was in the same position as when he'd looked in first thing to let her use the bucket, lying on her side on the pallet. Her mouth was still taped up and she was chained by one wrist. He'd told her he'd break her fingers if she tried to pull the gag off.

She shifted her head as he came in, looking up at him accusingly, her face white and pinched. She was shivering, from pain or cold, he couldn't tell which – not that he cared. There was more life in her than there had been the day before.

He bent down and held the soup where she could see it.

'You can have that,' he said, 'if you do what I tell you. OK?'

She just stared at him defiantly. Was he going to have to tame the little bitch? Knock her into line so she'd see there was no choice but to do as she was told?

He moved closer and she edged away from him. Then he realised. It wasn't rebellion but fear.

'I won't hurt you,' he said. 'I won't lay a finger on you, but you've got to do what I say. Right?'

She nodded her head.

He put the soup and the other things on the floor.

'I'm going to take the tape off your face so you can drink this. If you scream . . .'

He didn't finish the sentence. There was no need.

He'd used wide brown parcel tape, a lot of it, wound round and round the bottom half of her face. He had made sure to leave her nose clear so she could breathe.

He took a folding knife from the pocket of his overalls. Opened it. 'Keep still,' he said, then slid the metal blade between the sticky strip and the skin of her cheek. He held it there for a few seconds, with her frozen, terror struck, not even breathing through her nostrils. He let her feel his power – it was necessary. If he wanted he could turn the blade just fractionally. Slice her face open as easily as cutting a peach. They both knew it.

He slit through the tape. Yanked the strip from her lips.

She made no sound. There was just the ragged intake of breath as she gulped air into her lungs.

He stepped away from her, folded the knife and put it back in his pocket.

'Drink the soup,' he said.

She sat up, moving slowly and painfully.

'What are you going to do with me?' she asked in a small voice as she reached for the mug.

'Don't ask questions,' he said. There was only one master here. The Beast was enjoying this.

There was a wooden straight-backed chair in the corner. He placed it next to her and put the paper and pencil on top of it. It would do as a surface to lean on.

'You're going to write a letter,' he said. 'To your mum.'

She looked at him over the top of the mug. 'She's dead.'

'Your dad, then.'

'He lives in America.'

Shit.

'Who's your closest family? Here in England.'

'My gran. But she's in a home. I can't write to her for help or anything.'

Keith was annoyed. 'What are you? A fucking orphan or something?'

She said nothing, just stared at him, her eyes full of reproach.

Then it came to him. Why change a winning formula, after all?

'You're going to write to the editor of the *Racing Beacon*. Say you're being treated all right but you're a prisoner and won't be allowed to go unless he does what he's told. Say please help me or something like that. Make him feel sorry for you. Then sign your name.'

'Do I have to have this on?' She raised her hand with the shackle on the wrist.

He considered the request. Right now he needed her to cooperate.

He unlocked the shackle and pocketed the key. Then he thrust the pencil towards her. 'OK. Now get on with it.'

As she pulled the paper towards her he heard the car. They both did.

Who the fuck could that be?

His first impulse was to stay right where he was, keeping an eye on her until the unwanted visitor had buggered off. But suppose whoever it was didn't go? He'd left doors open and the wagon was in plain view. It was pretty obvious he was about the place. Suppose it was Jellicoe? It would be just like him to turn up out of the blue. He didn't want him sniffing around the buildings. Coming in here . . .

He pulled the parcel tape from his pocket – he'd come prepared to muzzle her when he'd finished. Now he pulled a band of tape from the roll and advanced on the girl.

For a split second he could see her hesitate, wondering whether to make it difficult for him.

'Don't you fucking dare,' he growled as he slammed the tape over her mouth. He wound it round and round her head, stifling the squealing from her throat as she tried, too late, to cry out.

He was a bit rough with her but he had to be quick. There was no time for niceties.

He cut the tape, checked the knife was back safely in his pocket and moved swiftly to the door.

'Don't you even move,' he whispered before he locked her in.

He ran to the house and in through the back door, half expecting to find Jellicoe on the way. The bastard treated the place like he owned it – which, as a matter of fact, he did.

But, to his relief, the hall was empty. He slipped into the front room and looked through the net curtain into the yard. A muddy Volvo estate he did not recognise was parked there.

At that moment the doorbell rang.

Keith retraced his steps into the hall, coming face to face with his image in the mirror by the coatstand. It was just as well he did.

There was no plausible explanation for wearing a woollen hood over his face.

He snatched it off with one hand as he opened the door with the other.

Rebecca's mind was racing. Now she knew for certain she was being held by the man who'd attacked Louise's father – surely no one else would get her to write to the *Racing Beacon*. In some ways that was a relief – at least she wasn't being held by a sex pervert. On the other hand, he was the brute who'd half killed Gerry Fowler and that poor jockey who'd been shot with a crossbow. Who knew how he'd behave if the paper didn't pay him the money he demanded? Or what if things went wrong, like the other day when they'd messed up the handover? What might he do to her if that happened again?

And now, out there, someone had turned up in a car who her captor had not expected. Was there something she could do? Some way she could call attention to herself?

She put her feet on the floor and slowly stood up. It hurt – God, how it hurt, at the base of her spine and all down her left leg. She'd hobbled to the bucket in the corner earlier on and it had been agony. Now it was even worse.

She forced herself to breathe in deeply through her nostrils. She mustn't panic. This might be her one chance to save herself.

She had to do something.

At first Keith didn't recognise his visitor. The grey moustache and walking stick were familiar, but it took a moment for him to make the connection. Henry Carrington, the man who'd asked him to slaughter his horse, was the last person he expected to see standing on his doorstep.

The pensioner had a bellicose set to his jaw and a glint in his beady eyes behind his spectacles.

'So there you are, Jeffries. Thought for a moment you weren't around.'

The patronising tone added to Keith's irritation. 'I was just out the back with the hounds.' He reminded himself to be servile. 'How can I help you, sir?'

'Well . . .' The little man looked up at him, craning his neck and sticking his chin out. 'You took care of my old hunter, didn't you? Put him down for eighty pounds cash, as I recall.'

'That's right, sir.'

'So what would you say if I told you a friend of mine has seen my horse as large as life, out hunting in Derbyshire, just last weekend?'

'I'd say your friend has made a mistake, sir.' Keith put as much confidence into his voice as he could muster.

The old man blinked. 'Would you indeed?' he said. 'My friend knows Monty well. Used to hunt regularly with me down here until he retired. Then he moved north, you see.'

'How long ago would that be, sir?' Keith tried to adopt as conciliatory a tone as possible. He needed to fob the old boy off – and quickly.

'Granted, it's a while.' Carrington had pulled his chin in – a good sign, Keith concluded. 'Must be three years since he moved on.'

'Anyone can make a mistake after that length of time, sir. And, forgive my saying so, but nobody's eyesight's as good once they get past a certain age.'

'Don't I know it.' The old man barked out a mirthless laugh then stuck his chin out again. 'So you swear to me that you put Monty down as I requested?'

'On my word of honour, sir. I did it the moment you drove out of the yard. You didn't want to watch, if you remember.'

'I see. Well . . .' He took a step backward, his chin now tucked into his muffler. 'I'm sorry to have troubled you in that case.'

'No trouble at all, sir. I quite understand.'

Carrington nodded and turned towards his car. He called a curt goodbye over his shoulder. As he opened the car door, a loud crash split the air, followed by a cacophony of barking.

The crash came again. A regular and deliberate thud of something solid hitting metal.

Carrington whirled round to look back at Keith. 'What the devil is that?'

Keith hadn't a clue, but it had to be something to do with the girl.

The old man walked back across the yard. 'Is everything all right?'

'It's the hounds, sir. I've got to go and sort them out.'

'What on earth are they doing to make a noise like that?'

Carrington's dander was up, and he was gazing down the passage at the side of the house, towards the kennels.

Keith thought fast.

'There's a bloke out back doing some work on one of the pens. Bit of a noisy job, I'm afraid.'

'I thought you were here on your own.'

Had he said that? He didn't think so.

'No, sir. Fred's up from the village.'

He noted Carrington's perusal of the yard, empty but for the Volvo and the wagon; his own car was in the garage with the quad bike.

'Fred parks his cycle out the back,' he added to forestall the inevitable query. This nosy old fart was getting to be more than a nuisance. If he knew what was good for him he'd be on his way quick.

The banging continued, maybe at a slower tempo now but the noise was still loud and insistent, stoking the hounds into a frenzy.

Carrington had evidently come to a decision. 'Bloody awful racket,' he said, turning on his heel. 'I'll leave you to it.'

Keith watched him go from inside the house. Not until he'd seen the Volvo reach the bottom of the track and then, through a gap in the hedgerow, glimpsed it drive off along the road did he retrieve the Balaclava and head towards the back door.

Keith surprised himself with his self-restraint. The Beast was excited, slavering within him at the prospect of blood, but Keith kept him under control. He was impressed with himself.

The girl was using the chair to batter the corrugated-iron wall of the shed. She turned as he unlocked the door, her hair flailing, her cheeks flushed red, her eyes wide with desperation. When she saw it was him she came at him, swinging the chair. But the blow was feeble and he caught the chair in one big hand.

She tried to kick him in the crotch but he'd taken her footwear and her sock-clad foot bounced harmlessly off his thigh. Deliberately, and without malice, he felled her with one well-aimed shove. She crumpled on to the floor.

He pictured crashing his boot into her pale face. Jumping on her leg and hearing the bone snap. Stringing her up from the ceiling with his belt and watching her dangle.

He let the Beast enjoy these images as she grovelled on the floor at his feet.

He dragged her to the bed then dumped her on the straw. Using cord, he tied her hands and feet together till he was convinced she couldn't move.

He took hold of her chin and forced her to look into his eyes. Only then did he speak.

'According to the newspaper,' he said, 'you're a clever girl, Rebecca. But that wasn't very bright. That's the kind of behaviour that's going to cause you a lot of unnecessary pain.'

Her clear hazel eyes were overflowing with unreadable emotion.

'I'm sure you don't want me to feed you piece by piece to the dogs, but if you do anything like that again I will.'

Her face blanched.

He got up. 'I'll leave you to think about it. And what you're going to say in that letter.'

All in all, he reflected as he locked the door behind him, very impressive. He'd sorted her out and he'd kept the Beast under control. And he'd seen off that interfering old busybody, Carrington. He smiled as he went to quieten the hounds.

Rebecca wanted to sleep. The pain and the terror were exhausting. She'd taken a lot out of herself in battering the wall, trying to attract attention. But sleep wouldn't come.

She'd thought he was going to kill her when he'd come back in and found her with the chair. For a second she'd seen it in those mean muddy-brown eyes that showed through the slits of his woollen mask. Instead he'd smacked her down like a grown-up with a child. Against his strength she was powerless.

So, was she just going to give up? Pin her hopes on a ransom? God knows how long that would take. Could she bear it, rotting here in this dreadful place?

Did she have a choice?

She must have slept. Drifting back and forth between slumber and wakefulness, her thoughts were a jumble. One moment she was lying safely, her face on Kit's bare chest, his arms around her. The next she was wide awake, straw tickling her cheek and jolts of electric pain shooting up and down her leg.

She knew her night with Kit had been just a beautiful illusion. Already it seemed distant, part of another, unreal life that she'd never see again.

Lying bound and gagged, gripped by pain, thirsty and in terrible need – this was now her life.

She'd promised herself she wouldn't cry, but what did it matter now?

Keith gave the girl an hour. Time enough for her to realise that there was no point in trying to resist him. He'd have liked to have left it longer but he had to get this letter sorted.

He took her more soup and a couple of aspirins – that should show her there were advantages in playing ball with him.

He hauled her into a sitting position and took out his knife. Once more he slid it under the tape around her mouth.

'No noise,' he said, and waited for her to nod feebly before he cut the gag away.

He cut the cords around her wrists too but left her legs tied. She wouldn't need her feet to write a letter.

She warmed her hands on the mug and sipped as he once more set out the chair and paper.

'Remember what you were going to do earlier?'

She nodded. He put the pencil in her hand.

'Write like I told you.'

'Can I . . .?' She stopped. 'I want to use the bucket.'

Jesus! He felt like saying no and ordering her to do that letter first. But that was the Beast thinking. Keith knew he needed her cooperation.

He bent and roughly hacked through the cord that bound her feet. 'Hurry up,' he said.

*

Rebecca hobbled slowly across the stone floor, trying to ease the stiffness from her aching limbs. She fumbled with her jeans as she pushed them down her hips, squatting awkwardly on the cold metal rim of the bucket.

He stood there by the door, watching her every move.

If anyone had told her that one day she would relieve herself in front of a stranger without shame she would not have believed them. It was weird how quickly life could change.

She felt no shame because she could think only of survival. For the first time since she had been captured she wore no chains or bonds – and the door to her prison was unlocked.

There was only him.

Keith told her again what he wanted her to say and, at last, she began to write. He stood over her and tried to read what she was writing, but she protested. 'I can't do it with you standing there like that.'

He backed away and forced himself to wait. She seemed to be taking an age. His patience was running out.

Finally he peered down at the paper.

Dear Editor
Please help me. I'm being kept prisoner. I don't know where I am exactly but it's not more than an hour by road from Greenhills Yard. I'm locked in a shed out in the country and I'm surrounded by dogs—

The little cow. He couldn't send that!

He didn't see it coming. There was just the blur in the corner of his vision and the piercing needle of fire entering his left eye. His body convulsed in agony and his hands flew automatically to his face, knocking aside the skewering piece of wood.

The bitch had blinded him with the pencil!

He heard the scuffle of her feet on the floor and the rattle of the door behind him.

She was getting away.

He blundered after her, holding a hand to his head, squinting through his right eye. He could see her turning past the first hound pen. He ran after her. He had to catch her.

He found himself at the back door to the house. Had she gone inside?

A sudden howling and yapping from the last of the pens next to the field informed him otherwise. The hounds were telling him something.

He caught her getting through the gate into the cow pasture beyond the pens. She cried out as he grabbed her by the shoulder, throwing her to the ground.

Then the Beast took over.

Keith squinted at the broken doll down by his feet.

He never meant it to happen. He'd thought the Beast was under control.

But she'd pushed the Beast too far and paid the price.

What a bloody fiasco.

Keith had lived with the Beast long enough to suffer, many times, for his excesses. But there'd never been anything like this.

He mustn't allow himself to dwell on it. As ever, it was up to him to sort out the mess.

First he got the body out of sight and cleaned up the shed where she'd been, raking it out and hosing it down. He'd burn the straw bedding in the incinerator along with the body.

He wasn't squeamish about disposing of the corpse – she was just another dead animal when it came down to it – but he'd have to take exceptional care. No trace of the girl must be left. It would be a laborious task, and his eye was hurting so much he couldn't start just yet.

He should have put ice on the wound at once, he thought as he looked at the swelling around the ripped flesh. He'd been lucky, though. The little bitch could have blinded him, but the pencil point had missed the eyeball, gouging into the outer rim of the socket. He remembered it had stuck there, entangled in his skin and the wool of the Balaclava, until he'd knocked it away.

The eye was full of blood and gunk and his vision was misty. The deep furrow running almost to the top of his ear needed stitching. That was too bad. He washed the eye and disinfected the wound. By the time he had applied a strip of lint and fixed it to his face with a strip of Elastoplast he looked horrific. What he needed was an eye patch – and a good cover story.

As he worked he thought more rationally. He could yet make something of this disaster.

When he went back to the outhouse he put the body in a large plastic refuse sack and transferred it to the wagon. He reckoned he could drive with one eye if he took it carefully.

He drove the wagon slowly through the lanes. He'd be better out on the motorway. He planned to take a long circuitous route back, taking his time so he could pitch up at Middleton's farm to collect a dead heifer – just like normal.

He'd find a good spot for the girl. He'd considered a note, but what was the point? The message was clear. Next time they'd pay up without pissing him around.

Maybe there was method in the madness of the Beast after all.

Chapter Ten

Louise was trying, really trying, not to show Justin Delancy that she was falling apart. The banker was not the easiest company at the best of times – he seemed to have no small talk whatsoever – and these were far from the best of times. She suspected the only reason Greenhills was still running Delancy's horses was that he'd not been able to move Easy Does It to another yard ahead of today's Grand National trial. It followed, therefore, that their best hope of retaining his business – short of a miraculous recovery by her father – was for the horse to put up a good show that afternoon. Winning well might solve the problem.

Meanwhile anxiety about Rebecca was eating her up. She should be in Becky's place. Charlie Lynch had brushed it aside, but she knew the kidnapper had really been looking for her. The thought was hard to live with, and it got worse as time went by.

Her mother had begged her not to make the trip to Haydock, but what else was she to do? It was important she was available to glad-hand their most difficult owner. Besides, she'd go mad back at Greenhills just waiting for news of her absent friend.

Delancy had taken a hospitality box to entertain his City cronies and their wives. To be fair, most of them were solicitous towards her. A woman she'd never met before put her arms around her and said she was an inspiration. Louise had thanked her, biting back the tears. Tell that to Becky, she thought.

On the whole she preferred hobnobbing with the men – balding, bejowled and sleek, pneumatic stomachs straining at their waistbands. They talked money and horses, topics that went hand in glove. And when, briefly, mention was made of her father's assault and Rebecca's abduction, they were of the opinion that a swift bullet between the eyes of whoever was responsible would save a lot of time and trouble. Normally Louise would have recoiled at such sentiments, but right now they gave her some bitter comfort.

Delancy himself was not sleek or jowly. He was tall and lean with an angular face that scarcely moved. Only his eyes were animated, flicking from side to side, recording like a camera shutter, missing nothing. His hair was thin and grey, plastered to his scalp with some kind of gel. A lizard of a man who made Louise's flesh creep.

They'd not come face to face before.

'You're prettier than your father, I'll say that for you,' had been his opening remark.

She supposed it was a compliment but it unnerved her, and she tried to overcome her awkwardness by talking earnestly about Easy Does It, how well he'd been working and how the soft ground would suit him.

Delancy listened to her prattle on and said, 'Have you spoken to O'Neil yet?'

Jimmy O'Neil, a well-known Irish rider, had been booked to partner Easy Does It at Delancy's insistence.

Before she could reply he added, 'I hope you've told him to hold the horse up. Now we've got a decent jockey on board we can ride a proper race.'

Louise's heart sank at this mention of race tactics. Her dad had told her that all the horse did was gallop and stay. His best means of winning was to set the pace from the start and wear his rivals down. Honest performer though he was, the one attribute he did not possess was a turn of speed.

Unfortunately, his owner did not see it that way.

Louise replied that she'd had a preliminary chat with the jockey and he was full of enthusiasm for the horse. She didn't reveal that, when she gave the jockey a leg-up in the parade ring, she intended to instruct him to get after Easy Does It from the start and let the rest of the field try and keep up.

Delancy's eyes narrowed. He had his suspicions, she could tell.

'You don't want to discuss it, do you? Answer me this, then – is he going to win? Yes or no?'

She should have ducked the question, laughed it off somehow as her father would. Instead she hesitated, gulped and said, 'Yes, of course.'

The lizard eyes flickered over her. 'So I can expect a refund of my training fees if he doesn't?'

He was a horrible man. He didn't deserve to own horses.

Phil was prepared for the ribbing that greeted him as he walked through the weighing area and into the changing-rooms. Nothing and nobody was sacred in the confines of the jockeys' quarters – least of all the disappearance of a pretty girl. As jump jockeys the lads were optimists to a man – as far as they were concerned Rebecca was going to turn up at any moment, and Phil's article was a source of amusement.

'You crafty sod. I bet you've got her locked up somewhere yourself,' yelled one of the Geordie lads.

Phil had no choice but to take the flak – the changing-room was that sort of place. He was more worried about how he would handle a call from the kidnapper should it come through. The police had given him a mobile phone designated for the purpose and he handled it like a primed hand grenade.

Thankfully he had only one ride to worry about, in the Grand National trial. Captain Redbeard was a relatively inexperienced horse for a gruelling three-and-a-half-mile chase over Haydock's big, scary fences but, if he put his best foot forward, Phil knew he should go close.

Suddenly the police mobile burst into life, blotting all other matters from his thoughts.

He took a deep breath and answered the call.

Louise excused herself from the Delancy box, promising to see the banker in the parade ring shortly. She needed a break to prepare herself for the next act in this ordeal. She pushed her way through the crowd. When she found Jimmy O'Neil she would tell him to disregard any instructions Delancy might give him about Easy Does It.

She was so preoccupied she did not see Hugh until he was on top of her.

'Louise,' he said, blocking her path.

She felt a rush of relief at the sight of him.

Hugh grabbed her arm, pulling her out of the crowd. 'Come with me.' His voice was insistent.

She protested. 'I'm in a rush, Hugh. I've got to talk to my jockey.'

'They've found a body, Louise.'

The shock sucked the air from her lungs. The people around them seemed to disappear. There was just Hugh in front of her, his face grave.

He lowered his voice. 'It's not official but they think it's Rebecca.'

Someone was moaning, a high-pitched keening like an animal in pain. The sound was coming from her.

'I'm sorry,' Hugh murmured, pulling her into the shelter of his arms.

Phil weighed out in a daze. He flicked his whip against his boot as he walked towards the parade ring and flexed his left arm, the one he'd broken. He went through all the regular reflex actions he performed before a race. They helped somehow.

The phone call had not been from the kidnapper. A DS Stone had told him a young woman's body had been discovered in a ditch behind a lay-by on the M5. It was probably the missing girl. In the circumstances, Stone had said, they doubted they would be forwarding any calls.

Though Phil said nothing, news of the discovery spread round the changing-room and the atmosphere became subdued. A couple of the lads who had been taking the mickey came up to Phil and apologised – not that Phil had even met Rebecca.

Phil had never felt less like riding in a race. It seemed a ridiculous thing to be doing in these circumstances. What did a contest between a bunch of horses matter?

'Are you all right?' Russell said.

Phil realised the trainer had been briefing him on the race ahead and he'd not taken in a word he'd said.

'Yeah,' he said. He didn't want to go into it. He had no idea what Russell had made of the kidnapping or his article in the paper that morning. But, whatever he felt, Russell wouldn't want to discuss it right now. He made his living training racehorses, and he was the best in the business. At moments like this, five minutes before a race, that was all that mattered to him.

'I'm fine, honest,' Phil added, lying through his teeth.

By the time Chris got word to stand in for Louise, Delancy and his wife had been chatting to the jockey in the parade ring for a couple of minutes.

'Where's little Miss Fowler got to, then?' demanded the owner.

'She's been taken ill. She's gone to the ambulance room.' That was all that Chris was inclined to tell them. He'd head over to see how she was coping once he'd got shot of the Delancys.

'I thought she wasn't looking well,' said Mrs Delancy. 'She didn't eat a thing at lunch.'

The owner put his hand on Jimmy O'Neil's shoulder. He seemed about twice the height of the diminutive jockey. 'You've got your marching orders. Give it your best shot.'

Chris gave Jimmy a leg-up on to Easy Does It.

'Do you know how to ride this fellow?'

'I reckon so. The owner's been chewing my ear off. He says I'm on an extra present if I get him home in front.'

'Lucky old you.'

Jimmy set off round the ring. The Delancys were already striding across the grass, eager to get in position for the race. Chris had barely managed to be civil to them. He felt bad enough that Rebecca had been snatched while he'd been giving her a hard time. He rushed off in search of Louise, guilt eating him up.

A nurse ushered Chris into the ambulance room, where Louise was sitting on the bed with a blanket around her shoulders. A large fellow in spectacles who Chris recognised as a reporter was perched on a chair near by.

'I heard,' Chris mumbled.

He sat on the bed next to Louise and took her hand. She gazed at him with red-rimmed, haunted eyes. He didn't know what to say. His gaze strayed to the reporter, who was staring at the television above their heads on a wall bracket.

'What's he doing here?' he muttered and, without waiting for her reply, said aggressively 'Oy, you, push off. No press.'

The big bloke looked at him. He didn't move.

'I want Hugh to stay,' she said softly. 'Be friends, please, Chris.'

He nodded. Whatever she wanted.

'Some bastard's going to pay for this,' he said. It didn't make him feel any better.

The three of them sat in silence as the racing commentary washed over them.

*

Phil was riding as if on autopilot – he'd never done that before in a race. He looked down on jockeys who admitted to riding with their minds on other things. To Phil's way of thinking, the guy rehashing last night's row with his girlfriend had no place in a horserace. To ride well, to get the most out of the horse beneath you, required a hundred per cent concentration – more, if possible. That was what set winners apart from losers. The longer he kept at it, the more he realised that racing was a mind game.

But right now his mind was elsewhere – on the broken body of some poor girl he'd never met. He'd often felt sympathy for murder victims, like everyone did. They were someone's sister or mother, husband or brother. But this time he felt more than just sympathy. He'd been asked to play a part in saving Rebecca – and he'd failed. Failed in a spectacular, public fashion. The carefully composed newspaper article that was meant to offer the poor girl a lifeline had been answered in the most damning way possible. There had been no chance for Rebecca after all. He just hoped what he'd said in the paper hadn't made things worse.

Captain Redbeard was in a good rhythm and jumping easily out of the soft ground. There were only ten runners and Easy Does It, who usually made the running, was being held up, so the pace was sensible. They were at the end of the first circuit already, and he could hardly remember how they got there. Perhaps there was something to be said for autopilot after all.

Chris finally broke the silence.

'What the hell does O'Neil think he's doing? He's never going to win from back there.'

They'd all been watching the race. It was their lives. It was what they did. Innocent girls died cruel deaths, but the business of racing went on.

'I never got to brief Jimmy,' said Louise. 'I was on my way to talk to him when I heard about Becky.'

Chris turned to her. 'That shouldn't have made any difference. Mr Delancy talked to him.'

'But Delancy wanted him held up. He said now we had a proper jockey we should ride a proper race.'

Chris groaned. He too had thought Delancy had ditched his half-baked ideas about how his horse should be run.

'I guess we'll see who's right, then,' he said. 'He's got to make a move now or he'll be run out of it.'

In a weird way, Phil found the burden of his knowledge helpful. As they entered the back straight for the second time, with four menacing fences and an open ditch ahead, he felt the familiar bubble of panic form in his stomach. Other runners were around him now, the big shape of Easy Does It bearing in on the outside and a tiring horse pecking at the jump ahead. This was shaping up as his nightmare scenario – travelling at speed on an iffy jumper, hemmed in on all sides with no chance of escape should someone make a mistake.

He thought of Rebecca, dead in a ditch at the age of nineteen, and of his pathetic attempt to help her. The bubble in his belly shrank and he sailed over the fence ahead, landing upsides of the tiring animal in his path.

He nudged the Captain on, lengthening his stride into the next.

Though she'd never admit it, Julia was happy not to be at Haydock with her husband. Seeing Phil through his psychological bad patch was hard work, and she could do with a break. Today she had her own worries, but the possibilities were exciting. Callisto was having his first run for two years in a race for horses who hadn't won anything for more than twelve months.

Because Callisto had been such a good horse, finding a suitable race for his comeback hadn't been easy. Julia didn't want him to lump top weight around in a handicap. Neither did she want to throw him in against top-class horses who were race fit. In the end, she had decided on this three-mile hurdle at Kempton. It was a bit too far for him, but at least there wouldn't be the strain on his pelvis which he might get from jumping fences. And if he got tired, Mark could simply pull him up.

It had been a last-minute decision to enter the race, but it felt right and she had no regrets, nervous as she was about the outcome. Phil's dad, Ted, was acting as groom, and the owners, Jack and Yvonne Mitton, were in attendance. The only thing that could have improved the day was if Phil had been riding. Instead, Mark – at Phil's request – was in the saddle. He'd put quite a bit of work into the horse and deserved to be on board.

Julia had spent time on the phone with Yvonne but she'd not met her before. She was unprepared for the sight of a tiny, water-thin woman who walked with a cane and leant heavily on her husband's arm. Her voice, though, was full of vigour as she said, 'I can't believe Callisto is racing again. Do you really think he's ready?'

They'd been over this before on the phone, but Julia hadn't been entirely straightforward. Now, seeing the anticipation in Yvonne's face, she had the urge to confide in her further. She detached the frail woman from Jack, who took the hint and disappeared to check out the bookmakers' expectations of Callisto's chances.

'To be honest,' Julia said, 'I don't know if he really is ready. I just know he wants to have a go.'

Yvonne cocked her head on one side and looked at her shrewdly.

Julia continued. 'He ambles around most of the time like he couldn't give a monkey's, but when I get him to do a piece of work he wakes up. The more you ask him to do, the more he does. I was wondering one morning if he'd like to go racing again and—' She hesitated. This could be embarrassing.

'Go on.'

'He just looked at me and it was as if he'd said "Of course I bloody well do".'

Yvonne didn't say anything. Julia wondered whether she should have kept her mouth shut.

'It's stupid of me,' she said hastily. 'I often imagine I can hear horses speak.'

Yvonne squeezed her arm. 'You're not the only one, my dear.'

Captain Redbeard was jumping like a stag, which was rather out of character. He'll cock one up in a minute, thought Phil, as they came out of the bottom bend into the home straight for the last time. There were nearly four furlongs left to go and just three fences to negotiate.

They'd made progress through the field and now they were lying fourth with the fancied Easy Does It a length adrift. Phil was feeling confident. The favourite looked like he was going flat out just to keep up the pace, and the horse ahead was beginning to wobble. The Captain, on the other hand, seemed to have plenty left in the tank.

A tremendous leap at the second last took them within two lengths of the leaders. The Captain was turbocharged and the rest were going backward.

I'm bloody well going to do this, Phil thought as he galloped towards the last.

The riderless horse came out of nowhere, rushing gleefully past them on the inside and then veering away from the fence into their path. There was nothing Phil could do.

Suddenly he was spinning through the air in slow motion, instinctively curling into a ball and bouncing on the turf as he took the impact. The ground shuddered as horses thundered over him, showering him with mud, deafening him with the thumping hooves and their riders' shouts. Then the din receded and all was quiet.

Phil wiggled his toes, left foot then right foot. He twisted his pelvis gingerly and moved his legs. It was OK, he was in working order.

He was on his feet before the paramedics reached him, unplugging earth from his ear. He was still alive – unlike some.

Captain Redbeard's fall left Easy Does It in fourth place. Next to Louise in the ambulance room, Chris was on his feet, yelling at the screen. Hugh too was transfixed, exclaiming loudly as the loose horse wiped out Phil Nicholas.

Louise also stared at the television, but for once the sight of a horse race did not work its familiar magic. It was simply a diversion. She wished the race would never end so she could keep the reality of Becky's death at arm's length. Did it really matter who won or lost?

She could see Easy Does It was not going to get past the horses in front of him. As all Greenhills knew, he was a one-paced horse and had to be ridden accordingly. Unfortunately, Jimmy O'Neil had never ridden him before and he'd been given the wrong instructions.

As Easy Does It crossed the line five lengths behind the horse in third place, the consequences were clear to Louise. Justin Delancy would blame her for the defeat and send his horses elsewhere.

Well, so what?

Phil refused a lift in the ambulance and trudged back to the unsaddling enclosure to find Russell waiting for him.

'So what happened?'

'Is the Captain all right?' Phil said. He'd not seen the horse since he'd been dumped on his backside.

'He's fine,' Russell replied shortly, not to be deflected. 'What went wrong?'

Phil shrugged. 'I ran into a loose horse.' What else was there to say?

'You shouldn't have been back in the pack like that. I told you to get him out and make the pace.'

Phil was puzzled. 'We were all expecting Easy Does It to do that.'

Russell sighed in exasperation. 'But he didn't, did he? And I happened to know he wouldn't, which is why I told you to get out there and take advantage. Only you weren't listening, were you?'

Phil couldn't deny it. He remembered the trainer's words before the race completely passing him by in the shock of hearing about the girl's body. 'Sorry, boss.'

Russell gave him his death's-head glare. 'I don't know what's up with you these days, Phil.'

The return to Kempton of the old favourite, Callisto, had attracted much enthusiasm from a generous crowd, and sentimental money had pushed his price down to 5–2.

'Ridiculous,' snorted Jack. 'He hasn't run for two years.'

To Julia, Callisto had the air of someone trying to look blasé but who was really as pleased as punch.

'See,' she said to Yvonne as they watched him go down to the start from the balcony of Jack's box, 'he's trying to look cool, like he's won here many times before, but he's drinking it all in.'

Yvonne laughed, the paper-thin skin wrinkling around her eyes. 'He can't get enough of it. Of course, he has won here in the past.'

'And he was second in the King George,' chipped in Jack. 'He even led the field turning for home but it was too far for him.'

He was hopping from foot to foot, like a schoolboy putting off a trip to the toilet. Julia realised he suffering from nerves, as she was herself.

'Just as long as the old boy doesn't trail in half a mile behind,' he said.

Amen to that.

'Too bad if he does,' said Yvonne, fidgeting in her handbag and producing a packet of cigarettes.

Jack glared at her. 'Where did you get those?'

She shrugged and peeled off the cellophane.

'Macpherson would have a fit,' Jack continued.

'Stuff the bloody doctor,' she said blithely, and offered the packet to Julia.

She shouldn't. She'd sworn off them since the last time.

She took the thin white tube and eagerly accepted Yvonne's lighter. She lit both of their cigarettes. Bliss. With the first drag that nagging uncertainty in the pit of her stomach disappeared. Good luck, Callisto. What will be, will be.

Jack was still hopping. His face a scowl of disapproval.

'And I thought you'd be good for her,' he muttered at Julia.

Yvonne giggled and waved the packet under his nose.

'Oh, sod it,' he said, and took one.

Mark had been thrilled when Phil had asked him to ride Callisto, though he'd taken care not to show it.

'What's up? Don't you fancy it yourself, then?'

'I can't, I'm too busy.'

Mark was well aware of that. Phil was too busy cocking up rides he should have had.

'You'd be doing Julia a real favour,' Phil continued.

'In that case – anything for the gorgeous Julia' – which was a stupid thing to say, but Phil didn't appear to mind.

'Thanks, mate,' he'd said, clapping Mark on the back.

So, for the past few days, Mark had made himself available to ride Callisto out and discuss progress and tactics with Julia. It had all been strictly above board. There'd been no return to the flirting of a few weeks back, but a man could dream, couldn't he? And spending time with the curly-haired blonde in her tight jodhpurs gave rise to some pretty interesting dreams. Phil was such a lucky bastard. Of course, a word in the right ear about his visits to a shrink might change that luck. He'd been hoping that Russell might have drawn his own conclusions about Phil's recent performances, but apparently not. Maybe he'd have to give the trainer a nudge.

Mark put the thought to one side and concentrated on the race ahead. Callisto had come on a treat. He'd shed weight and, thanks to Julia's regime, built up muscle on his weakened right side, so he now moved in a straight line. The big question – among many smaller ones – was whether his long-term injury would hold up under race conditions.

So far, so good, thought Mark. There'd been a spring in the horse's step as he'd gone down to the start, as if he was eager to get on with business. That suited Mark just fine; he was eager to get on with it himself and show Julia what he could do. He'd give the horse a damn sight better ride than her old man could, that was for sure.

Julia's instructions had been to take it easy, but Mark was not inclined to plod around at the back of the field.

'Why don't I just play it by ear?' he'd suggested. 'You know, see how he gets on. If he doesn't fancy it I'll pull him up.'

Now, as the tapes went up and the horses surged forward, he tried to get a feel for the animal beneath him.

At home, everything Callisto did seemed like a real effort. Now, as they raced towards the first flight of hurdles, Mark was shocked by the horse's power. He took a firm tug on the reins and concentrated on getting him settled. But as they got within a dozen strides of the small obstacles, Callisto took control and surged forward. It was as if he were saying, 'You sit still and I'll show you what a real horse can do.'

He stood off the hurdle what seemed to Mark to be a stride too soon. Mark held his breath, but Callisto sailed through the air, landing just as far the other side and passing four horses as he did so. The old fellow fancied it all right.

Towards the end of the afternoon, Louise summoned up the courage to seek out Delancy.

'You don't have to see him, you know,' said Hugh. 'I'll take him a message, if you like. Explain the circumstances.'

'He won't care about the circumstances. In any case, it's my job to go.'

He offered to accompany her but, much as she would have liked that, she stepped into Delancy's box on her own.

'I'm glad to see you're feeling better,' the banker observed. Why did everything he said sound insincere? Surely that was a drawback in the business world?

'I'm sorry I wasn't on hand before the race,' she said.

He dismissed her apology with a blink of his reptilian eyes. 'I've decided to move Easy Does It. I'm sure it won't come as a surprise.'

It didn't, but it still hurt.

'That's not fair,' she protested. 'He would have done much better if he'd been allowed to make the running.'

'It's not just one race, Miss Fowler. It's my observation that your yard is a shambles without your father at the helm. I'm sorry for what's happened to him but I can't make decisions based on sentiment.'

'But Dad will be back soon!' she blurted out. 'What shall I tell him?'

'Tell him that I'm moving my horses to Russell Dean. I'm sure Greenhills will soon be back on form but I can't afford to wait.'

'You bastard,' she said without thinking.

He was unfazed. 'You're not the first to call me that, Miss Fowler. I take it as a compliment.'

Julia took great pleasure from watching Yvonne Mitton as Callisto led the field around Kempton Park. The small, thin woman squealed with excitement as the horse stretched out, soaring over the hurdles. Yvonne's delight was almost as pleasing as Callisto's performance.

'My word,' said Jack, 'it's as if he's never been away.'

The horse was ten lengths clear at the two-mile marker, despite putting in enormous and unnecessary leaps at the hurdles.

'You can see he's really a steeplechaser,' said Julia. 'He's not touched one of those hurdles.'

'We're going to win,' cried Yvonne, gripping Julia's hand so tightly it was painful. 'Jack said you were a miracle-worker.'

It was all going so well that Julia bit back her words of caution. Maybe Callisto would win – what a triumph that would be.

But a triumphant comeback wasn't really on the cards. Halfway down the back straight on the second circuit, Julia saw Callisto flag. Suddenly he was treading water and the chasing pack were closing fast. He took the next hurdle in customary style, but by the time his back legs had cleared the obstacle the next horse was level. Three animals went past him in a knot as Callisto laboured in their wake.

'Oh, no,' cried Yvonne.

'He's pulling him up,' muttered Jack. 'I guess he did pretty well to get so far.'

'Never mind,' said Yvonne, her disappointment obvious.

Julia had her eye on the horse as Mark led him slowly back. She just hoped he hadn't broken down.

*

Keith had only had two awkward moments so far – three, if you counted explaining the state of his eye. Neither Fred nor his lad, Jeff, who'd come up to help exercise the hounds, had looked convinced when he'd told them about slipping on to a garden stake when clearing the vegetable patch. Jeff had laughed and asked him to demonstrate, but Fred told him to belt up. Then he'd winked at Keith and said, 'I'd hate to see the other fellow.'

Keith had let that pass, but he'd had to think on his feet when they'd let the hounds out and they'd made straight for the gate into the cow pasture – the spot where the Beast had dealt with the girl. To Keith's alarm, the hounds were all over it.

'Something's gone on,' said Fred.

'A fox must have had a rabbit out here,' Keith said.

Jeff was peering intently at the ground. The boy had sharp eyes as Keith knew well enough. 'I don't see no fur or nothing,' he complained.

Keith was relieved when they moved off. He'd cleaned up by the gate as best he could, so there was nothing obvious to see. Of course, if police forensic people were to go over it that would be a different story.

But his biggest fright came later, when he got Fred to help him with the heifer. They'd got it inside to skin and cut up when Keith saw, standing on the floor by the incinerator, the girl's boots. He'd meant to burn them but there they still were. Shiny leather riding boots, size four or five, just screaming out for Fred to notice and say, 'Whose are those?' And what would he say then?

But Fred was such a pillock he never saw a blind thing and Keith sent him off to fetch him some headache pills – which he needed, that was no lie.

As he tucked the boots out of sight, Keith thanked his lucky stars sharp-eyed young Jeff was still in with the hounds.

The whole business with the girl had been a cock-up. He'd acted on impulse and everything had gone wrong. He had to learn from his mistakes.

Next time he'd have a proper plan.

'Is he all right?' Julia called to Mark as he rode Callisto back to the unsaddling area. She was relieved to see that the jockey was smiling.

'Sure,' he said. 'He just ran out of puff. I didn't want to take any chances so I pulled him out.'

Julia took the reins as Mark slipped from the saddle. Callisto blew a plume of hot air into her face as he lowered his head to be patted.

'I though he was going to pull my arms off at the start,' said Mark. 'He's still got the guts for it, all right, but next time don't waste him on pissy little hurdles.'

'I don't know that there will be a next time.'

Mark looked shocked. 'It would be terrible shame not to give him another go. He loves it.'

'Don't tell me – tell them.' Julia pointed towards Jack and Yvonne Mitton, who were slowly walking towards them across the turf. 'This might be just a one-off.'

'Do *you* want to run him again?' the jockey asked.

She considered the veteran horse. He was breathing easily and his ears were pricked. He looked pretty pleased with himself, she thought.

'You bet,' she said.

Phil was in the weighing-room, still only half dressed, when Julia called. He could tell she was excited, and remembered in a flash that today had been Callisto's comeback race. He should have looked out for the result. It had completely slipped his mind.

He listened to her cheerful account of the afternoon's race. Mark had pulled the old horse up before the finish but not before he'd torn the field apart over two and a half miles.

'He needed that race,' she said gleefully. 'We're going to run him at Cheltenham. Maybe in the Grand Annual or the Mildmay of Flete. A shorter race over fences will be perfect for him.'

'Sounds good, Jules. Congratulations.'

'How are you, darling?' He could tell she'd picked up that things weren't good.

'I came off. But it's OK, I've just got a couple of bruises.'

'And?'

Obviously she didn't yet know about Rebecca. He wished he didn't have to tell her.

Chapter Eleven

Charlie sat wearily on the bed and bent to untie his shoes. It was almost midnight, and he'd had about six hours' sleep in the last two days. He was determined to get his head down for a few hours, till daybreak at least. He was getting too old for this.

The irritating chirp of his mobile phone broke the silence. Grumbling to himself, the detective got back to his feet and searched through the jacket which he'd tossed on to the chair by the window.

As expected, John Petrie came on the line. He'd been trying to trace Rebecca's father in the States, which had proved to be a difficult task. Richard Thornton ran an antiques business in Philadelphia and spent a lot of time on the road.

'We've finally tracked him down,' he said. 'The Philadelphia PD say he's on an overnight flight. He lands at Heathrow at around half-six in the morning.'

'Thanks, John. Get Terry to pick me up at four.'

'Due respect, boss, but can't someone else fetch him? Give yourself a couple more hours in bed.'

'No.' He realised he sounded angry. He wasn't angry with John, though. 'Put yourself in that poor man's shoes. If I were him I'd want the Chief Constable himself to show up and tell me what was going on. But he'll just have to make do with me.'

Across the road a silver BMW drew to a halt and a man and a woman got out. He was tall and broad, in a well-cut suit; she wore a figure-hugging evening dress and carried a wrap. Their laughter floated up into the bedroom.

'Anything else?'

As the couple walked beneath a streetlamp, Charlie realised Amy was being escorted home from an evening out. The man had his arm around her shoulder.

'We've had two calls from Phil Nicholas. He says he doesn't want to be a nuisance, guv, but can you ring him? Any time till midnight.'

Phil Nicholas? Charlie had to think. Of course – the jockey.

A light came on in Amy's porch as she searched in her purse for the key. The man, Charlie realised, was younger than her. Much younger than himself.

Amy opened the door and stepped inside, the man following. He had his hand on the swell of her hip. The door closed behind them.

Charlie said goodnight to Petrie and rang off. He stared at the house opposite, waiting for the lights to come on. But in which room? The living room – or the bedroom?

He chuckled and pulled his own bedroom curtains closed with a jerk.

Good luck to you, BMW man, he thought.

Even though it had now gone midnight, Charlie rang Phil. It was now or never – he wouldn't have time tomorrow.

The phone was snatched up on the first ring. The jockey sounded agitated.

'I'm sorry to pester you, Inspector, but I just wanted a word about what's happened. You don't think my article in the *Beacon* had anything to do with Rebecca being killed, do you?'

Charlie had no idea but he wasn't going to say that. 'No, Phil, I don't think that's the case.'

'It's just that, having stuck my oar in, I'm worried I've made everything worse.'

The policeman heard the anguish in the other man's voice. He did his best to reassure him. 'Mr Nicholas, we're all very grateful for your help. Personally, I can't believe that what you wrote had anything to do with the murder.'

The jockey took a moment to reply. 'Thanks, Inspector. That makes me feel a bit better.'

As Charlie put the phone down he reflected that the jockey didn't sound better at all.

Phil drove to Deanscroft early the next morning, determined not to dwell on Rebecca's murder. He'd thought for a moment he had a chance to do some good, but it hadn't worked out. He'd just have to live with it.

He wouldn't normally have turned up for work on a Sunday but, with the Cheltenham Festival just over a fortnight off, the Deanscroft runners were cantering every day. One of Phil's favourites, Wolf Patrol, was running at Leicester in two days' time. If he came through that in good shape, Russell planned to have a tilt at the Royal & Sunalliance Novices' Chase on the Cheltenham Wednesday card. Phil could honestly say he was looking forward to it. Maybe he really was putting his riding problems behind him.

As he got out of his car, Russell called him over.

'How are you feeling today?' he asked. There was an edge to his voice.

'Fine.'

'Are you sure?'

Phil was puzzled by this sudden interest in his wellbeing.

'Only you weren't exactly on top form yesterday, were you?' Russell continued.

Phil was on the point of explaining why his mind hadn't been on the job, but thought better of it. No excuse, not even the discovery of Rebecca's body, would be reason enough for Russell.

He shrugged. 'I'm raring to go today, boss. We've got some big races coming up.'

Russell nodded slowly, as if weighing his words. Phil had a feeling he wasn't going to like what was coming next.

'I was going to suggest, Phil, that you took it easy for the next week or so. Get yourself in shape for Cheltenham.'

'But I am in shape. My knee's not playing up any more. I'm as fit as a fiddle.'

Russell's grey eyes narrowed. 'I didn't mean physical shape so much as mental.'

'Mental?' Phil could feel his face begin to colour.

'I know you've been having a few problems. I wish you'd told me you were seeing a shrink.'

Phil was speechless. How the hell did he know that?

'To be honest,' Russell continued, 'I feel a bit let down. I trust my jockeys to tell me if they get a knock and can't ride. If you've got a mind problem it's the same thing.'

'I haven't got a mind problem.' Phil found himself shouting.

Russell put a fatherly arm across his shoulder and Phil fought the impulse to brush it away.

'Listen to me, Phil. You are the best race-rider I've ever had on my horses but, right now, you're not in top form. I need you in good shape for Cheltenham. Take a break between now and the Festival.'

Phil made a conscious effort to control his temper as he replied. 'I'd rather not do that, Russell. I want to keep riding.'

The trainer stepped away from him. 'Well, I don't want you on my horses this week. Take a few days off – it's in your own interests.'

Phil stared at him.

'What about Wolf Patrol?' he demanded. 'At least let me ride him.'

'Sorry, Phil.' The smile had returned to Russell's face now he had won the argument. 'You need a complete rest.'

'Who is going to ride him, then?'

But Phil knew the answer to that. Mark would be riding Wolf Patrol and all the other horses that would have come his way. And if he performed well, who was to say he wouldn't keep the ride at the Festival?

Phil drove out of the yard in a rage.

At first Julia had shared Phil's outrage at his being banned from Russell Dean's horses, though privately she wondered whether a few days' rest from the strains of race-riding might not be good for him. Then, as Phil began to speculate about how Russell could have learned of his appointments with Simone, she fell silent.

As Phil's suspicions roamed from a hospital receptionist who might have recognised him to Simone herself, Julia realised at once who it was likely to be. Mark. She'd not meant to tell him and she'd asked him to keep it secret, but it made sense. Who else was liable to profit from Phil's absence? And she knew how much he resented being number two to Phil.

She was deeply disappointed in Mark Shaw. But nowhere near as disappointed as she was in herself.

Gerry Fowler was in a state. He badly wanted to get home but the doctors were insisting he remained where he was for the moment. He could get around the ward on crutches but he remained very sore. He still had a lot of mending to do.

For two pins he'd ignore the doctors and discharge himself, but he couldn't ignore his wife.

'I should be in the yard,' he begged. 'It's too much for Chris and Louise to deal with.'

'They're doing fine,' Anne said. 'Considering the circumstances.'

Gerry fell silent. They'd discussed those circumstances endlessly, particularly Rebecca's murder and the permanent police presence in the yard. Louise was obviously in danger.

'I want to keep an eye on her myself,' he said. 'She needs her father close by.'

'She needs her father fit and well,' Anne replied. 'You can't walk, Gerry. I'd have to wait on you hand and foot and I've got enough to do at the moment.'

'God, you're a stubborn bitch.'

She laughed. 'Anyway, you wouldn't like our new house guest. Some reporter Louise has brought home.'

His head spun as the words sunk in.

'You should see your face, Gerry.'

'Not Hugh Pimlott?'

'He's all right. He knows how to make a cup of tea and he pours a mean gin and tonic.'

'He's a great mouthy lump.'

'He's no glamour puss but I like him. And he's in the spare room, so you needn't worry.'

Gerry glared at her, speechless.

She leant closer and took his hand. 'He's just a friend, Gerry. That's what she needs right now.'

He closed his eyes. Talk about the last bloody straw.

On Sunday evening Keith caught up on his backlog of newspapers.

He read about the discovery of the girl's body dispassionately. The sensational tone of most reports was just what he would have expected. Many of them ran the same picture – of a smiling Rebecca sitting on a horse – and went on about how young and innocent she was, and how she'd led a blameless life. A load of balls. None of these bleeding-heart writers had been nearly blinded by her. Like most women she was a scheming little bitch when it came down to it. Like the whore Denise and Belinda, his first wife, and even – let's be honest – his mother. All of them pretended to be on your side and then gave you the shaft when you were looking the other way. And now, praise be, one of them had got caught. This Rebecca had run into the Beast and paid the price. Well, tough shit.

Keith laughed to himself as he tossed the Sunday tabloid aside. He could have predicted every word.

Yesterday's *Racing Beacon* was in the pile, and he read Phil Nicholas's letter through again. This time it stuck in his throat.

Nicholas said he had no axe to grind but that was a bit rich. The *Racing Beacon* was part of the Hoylake News Group. The same company who published the Sunday tabloid he'd just dumped on the floor. The jockey was part of all that, pocketing Hoylake's money, while pretending to be an independent shoulder to cry on. This was a transparently put-up job. Did Phil Nicholas think he was born yesterday?

What an arsehole.

Phil was twiddling his thumbs at home when the phone rang. Julia was off to check on Callisto, and he knew he should have gone with her. But he wasn't fit company. He was turning his conversation with Russell over and over in his head. If they'd had a cat he'd have kicked it.

So he was grateful when Hugh Pimlott called.

He'd last seen Hugh at Haydock across the unsaddling enclosure. He hadn't felt like talking at the time.

'What's going on?' the journalist said. 'I hear Russell's standing you down for a bit. He says you need a rest before Cheltenham but you don't agree, particularly where Wolf Patrol's concerned.'

'How do you know all this?'

'I'm a reporter, mate. I have sources I cannot reveal.'

Phil was suspicious. 'You're not ringing me up for a quote, are you?'

'I'm just concerned about your wellbeing.'

'You're concerned about me having nothing to say in your paper next week.'

Hugh chuckled. 'There is something on my mind, actually.'

Of course there was. Phil had never known Hugh call just for a chat. However, he could not have anticipated what the journalist said next.

'How would you like to ride for someone else at Leicester on Tuesday?'

Phil was flabbergasted. 'You're offering me a ride?'

'I know you're free, Phil. Are you interested?'

'Only if I've got a chance going up against Wolf Patrol.'

'You can judge for yourself. Come and ride him out tomorrow morning.'

Phil laughed. This conversation was bordering on the ludicrous.

'Pardon me saying so, Pim, but what the fuck would you know about riding out? Or anything to do with a horse that's not written on a bit of paper?'

'I don't, maestro. But Louise Fowler does and she's got an eight-year-old chaser who needs a run before Cheltenham. Are you interested or not?'

Out Of Time, the Greenhills chaser, was not a horse who caught the eye for the right reasons. He was a small, wiry beast with an ungainly walk – 'like a bag of bones', Phil thought as the horse was led towards him – and his coat was scruffy. Phil wasn't all that thrilled but he didn't want to offend anyone so he kept his mouth shut. Besides, as he knew well enough, looks didn't win horse races.

He was glad he'd kept his thoughts to himself almost as soon as he climbed on the animal's back. The horse felt totally different from on top. The ungainly walk now felt balanced and sure-footed. As he urged Out Of Time into a trot, the horse flowed across the turf, all the angles and jerks gone from his movement.

Phil jumped him along a row of practice fences at a gentle pace, enjoying every stride. He didn't ride too many like this in a season – the horse was an absolute joy. All he had to do was stay balanced and the animal did the rest. He had the fences weighed up long before his jockey.

Phil turned to take the fences again. He put his foot down this time, asking Out Of Time to show him what he could do at racing pace. The little horse was even better at speed, whistling over the obstacles with relish and clearly enjoying his work.

'Well?' said Chris as Phil trotted over to where he stood on the path by the gallop, Louise by his side.

'What a gem,' Phil said, patting a caramel-coloured shoulder in approval. 'I'd be happy to ride him anywhere.'

Louise smiled for the first time since he'd met her that morning. He'd seen her around at meetings but they'd never spoken before. She looked him in the eye and said, 'Fantastic.'

Phil supposed it was – now all he had to do was to get his little mount around Leicester racecourse ahead of Wolf Patrol.

Mark looked up as Phil dropped his bag on to the changing-room bench next to him.

'Bit of a surprise to see you,' the Irishman said. 'Russell said you'd taken a few days off.'

Phil had been wondering what might have been said about his absence.

'You know me,' he replied. 'Can't keep away. Anyway, I can't let you have it all your own way, can I?'

Mark shook his head. 'You're unbelievable, you know. You're the bloody champion jockey, with the pick of the horses and a stack of money in the bank. And you'll pitch up at some gaff track on a Tuesday just to make sure I don't get my nose in front of you.'

Phil looked at the lad in surprise. 'Is that what you think?'

'Yeah, I do. And I'll tell you something else – you're right to be worried. This time I'm on the good rides and you're not going to get a look-in. By the time I've finished this week, there'll be no point in you coming back.'

Phil stared at him open mouthed. He had no quarrel with Mark – at least, he'd not thought he had.

'Look, mate, I worked for my position. No one gave me top spot – I earned it.'

Mark smiled, but there was no humour in his eyes. 'Sure you did, Phil. But that was before you had your little problem, wasn't it?'

'What do you mean by that?'

'I mean that you haven't got a prayer of finishing ahead of Wolf Patrol. What did you think I meant?'

Phil said nothing, but his mind was in turmoil. When he found out how his psychological difficulties had become common knowledge at Deanscroft someone would suffer.

*

For once Keith was lucky – he got the first appointment when the walk-in surgery opened at three. The doctor was a thin Asian girl in spectacles who looked like she should still be at school. He'd never seen her before – another locum, he thought. He visited the doctor about twice a year – and saw a different GP on each visit.

His wound wasn't getting any better – the furrow ploughed by the pencil gaped moistly between two bruise-blackened hillocks of skin, and the eye, still bloodshot and weeping, ached with a dull throb. He was worried some serious infection was setting in, particularly as he couldn't dress it properly. Finally he'd decided to seek help.

'Nasty,' the doctor said simply as she removed the dirty lint covering. 'How did you do this?

He told the truth – in a manner of speaking. He was worried a bit of lead might have stuck in the wound.

'I did it with a pencil.'

'How on earth did you manage that?' She sounded a lot more grown up than she looked.

He shrugged. 'I slipped when I was sharpening it.'

She still looked quizzical so he added, 'I was a bit pissed,' which neatly cut off that line of enquiry.

She cleaned the wound carefully and shone a light into his eye, finally announcing that no permanent damage had been done. He was out of the surgery in five minutes with a nice clean dressing on his injury and a prescription for an antibiotic in his pocket. While he was in the chemist's he bought an eye patch which the girl behind the counter said would make him look like a pirate.

He felt quite cheered that things had gone so smoothly and, though he should have gone straight back to the kennels, he ducked into the bookie's by way of a celebration. There wasn't much doing – just two meetings, Catterick and Leicester – but that suited him fine. He'd have a quick look at the runners and maybe watch a couple of races. After all, he could easily still be sitting in the doctor's reception, surrounded by scabby children.

He peered at the newspaper guides to form pinned up around the poky little room. As he glanced at the runners, one race immediately caught his eye – the 3.50 at Leicester.

What the hell was Phil Nicholas doing on a horse trained by the

Fowlers? And, what was more, riding against a Deanscroft horse like Wolf Patrol?

Nicholas had won on Wolf Patrol at Folkestone just six weeks ago, so why had he switched?

Keith read the form on Out Of Time, mostly based on last season's performances, which were reasonable but not spectacular. The horse had been out of action since the autumn when he'd strained a ligament while winning at Chepstow. If all went well, today's race was intended as a pipe-opener for Cheltenham.

Keith considered the situation. Wolf Patrol was the short-priced favourite and the obvious choice. But why had Nicholas – the Deanscroft top jockey – turned him down for Out Of Time? There had to be a reason.

He had £45 in notes in his pocket and some loose change. He kept the change and slid the notes across the counter with his betting slip. It was against his rules to bet on impulse, but the signs were too good. Greenhills and Phil Nicholas – that had to mean something. It had to be an instant red-ink punt.

As he fastened his good eye on the TV monitor, he realised that it was at moments like this that he did not care about the Beast.

The runners were lining up and, for the moment, the Beast had ceased to exist.

Phil was still seething over the row with Mark when the tapes went up for the three-mile chase. He rode by instinct, his body instantly in tune with his horse, his mind replaying the angry words in the dressing-room.

How long had Mark felt that way about him? He'd thought the bloke was a friend. They'd changed side by side, shared lifts, worked out in the gym next to one another – put their necks on the line together, for God's sake. And all the time, it seemed, Mark resented him and couldn't wait for him to move over so he could take his position at Deanscroft.

Jesus! Phil had accepted Louise's ride so he could score points off Russell Dean, but now he was taking on Mark as well. If Mark wanted the number-one spot, he'd have to bloody well prove he was worthy of it.

Though there were ten runners, it was evident that Wolf Patrol and Out Of Time were the class horses. Phil tracked Mark round for the first half of the race, his little horse matching the big, race-seasoned Wolf Patrol every inch of the way. By this time, the pair were six lengths clear and pulling away.

Just as he had on the gallops the morning before, Out Of Time flowed easily over the fences, his footwork neat and economical. By contrast, Wolf Patrol was a powerhouse, putting in enormous leaps and conquering the obstacles by brute strength. Though his horse was matching Mark's so far, Phil wondered if he'd be able to maintain the effort when things got tough. He well knew Wolf Patrol's bottomless reserves of stamina.

They were running into the dip on the far side of the course, already going at a fair gallop, when Mark gave his mount a smack and the big horse lengthened his stride.

No you bloody don't, thought Phil, asking his horse for more speed and getting an instant response.

The pair were flying now, going flat out downhill, still with some five furlongs to go. *Watch it, you're going to get hurt*, said a voice in Phil's head. *So fucking what?* said another voice – Phil's own. Right now, he didn't care.

They cleared the last fence on the back straight neck and neck and careered round the bend to take the open ditch. As they landed on level terms, Phil looked across at Mark.

'We're going too fast,' he yelled.

Mark turned his head, his eyes flashing. 'You're fucking chicken,' he screamed back, and hit Wolf Patrol with his stick.

Mark might as well have hit Phil too, the effect of his words was the same. *Chicken?*

Phil urged his horse on. He'd die rather than be beaten by Mark in this race.

Wolf Patrol was half a length in front as they turned for home, but Out Of Time wasn't giving up. He surged alongside his rival as they approached the first fence in the home straight.

They were still a distance from the obstacle when Phil saw Mark launch his horse. *That's ridiculous*, he thought, as Wolf Patrol took off.

Then his own horse sprang forward, straining every sinew, his hooves up by his nostrils as he flew through the air. Phil scarcely registered the sound of snapping birch to his left.

Phil was galloping hard towards the next – just two to go – uphill towards the stands and the winning post, when he realised he was out on his own.

'Yes!' muttered Keith under his breath as, on the betting-shop screen, Wolf Patrol ploughed into the fence. His front feet hit the take-off board and he flipped up into the air. He saw the jockey diving over the fence and the horse flying, upside down, the sinews of its neck bulging, its legs pumping.

'Oh my Lord,' said an old man in a threadbare overcoat next to Keith. 'That's a nasty one.'

'Jockey needs his head testing,' said a building worker in dusty overalls. 'That's if he's still got a head.'

Keith didn't join in the general discussion. He didn't give a monkey's about Wolf Patrol or his jockey. His good eye was on the TV monitor as Out Of Time jumped the last two fences safely and crossed the finishing line with no other runner in sight.

He'd got it right! Something funny had been going on and he'd sussed it out. That feeling of being right was almost as satisfying as the thought of the £250 he was about to collect.

'Shame about Wolf Patrol,' he said to the old man. He wouldn't want anyone to think he didn't have a heart.

A small crowd applauded Phil and Out Of Time as they turned in to the winner's enclosure.

Louise took the horse's bridle, Hugh by her side. They congratulated him warmly, but Phil couldn't return their smiles.

'What happened to Mark?'

'He got completely buried. The horse landed on top of him.'

'Did he get up?'

'Not yet. They've got the screens round Wolf Patrol.'

Phil knew what that meant. A vet was probably putting the horse down right now.

Hugh had a hand on his arm. 'What was going on out there, Phil? Both of you were riding like lunatics.'

Phil didn't know what to say now the red mist of battle had faded. 'It's a tough sport, Pim. You want to try it some time.'

Behind the reporter Phil spotted the rest of the press pack heading his way.

'Sorry, Hugh,' he said, and stopped, his voice trapped in his throat.

'Phil,' called Arnie Johnson. 'Can we have your reaction to Mark Shaw's accident?'

Phil shook his head. He couldn't speak. He waved a hand in front of his face by way of apology and ran for the weighing-room, straight past the scales and into the changing-room.

Keith pushed his betting slip under the grille. Perhaps he'd treat himself to a decent bottle of Scotch for once. None of that supermarket own-brand gutrot. One of those fancy Scottish malts.

'Can you wait a moment, sir? There's been an objection.'

'What?'

The bookie pointed to the screen. The commentator's voice was announcing an objection by the Clerk of the Scale. The winning jockey had failed to weigh in and Out Of Time was certain to be disqualified.

Keith didn't listen to the rest of it. He stormed from the shop, angrily shoving other punters from his path.

He couldn't believe it. He couldn't fucking believe it.

Phil Nicholas had cheated him. Mr Nice Guy jockey, the bloke who'd held out the hand of friendship and offered to 'speak for him' – he'd robbed him.

He shouldn't be allowed to get away with it. And he wouldn't.

Keith knew there must be a way to make the jockey really suffer. He'd find it, and this time he'd think it out properly.

Then he'd act – him and the Beast.

Gloom hung over the changing-room like a pall of smoke. Jockeys changed into their silks for the next race – the afternoon business had to go on. The usual loudmouthed chat was banished for the moment, while they waited for news of Mark's condition. All they had heard was that the ambulance was on its way to hospital.

Phil sat motionless and dejected. It was like watching a movie for the second time and seeing things he'd missed. When he'd had his crash at Wincanton, it had been him in the ambulance, drifting in and out of consciousness, wondering how bad it was and how long he'd be out, replaying the split seconds before the world had turned upside down. He'd not felt much pain at the time – that had come later, after the operations and during the weeks of slow recuperation. Mark had all this to come. That was if he were still alive. Phil had watched the fall on close-circuit TV. He'd never seen one worse.

One of the other lads came over. Russell Dean wanted a word.

The trainer was waiting for him outside.

Russell didn't comment on Mark's fall or Wolf Patrol's death.

'I need a jockey for the next.'

Phil couldn't resist. 'So my mind problem doesn't bother you any more?'

Russell glared at him. 'Will you do it – yes or no?'

'Yes.'

The trainer's face relaxed. 'As a matter of fact, Phil, I don't think you've got a mind problem at all. You're the same tough bugger you've always been.'

Phil supposed he meant it as a compliment.

He changed quickly into a new set of silks. He'd try his damnedest to win the next for Mark.

Phil found Louise after the next race. He'd not won after all. He'd finished well down the field on a horse who'd faded at the death, having given his all. He hoped it wasn't bad omen for his injured colleague.

Louise was fussing over Out Of Time as he was loaded into the horse-box for the journey home.

The horse stuck his head into Phil's face and snorted.

'He likes you,' she said. 'Even if you did frighten him out of his skin. He's never run so fast in his life.'

Phil looked at her and held out a piece of paper. 'I'm sorry about the disqualification. Really sorry.'

'What's that?'

'A cheque. You and the owner ought not to miss out just because of me.'

Her eyes widened in surprise.

'Go on, take it,' he said. 'It'll make me feel better.'

'Why didn't you weigh in?' she asked. 'Did you just forget?'

Why hadn't he? He still wasn't sure. Unless it was the feeling that Mark's fall had been his fault somehow. That he'd goaded him into that reckless leap. That, after what had happened to him at Wincanton, he at least should have known better.

'Yes,' he said. 'I wasn't thinking.'

She looked like she was going to argue the point, then evidently thought better of it. Phil noticed the deep shadows under her eyes – here was someone else who was getting through the dark days as best she could.

Louise took the cheque and stuffed it in her back pocket without looking at it. It had not been an expensive race – first prize was fifteen hundred quid. He didn't know what he would have done if it had been the Gold Cup. Some principles were more affordable than others.

Hugh navigated as Phil drove the busy network of unfamiliar roads. Leicester General Hospital wasn't that easy to find. Word was that Mark had suffered a broken hip. He probably wouldn't be in a fit state to be seen but Phil intended to stay until he was. Mark's family in Ireland had been informed but it would be a while before any of them could get over. Phil knew how important it was to have someone you knew near by when you woke up in a hospital bed. Even if Mark now hated his guts, at least he'd be a familiar face.

'So what's with you and Louise?' he asked the journalist. She'd protested when Hugh had said he had to get back to London and that he'd ride into Leicester with Phil to catch the train.

Hugh sighed heavily. 'Don't you start. The press boys have been giving me an earful all day. Beauty and the Beast and all that.'

Phil laughed. 'Goes with the territory, mate. It's envy. You've got a fantastic woman and they haven't.'

'I haven't "got" Louise at all. I just stayed over the weekend because she needed a friend.'

'Right.'

'And that's all we are. Friends.'

'OK.'

'For crying out loud, Phil, I've got five stone and ten years on her. Why would she ever get involved with me?'

Phil just concentrated on the road ahead and tried to keep a straight face. At least he had something to smile about.

Hugh kept Phil company at the hospital for a couple of hours while a medical team worked on Mark. When he finally left in a taxi for the station, Phil was relieved. He'd rather not have a witness to his meeting with the injured jockey.

At around eleven a cadaverous Australian doctor led him to Mark's bedside. He looked small in the big hospital bed, propped up on a mound of pillows and surrounded by drips and monitors. His face, always pale, was tinged with blue. He stared at Phil in surprise.

'Oh, it's you.'

'Yeah, bad luck. Your mum's on her way. And Russell was here earlier but he had to get back.'

Mark stared at him without comprehension. Phil wondered how aware he was of what had taken place.

'I can move my toes,' he said suddenly. 'On both feet. That's good, isn't it?'

'Bloody marvellous,' Phil said. 'You'll be back before long.'

'Not before Cheltenham and Aintree, though.'

'Next year, mate.'

Mark nodded and they lapsed into silence.

Then, out of the blue, Mark apologised to him. Said he'd told Russell about Phil's shrink.

Phil was shocked. 'How the hell did you know about that?'

'It's all my fault, Phil. Don't blame her.'

Her. There was only one her it could be.

'Julia told you?'

'Only because she thought I was your mate. She told me in confidence.'

Which you didn't keep.

Phil said nothing. He didn't know what the hell to think.

Keith was wary of using the computer for any incriminating activity. He could have communicated with the *Racing Beacon* by e-mail but that would have been like putting his address at the top of a letter. Naturally he had copied the letters on-screen for the purpose of printing them off. But he'd not saved them and had deleted the text as soon as it had printed. He was pretty sure that was all right.

The internet was another matter. He'd read about perverts who'd stored child pornography on their computers. Some of them had erased the images and still been found out. Obviously the police used smart technicians who could discover just about anything you did with your PC. Which was a nuisance because he had a feeling the information he needed was available right there, a mouse click away. Only, if he logged on to the pages he had in mind, one day in the future some four-eyed adolescent would discover what he'd been up to. It might be that one extra detail in a court case that would turn a jury against him.

He pondered his predicament.

Then he realised that he had already damned himself. He'd probably left the computer fingerprint he was anxious to avoid. Months ago, in the course of his night-time surfing, he'd visited this particular website, just as he'd visited every racing page he could find. In which case, why shouldn't he revisit it right now? It was too late to worry.

He logged on and began searching. It didn't take long to get the home page he wanted on-screen. There'd been a bit of a fuss about it in the press when Deanscroft had launched its own website. Being one of the most progressive training facilities in the country, it had naturally come up with some well-designed and user-friendly pages. When Keith had examined it before, he'd focused on the content listed under 'Horses'. Now he clicked the icon for 'People'.

There were a lot of staff employed at Deanscroft. Some of them merited photographs and lengthy CVs – jockeys like Phil Nicholas and Mark Shaw. Others were listed as associates or consultants – vets and blacksmiths, for example. Some were in the market for freelance work – they listed e-mail addresses and contact numbers.

He made a note of the one he was looking for.

He was in business again.

Phil didn't know what to say to Julia about Mark's confession. He'd thought he could count on her, that he'd been wrong to conceal his visits to Simone and that speaking frankly was what marriage was all about. Now it turned out he'd been right in the first place. The moment he'd confided in her, she'd rushed off and told someone else.

In other circumstances she could have killed his career stone dead. To say he was disappointed in her was an understatement, but he didn't trust himself to have it out with her. He'd only lose his rag and make it worse.

So, after his late night in Leicester on Tuesday, he'd said little to her on Wednesday morning, just updated her on Mark's condition. He was riding at Chepstow later, back on Russell's horses, just as if their disagreement hadn't happened. He told her he was going to a charity dinner in the evening – a last-minute engagement which did not include her.

He read the disappointment on her face. It stayed with him all the way to Chepstow.

'My God, man, what have you done to your eye?'

Captain Adam Jellicoe peered down at Keith from his horse as the Latchbourne Hunt assembled. The hard ground had softened and the Wednesday meet was on.

Keith mumbled his excuse about the garden cane but fortunately Jellicoe wasn't really interested in the cause of Keith's injury. 'Just as long as you can ride that infernal thing,' he said, referring to the quad bike. Then he added, 'I want a word with you about Henry Carrington. He says you've bilked him over some old hunter of his.'

'He's got it all wrong, sir,' said Keith with some irritation, but Jellicoe wasn't listening. One of his pals was hailing him across the yard, which was teeming with hounds, a group of horsemen and a larger band of hunt followers who kept up with the action either on foot or by car. Some of the old boys had been followers for years. They knew where a fox would be found and which way it would run as well as any huntsman.

'He asked me to put his old horse down and that's what I did,' shouted Keith into the hubbub, 'and now he's hanging around the kennels, making a nuisance of himself.'

'Sorry – can't talk about it now,' Jellicoe stated, conveniently forgetting he had raised the subject. 'Got to get the show on the road, eh?'

Then he whirled away to jaw to one of his other cronies. A typical Jellicoe performance, Keith thought, all piss and wind.

His left eye was throbbing this morning but he could drive the quad OK by squinting through his right. It demanded all his concentration. There would be no racing around on the bike like he sometimes did.

Soon he was out on his own, following the hounds by keeping to the high ground. Thank God he wouldn't have to put up with self-important twits like Jellicoe much longer.

For years he'd thought his way to a better life was through a hot betting streak. But now the game had changed and the stakes were higher. Much higher. He'd be asking for a damn sight more than a hundred grand next time.

The pack had disappeared into the spinney just ahead. Yelping and barking split the air, and a cloud of steam rose from the wood. Keith gunned the bike over the damp meadow towards the site of another kill.

Chapter Twelve

Julia took the call mid-morning on Thursday, just after Phil had set off for Ludlow.

'Is that Julia Nicholas? The horse therapist?'

The voice was unknown to her but the West Country burr was warm enough.

'I got your number from a friend. I need help with an injured horse.'

'I'm busy at the moment,' she said.

'I'm not surprised,' the man said. 'They say you can bring back the dead and that's bound to put you in demand, isn't it? I reckon old Solomon's for the knacker's if you can't help me.'

Despite herself, Julia was intrigued. But then she usually was. She had resolved to be firm with these unsolicited calls.

Her caller continued to talk, his voice soft. 'I've had him with two different vets and they can't get him sound. Those kids up at the farm are going to be heartbroken if he's put down.'

'Why are you talking of putting him down.'

'Oh, it's not me. I just keep an eye on him. Mr Lawrence says if I can't do something about him he'll have to go. He's just hobbling around, getting fat, see? Mr Lawrence like his animals to be cost effective.'

Julia didn't like the sound of this. 'You mean because the horse is injured his owner's going to put him down?'

'That's about it. Are you sure you couldn't manage a quick look at him? I reckon it's only about a half-hour drive from your place.'

How could Julia say no? She scribbled the directions down on the back of an envelope. She'd get over there during her lunch-time break.

*

After his second reading of the fibre-analysis report on Rebecca Thornton's body, Charlie had taken himself off to the gents' and splashed water on his face for a full minute. The lines of text had been swimming before his eyes. It's your own fault, he told himself. You can't work round the clock any more at your age.

His best hope of catching Rebecca's killer, he'd thought, would come from forensic analysis of her remains. Happily, there was no sign she'd been sexually abused – though that might have yielded a clue to her attacker's identity. He'd had a dream the other night that human tissue was found beneath her fingernails and they'd matched the DNA to a known offender. He'd clung on to the hope until the pathologist had dashed it. Nothing had been found beneath the girl's fingernails but dirt – dirt which had now been analysed in the report he'd been reading.

'OK, John,' he said to DS Petrie when he returned to his office, 'just summarise it for me. What's unique about all this stuff they found on her?'

Rebecca's body had been in a filthy condition, covered with earth, straw and other materials.

'Dog hairs,' said Petrie. 'In her hair and all over her clothes.'

'Any particular kind of dog?'

'Short-haired. Light brown, dark brown, white – all sorts. Doesn't give a breed.'

'So it could be anything? Or lots of different dogs?'

'I suppose so, guv. Terriers, lurchers, spaniels – those types.'

They looked at each other. This was helpful. If they had a suspect who owned dogs of that description it might be very helpful indeed. But they didn't have a suspect.

The phone rang on Charlie's desk. Petrie was nearer to it.

'Shall I?'

'Go ahead,' said Charlie.

He'd developed a buzzing in his ears. He put it down to lack of sleep. The truth was he didn't like sleep at present – prophetic dreams about DNA were not the only ones he was having. Some of them simply reran the terrible day spent with Rebecca's father. Watching the man's glossy self-confidence evaporate as he learned the pitiless details of his daughter's death – beaten and brutalised and tossed on the side of the road in a rubbish sack. Then there were the dreams about the dead girl herself, of him standing over her broken corpse in the mortuary. But in those dreams it was Charlie who was the father and the girl on the metal trolley was Claire.

'Guv!'

How long had John been staring at him? Charlie shook his head to clear the buzzing, like shaking water from his ears. John's eyes were gleaming.

'What is it?'

'There's been another letter. It arrived second post at the *Beacon*.'

They both rushed for the fax machine.

The journey took more than half an hour, as Julia had guessed it would. People always gilded the truth when they wanted you to do something. This Geoff Lamb she was meeting was no different.

As she drove she reflected miserably on Phil's coldness towards her. She hadn't plucked up the nerve to ask him what the matter was – maybe she'd talk to him this evening. She supposed this was what her mother had meant at her wedding when she'd told her marriage was a long road. At the time she'd thought it was a funny thing to say, especially since her mother had never actually been married. Whenever she'd found the going tough she'd simply looked for another man. Julia was determined that wouldn't happen to her. She was with Phil for keeps.

She'd turned off the A road two miles back and driven through the village of Down Sutton, as directed. She found the unpaved track she was looking for on the left, past a ploughed field. As she drove along it she could see nothing through the high hedge on either side. The track was deeply rutted and obviously little used. She was pleased to note fresh tyre tracks through the puddles ahead – it looked like Geoff Lamb was here already.

Her way took her uphill and, as she rounded a bend, the hedge to her left was replaced by trees. Through their bare winter foliage she could see a horse in a muddy paddock. She had arrived.

She got out of the car and walked towards a brown pick-up with a lifting device on the back parked by a gate into the field. A big, barrel-shaped man in a cap was standing by the vehicle. The first thing that struck her about him was the patch he wore over one eye.

'Mr Lamb?'

He nodded and held out his hand.

Julia looked over his shoulder at the horse, who was ambling towards them. Moving easily.

'There doesn't took much wrong with him,' she said as she accepted his handshake.

'There's nothing wrong with him at all,' the man replied, his grip like a vice.

Charlie and John read the letter, shoulder to shoulder.

It is beyond my powers to say how much I regret what happened to Rebecca Thornton. I offer my heartfelt commiserations to her family and friends for their dreadful loss. That such a young girl should loose her life is an awful thing and, believe me, I would give anything to bring her back. BUT IT WAS NOT MY FAULT.

If Rebecca had done as she was told she would be alive today. But she would not listen to me and her death is the tragic result of her own stupidity. Let this be a lesson for us all.

In future, I will be better prepared. I am determined to succeed and will not finish my campagne until I have got what I want.

Next time follow my instructions to the letter. For Rebecca's sake.

'They don't pay us enough, do they?' said John. 'I feel like some of this bloke's slime is rubbing off on me.'

Charlie grunted. He knew just what his colleague meant, but now was no time to analyse their feelings.

'I don't like this talk of next time,' he said.

'You mean you think he'll kill again?'

'I've no doubt he's prepared to do that but it doesn't earn him any money, does it? I think it's more likely he'll take another hostage.'

It was a sombre thought – especially since there was no easy way of preventing it.

'I'll warn the guys watching Greenhills,' said John.

Charlie nodded. 'Talk to Phil Nicholas as well, will you? Tell him to be careful.'

'Why him?'

'Because, apart from that open letter he wrote to our man, he forgot to weigh in after winning a race at Leicester.'

Petrie looked puzzled.

'You don't follow the horses, do you, John?'

'I didn't think you did either, guv.'

Charlie proceeded to explain how Phil had inadvertently disqualified himself. He could see John was impressed.

Charlie allowed himself a grin. Such minor satisfactions apart, there wasn't much else to be cheerful about. Once they'd alerted Greenhills and Phil Nicholas there was still the rest of the entire racing community to keep watch over.

Compared to the other one, dealing with Julia was a doddle. Once Keith had shown her the knife she was putty in his hands. It was like she understood everything instantly. That he was the boss and, if she wanted to stay alive, she had to do everything he said. And she did.

He'd prepared for the moment when he'd take her. He didn't want a repeat of the struggle with Rebecca. She'd been bigger and full of fight. She'd taken a lot of killing. This Julia seemed paralysed with fear, which made life much easier.

When he told her to take off her Barbour and put on the anorak that was in the back of the wagon, she did it without protest. The anorak was old – it had once belonged to a skinny kid who did a bit of gardening up at the kennels. Keith had adapted it, sewing tapes and buckles on to the sleeves with thick thread. So now, when Julia put it on back to front as he ordered, it was like a straitjacket. He zipped up the coat at the back and pulled the sleeves around her body, buckling them behind her.

He'd brought two belts; one went round her thighs and the other round her ankles. She wasn't going anywhere in a hurry.

That just left the matter of keeping her quiet. He'd thought about that a lot. He couldn't see any way round gagging her, much as he had the other one. But Rebecca's hair had been a nuisance, getting stuck in the tape and making it difficult to get a tight grip. And this one had even more than the last, a mass of shoulder-length golden hair. He'd decided it would have to go.

He took a pair of scissors and the battery-operated clippers he used for trimming the hunters out of a plastic bag. She gasped.

He held them in front of her face.

'I've got to cut your hair, it's in the way. I won't hurt you unless you make it difficult for me – then you'll wish you hadn't. Understand?'

Her eyes, huge with fear, stared up at him.

'Please,' she begged.

'You'd rather I cut something else?' He held the blades of the scissors against her cheek.

She bent her head in submission.

Keith looked round. He'd chosen the most isolated spot he knew, but some nosey buggers always seemed to turn up where you least expected them.

There was no one about. Keith sat her on the floor of the wagon with her feet hanging over the end and doubled her over so her head hung between her knees. It was easy to get at her hair in this position.

First he used the scissors, slicing off silky clumps and placing them in the plastic bag. Though there was no time to be neat, he worked methodically, from the back of her head to the front, cutting the hair to within an inch or two of the scalp. Then he used the electric clippers to shave the back of her head, where the gaffer tape would go when he gagged her.

When he'd finished he admired his handiwork. Without the blonde cloud surrounding it, her face seemed more sculpted, its heart shape more obvious. Her cheekbones were high and sharp, her lips wide and full. She was a beauty, no doubt about it.

'If you ask me,' he said as he pulled the roll of brown tape from his pocket, 'you look better than ever.'

She said nothing, but her tears wet his fingers as he taped up her mouth.

Phil had three rides at Ludlow, two hurdles and a steeplechase – the last of which gave him food for thought. He was conscious every time he lined up for a race over fences that a demon was still lurking in his mind, ready to waylay him. But he'd also learned, through Simone, that the best way to keep the demon at bay was not to run from it. He had to face up to the possible dangers that lay ahead.

He was reminded of this at the end of the three-mile handicap on Airbus, a big, clumsy horse, hardly the right type to be lumbering round Ludlow's tight little track. Phil had tried to break away from the field down the back straight but had failed to slip the opposition. Coming out of the final bend into the home straight, with three fences in quick succession, Airbus was slowing fast. He pecked at the first of the three fences, almost falling to his knees, then crashed through the top of the next.

The pack was all around them by then, the race lost and the demon panic gripping Phil by the throat. He was going to fall. Airbus was going to pitch him under the hooves of the runners behind. He'd end up smashed in a hospital bed . . .

But these thoughts had invaded his head before. He told himself to ignore them. They'd not brought him down the last time or the time before that.

Phil steadied the faltering horse beneath him and they jumped the next safely. He kicked him on but Airbus had nothing left; the needle was stuck on empty.

They finished down the field, overtaken by five or six other runners. Phil didn't mind about that. The horse had given all he could and he himself had fought off a panic attack. He could have frozen like before but he hadn't.

He'd often questioned the wisdom of visiting Simone, but there was no doubt that, without her advice, he'd still be struggling. He wasn't out of the tunnel yet, but at least he could see light ahead.

Back in the changing-room he thought of phoning Julia but changed his mind. He was still angry with her.

He didn't bother to check his messages

Hugh felt a right prat as he lumbered across Clapham Common in his black Nike sweatpants. He'd always been loud in his condemnation of the conspicuous exercise habit. In his opinion, which he'd shared frequently with anyone who cared to listen, exercise should be done in private, like masturbation or nose-picking. But here he was, breathing hard, sloshing through puddles in his new trainers, fighting the stitch in his side. Pray God no one he knew would spot him in the evening gloom. It was enough to ruin a hack's reputation.

He'd slipped it casually into the conversation he'd just concluded with Louise.

'Gotta go,' he'd said. 'I'm just off for a run.'

She hadn't commented at all, which, on reflection, was a good thing. He'd half expected a splutter of laughter or a sarky remark, but Louise wasn't like that. In fact she wasn't like any of his other friends in the slightest. Which was another reason why there couldn't be anything between them.

And he certainly wasn't exercising to try to impress her, nor cutting out the buns and biscuits and ducking into trendy men's outfitters in his lunch break on her account. He was doing all this because of his beloved sister-in-law, who'd been making noises about him coming round to dinner again. And this time, she'd reminded him, he was bringing his own date. He wished he'd kept his mouth shut.

The stitch had faded now, which was something. He remembered that about running when he'd done it at school – if you kept going you got a second wind. He was in a steady rhythm as he headed for the pond. A thinking rhythm. And his thoughts were of the latest letter from the nutter – the murderer – which Gemma had brought him that morning.

The man was working up to some other atrocity, wasn't he? But where and when? And who would be the next victim?

It occurred to him that he shouldn't be here in London. Louise had said there was a policewoman permanently at Greenhills but would that be enough? Suppose the killer really was determined to get to Louise – would one policewoman be enough to stop him?

He'd ring Louise again when he got back – just to make sure she was all right.

It was gone seven by the time Phil turned up the lane to Barley Cottage. The place was in darkness, which was a puzzle, and there was no sign of Julia's car. He wondered where she'd got to.

Standing in the hall, he called her mobile number but it was switched off. Then he rang his mum and Russell – but she wasn't at the farm or Deanscroft. Russell made some enquiries and told Phil she'd left at lunch-time to do a freelance job.

What freelance job? Perhaps it had turned into something complicated and she was still working. Or maybe she was stuck on the road somewhere. Phil listened to the answer service on the home phone, but there was only his own message, saying he was on his way, and one from DS Petrie.

He dug out his mobile and checked his messages. Two more from Petrie, the second requesting he ring back urgently.

His stomach contracted. This must be to do with Julia. He misdialled in his eagerness to return the policeman's call. His anger had vanished, replaced by anxiety. And fear.

Car tyres rumbled on the gravel at the front of the house and headlights flooded the unlit front room to his left.

She was back. *Thank God*. He put the phone down.

But it wasn't Julia's car. Two uniformed policemen were striding towards the front door as he opened it.

'Mr Nicholas?'

'Yes?' His heart was pounding and his insides were in a knot. This was real panic – not some neurotic flight of fancy. What had happened to Julia?

The policemen did not look concerned; indeed, the man who had spoken was smiling.

'There's nothing to worry about, sir. CID couldn't get you on the phone so we've come to see if you're all right.'

'Me? Why wouldn't I be?'

'There's been another letter from the kidnapper. We're just checking on possible targets.'

'Like me?'

'Yes.'

'And my wife?'

The two men looked at each other.

'I've just got back and I don't know where she is. No one's seen her since lunch-time.'

The policeman's smile had vanished and his colleague was reaching for his radio.

'Do you mind if we come in, sir?'

Phil said nothing as the officers ushered him back inside, a vista of hideous possibilities opening up in his mind.

Julia was cold. He'd put a blanket on top of her but she still shivered as she lay in the dark, the straw of her bed scratching the raw skin of her neck. Not that she cared about her physical discomfort or even the loss of her hair. What did it matter? Apart from the monster who had kidnapped her, no one was ever going to see her alive again. She knew he must be intending to kill her. Why else had he allowed her to see his face?

He'd taken the straitjacket off her, that was something, but he'd chained her to the low frame on which she lay. She recognised it as a dog's bed. The smell of dogs was all around, and she was aware of animals, lots of them, in buildings near by. She could hear them shifting around. They were aware of her too, she knew, and curious about her. Their presence comforted her.

Perhaps she could come back as an animal in her next existence. A horse would be best, of course – especially a thoroughbred racehorse, pampered and praised all its life – but a dog would be almost as good. She'd always lived with dogs, though she didn't have one now. Suddenly it seemed a terrible omission. If she ever got out of here she'd get a dog. A big, bounding Labrador. If she'd had a Labrador with her today, would the monster have been able to snatch her?

Of course he would. He'd have killed the dog with his knife, that's all.

She wondered how he was going to kill her.

Charlie was contemplating a bowl of bran flakes when the phone rang. It was 7.30 in the morning. Jan had always said bran flakes were good for you and he had no doubt they were. He just wished they didn't taste like wood shavings.

An excited DC Jenkins reported that a navy-blue Fiesta had been found abandoned on farm land near Down Sutton. The farmer had discovered it in the early hours of the morning up a track behind a field where he kept his daughter's horse.

The car was unlocked; a Barbour jacket was bundled on the driver's seat and a woman's handbag lay in the footwell on the passenger side. Amongst other possessions in the bag, the farmer had found a purse and a driving licence belonging to a Julia Nicholas.

A preliminary examination suggested that Julia had been snatched, but there were plenty of places where she could be lying out of sight.

Down Sutton was fifty miles off, but Charlie reckoned he could do it in half an hour if he stepped on it. He abandoned his breakfast and fled the house clutching his jacket and mobile phone.

By the time Charlie reached the farm, the area had been cordoned off and Scene-of-Crime Officers were examining the location, in particular the spot by the gate leading into the horse's paddock.

'They've found tyre tracks that don't match the Fiesta or Mr Watt's

Land Rover,' said Terry. He pointed out Mr Watt, the farmer, who was sitting in the back of the squad car making a statement. 'He says he won't go down to the station because he's already lost half the morning.'

Charlie nodded. He'd have a word with him in a moment and smooth his feathers. They'd be camped on his land for a bit and it would be best to keep him sweet.

He approached a SOCO he knew well from past investigations.

'What do you reckon, Pete? Any sign of a struggle?'

Pete shook his head. 'There's a whole mess of boot and shoe impressions in front of the gate but that's what you'd expect. I imagine the farmer and his kids are up here often to keep an eye on the horse. He's a friendly fellow.'

Charlie looked over the gate. A chunky brown horse wearing a thick waterproof rug was surveying them with considerable interest, his ears pricked.

'Pity he can't make a statement,' said Pete.

Charlie ignored the remark. 'So what have you got?'

The officer held up a plastic envelope with something yellow inside. Charlie took it. The envelope contained strands of curly blonde hair, eight or nine inches long.

'We've found quite a lot of it,' said Pete. 'On the ground there and in the grass fringe beneath those trees.'

'Any idea how long it's been here?'

The other man thought. 'Based on the fact that it's relatively dry and contained within this small area, I'd say a couple of days at the most. Probably less than twenty-four hours.'

Charlie handed the envelope back. He didn't know what this meant but he didn't like it. It was creepy.

'The missing woman's a blonde, isn't she?' said Pete, stating the obvious.

Charlie nodded. 'Have you looked inside the handbag they found in her car?'

'Not yet.'

'When you do I bet you'll find a hairbrush. And I've a good idea this hair you've found will match the hair on the brush.'

'What's he doing cutting off her hair, Charlie?'

Charlie had no answer to that. He looked beyond the parked vehicles and the men scouring the hedgerow, over the head of the inquisitive horse, at the soggy acres of field and trees ahead. He wondered whether Julia's body was out there. If so, it would take some finding.

Phil didn't know what to do with himself. He'd been scheduled to attend the two-day Newbury meeting and he had a full book of rides. When he'd explained to Russell the reason he couldn't go, the trainer had been shocked. So far, Julia's disappearance had been kept from the media. Nevertheless, Russell had rung off pretty quickly – to fix himself up with a substitute jockey, Phil assumed.

A policewoman had been instructed to keep an eye on him – Maureen, a middle-aged Family Liaison Officer who offered him food and drink at regular intervals as he prowled Barley Cottage. He couldn't see the point of Maureen's presence – was she supposed to prevent him harming himself? In the event, since his dad had also elected to stay with him, the pair of them chatted away and he was left with his thoughts – which were increasingly dark.

The phone rang mid-morning and he rushed to answer it. The call was for Maureen, who took it on the upstairs extension. When she came down she told him they'd found Julia's car at Down Sutton. Down Sutton? He couldn't understand it. As far as he knew, she wasn't even aware of its existence.

He wanted to go to the place but Maureen said no. Police teams were searching the area and DCI Lynch promised he'd drop by later to talk to Phil.

She told him they'd found Julia's bag and personal effects, including her purse containing £60 in cash. What about her mobile phone? Phil asked. He'd been ringing it hopefully, without success, since last night.

She'd called Charlie and asked about it. The phone, it seemed, was missing.

Phil bombarded her with more questions. Were any of Julia's clothes at the scene? Did it look like she'd been harmed? Was there blood in the car?

She stonewalled him nicely. Phil would have to wait for a full report till DCI Lynch came but he shouldn't torture himself. There had been no blood or signs of a struggle. Phil wondered whether she was telling him everything.

His father suggested they take a look at the horses down at the farm. Maybe Phil would care to ride Callisto out? Julia would like that.

Phil felt guilty for not having thought of it himself, and the three of them drove down the lane to Ted's stables and Phil spent an hour exercising the old champion. It didn't exactly take his mind off his predicament but it helped pass the time. This was proving to be the most terrible day of his life.

When they returned to the cottage it got worse.

A padded cardboard envelope, too big for the letterbox, was propped against the cottage door. The printed label on the front was addressed to Phil, care of Deanscroft; someone at the yard must have brought it over in their lunch break.

Phil opened it without thought. He didn't think it had any relevance to Julia's disappearance. But he was wrong.

The silky golden locks tumbled from the envelope into his hands, filling the kitchen with a familiar perfume.

There was a handwritten note with the hair.

Darling Phil

I am being held hostage but it's all right. I am given food and have not been hurt though my hair had to be cut so I could be gagged with tape. Honestly, it doesn't hurt.

Tell my mum and my sisters I'm OK and I love them very much.

Please look after Callisto for me. Whatever happens I want him to run at Cheltenham for Jack and Yvonne.

Please, please do what he asks or else I will never see you again.

I love you so much.

Your Jules

Phil buried his face in his wife's butchered hair and wept.

The ransom demand turned up at the *Beacon* on Saturday morning. DS Petrie, the policeman with the violent tie, opened the envelope in front of Hugh and Frame. He quickly scanned the sheet of paper inside and then placed it on the editor's desk for the two journalists to read.

Re: Mrs Julia Nicholas

At present this woman is in my custody. My only concern is to return her safely to her family and friends. This letter sets out the terms on which that event can occur.

At 7.30 pm on Saturday 3rd March a courier will drive to Hillminster town centre. He will have a full tank of petrol. He will also have with him a hold-all with a carrying handle containing half a million pounds (£500,000) made up as follows. £400,000 in used £50 notes, £80,000 in 20s, the rest in 10s. The notes must be wrapped in bundles of clear sellophane, three parcels of £50 notes, the other dennominations all separate.

There must be no police, no radios, no helicopters. If I see signs of the courier being followed I shall call it off. And don't think of putting a bugging device in with the money. I have electronic detecting equipment and will find it.

At 7.45 the courier will wait by the telephones outside the town hall. He will answer the phone that rings and follow the instructions that are given.

The courier is to be Mr Phil Nicholas. If you send a policeman instead Mr Nicholas will never see his wife again.

If he wants his wife back this is one appointment he better not forget to weigh in for. He must follow the instructions he will receive to the letter.

I have had it with racing. It is rotten to the core. After this I am giving up my campagne for good. At half a million pounds you are getting off light.

May I remind you that Julia's life is in your hands. Think of poor Rebecca. It would break my heart for another young woman to die because of the callus attitude of the racing world.

Petrie turned the envelope over in his hand. 'Posted on Thursday,' he said.

So it had taken two days to arrive, Hugh thought. It should have been delivered at the same time as the package Phil had received.

Petrie was already on the phone, talking to DCI Lynch. They were relieved the demand had turned up but concerned that the deadline was so close. Seven-thirty that evening.

The detective replaced the receiver and said, 'We've got to go for it.'

'What about Phil Nicholas?' asked Frame.

The editor was looking at Hugh, but Petrie answered. 'Charlie's off to talk to him now.'

'He'll do it,' said Hugh. 'He'll do anything.'

'So will the *Beacon*,' said Frame. 'But it's going to be tight getting the money together on time.'

He picked up the phone. 'And bang goes my career if we don't get it back.'

In an ideal world Charlie would not be asking the husband of a hostage to carry the ransom money to her kidnapper. But there was nothing ideal about this situation. And after the balls-up when Patsy had stood in for Louise, Charlie was going to go along with whatever Bernie asked for.

If he wanted the husband, he got him. If he said no trace on the money, then there'd be no trace. A woman's life was at stake.

Charlie briefed Phil as best he could. He assured him that police surveillance teams would be watching at all times and instructed him on the use of the two-way radio they had fitted in his car. They also agreed he'd be carrying his own mobile.

'Your task,' he told him, 'is to follow Bernie's instructions and keep us informed. And once you've handed over the money your job's finished. Don't be a hero – leave the rest to us.'

Phil murmured agreement.

'Can I ask a question?' he added. 'Do you think Julia's been mistreated?'

'She won't be having a comfortable time. She'll be restrained. Tied up and gagged probably.'

'What else?'

The detective hesitated. 'I don't think she's been sexually assaulted, if that's on your mind.'

Phil's face gave nothing away but Charlie carried on – he might as well spell it out.

'I've got two reasons for saying that. One is that Rebecca wasn't attacked in that way. The other is that I don't think this man would do it. He fancies he's clever. He likes playing games with us – that's why he wants you to carry the money. He would consider deviant sexual behaviour beneath him.'

The jockey nodded, lost in thought. Finally he said, 'What kind of a place was Rebecca kept in?'

Charlie thought hard. He didn't want to distress Phil if he could help it. 'Difficult to say, except that it's probably not in a town. Rebecca and her clothes were covered in the kind of fibres you'd expect to find in a farmyard. Mud, straw and a lot of dog hair.'

Phil nodded. 'Jules loves dogs,' he said.

All the same, Charlie wasn't sure it was much comfort.

Julia lay on her back, scarcely able to move. The monster had tied her to the supports of the dog bed and put sacking over her head. At first she'd thought that was to prevent her seeing; now she realised it was to conceal her.

She could make no noise – the gag was in place – but she could hear what was going on. When the dogs were moved she listened to them banging and thumping against the metal sides of her prison. They knew she was in here and they wanted to come and say hello. She could imagine their wet little snouts sniffing and prodding, their tongues licking her skin. She longed for their company, but they were chivvied past.

She recognised the monster's voice urging them on. But there was another voice as well, another man out there. An accomplice? Or a possible friend? She didn't know. But why was she gagged and covered up unless the other one didn't know about her?

She had a craving. Not for water or food or a bath – or any of the things she might have imagined.

He'd offered her food and drink first thing that morning. And made her pee into a bucket.

Then he'd asked if there was anything else she wanted before he tied her up, and she'd said, 'A cigarette.'

That was her craving. A desperate urge to wreathe herself in tobacco smoke and blot out, for just a split second, all the other hurts in her life.

He'd refused her, said he didn't have any.

She'd pleaded with him. Asked if he could get some. Begged as she'd not done for anything else.

He'd laughed and said cigarettes were bad for her health.

Very funny.

She knew he was going to kill her eventually because he didn't care whether she saw his face. And the dogs. She'd worked out she was being held in a kennels and that these were hunting dogs. Either hounds or beagles.

If she got out she could easily identify him. And she knew how long they'd been travelling yesterday. There couldn't be that many kennels in the area they'd covered. If she ever spoke to the police, he'd be caught.

And he'd killed Rebecca Thornton. So there was no reason why he wouldn't do the same to her.

In the circumstances, he owed her a cigarette.

Like any condemned prisoner, she was entitled.

Chapter Thirteen

Phil nervously eyed the row of three pay-phones outside Hillminster town hall. He had the collar of his waterproof jacket turned up against the weather. Rain was falling in a fine sheet, gusting in the swirling wind, dancing in the glow of the streetlamps lighting up the old town square. It was a nasty night.

A girl was arguing with her boyfriend on the middle phone. She wore a pelmet-sized skirt and a silver jacket which exposed a lot of robust white flesh. She didn't appear to notice the rain blowing into the open-sided booth as she shouted into the receiver.

It was 7.49 by Phil's watch, four minutes after the specified time. Suppose Julia's kidnapper was trying to get through on the engaged phone? Surely things weren't going to screw up right at the start?

Charlie had warned him to expect the unexpected. And, as Phil had left, the inspector had gripped his hand and looked into his eyes. 'You'll do a grand job. You do far more dangerous things every day of the week.'

Phil only wished he could share the policeman's confidence. He'd ride the National blindfold in preference to this.

'If you ain't down here by eight, Jason, don't bother coming down at all.'

The girl smashed the receiver into its cradle and glared at Phil. 'Had your money's worth, you nosey prat?' she spat at him as she stalked past.

He watched her cross the square, towards the pub opposite. Whatever her problems, he'd swap them for his like a shot.

The ringing of a phone captured his attention. It was the middle one. He ignored the reek of perfume as he snatched up the receiver.

'Yes?' he said.

There was a pause. Then a soft voice. 'Who's that?'

'Phil Nicholas.'

'*The* Phil Nicholas? The champion jockey? I'm honoured.' The voice dripped with sarcasm.

'That's what you asked for,' said Phil. 'I've got the package you want.' It was important to play it straight. He mustn't allow this creep to unsettle him.

'One thing before we start. Just so I know you're telling the truth.' Phil held his breath. Charlie had warned him this might happen.

'Describe your wife's tattoo.'

Jesus Christ!

'It's a daisy.'

'And where is it?'

Phil hesitated. 'On her left hip.'

The man chuckled, a rich, throaty sound that in other circumstances might have been appealing. But not now.

'On her bum cheek, you mean.' The voice was exultant. 'You're wondering how I've seen it, aren't you?'

Phil said nothing, though he wanted to put his hand down the phone line and rip the man's tongue out.

'Don't worry, Mr Champion Jockey, I've no intention of touching her. But if you don't play straight with me you won't ever see her pretty little arse again. Understand?' The voice was loud now, the man's anger unconcealed. It dwarfed Phil's own.

'I understand.'

'Good. Now listen.' The softness was back but Phil was not fooled. This man was frightening.

'Drive north out of town towards Buckworthy. After six miles there's a pub on the right called the Pheasant. Turn left directly after the pub and drive three hundred yards to a phone box. You've got twenty minutes.'

Phil repeated the instructions and the connection was abruptly cut.

When he replaced the phone his hand was trembling.

As he drove he tried not to look out for the surveillance vehicles that would be following. Charlie had warned him to pay his minders no attention. 'Don't worry, we'll be there with you. You just concentrate on doing what he tells you.'

The rain was still falling, heavier if anything, and driving conditions were not good. Phil drove carefully, anxious not to miss a landmark, his slow progress annoying a few local drivers. That was too bad; he couldn't afford to make a mistake.

Eventually he came to the pub, a large, well-lit building on the edge of a built-up area. He turned up the lane as directed, along a wet and empty suburban street. He reached the phone box with three minutes to spare.

He waited that length of time and more. The phone didn't ring. He guessed this was part of his tormentor's game – to frustrate at every turn.

A man approached under a large umbrella. *This could be him*, Phil thought – *anybody could be him*. The man didn't even glance in Phil's direction as he passed by, a sausage dog waddling at his heels.

Phil stared at the phone. *Ring, you bastard.*

Eventually it did.

This time the conversation was short.

'Go back on to the main road and drive to Buckworthy. Park by the toilet block in the centre and wait by the phone kiosk.'

For crying out loud! Why the hell hadn't he been told to drive straight to Buckworthy from Hillminster? He said as much over the radio and Charlie came on the line.

'He just wants to muck you around. It gives him a thrill.'

'Jesus Christ!'

'Keep as calm as you can, Phil. Just be prepared for a long night.'

Phil turned these words over in his head as he drove through the rain. At least he'd made contact and the operation was on. There was no point in letting the kidnapper's mind games get to him. No point in imagining the precise circumstances in which this bastard had seen Julia's tattoo. Bernie wanted to unnerve him so he could catch him out and get away with the hold-all in the boot of the car without being detected. The hold-all containing half a million pounds.

It was Phil's task to comply. That was all.

Don't be a hero.

He was just a courier.

'Well, that was a pleasant day out, wasn't it?' said Moira Carrington as they turned into their drive. 'It was so nice to see Selina and Jumbo again, don't you think?'

Henry Carrington grunted. He didn't mind her repeating herself – and she had said the same thing several times over on their journey back from Derby – it was the way she turned every statement into a question. As if every opinion of her own demanded a matching response from him. As it happened he had also enjoyed catching up with their old friends. He just didn't feel the need to keep banging on about it.

'Henry,' she said as they got out of the car, 'you're not still brooding about old Monty, are you?'

'I'm not brooding about anything.'

He turned his back on her as he fumbled with the keys to the garage. As a matter of fact, he was a trifle put out by the Monty business. 'Brooding' was not how he'd put it, however. Hopping mad was more like it.

'You could have been mistaken, you know. One old horse looks much like another.'

He snapped his head round. 'I know my own damned horse when I see him.'

She shrugged. 'I can't see what you're complaining about. You wanted it off your hands, didn't you?'

He glared at her. 'First of all, Monty is not an *it*. Secondly, it's not fair on the horse. He deserves a merciful end instead of being flogged into the ground.'

'Oh, I see,' she said in a tone designed to irritate. She'd perfected it over the years.

She watched as he drove the car into the garage and closed the door. 'I'm for a cup of tea. Would you like one, too?'

'No, I wouldn't. I'm having a large Scotch.'

Phil's journey was now well into its second hour. He must have made half a dozen stops or more, each at a remote phone box on a minor road. No leg had lasted more than ten miles, though he was aware he'd doubled back on himself several times.

'Don't worry,' Charlie told him over the radio. 'He's trying to lose us but we've still got you in sight. Just keep going.'

At the next stop, at the end of a dreary village street, the phone sat in its rest but the cord hung limply to the floor. Vandalised. What the hell did he do now? Was this the end of line? Surely not. Not after all this.

He returned to the car and radioed in.

'Does the phone damage look recent?' Charlie asked.

It didn't. A hard cud of chewing gum was wedged into the connection at the base of the phone.

'Look around the box,' Charlie suggested. 'There might be instructions on the wall.'

There weren't, but taped beneath the metal shelf, was a package. It contained a mobile phone – Julia's phone.

He switched it on and it rang ten seconds later.

'About bloody time,' said that irritating West Country burr. 'Get back in the car and drive straight on till you come to a roundabout.'

Phil did as he was told, relieved that the game was still on. He couldn't bear to think what might happen to Julia if he screwed up.

As the road signs for the roundabout loomed, the phone rang again. He pulled over.

'See the signs for the motorway? Take it heading north. I hope you filled your tank like I told you.'

'Why?'

But the line was now dead. He reported the conversation to Charlie and put his foot down.

In the incident room at Maybrick Street, Charlie Lynch and John Petrie were breathing down the neck of a Traffic sergeant directing the surveillance team. They were trying to plot Phil's erratic journey. There didn't seem much sense to it beyond the need to create confusion.

'The bugger knows every back road in Somerset from the look of it,' muttered John.

Charlie nodded. It was a relief to think Phil was taking to the motorway, where it would be easier to control the exits. He had a feeling they were getting to the point when Bernie would make his move. Now he looked at the map, he could see that the seemingly pointless back and forth had taken Phil ever closer to the motorway.

'Have we got anyone on the motorway itself?' he asked John.

'Yeah. Ivan and Terry will pick him up off the slip road and we've got motorcyclists watching the junctions. Don't worry, guv.'

But Charlie did worry. The operation had had to be mounted at speed and there was a seat-of-the-pants feel to it that petrified him. A few years ago, he realised, he would have loved the buzz. Now he just prayed for a successful conclusion – which meant getting the girl out in one piece. Though there would be hell to pay, he'd even let Bernie keep Hoylake's money if he could be guaranteed Julia's safety.

He was definitely too old for this.

On the motorway, Phil put his foot down. It was a relief to be on a broad and friendly carriageway without having to keep an eye open for some barely visible turn-off. He knew this route well. The next exit was a good ten miles ahead.

The bleep of the phone cut through the purr of the engine. He pulled into the inside lane and answered it with one hand. He had the radio open to the incident room.

'There's a bridge marked with a blue light coming up in the next two miles. Stop on the hard shoulder beneath the bridge. Do you understand?'

'Yes.'

Phil repeated the instruction, hugging the inside lane and trusting that the police were picking up his side of the conversation.

'Can you see him, Tel?'

Terry had never much liked being called Tel. He'd once bollocked a boy at school about it and after that everyone had taken the piss, addressing him as 'Terrance' in a la-di-da sort of voice. Yet here he was being called Tel by his partner, a detective on a high-profile kidnap-and-murder case. And loving it.

'There's a white saloon in the inside lane about a hundred metres ahead,' he said. 'Could be a Saab.'

Ivan moved into the slow lane, putting an old VW Beetle between them and the white car. They were closer to it now.

'That's him,' said Terry. 'I saw the registration.'

'Good stuff. So if we just sit tight here . . . Aye-aye, what's he up to?'

The Beetle in front suddenly pulled into the middle lane without signalling and they found themselves heading for the rear of the rapidly slowing Saab.

Ivan switched lanes too, taking them past the white car, which seemed to be standing still as they drove under a bridge across the carriageway.

'He's stopping on the hard shoulder, Sarge,' cried Terry. 'Shouldn't we pull over?'

'Not unless we want to cock up a possible handover. It could be going down.'

*

Phil only spotted the light at the last minute and stamped on the brake, causing confusion in the traffic behind. He came to a halt just before the bridge. He picked up the mobile from the passenger seat and spoke into it.

'OK,' he said. 'I'm parked by the bridge.'

'Can you see the rope hanging down below the light?'

'Yes.'

'Get out of the car and bring the money bag. Tie the handles of the bag to the rope. Then get back in the car and drive off.'

He repeated his orders for the benefit of the police.

'What about Julia?' he said. 'Will you let her go?'

'When I've got the money.'

Phil took the hold-all from the boot and walked up to the bridge. He stared at the circle of light on top of it, hoping to catch sight of his tormentor, but there was no one in sight.

The end of the rope was coiled at the base of the steep bank of the cutting. He slipped it through the handles of the black canvas hold-all and tied it on firmly. He tested the knot to make sure it would hold, then let go.

He took two paces backward, towards the car. The bag lifted off the ground.

Phil looked up. He still couldn't see anyone – the bastard must be standing back from the parapet. But he was up there somewhere.

The bag was ascending in jerks, a few feet at a time, turning slowly in the eerie light. Half a million pounds disappearing into the grasp of the man who had killed Rebecca Thornton. And held Julia's life in his hands. Phil just had to hope he would keep his word.

That wasn't good enough.

The concrete base of the bank was wet and slippery. The first few feet were easy to climb, then the slope got steeper. His fingers scrabbled for purchase as he assaulted the coarse gradient, his knees scraping on the hard surface even through the thickness of his jeans.

He had scrambled halfway up the bank when the man-made face turned into earth and stone. The ascent was almost sheer, but now it was easier to grip. He hauled himself up by his hands, his feet skidding, one leg flailing in the air before he rammed it into the wall of earth.

He looked around.

Below him the headlights of motorway traffic swept by, the sound of tyres washing over him like waves. Above and behind him the rail of the parapet shone in the blue light, wet with rain. The hold-all was no longer in view.

He had to hurry.

He reached above him, feeling the surface for a hold and finding a mass of roots. He plunged his hand deep. Then gripped and pulled. Inch by inch, he rose upward, breathing hard, desperate. His hands were in foliage now. Brambles and soggy leaves. He was panting with effort, lying half over the edge of the embankment.

He pushed a fringe of grass out of his face and raised his head. In front of him was a fence topped with barbed wire, acting as a barrier between the field and the motorway cutting. Across the angle of the irregular-shaped pasture stood a low hedge which bordered the road leading to the bridge, just a few yards away. Was the kidnapper still there?

Phil eyed the barbed-wire fence. He'd come this far and he wasn't going back. He pulled off his jacket and threw it on top of the jagged spikes, which bit into the material as he clambered over. He yanked hard at the jacket on the other side, hearing the material rip as it came free. Then, in a few strides, he was pushing through the hedgerow on to the road.

The sound of motorway traffic had receded. It was still loud but not as loud as the engine noise that burst upon his eardrums from a few feet away.

As he scrambled through the hedge, a quad bike shot across his vision, down the road that ran away from the bridge, into the darkness on his left.

He was too late. Bernie had got away.

Charlie knew they had to act fast. They'd heard Phil repeat the kidnapper's instructions.

He turned to the Traffic sergeant. 'Can you get people on the bridge?'

'On their way already,' the sergeant replied. 'And I've got bods on the motorway. Do you want them to go in or hold off?'

What the hell.

'Go in. There's no point in hanging back now.'

*

Si Pritchard got the call to check out the bridge at Cowcroft as he was heading for the White Leigh motorway turn-off. It was a stroke of luck, as the junction was a good ten minutes away by these little roads and he was right by Cowcroft.

He went round a stand of tall pines and turned left to pick up the bridge road. He saw the lights of a vehicle ahead and flashed him. For a moment he was confused by its shape, then he realised he was looking at a quad bike.

He slowed his motorcycle to a halt and parked it on its stand in the middle of the narrow carriageway, leaving the engine on. Then he dismounted and signalled to the oncoming vehicle with his torch. This joker wasn't going anywhere till he'd checked him out.

The quad bike slowed to a halt and Si's torch beam picked out the bulky shape of a man.

'Would you please turn off your engine and walk away from the vehicle, sir,' he called.

The man hesitated, as if he were considering whether to comply or not. Then the motor died and the man got off. He was big, taller than Si, who was a size himself, especially in his cycle kit.

'Evening, Officer.' He sounded friendly enough. 'What's the trouble?'

'No trouble, sir. I'd be grateful if you'd—' Si stopped in mid-sentence as the torch beam illuminated the man's face. An ugly gash ran from the top of his ear to the corner of his left eye, where it disappeared beneath a black eye patch. The gash was only half scabbed over, and a stream of blood coated the stubble that covered the man's leathery cheek.

'What have you done, sir? That looks like a nasty wound.'

The man stepped up close, turning his head so Si could get a good look.

Then he moved quickly. He must have had something in his hand and Si hadn't noticed. Too bloody busy playing the Good Samaritan, he thought, as a needle of ice slid into his neck, into the unprotected chink between helmet and leather collar.

Keith leant on the motorcycle policeman with his full weight, pinning him to the road as he coughed and shook. The knife was sharp and efficient. It had dispatched many other mammals; this one just happened to be larger than usual.

When he was certain the man was dead he got to his feet, avoiding the worst of the blood.

He turned his attention to the copper's motorcycle, wrestling it out of the middle of the carriageway.

It was an interruption he could have done without. It had set him back five minutes. But he could live with that.

Phil watched as the quad bike accelerated away. He'd come so far, he'd got so close – to miss him by a whisker! He couldn't bear it.

The road curved ahead and the bike was soon out of sight, though he followed the progress of its lights above the gorse bushes that bordered the carriageway. Then the light seemed to hesitate in the sky and he heard the pitch of the engine change. The bike was slowing down!

He took off after it, sprinting towards the bend and the lights. There was a lot of light, he thought, for one vehicle. Then he realised that there were two, one pointing its single headlamp across the road, illuminating trees and fields.

Now he could see a figure, dragging one of the machines off the road. A machine with familiar markings – a police motorcycle.

Suddenly he had more air in his lungs. He kicked on faster, revitalised by hope. Police! They'd got the bastard now!

With a roar the quad bike burst into life and was away again, speeding off down the road. Phil could scarcely believe it.

He almost fell over the man in the road. A motorcycle policeman in a crash helmet and leathers, lying in a puddle.

'Are you all right, mate?' he asked, bending down.

'Oh, Jesus,' he said as he took in the lifeless face, the gaping hole in the man's neck and the puddle that he now realised was blood. He pulled off the man's leather gauntlet and felt for a pulse at the wrist.

He knelt there in the poor fellow's blood, desperately searching for a flicker of life.

Nothing.

He reached into his jacket pocket for his phone, but the pocket was torn and the phone wasn't there. He remembered yanking his coat free from the barbed-wire fence and the sound of ripping fabric – he must have lost it then. And Julia's mobile was back in the car.

He stared over the body of the policeman, down the road in the direction the killer had gone. A few yards away, the motorbike lay on its side, the engine still grumbling.

He should get on the bike and fetch the emergency services.

The quad bike was out of sight but he could see its lights above the hedgerow. Julia's kidnapper was accelerating away on the road ahead.

He ran to the motorcycle and heaved it upright. It was heavy but he swung his leg over and kicked away the stand.

The policeman was dead and there was nothing he could do for him.

He opened the throttle and the powerful machine punched into the night.

Charlie knew events had moved out of his control. Given the nature of the operation that was no surprise. But for things to slip so disastrously through his fingers was another matter.

Phil's car had been recovered on the hard shoulder of the motorway. But where was Phil?

Had Bernie taken Phil hostage along with the ransom? Maybe the rope had been a ruse and he'd not been on the bridge at all? He could have hidden in a vehicle beneath the bridge on the hard shoulder and, right now, be spiriting Phil away along the motorway. In which case, how the hell would Charlie ever find them? They could be halfway to Bristol by now – or Exeter if Bernie had headed back in the opposite direction.

He had no doubt that both Phil and Julia could end up being murdered by this maniac – just like Rebecca.

Charlie was looking forward to retirement. But retirement with dignity at the end of a long and productive career. He didn't want to finish with a case which involved a lost half-million, three corpses and no suspect.

Right now that was a distinct possibility.

The rain had stopped but the night was black and getting blacker the farther they moved away from the lights of the motorway. It was sheer stupidity to be charging along unlit roads on an unfamiliar machine without goggles or helmet. He was less protected on the powerful monster between his legs than on a racehorse.

The darkness gave him one advantage. He could follow the light of the quad bike as it shone over the fields, separated by hedges of gorse and hawthorn. Even when the quad lights vanished, hidden in the lee of a building or behind a stand of substantial trees, he was able to pick it up again. But for how long?

'Aren't you coming through, Henry?' Moira hovered in the kitchen door, a polite smile fastened to her lips. Moira was always polite – even to her husband of forty-three years.

'No,' said Carrington.

'I thought we were going to watch the Morse video.'

'For God's sake, woman, you don't need me to watch television with you.'

That flustered her a little. He wasn't often so ungallant.

'Sorry, old girl,' he muttered, 'didn't mean to be . . . you know.'

She knew well enough. She'd closed on him now and had her hand on his arm.

'Forget about Monty, please, Henry. It's not worth getting in a stew over.'

There was a lot he could have said but he bit his tongue and said nothing.

She sighed expressively. Even ten years ago they might have thrashed the matter out all over again, but not now.

'I'm off to bed, then,' she said, turning for the door. 'Don't stay up too late.'

He knew her eyes were on the level in the whisky bottle.

'No, dear,' he said, and waited for her footsteps to recede up the stairs before pouring himself another.

Phil had lost him. At least, he thought he had. The countryside was becoming hilly, and it was getting harder to keep track of the quad bike. And suddenly the light ahead vanished.

Phil drove down the stretch of road where his quarry had disappeared. It was empty, with no turnings on either side. Was this where his foolhardy pursuit finished?

He drove back down the road, and this time he noticed a gate. He angled the bike's headlight into the shadows off the road and spotted the track, little more than a ditch between an alley of trees. It was big enough for a quad bike to pass through, however. Where else could he have gone?

Maybe Bernie had realised he was being followed. Perhaps he was lying in wait for him down there. Waiting to do to him what he'd done to that motorcycle policeman.

Phil had done his job. He didn't have to go after the kidnapper. Bernie would let Julia go now he had the money. He'd said so.

Phil dismounted and opened the gate. He set off into the undergrowth, the wheels crunching over rotten logs and plunging him into sudden dips. A machine like this was built for slick tarmac, not an unpaved switchback full of hidden perils. He was crawling along, aware he might overbalance any moment.

Then that familiar and paralysing bubble of panic was in his gut, growing larger, pressing up beneath his lungs, squeezing the air out. His breath came in short gasps, and sweat trickled down the small of his back as he clung on to the handlebars, as paralysed as he had ever been on a horse.

He closed his mind to it. Opened the throttle and bumped along faster. This was nothing compared to a steeplechase.

He wasn't going to bottle out now.

Keith turned off his headlight for the last stretch up the lane to the kennels. He could travel this section blindfold if he had to.

He sat in the yard on the bike, looking back down the hill. At one point he'd thought he was being followed. But he could see no pursuing headlights, hear no rumble of a car's engine. And the hounds, who had been disturbed by his arrival, were settling.

Keith wasn't foolish enough to think he was home and dry. A long night lay ahead, and a lot of work. All his clothes would have to go in the incinerator, for a start. He'd not anticipated that, but then he'd not thought he'd run into a motorcycle copper. He'd had no alternative but to get rid of him. The man was hardly likely to forget Keith and his eye patch.

But, by God, he'd dealt with him like a pro. At least, the Beast had. And the Beast had more work to do before the night was over. There was the girl to take care of.

But before he could continue his night of toil, there was the most important task of all.

He carried the hold-all into the front room and pulled the curtains. He examined the bag. Had they played straight with him? Someone close by would suffer if this did not contain what he'd asked for. He'd send the jockey's wife home in little pieces if the money wasn't here.

But it was.

He unzipped the bag and pulled out a brick of £50 notes. Incredible. And there was much, much more. Half a million pounds in cash. He'd pulled off the biggest gamble of his life.

Then the hounds started up. Keith froze.

The barking grew more agitated, and lights swept across the curtains from the yard outside.

He had been followed after all.

Phil had always imagined that coming off a motorbike would be worse than falling off a horse, but he'd had more painful falls on the practice gallops. He wasn't even concussed – at least, he didn't think so. He'd been lucky, though, there was no doubt about that.

As he'd driven along, the rutted track had got steeper, picking up water as it progressed downhill. Trying to avoid the wet, Phil had stuck to the side as the pathway broadened, and he'd found himself riding along a raised bank as the track turned into a proper stream. Suddenly the bank veered left under the trees as the waterway diverged and a branch at chest height separated Phil from the bike. He had landed on his back in a mound of pulpy end-of-winter leaves, and the bike had continued its journey without him.

Now, as he dragged himself to his feet, he heard a fully fledged river flowing some ten yards off to his left. And through the trees he saw a dim glow he took to be the motorcycle headlight. It occurred to him that, if he hadn't been knocked off, he'd now be in the water.

The track ahead, he noticed, was paved. He followed it over a bridge across the river and passed through a gate on to a road.

What the hell should he do now?

The door swung open before Henry had even pressed the bell. Keith Jeffries stood in the doorway.

He looked a sight, even more dishevelled and scruffy than usual, with dirt on his hands and face and that ghastly eye injury. Why Adam Jellicoe employed him, Henry couldn't imagine.

He was big, though. And menacing. He stared down at Henry with barely concealed malevolence.

'What the hell do *you* want?' he said.

The words hit Henry like a slap in the face.

'I beg your pardon, Jeffries?'

The man glared at him insolently. 'Don't pull rank on me, you old git. Say your piece and bugger off.'

Henry took a deep breath. 'It's about my horse. He's alive. I saw him myself this afternoon.'

'So what?'

'You lied to me, Jeffries, that's what. You took my money and broke your word. And, I've no doubt, money changed hands when you sent my hunter to Derbyshire.'

Jeffries took a step forward, angry and threatening. Henry wasn't a man to be intimidated, but it took all his nerve to stand his ground.

'Wait here,' the big man said, and turned into the house.

A few seconds later he was back, holding some banknotes in his hand.

'Here's the eighty quid you gave me to put him down. Plus five hundred, which is half what I got for him when I flogged him off.' He twisted the notes into a roll and thrust it into Henry's breast pocket.

Henry stared at him, confused at this turn of events.

'It's all right, Mr Carrington, there's no need to say thank you. Just bugger off.'

Henry's heart was pounding in his chest. This wasn't good for his blood pressure. He crossed the yard to his car, telling himself to retire with dignity. As he started the engine he lowered the window.

'You should take a look at yourself, Jeffries. You're a disgrace.'

'Fuck off, you nosey old fart.'

Really!

'I shall be speaking to Captain Jellicoe about your behaviour. I wouldn't bank on being employed here much longer, if I were you.'

The man shouted something back but Henry didn't catch it over the car engine and the racket the dogs were making. He put the car in gear and drove carefully back down the lane, conscious that he was probably a peg or two over the limit.

As he drove he calculated. Fancy Monty fetching all that money. He was going home £580 better off. And he'd given that insolent oaf a piece of his mind.

He'd always believed it paid to stick up for yourself.

*

Phil stared at the road. The man on the quad bike could have turned left or right – he had no way of knowing.

As he pondered his options, he became aware of noise – a loud barking that split the night. He tried to pinpoint the sound. Dogs meant dwellings and telephones. He could knock on the door and ask to make a call.

Lights flickered ahead, from behind the trees that bordered a sloping pasture. Headlights lit up the sky, then were hidden again.

Suddenly, a car emerged from a break in the hedge twenty yards to Phil's left, on the other side of the carriageway. For a second Phil considered flagging it down and begging the driver to get him to a phone.

But the car was too far off. It turned smartly on to the road and sped off in the opposite direction.

Too late. But up that lane must be a house. He set off.

As Phil walked up the hill the barking of dogs grew louder. There must be a hell of a lot of them to be making such a noise.

He remembered his conversation with Charlie about Rebecca, when the detective had said she'd been covered in dog hairs.

The quad bike need not necessarily have taken the road below. It could have come up this lane. To the house with the dogs.

At the top of the hill the road ended at an open gate. Phil stepped cautiously through the gateway into a yard flanked by a field and a cluster of buildings, among them a sprawling two-storey building – the main house, Phil guessed. The front door was open and light spilled across the yard, illuminating a parked vehicle.

A quad bike.

Was this the machine he'd been following? He couldn't tell for sure.

He bent low as he ran across the yard, keeping in the shadows. He placed his hand on the bike's engine casing.

It was hot.

He was convinced now. This was the bike.

So where was Bernie?

He eyed the house and its dark windows. And the open front door. The kidnapper could be in there.

And so could Julia. He'd not be able to save her standing out here.

*

Keith checked the diesel in the incinerator. Once he pressed the start button the doors would lock and it would burn for twelve hours straight, reducing everything inside to ash. In a way it was a bit like a washing-machine, but with better results. This machine got rid of everything, not just dirt.

He considered the tasks that remained. First he had to kill the girl – a ligature round the neck would be simplest. He'd put her out of her misery in the shed and carry the body through for burning. He'd have to load all her clothes as well, and the straw and blankets she'd been sleeping on, just as he'd done with the other one. And when he'd done all that, he had to add his own gear. And the bag the money was in.

Which reminded him – he'd forgotten about the money. That stupid old fart Carrington had distracted him. Just as well he'd fucked off when he had or there would be another corpse for disposal tonight. And that would have been a disaster. Once he'd got rid of Julia and hidden the cash he'd be in the clear. But Carrington would have been traced to him for sure.

He trudged back across the yard. He knew a few good spots round about where he could bury the money, but he'd wait a day or two. In the meantime, he had just the place to hide it from sight.

The house smelt. Of stale food, sweat, dogs – and neglect. Phil looked into the front room, off the hall to the left. It had probably once been quite cosy, but most of the floor and the furniture – a three-piece suite and glass coffee table – was covered in bundles of newspapers, empty food packets and crumpled beer cans. The room on the other side of the hall was dark, but he could make out a table and computer equipment and piles of books on the floor.

Julia wouldn't be here on the ground floor. Maybe there was a cellar. He looked for a door but found only a back room littered with coats and boots, a small, foul toilet and the kitchen. He ignored the mess and peered into drawers for a weapon. He found a carving knife.

He hesitated at the bottom of the stairs. Once up there he'd be trapped by a killer. A man who'd already slaughtered a policeman tonight. What chance would he have?

But suppose Julia was up there? The man might be about to kill her too.

Phil took the stairs as quietly as he could.

Facing the staircase was a bathroom and next to it a bedroom. He noted a double bed with dirty sheets. Clothes heaped on the floor. An overflowing wastepaper basket and a half-empty bottle of Scotch.

The door opposite was closed. Phil tried the handle and it swung open. The smell of must and damp was worse in here. He peered into the gloom, trying to make out the shapes. A dressing table and a floor-length mirror. Clothes racks full of dresses and coats. A heap of shoes – high heels and sandals and fluffy mules. Plastic bags from designer boutiques, overflowing with female underwear, leotards and tights. An exercise cycle with a pink cushion and a pair of small dumb-bells. All women's stuff.

But no Julia.

He heard the sound of heavy footsteps coming up the stairs.

Julia's torment seemed endless. She'd been lying on the straw bed since the afternoon, bound and gagged but able to see this time. So it had been late afternoon, she guessed, when the monster had gone off – in a different-sounding vehicle to normal, setting the dogs barking. Finally they'd settled down, and she'd been left to watch the light thicken in her grim prison.

It had been a relief when he'd left. He terrified her so much. She hoped he'd never come back. Perhaps he'd have an accident or be struck by lightning or – wasn't this possible? – be caught by the police. Then someone else would come to tend to the dogs and find her.

She tried to fill her mind with good things and happy times – of riding ponies as a little girl and the excitement of her wedding day and the look on Yvonne Mitton's face when Callisto had strode magnificently down to the start at Kempton.

But these thoughts didn't stay in her head. Not even the loving look on Phil's face and the sweet sound of his voice. Instead she thought of the girl in the papers – Rebecca Thornton – and how she must have lain here, too, cold and miserable, listening to the dogs, waiting for the monster to come back and snuff her life out like a candle.

Then she'd heard the unfamiliar vehicle come back and a commotion from the kennels shortly after. Her heart had leapt when she'd caught the sound of a car and a different voice raised over the barking. But she'd heard the monster too. Then the car had gone and the dogs had calmed down.

He hadn't come in yet, but she knew he would.

Was he going to kill her tonight?

Or would her torment drag on?

The footsteps reached the top of the stairs. Phil heard the creak of a door. Then a thump and a grunt, as of a heavy man lowering himself to his knees. Followed by a banging, like someone trying to dislodge a large piece of wood. What was he doing?

Phil leaned out carefully from his position in the doorway. Ten feet away, a man was on his knees in the bathroom. He had removed the wooden side to the bath and was pushing something into the gap. By his side was a black hold-all.

The kidnapper was hiding the money.

Phil was frozen to the spot. Should he run or should he hide? Or should he attack while he had the advantage of surprise?

He took a pace forward. The floorboard beneath him creaked.

The man turned his head slowly and stared at Phil. If he was surprised he didn't show it. His face was huge. Monstrous. Covered with blood, dirt and stubble. He wore a patch over one eye and his mouth was twisted. Phil realised he was smiling.

'It's the champion jockey,' the man said in that soft, familiar voice. He got to his feet, filling the bathroom doorway. He was huge.

'What have you done with my wife?' Phil shouted.

The kidnapper took a pace towards him down the hall, cutting off his path to the stairs.

'Tell me where Julia is,' Phil demanded, raising the knife. It did not seem much of a weapon against this giant.

Bernie's one brown eye regarded him steadily. 'I don't think so.'

His fist came out of nowhere. Phil took the blow on his left shoulder and thrust with his knife at the centre of the man's chest. But he was off balance and the blade found nothing more solid than the woollen folds of Bernie's sweater.

Phil crashed against the door jamb. The man took hold of his wrist and twisted. The knife dropped to the floor.

Phil hit him with his left. It was his weaker hand and his arm was numb from the other man's punch – not that it would have made any difference. It was like hitting a wall.

The man picked him up and threw him backward into the room full of women's things. Phil's head slammed against the floor. The man stood over him and kicked him like a football. He kicked him again. It was like being hit by a sledgehammer.

Phil rolled away and stumbled to his feet, swaying in the half-light. The man watched him, calculating his next thunderbolt. This was no contest. Phil knew he was going to die.

Bernie smashed him in the ribs. Phil fell backward, tumbling into a pile of shopping bags and spilling their contents across the floor.

He tried to get away across the room, crawling on all fours, his knees crunching on small hard objects – a hairbrush, perfume, a tube of some ointment. A blow on his back brought him to a halt. His gasps were loud and tortured. He rolled on to his side. This was the end.

He watched the man pull a long, thin scarf from the clothes rack and double it round both fists.

The giant bent over him to loop the makeshift garrotte round his neck.

Phil lifted the aerosol can. It was his last chance.

From a distance of six inches, he squirted hairspray into the man's good eye.

Bernie roared, clapping his hands to his face.

Phil dragged himself clear.

The man blundered after him, crashing blindly into one of the racks of clothes. He fell like an oak and the floor shook. He still had a hand pressed to his eye; the other flailed in the air, searching for Phil.

Phil pushed himself away from him, clattering into the exercise bike, bumping his knees on something solid. An exercise weight. A compact, three-pound dumb-bell, just right for a woman.

Phil picked it up and swung. One end smacked into the man's skull as he clambered to his knees. He said nothing, but the solid clunk of metal on bone reverberated round the room.

The man swayed on his knees.

Phil hit him again, as hard as he could. The weight thumped into the giant's face and blood fountained over the pair of them. He grunted, as if acknowledging the hit, and groped for Phil.

A big hand fastened on Phil's shirt and gripped fast. Phil swung the weight again, and it landed on the man's temple above the eye patch.

The hand lost its grip and Bernie fell again. He moaned and twitched on the floor.

Phil didn't have the energy to deliver another blow. He sat on his haunches, panting, watching the big figure sprawling in front of him.

If he had to beat the bastard's brains out he'd find the strength from somewhere. But, as the minutes dragged by, he realised he wouldn't have to.

The man groaned and twitched as Phil bound him with belts and scarves he took from the clothing racks.

To all appearances Charlie Lynch was unflappable. A commander in control of his troops. All his manpower was concentrated on thirty square miles of Somerset either side of the motorway bridge where Phil Nicholas had last been seen. And where a motorcycle policeman had been discovered lying in the road with his throat cut.

Inside, Charlie was dying his own kind of death. A man's life had been lost on his operation – it was too dreadful to contemplate. But, for the moment, there was no time for reflection. They must find this killer before other lives were lost.

But how? The murder scene might yield good evidence, but it would take time to analyse and he had precious little of that. All he could do was search the area with the maximum force at his disposal. He didn't even know what kind of vehicle he was looking for, though an alert had gone out for a missing police motorcycle.

'How do you keep so cool, guv?' muttered John Petrie as he poured over the map sections laid out on the incident room table.

Charlie was about to say 'Prayer' when the Traffic sergeant raised his hand. 'I've got the emergency operator.'

A 999 call had just come in from a man requesting police and ambulance services. He'd asked for DCI Lynch.

'That must be Phil,' said John.

The caller claimed not to know his location but he'd left the phone line open so it could be traced while he went to search for his wife. He'd left a message for the inspector – 'Bernie's shot his bolt.'

'Bloody hell,' said John. 'What do you think of that, guv?'

Charlie didn't know what to think. 'I told him not to be a hero. Might as well have saved my breath.'

*

Julia was drifting. It wasn't proper sleep but a kind of hallucination. And it was nice – she could hear Phil. His voice calling her name. He was coming to rescue her from this nightmare. To wrap her in his arms and never let her go.

'Julia!'

Her eyes flicked open in the dark. It did sound like him.

'Jules, are you in here?'

It was him.

'Where are you?'

She couldn't shout back. She couldn't move from the bed. She couldn't make a sound.

There was a rattling at the door of her prison. Then a smashing sound of metal on metal and a beam of light pierced the darkness.

The light was falling on her. He had found her.

Thank God.

Chapter Fourteen

'Aren't you tempted,' said Yvonne Mitton to Julia, 'to wear a hat?'

They were sitting in the panoramic restaurant at the top of Cheltenham's grandstand which, as can be imagined, gives its lucky patrons a marvellous view of the course below. It was the second day of the best jumping festival in the world but, in between races, many eyes turned inward across the room to focus on Julia.

It had been a fortnight since Keith Jeffries had massacred her hair, and the first thing she'd done when she'd regained her freedom was to shave her head completely. Now the hair had grown just enough to soften the outline of her skull. She'd made no attempt to hide her gaunt and striking looks. Her eyes were huge, the skin stretched tight over the bones of her face, the blue shadows like bruises.

'No,' she said in response to Yvonne's enquiry. 'No hat, no wig, no make-up. Sorry.'

She couldn't fully explain it to herself but it was to do with starting all over again. She'd thought she was going to die, and now she had another chance at life. She wanted to begin again from scratch. No artifice, no prettifying, no hiding behind other people.

'Don't apologise, darling. I think you look beautiful,' said Yvonne, offering her a cigarette.

'No thanks,' said Julia. The craving was gone. She'd escaped her execution and had no need for tobacco any more.

'Good for you,' said Jack, lighting up. 'I wish I had your willpower.'

There was over an hour to go to Callisto's race and the Mitton party were already consumed by nerves at the prospect.

Julia glanced at Ted, Phil's dad, who made up the group. Even he looked apprehensive, but maybe that was because Phil was riding in the next. They'd watch it up here and then fight their way through the throng below in readiness for Callisto's race.

Phil had high hopes for the Royal & Sunalliance Chase. In a day and a half of racing he'd not even been placed, despite riding some fancied horses for Russell. That was the way of Cheltenham, he knew that, but it worried him. He'd conquered his demons. He'd proved to himself and the whole world that he was no coward, but he wasn't riding well. It was nothing to do with being scared any more, just something that wasn't right. Something he couldn't put his finger on.

And so, when Hollow Crown dumped him in the ditch after the water at the start of the second circuit, he wasn't looking forward to the post-race inquest with his boss. But it wasn't Russell who was waiting for him when he arrived back at the weighing-room. It was his dad.

Phil spotted Ted by the double doors as he approached and assumed he was checking to make sure he wasn't injured.

'I'm OK, thanks,' he said, forcing a smile.

'You know why you fell, don't you?' said Ted without preamble.

Phil was surprised rather than offended. He couldn't remember the last time his father had commented on his riding.

'You're letting go of the horse's head as you approach the fence,' Ted said earnestly, leaning closer so as not to be overheard. 'I've noticed you doing it for a few weeks.'

Phil was listening intently. His father had taught him just about everything he knew about riding.

'Go on.'

'You probably don't even realise you're doing it but, as soon you take even the slightest pressure from the horse's mouth, the line of communication changes. The horse is relying on you to help him balance and suddenly, just when he needs you most, you desert him. He has to adjust his balance and, worst of all, you lose the feeling through your fingers of how the horse is reacting to the fence in front of him.'

Phil digested this information. He wasn't aware of doing anything wrong but perhaps his father had a point.

Ted was looking at him keenly. 'I don't like to interfere – you're ten times the rider I ever was. But no matter how good you are, it's not always possible to work things out for yourself.'

Phil knew this was true from his attempts to play golf. A pro had once videoed his swing and it had been an eye-opener. Phil had thought he was doing one thing but how he actually swung the club was quite another.

Phil put his hand on his father's shoulder. 'What would I do without you, Dad?'

The weather was unseasonably hot for mid-March and Hugh was down to his shirtsleeves in the press room. The sight raised a few eyebrows among his fellows, who were not used to seeing him in a bow tie and cuff links. The yellow stripe in the shirt was possibly a mistake, but the salesman had been most enthusiastic. This was day two of his new look and he'd had approving glances from some of the many French scribes in attendance, even if the local hacks thought he looked a bit of a ponce.

So far, however, he'd not had the one reaction he really wanted. He'd not caught sight of Louise, though she'd said she'd be at the Festival. Maybe, with her father just out of hospital, she'd not been able to come after all.

Not that it mattered. He could pick up the phone to Louise any time. He'd bump into her soon enough at a smaller meeting, where they wouldn't have to compete with the crush of thousands.

He dismissed Louise from his mind and went downstairs to mingle with the exuberant crowd. But as he made his way to the bar his eyes searched the throng for a head of copper curls.

Charlie couldn't remember the last time he'd been at home on a weekday afternoon. But he'd been working flat out for long enough, and this afternoon was special – and not just because it was his birthday. Frankly, a birthday was just like any other day. He'd dutifully opened half a dozen cards and stuck them on the mantelpiece. You'd think your only daughter might remember, even if she was having a whale of a time at university with her fancy new friends.

He took a beer from the fridge and tuned the television to Cheltenham. He'd never heard of the race before, but this afternoon's running of the Mildmay of Flete Challenge Cup was not one he intended to miss. Not after spending so much time recently in the company of Phil and Julia Nicholas.

He watched Phil come off his horse in the fourth race of the afternoon with some concern, shared by the TV commentator. After the Keith Jeffries affair, the jockey was a national hero. The story of Phil's battle and of Julia's rescue was still headline news. Fortunately the prospect of the forthcoming trial had muzzled the media to some extent, but Charlie knew how uncomfortable Phil was with all the sensation.

As a policeman, Charlie had long ago learned not to get too involved with the victims of crime. But sometimes it couldn't be helped.

He went into the kitchen and opened another beer. Outside in the sunshine the garden was looking a little ragged. Since the silver BMW had become a fixture across the road, it seemed Amy was no longer inclined to keep an eye on it. That suited Charlie just fine.

Phil looked down at Julia from Callisto's back. 'What're my instructions, then, boss?'

She laughed. It was good to see.

'Just both of you come back in one piece.'

'Don't you want us to win?'

She shook her head. 'You're carrying too much weight. Anyhow, it's being here that counts.'

'You'll never make another Russell Dean, Jules,' he said as Ted led him off on a circuit of the parade ring.

She had a point, however. The horse was carrying a heck of a lot of weight. Past form, even though it was over two years back, had lumbered Callisto with twelve stone, a good seven pounds more than his nearest rival and a whole two stone more than some of the others.

And yet Phil did want to win. This horse had kept Julia going. Callisto had been the focus of her life while he'd been having his psychological problems and, again, after her kidnap and imprisonment by Keith Jeffries. She'd not had time to brood over her narrow escape while she had the old horse to worry about. Maybe it was wishful thinking, but Callisto ought to win here at Cheltenham. For Julia's sake.

The sound of a key turning in the front door took Charlie by surprise. He heard the door open and the familiar rustle of carrier bags as they were dumped in the hall. For a crazy second, he thought his wife had returned from shopping.

'Dad!' The voice rang out and he jumped to his feet, heedlessly spilling the dregs of his beer.

'Surprise!' cried Claire as he dashed into the hall and grabbed his daughter in a bear hug.

Hugh found a monitor in one of the bars. There was no point in fighting his way to the stands outside – not if he wanted to follow the action. Even so, it was pretty much a scrum. It felt like someone was boring a hole in his back.

He turned his head abruptly and bit back a complaint as he nearly got a mouthful of curly red hair.

'Are you hiding from me?' said Louise.

He grinned. It was good to see her.

'And what's this?' Her fingers were plucking at his bow tie. 'You *are* hiding. You're going round in disguise.'

'It's my new image.'

'What do you need a new image for?'

'Er . . .' It was a good question. 'My sister-in-law thinks I'm a bit of a scruff.'

'Doesn't she like scruffs?'

'No.'

'She sounds a bit odd to me.'

'I never knew you liked horseracing,' Claire said as she lolled against Charlie on the sofa, sipping beer directly from the bottle.

'You keep telling me to develop my interests. Get a life, I believe you said.'

'I was thinking of something more active. Golf, maybe. Or ballroom dancing.'

'You're joking.'

'Just as long as you don't go with the merry widow across the street.'

He turned to her in surprise. 'You mean Amy Baylis?'

'Promise me, Dad. Mum couldn't stand her.'

Really? He'd had no idea. Not that it mattered. He squeezed his daughter's hand.

'Don't worry, sweetheart, I'm not interested in Amy. Now, will you belt up so I can watch this race?'

*

Callisto took up the running on the uphill climb on the second circuit. It was a joint decision. The horse wanted to go and Phil agreed. His father's advice had been spot on. From the first jump he'd concentrated on keeping an even contact with Callisto from one side of the fence to the other – and it had worked. Suddenly it all felt so easy. He was back in control again.

Callisto was loving it, too. He powered up the incline, past a flagging front-runner, as if his years and the extra weight were a trifle.

Every fence saw them gain more ground. As they turned downhill and kicked for home, Phil was buzzing. No matter where they finished, they'd given an unforgettable display of steeplechasing.

Callisto turned into the home straight six lengths in the lead.

'Go on, Phil!' Hugh roared at the top of his voice, but the sound was drowned out by the shouts of those around and above and below. The whole of Cheltenham racecourse, it seemed, was shouting Callisto home.

Louise was in front of him and his arms were somehow wrapped around her, the pair of them jumping up and down with excitement.

When this race was over Hugh was going to tell her about Emma's dinner party next Saturday. She was coming whether she liked it or not. Just to offer moral support as a good friend should.

The uphill run-in at Cheltenham is a famous destroyer of hopes, dreams and near-certainties. Not this time, though.

Callisto sailed over the last fence and Phil rode him to the finishing post in style. There was no other contender in sight.

'How much will you get?' asked Claire, her face flushed with excitement.

'I had no money on it. I just wanted Phil Nicholas to win.'

She nodded. 'This is all to do with your case, isn't it?'

'It's a long story.'

She smiled. 'That's fine by me, Dad. You can tell me all about it while I cook your birthday dinner.'

Phil had never heard such a noise. The crowd were going potty and everyone wanted to slap his back or shake his hand or give him a hug. He returned their greetings with a smile, but there was only one person he wanted to embrace.

A woman with no hair, no make-up and a light in her eyes that was meant just for him.